Gary Dennis

They call me the Wildrover. Among other things, I have sailed around the world with my wife and children, fought with pirates of the Arabian Gulf and found the Promised Land. The Christening is my "BIG IDEA."

By buying this book you will help to raise millions of dollars for many worthy causes around the world. One is to support early education and inclusion of children with Down Syndrome in New Zealand. Another is to make The Christening into a "BIG MOVIE" from which some of the profits will be used to support children with Down Syndrome worldwide.

Check out our BIG website www.trysoftaproductions.com

Thanks a million for your support!

Dream no small dreams
for they do not have the
power to move the hearts
of men!

May all your dreams come true!

from

Gary

The Christening

By

Gary Dennis

Trysofta Productions

First Published September 2010

Trysofta Productions
Box 300872
Albany
Auckland
New Zealand

Email: gary@trysoftaproductions.com

Website: www.trysoftaproductions.com

Copyright: Gary Dennis 2010

The author assess his moral rights. This book is copyright under the Berne convention. All rights reserved. No reproduction without permission. Enquiries should be made to the publisher.

Typeset in Cambria 11 pt
Cover design by Brown Dog Design, Auckland, NZ.

Printed by Kalamazoo in Auckland NZ

ISBN: 978-0-9864566-0-2

For

Lorene
Tara, Jake and our 'unsinkable' Molly
Wildrovers all
Your love is the landscape of my heart
the silken thread that weaves our story
and binds us all together

Special Thanks

to

Adrian Hirst and Philip Doyle for recognising the 'Pure Genius' in this story and to Guinness and Diageo for helping to make it a reality

Thanks lads!

'Happiness is easily secured.
What fearful prices some men pay for imitations!'

Dr Daniel David Palmer

Celebrate life, every day, everywhere

Diageo

Introduction

Once upon a time I lived in a house on the top of a hill in New Zealand. In that house I had a dream and in that dream I met Kate on the far side of the world in Ireland. As she told me her story, I thought that I should write it down, but before she had finished I was awoken by a sound so loud that the whole house shook. I thought that it must be an earthquake until I went outside to the garden and looked up to see a Spitfire diving time and time again across our roof. It was so close that I could see the pilot who stared back at me with a look of fierce determination. There was a green shamrock painted on the cowling in front of the cockpit. The first thing that came to mind was that he must be part of Kate's story, but it was too bizarre, so I didn't write it down.

    Years later I attended a jumble sale at a village in a town square in Wales. There was a book that caught my eye with the picture of a Spitfire with its pilot sitting in the cockpit on the cover, staring straight at me. To my great surprise there was a shamrock on the cowling in front of him! I realised then that he had been a fighter ace and had lived in that faraway place that we are separated from by time rather than space. But he had lived all the same, and I believed then that what Kate had told me was true.

This is their story.

Chapter one

The speedometer read forty before he applied the clutch and changed gear into fourth. There was a terrible sound of grinding in the manoeuvre.

'One lady owner!' the salesman had told him with a smile as he glorified the car's history to try and secure the deal. Michael had doubted this. The price had been more than he wanted to pay, but he had run out of options and had little time to spare. The last thing he had wanted was a convertible. The salesman could sense that Michael was under pressure.

'I'll throw in a full tank,' he whispered, looking over his shoulder to make sure he was not overheard. With that Michael was swayed. Because of wartime petrol rationing and the long distance he had to travel, the first thing he did was put the car on the train. His final destination was the south-west of Ireland. It was a long way away from Dublin and would use valuable fuel. He sat at a window with a book he had intended to read, but he spent most of the journey thinking instead about the mission that lay ahead and how he had been saddled with such a lousy job.

'Don't think of it as a demotion,' his superior had advised. 'This is a delicate matter that needs a world of experience. We feel that you are the best man for the job. Upon success we have a challenge for you that will more than satisfy your ambitions!'

He took his boss at his word and prayed that it would be sooner rather than later. The trip seemed endless, with too many stops before Michael finally got to unload at the far end. From the station he drove the last twenty-five miles or so out towards the coast. The workers in the fields waved at the rare spectacle of a car in these parts. Michael waved back without enthusiasm. While it had seemed okay during the test drive, the car now struggled to keep up with his easy demands. With only a few miles left to go, a queer-coloured smoke started belching from the exhaust.

Carrick Hill lay ahead and he was beginning to wonder if he would make it to the crest, when, like all bad beginnings it started to rain. He put his hand into the slipstream just to be sure and, as if on cue, the heavens opened.

'Ah no...not now...Bollocks' he cried in exasperation, jamming on the brakes. The car skidded to a halt just as the rain began pelting down. Michael jumped out to pull up the top before the inside was saturated.

'Two minutes is all it takes to convert her,' the salesman had told him. Two minutes to undo the collar, unfold the top and clip it to the edge of the windscreen before getting back into the car, soaking wet, because the salesman had lied about that part as well. Ten minutes is what it really took before Michael slumped back into the driver's seat, soaked to the skin.

'Damn you,' he cursed, but more for his own stupidity in believing the salesman. The gears ground again as he started back on his way. The further he drove the heavier it rained. To make matters worse, the wipers were not working and he could barely make out the front of the car. When he finally managed to reach the top of Carrick Hill he was forced to stop and wait for the downpour to pass. Two Sweet Afton cigarettes and twenty cold minutes later the rain finally blew over, but not before he had cursed the salesman again after finding a leak directly over his head.

From the top of the hill he had a spectacular view of Tralee Bay and the Atlantic Ocean, with its white-capped waves. In the distance, behind the Maharee Islands, the setting sun cast great beams of light in enchanted patterns, as if in an attempt to ease some of Michael's vexation. But frustration rose once again when the car refused to start. This time it was water in the carburettor. The only luck he had was being parked on the downside of the hill. By releasing the brake he was at least able to make some headway. There was a small humped-back bridge at the foot of the hill. If he could make it over fast enough, there was a short flat stretch on the far side, giving way to another long downhill section that ran all of the way to the village of Clochan, his final destination.

He leaned forward in anticipation, wondering if the bridge was going to send him airborne and if he should hold back for the sake of the chassis. He decided that he would wait until the last second, to see how he was getting on, and jam on the brakes only if it was necessary. The car gathered speed and quickly reached fifty. He dabbed on the brakes to be sure he had control and was shocked to find himself in greater difficulty. The brakes wouldn't work, the bridge was coming up fast and he knew that he was now in serious trouble. He could save himself by putting the car in the ditch, but would probably write her off in the process. Or he could say his prayers and take on the bridge, an option that put the gods between him and obliteration. At fifty-four miles an hour he made his choice, and with his breath held, the car hit the foot of the bridge with a terrible wallop. The back wheels followed the front, the whole show got airborne, and it was all going reasonably well until a girl stepped out in front of him.

'Holy Mother of God!' Michael cried out, at the sudden apparition. With a double shot of adrenaline he managed to prevent the car from running over the girl, but it was so close

Michael could see the terror in her face as he shot by. Out of control and in panic, he found himself spinning wildly in the direction of the ditch. With a mighty effort he managed to swerve to a stop before ramming into it. Dazed and confused, he sat there without a scratch or a hurt to himself or the car. He'd have stayed there all day re-living the experience if the cries of a baby hadn't jolted him back to reality.

'Oh God,' he prayed, as he jumped out of the car. He'd have killed the girl if he'd been any closer. Still dizzy from the violent stop, he had trouble gathering his bearings. The persistent crying of a baby however, finally made him turn around, and there in the middle of the road lay a body.

'Sweet Mother of Jesus.' He staggered forward realising that the woman wouldn't have heard him as he came silently careering down the hill with the engine off. He must have clipped her with the rear of the car without knowing it. Guilt pierced him as he knelt beside the body and discovered to his horror that she had a small baby wrapped in a shawl beside her. He didn't know what he should do until she jerked suddenly and let out a groan.

'Are you all right?' he asked. 'Are you injured?' The young woman turned slowly to look at him. She was pale as death and looked like she was in a lot of pain. A quick survey of the situation found no blood, which was reassuring. The baby seemed fine except for it's bawling. The girl was young, twenty perhaps – it was hard to tell from the state she was in. Her clothes were soaked through and she was frozen. She had been caught in the storm as well, but her condition suggested worse than he might have expected.

'It's all right, it's all right,' Michael said in a reassuring tone as he helped her to her feet. She was dazed and incoherent, trying to settle her crying baby. Michael sensed that she had been in some sort of distress before the accident and was going to need his help. It started raining again and she made no resistance when he suggested they should make for the shelter of the car. Though she was small and frail, it was still a struggle to deal with the weight of her and the baby together. He prayed that some other idiot in a car was not about to repeat his mistake.

'Which way are you going?' Michael asked, as he settled mother and child in the passenger side. With the car he could have her home in a few minutes.

'Tralee, I have to make it to Tralee before it gets dark!' she repeated, her voice getting weaker. She was shivering violently and tears began to well in her eyes. Michael took a blanket from the boot of the car. When he went to cover her he found her unconscious. He felt her hand, and the cheek of the baby. Both were frozen. Tralee was out of the question. It was too far in the opposite direction and their condition now constituted an emergency. Michael decided to seek help at Clochan only a few minutes away.

'Dear God, don't let them die in my car!' he pleaded quietly. The engine started immediately, as if in answer to his prayer and this time he drove more carefully in the middle of the road. The rain was pelting down again. After a few minutes a lone streetlight in the distance flickered through the downpour, as welcome as a lighthouse to a soul lost at sea. Only a stone's throw from the ocean, Clochan stood deserted and miserable. It was pitch-dark save for the light that shone from the occasional window. Michael searched hopefully for an appropriate place to stop for help. He spotted a large two-storey house with signs on either end of the building. One had a picture of a Toucan bird with a pint of stout in front of it and the word Guinness written below. The other read 'White House Bed and Breakfast'. Just what he was looking for. He pulled up outside the entranceway. He pounded on the horn for several long blasts as if to send out a distress signal then climbed out of the car with the baby in his arms. The rain was unrelenting. He made a dash for the small porch way and was relieved to see a light come on in answer to his call. When the landlady opened the door he thrust the baby into her arms followed by orders to run a hot bath.

'I have a young girl suffering from hypothermia in the car,' he said and dashed out again into the rain. He struggled unsuccessfully to lift her dead weight, until a pair of massive work-worn hands reached in beside him and helped carry the limp body into the house. Dan O'Brien was sixty-five years old, but rose to the occasion with the strength of a young man who'd spent his whole life farming. He helped to carry the girl upstairs to a warm bedroom where a fire was throwing out a good solid heat. The cries of the baby could be heard from somewhere downstairs and by some primeval instinct the mother stirred from unconsciousness. Michael moved quickly, removing some of the sodden layers of clothing and rubbed the girl's arms and legs to encourage circulation. Mrs O'Brien, the landlady, returned with the infant wrapped in dry clothing. She had found a baby's bottle and filled it with warm milk and the baby was happy to drink it.

'Go and get Bridget and her daughter from next door to give us some help,' she ordered her husband. 'You wait outside,' she said to Michael as she thrust the child back into his arms and nodded towards the bedroom door. The neighbours had heard the commotion and were already standing at the foot of the stairs, ready for action. They were up like a shot when Dan told them what was happening. To Michael's great relief the teenager took the baby and her mother into the bedroom behind them.

'She'll be all right now,' said Dan as he led Michael downstairs and pointed him in the direction of the kitchen. He disappeared behind a curtain that hid a door connecting the bed and breakfast to the small pub next door. He reappeared two minutes later with a pint of Guinness in one hand drawn from a tap behind the bar, a half-full bottle of Bushmills whiskey in the other and two small tumblers. 'Here, get that inside you, it will do you good,' he said handing the pint to Michael. He placed the two glasses on the kitchen table and filled them with a generous portion from the bottle of Bushmills. 'The wife was a matron, and Mrs Kinane a nurse,' he explained. He steered Michael over to stand by the coal range that heated the kitchen. 'This will warm your insides,' he said and swapped one of the glasses of amber liquid for the empty glass of stout that his guest had finished in two long swigs. 'Slainte,' he toasted his guest and knocked back his drink in one large gulp.

'What in God's name was she doing out in that kind of weather?' Michael asked, after he'd demolished his own whiskey.

'I've no idea,' Dan replied. He refilled Michael's glass and then excused himself to go and see if 'the wife' needed any more help.

The kitchen, like most of the house, was richly decorated with heavy oak furniture, full-length curtains and an array of pictures and photos on the walls that lent a certain charm and warmth to the surroundings. A black cat, oblivious to Michael's predicament, purred softly in a basket close to the range. The cat reminded him just how cold and tired he was feeling. He was looking forward to putting his own head down for the night and began hoping that they had another room for him.

Chapter two

Dawn broke the next morning with a clear blue sky. Michael had slept well with the help of a hot-water bottle and one too many whiskeys. He woke with a pounding head and a dry mouth. His back hurt and he felt as if he had been run over. Conversation the previous night had been polite but rather strained after Mrs O'Brien had finally entered the kitchen.

'She'll be all right now,' she said, as she put on the kettle to make tea. 'The baby and herself are sleeping sound. I've made up the bed at the other end of the landing, I suppose you'll be staying too?' It had been more of a statement than a question, and had the ring of inconvenience about it. It struck Michael as odd at the time, but the last thing he wanted was to go back out into the miserable weather, so he accepted their hospitality, if that's what one might call it. Before he knew it they had excused themselves for bed and left Michael to nurse the whiskey bottle.

As he dressed now he regretted the whiskey. His brain was groggy and his forehead pounded with every movement.

Somewhere in the house a grandfather clock chimed. Nine times he counted and he was surprised at how long he had slept. He took some deep breaths to try and invigorate himself and splashed his face with water from a porcelain basin in the corner of the room. The coldness of the water reminded him of the rain the previous night and the nightmare image of the young woman and her baby lying on the road flashed before him. He took another deep breath and let it out slowly with the relief of knowing that the nightmare had not become a reality. It had been too close for comfort. Too close by far. The thought of seeing her again made him feel guilty. What would he say to her? What would she say more like? Michael wondered why a mother would take her baby out in such a storm and why the O'Briens had acted so strangely in such an emergency?

He finished dressing, brushed his hair back as best he could without a comb, opened his bedroom door and stepped out onto the landing. The smell of fried bacon rising up from the kitchen made his mouth water and reminded him that he had not eaten since early the previous day. He was famished. The delicious smell made him descend the stairs two steps at a time in anticipation, sure that a good feed would make him feel a lot better. The kitchen was deserted, save for the black cat, that still lay, disinterested, in the same place by the old range as the night before. He heard a raised voice coming from the next room, but it was the surprise of hearing a baby crying that drew him closer. On entering the dining area, he found Mrs O'Brien clearing dishes from the table. Seated with her back to him was the girl, cradling her baby. Mrs O'Brien visibly stiffened when she noticed him. Whatever she had been saying to the girl she left unfinished and turned instead to take a tray full of dishes back to the kitchen.

'I suppose you'll be having breakfast too,' she said, agitated, and she pushed past him. She walked into the kitchen leaving Michael and the girl alone in an awkward silence. Michael was stunned by the reception.

'Morning,' he said to the young girl leaving the 'good' out of it, for he had seen nothing so far that would warrant its usage.

She turned her head towards him as he approached her table. A quiet 'hello' was all she could say.

'Are you all right? How are you feeling? I was going to go out and get the doctor!' The words tumbled out of him. He was embarrassed and uneasy; he hadn't expected her to be out of bed yet. 'You should be resting,' he said. 'The last time I saw you, you were in an awful state.'

'I'm fine,' she said, in a weak voice. 'I was just about to be going. I'm sorry about last night,' she went on, 'and all of the bother that I caused you. I did not mean to be so much trouble!'

'Trouble!' Michael exclaimed. 'Are ya out of your mind? I should be apologising to you for what happened.' He sat down opposite her, but she avoided his gaze. Her eyes were hollow and drained and failed to hide the misery she was feeling.

'Is there anything I can do for you?' he asked softly with deep concern.

'No,' she replied.

'What about the baby?'

'No, we're fine,' she lied. 'I was just about to be going,' she added when Mrs O'Brien returned to the table. The girl feigned distraction with the baby and avoided looking at her.

'There's your breakfast!' said Mrs O'Brien, as if it served him right and plonked two plates down on the table. 'I'll bring your tea in a minute.' With a bothered look, she headed back to the kitchen before Michael had a chance to reply. His stomach let out a growl and he turned longingly to the food. It was nothing like he had anticipated: the fried bread was burnt, the eggs were hard and there was only one piece of dried up bacon.

'She can't be serious,' he said. The sight of it made him sick. His stomach churned and he started to feel queasy. 'Did you ever get the feeling you were not wanted?' he asked half-jokingly. The girl nodded, tears welled in her eyes and she got up to leave the table.

'Thank you for looking after me last night,' she murmured. She collected up her baby and their belongings and left the room before Michael could stop her.

'What the hell is going on here?' he said to an empty room and was about to get up and follow her when the landlady came back with his pot of tea.

'Don't waste your time with the likes of that one,' she said, having overheard him. 'We don't want her sort around these parts,' she said and placed the pot on the table.

'What do you mean her sort?' Michael said, shocked at the tone of her voice. It began to dawn on him that the mother and her baby were truly not welcome.

'She's only a hussy, that's all that one is,' the landlady replied offhandedly, as she cleared the dishes. Michael was horrified. He could not believe the way Mrs O'Brien was carrying on. She had been a saviour last night. Now she was harsh and judgmental. It was obvious that she resented the inconvenience. Michael realised that he was probably not welcome either and with this thought in mind, he got up to leave the table.

'What about your breakfast?' Mrs O'Brien asked, surprised that he was standing up to leave. 'Are you not going to eat it?'

'That food is only fit for a pig!' he said, as much in disgust at her attitude as to the food she had served. 'You eat it!' he said and left in pursuit of the girl before Mrs O' Brien had a chance to reply. In the hallway he stopped only long enough to place some money on a sideboard for the two rooms. He opened the front door and stepped out onto the street. He looked up and down either way to find the young woman. To the left stood a small grocery shop. Across the road, the church marked the beginning of the town, but there was no sign of her. On the right the road ran two hundred yards or so before disappearing around a corner into the village out of view. There was a man on a bicycle and two old ladies talking by a half-door of a small row of terraced houses on the opposite side. Otherwise the street was empty. The road on the left was the one that he had come in on the night before and he didn't imagine that she would attempt it again. He glanced to the right, considered his options and decided he should use the car. By now his anger had risen. He was determined to find out what was going on. He turned the key in the ignition to start the engine, but was goaded further by the silence of a long-dead battery. His temper flared and he hit the steering wheel with his fist before getting out of the car and heading down the road on foot. The old man tipped his hat as he passed by. The two old ladies' eyes followed him as they whispered together. Michael paid them no heed.

He ran quickly, praying silently that he would find the young mother. The street wound back again and opened up into the main part of the village. Ahead of him, several shop fronts, including two public houses, a post office and a petrol pump, lined the road. It was a Saturday morning and the town was already busy. Michael's eyes darted from person to person as he slowed his pace to a quick walk, conscious that he was drawing attention. Several times he peered into shop fronts, hoping that he might find her. He was about to stop an old couple and ask them if they had seen her when a raised voice attracted his attention. Michael turned and saw a crowd standing in front of a large granite cross that marked the centre of the town square. Something about the situation made him uneasy. He walked over to the crowd to see what the shouting was about. There were at least ten people standing in a circle around what seemed to be an argument. When he reached the group he realised to his horror that the girl was involved in the altercation.

'Please let me pass,' she said in a pleading tone to an intimidating figure that was blocking her way. Michael pushed through the crowd to see what was going on.

'What are ya doing back here?' the large man sneered. Micilin Og was well over six feet tall with the shoulders of an ox and a large jaw that was set against her.

'I've done you no harm,' she said trying to side-step him, but he would not let her pass.

'I thought it was made clear to you that you were to get out of town,' he shot back as if speaking for the crowd. 'Your type is not wanted in this community.'

'You're a hussy!' someone else cried out from behind Michael. It was then that he stepped forward.

'What in God's name is going on here?' he demanded and moved forward to stand beside the girl. He was shorter and lighter than Micilin, but his anger more than made up for the difference. It was time for some answers and he wasn't backing down, even if his aggressor looked like Goliath.

'Why are you picking on this girl?' he growled, challenging the crowd.

'And who wants to know?' said the giant returning his gaze with contempt and shifting his body weight to face him.

'Why are ye all picking on this girl and her baby?' Michael demanded once more, this time taking a step closer to Micilin, to emphasise the fact that he wasn't afraid of him.

'Why don't you mind your own business?' Micilin said and stood up to meet him in a pose that left no doubt as to what would happen if he didn't back down.

'Yeah, mind your own business!' a voice echoed from the crowd. 'Who do you think you are anyway?'

'My name is Murphy,' he replied with a level voice. 'Michael Murphy,' he added without taking his eyes off his aggressor. 'But my parishioners usually refer to me as Father,' he finished loudly and the last word struck the crowd dumb. 'I have been sent from Dublin by the Archbishop to replace Father Flaherty who passed on, Lord rest him.' His voice was calm yet authoritative and left the crowd in no doubt as to who was in charge.

'Now you!' he pointed to the aggressor. 'What are you doing picking on this girl?' The crowd stood back a little to disassociate themselves. It was obvious that they were all involved, but had collectively decided that Micilin was going to take the blame. No one volunteered to give any answers which made Michael even more angry. The big man, who only a minute ago determinedly blocked the girl's way now stood quiet, well aware that he no longer represented the moral majority.

'Why don't you pick on someone your own size?' Michael said, giving Micilin a shove.

'Ah, Father,' he replied all apologetic. 'I don't have any argument with you.'

'What do you mean you have no argument with me, you big bully,' Michael replied and pushed him hard in the chest. There was a statement to be made and he was not going to let the big oaf back down.

'Shame on you, shame on you all,' he lashed out and pushed his aggressor once more. His anger had passed the point of reason.

'Go on, hit me,' he demanded, almost pushing the big man off his feet, 'because I'm going to flatten you for being such a coward!'

It was one thing to be pushed by a priest, but to be called a coward was more than Micilin could handle. He launched forward, his anger now unleashed and with one swift action struck out for Michael's chin. In that single moment the crowd stood aghast, aware of the terrible hiding that Micilin Og was known to be able to give as a fighter. It would be bad news to lose a second priest before he even got started. Their concern turned quickly to surprise however, when Michael, in a single fluid motion, dodged sideways, tripped his opponent and landed him a blow that rendered him half-unconscious as he crashed to the ground. The big fellow lay on his side and Michael stood over him with one foot on his shoulder and his fists ready to strike again if he made any attempt to get up.

'The child has no father,' an old woman piped up in the crowd's defence as if it were a worse sin than their own behaviour. There were mumbles of support for her statement.

'She has too!' the young girl finally spoke up, wiping tears from her eyes. She felt courage now that someone was standing up for her.

'If you were telling the truth you'd tell us his name,' a young man called out in the hope that a moment of weakness might make her finally reveal who the father was.

'He's gone to the war. He doesn't even know!' she cried in anguish. There were more questions to be answered, but Michael could see that what was important now was to put an end to it immediately.

'What does it matter?' he said taking the baby in his arms. 'This is a child of God.' With a symbolic gesture he stood on the step of the granite cross behind him. 'He wouldn't have entrusted her care to this young girl if he had not seen her as fit to carry out His will,' he said as he cradled the baby. 'Who are you to question the will of God?' he demanded as he stared down on them with righteous indignation.

'But the child is not christened!' the old woman persisted with genuine concern. 'Father Flaherty wouldn't have anything to do with her,' she added, voicing the thoughts of the many that surrounded her.

'Now look here the lot of ya. I'm Father Murphy, your new parish priest and I won't accept this kind of nonsense. The father of this child is the mother's business and not up for your opinion, same way as what you tell me in confession is between you and God and no one else's business. Do you understand what I am saying? The child will be baptised when the time is right and I'll expect everyone in the village to attend,' he added.

'I'm not going to any christening,' Micilin was quick to say as he struggled to get off the ground.

'You'll be there all right!' Michael said as he stepped down from the step and stood threateningly over him, 'or I'll come looking for ye afterwards. Go on now the lot of ye and mind your own business and leave this girl to mind hers,' he ordered. 'You should be ashamed of yourselves,' he stated – 'in front of this boy no less,' as he pointed to a child of about nine years of age who stood at the front of the crowd. 'What's your name boy?'

'Seamus, Father,' the boy replied, red-faced at being the centre of attention.

'Why aren't you in school?' he demanded.

'I don't go to school,' he replied as if it was a waste of time and looked to Micilin for fatherly support.

'We'll see about that,' said Michael. 'There will be some changes taking place around here from now on,' he announced 'and you going to school will be one of them!' With that the crowd began to disperse. 'I'll see you all at Mass on Sunday, and make sure ye have attended confession beforehand,' he said reminding them of their own sins. It was not long before everyone was gone and Michael and the girl were left alone.

'Well, that's that!' he said with genuine relief.

'I'm Kate,' she introduced herself. 'Kate Spillane and my baby's name is Grace.' She was still a little bit shaken, but obviously grateful that he had interceded on her behalf.

'Well, you know who I am!' said Michael, smiling for the first time. He took the baby in his arms once again for closer inspection.

'For a moment there I thought I might be attending my own funeral instead of a christening,' he said to the baby as he stroked her cheeks. The baby smiled as if she understood and he and Kate laughed.

'How did you do it, Father?' Kate asked. She was in awe of him for knocking Micilin down with one punch.

'The power of God is always greater than the will of man,' he replied. 'He obviously underestimated it,' he winked, half serious, half joking. 'That and the fact that I was a champion boxer in my youth.' Kate laughed again, comfortable in his presence. For a brief moment her troubles were forgotten.

'I'm looking for the priest's house. Can you tell me where to find it?' he asked as they began walking back in the direction of the guest house.

'That's easy enough,' she replied and nodded in the way they were headed. 'The house is at the side of the church. I used to be the housekeeper,' she said, surprising him. 'When he found out that I was pregnant he asked me to leave. He was afraid of what the people would say,' she explained.

'That's why they were against you?' he said.

'Yes,' she said. 'There was Mrs Ryan with him after that until he died. I believe she has gone back to Tralee.'

'I see,' said Michael, starting to put some of the jigsaw together. 'So they think it's his child?' he laughed openly at the suggestion. Kate smiled at his amusement. He was the first one to believe in her innocence.

'I saw him one night in his pyjamas,' she explained. 'He was sleepwalking,' she half-smiled at the thought. 'I told someone whom I thought was a friend and we had a giggle and no more was said about it. When word got out that I had a baby, rumours started flying. They all assumed it was the priest. They hated him, you know. He was really quite bad to them and there was nothing they could do about it. I suppose since he died they have just been trying to get rid of everything that reminded them of him.' Kate's tone had softened. Despite the torment she understood what some of them had been through.

'Hello, Father!' rang out the voice of one of the old ladies at the half-door as they passed by. Word had spread quickly.

'Good day to you,' Michael said, but did not stop to talk. He was lost in thought and kept walking.

'I'm going to need a housekeeper,' he said to Kate, sensing it might be as much a help to himself as to her. 'Why don't you come and work for me?' He smiled at the expression of surprise on Kate's face and the amusing thought of all the gossip it would make throughout the town.

'Oh Father, I couldn't,' she replied. There was a terrible anxiety in her voice. She had lost her confidence and was reluctant to stay in the village.

'Of course you can. Sure there is no one to stop you except yourself,' he paused, 'or maybe you have a better option?' he probed. She realised then that he understood her position. Kate's pace slowed down, but her mind raced. So much had happened in such a short time, she was confused. One minute she was being driven out of a town that seemed to hate her, the next she was being invited to remain by the very institution that had contributed to her downfall. Her heart ached with a pain that no mortal should have to endure. She was exhausted beyond all reason. All she wanted was a bit of peace, but it was the very thought of nowhere to go that held her. By the time they had reached the guesthouse she had gathered her wits enough to realise that she was in no position to turn down his offer.

'On a temporary basis,' she replied and extended her hand in acceptance.

Chapter three

Michael and Kate stopped outside the guesthouse long enough to take his belongings from the car. From there they crossed the road to the post office to pick up the key to the priest's house and use the phone to call the local mechanic to come and fix the car which he now referred to as his 'banger'.

     The church was only a short walk away. In it's shadow the priest's house stood, forlorn and dreary. Michael turned the key and they stepped into darkness. The house had been shut up for months. The smell of stale damp air that wafted from the entrance hall made it feel like it was suffocating in its own sadness. Kate went from room to room to let in the fresh air and what little sunlight there was in the day. Michael looked for wood and coal to start the fire. By lunch time Kate had baked bread and made a pot of vegetable soup – the aroma was like a promise of better things to come. If the spirit of a house is a reflection of the people that live within then it can be said that by the time the sun set on the western horizon there was a certain glow from every room.

'I'm very thankful to you for all you have done for me,' Kate said, before turning in early that night. She was exhausted and pale. She had not fully recovered from her ordeal, but it was a great relief to her that for the time being, she had somewhere to stay.

'It's no trouble Kate, really, I'm glad of the company,' Michael replied. 'Sure it would be a lonely place without you. Make sure you lie on in the morning and catch up on your rest,' he called after her as she left the room.

Kate trudged wearily up the stairs. The fact that she had a roof over her head had given her strength during the day and she had worked hard to show her gratitude. Grace had been well behaved and was already asleep in their bed. Kate looked forward to snuggling in beside her. She would stay long enough to get her strength back, and then move on. Too tired to undress, she crawled under the covers and lay down beside Grace. The warm room and her tired bones had her asleep before her head hit the pillow.

Michael sat for a while, thinking about Kate and her baby and the work that lay ahead of him. She was a mystery and had made no attempt to explain what had happened to her. When he had inquired she clammed up and begged him not to ask. Under normal circumstances it would be unacceptable to have her and a baby in the house. He felt, however, that if he was to overcome the animosity he sensed in the town then he must begin by setting an example. She was bright to talk to and had done well in her situation. He felt that she might make a good ally for the days ahead if he could persuade her to stay. His superiors in Dublin had briefed him about the general situation, but he had no idea that his predecessor had been such a tyrant. He had used the fear of God to manage his parishioners, and, in abusing his position had left them deeply resentful. As he dozed off, Michael wondered how he was going to fit in.

The next morning started with sunny eggs and decent

bacon and fresh bread, fried golden brown on the skillet. Kate was humming to herself as Michael entered the kitchen. He was in two minds whether to admonish her for not staying in bed or compliment her for the way she had transformed the house. He decided the latter was the better choice when she served him up his breakfast, and took it as a sign that she was feeling somewhat better.

'Mrs O' Brien could learn a thing or two from you,' he remarked as he sat down at the table. 'How are ye getting on, are you all right?'

'We're grand, Father. We had a great night's sleep,' Kate replied. 'Grace is still out to it up in the room.' She had combed her hair and tied it back in a lazy knot behind her shoulders. Although the clothes she wore were the only ones she had, she had ironed them and somehow transformed them into something a bit more presentable. Her shirt sleeves were rolled up to hide the dirt on her cuffs and the apron she wore did a lot to hide the stains on her long skirt. Her big brown eyes were less troubled than the day before.

'You can't leave me now, Kate,' he joked as he cleaned the last of the egg off his plate with fried bread. 'Not after cooking up such a storm! Sure I'd die with the hunger if I had to cook and clean for myself.' He licked the grease off the tips of his fingers in an animated display, as if he was still starving.

Kate laughed as she picked up his empty plate. 'There's meat on you yet, Father!' she said, being familiar without thinking. She would never have spoken to the old priest in this manner.

'Not for long if you go,' he replied. 'Have you given any thought to staying on?' His tone became more serious. He wanted her to know that she was still welcome and very much needed.

'To be honest, Father I haven't.' In truth she had been giving it a lot of thought, but was reluctant to make any commitments until she felt better and had time to plan ahead. Kate was grateful, but unsure if she should stay in Clochan or not.

'Can I have a few more days to think about it?' she asked.

'Keep cooking like this and you can have as long as you want!' Michael excused himself from the table. 'There's work to be done. Why don't you just pick up where you left off last time you were here, and we can talk about it at the end of the week?' He made his way to the back room of the house that was used as an office. There was a pile of letters he had discovered the previous evening that would take him weeks to plough through. He hated paperwork, but had decided reluctantly that he should at least make a dent in the pile before starting on anything else. The envelopes had been wrapped in an elastic band by the post mistress and organised according to date. One of the letters in the middle of the pack had come from England.

He sat there wondering which end of the dated sequence he should start at when a loud knock on the front door of the house drew his attention. Kate was somewhere about. It was her job to answer it, but he sat back and listened in case she had missed it. When it banged for a third time a little bit harder he decided she must be busy with the baby. He got up to answer it himself, and saw through a window in the office that she was at the end of the garden hanging out some washing. A little embarrassed that they had been made to wait so long, he quickened his step so that he would not miss the caller. As he approached the front door he noticed through the frosted glass that the person standing on the far side had long blonde hair. The outline of her figure promised beauty. He was surprised at himself for having such thoughts. He was even more surprised when he opened the door. The young woman was very pretty.

'Hello!' she said cheerfully and offered her hand as an introduction.

'Hello,' Michael replied taken aback by her enthusiasm.

'I'm Elsabeth,' she introduced herself, 'from Brandon Manor.' She pointed in the direction from where she had come from. In the distant landscape, partially hidden by a row of old oak trees, stood an imposing house that dominated the view for miles around. It was the home of her family, the Finucanes, who had farmed over five-hundred acres of the finest surrounding countryside for generations. It was the biggest property in the district. Her father was a politician and a member of the district council.

'I just stopped by to welcome you and ask you over for tea,' she said handing him a letter of invitation.

'That's very kind of you,' Michael replied moving to one side, 'please come in.'

'No, I can't, really, I'm on my way to see a friend and I'm late as it is.' She seemed anxious to be away as quickly as possible – not rude, but clearly in a hurry.

'When should I call?' Michael asked. She was already backing down the steps to her bike, waiting on its stand. He had to follow her to get an answer.

'Tomorrow evening,' she replied. 'At six o'clock. It's all written down there,' she pointed to the envelope. She was just about to set off when, in the background, a baby's tiny voice cried out. Michael did not hear it for he was not yet attuned to Grace's cry, but Elsabeth stopped dead in her tracks. It was the strangest of sounds coming from the priest's house. Even stranger because she was sure she recognised it. Michael could see by her expression that she was mystified as she listened intently. For a moment there was silence and then he himself finally heard the baby. He was just about to explain when Kate came running into the hallway behind him. She stopped momentarily at the foot of the stairs when she saw Elsabeth. By the looks they exchanged he could tell that they knew each other, but without acknowledging her, Kate took off up the stairs to check the baby.

'Kate! Kate!' Elsabeth suddenly cried out after her. To Michael's surprise she dropped her bike and rushed past him into the house. 'Kate!' she called out again. 'What are you doing here?' She took the stairs two steps at a time in chase. Michael found himself not far behind her, wondering what the hell was happening. On reaching Kate's room Elsabeth found the door locked. She grabbed the doorknob and twisted it a few times, dismayed by the fact that she was forbidden entry.

'Oh, Kate, for God's sake,' she pleaded in desperation as

she leaned against the door. 'What is she doing here?' she demanded of the priest and started banging at the door.

'I found her on the road yesterday,' Michael explained. He tried to ease her gently away from the door, but Elsabeth was having none of it. She pulled free and banged on the door again.

'Let me in, Kate,' she demanded. 'Tell me what's wrong ... please!' she shouted, this time kicking the door in frustration. There was a loud crack and then it finally gave way. She burst in to find Kate nursing Grace. She was staring out the window at the far side of the room, rocking herself and sobbing. Elsabeth stepped across the room, knelt silently beside her and placed her hand gently on her friend's lap.

'Oh, Kate!' she said softly with sadness in her voice at seeing her friend in such a state. She could see that something terrible must have happened. 'I was on my way to visit you at the cottage. I've brought a picnic and some surprises for Grace,' Elsabeth tried to reach across the distance between them. 'What's happened?' she asked in a whisper. Tears welled up in her eyes and she began rubbing Kate's shoulder to comfort her. She seemed inconsolable.

'Am I allowed to ask what's going on here?' Michael inquired, thinking that Elsabeth might be forthcoming with answers, but the look on her face told him he was wrong. Whose house they were in did not make any difference, the only thing she cared about was her friend. 'Right,' he said. 'I'd say everyone could do with a strong cup of tea. I'll wait downstairs in the kitchen until you're ready!'

It was a long time before Elsabeth came down. It had taken an hour before she managed to get Kate to open up, and even then it was only through fits and starts that she got some explanation.

'She's asleep now,' Elsabeth said, gratefully accepting a steaming cup of tea. She gave a slight sob as she sipped it. 'I'm sorry, I didn't mean to behave like that. It's just that I was so shocked to see Kate and Grace here.' Her eyes were red and puffy from crying and she had smudged her mascara.

'I found her on the road the night before last,' Michael said. He hoped Elsabeth would give him some information about the situation.

'I know, Kate told me. She says that you're the best. I'm very grateful for all of the help you have given her.' Elsabeth placed her half-empty cup on the table. Michael was about to pour her more tea when she got up and made for the hall.

'Hold on Elizabeth you must......'

'Elsabeth. My name is Elsabeth, not Elizabeth,' she cut him off. 'It's French,' she explained not wanting to sound rude.

'I'm sorry,' Michael replied embarrassed. 'I just want to know what has happened,' he added.

'I'm sorry. I'm not sure,' she answered evasively. 'She didn't tell me everything. But she has had a terrible experience.'

'I know that!' replied Michael with impatience in his voice. 'You are her friend and you have been talking to her for ages. Surely you can tell me something!'

'I'm sorry, really, it is all very complicated,' she apologised. 'She asked me not to say anything. I think it's better to hear it from Kate when she's good and ready. I really must go now,' she said intent on avoiding further discussion. Michael followed her out to the front door. He was annoyed that she had not told him anything, but he decided to leave it for the moment. He did not wish to alienate someone who seemed to share the same concern for Kate as he did. Elsabeth stopped at her bike.

'These are for Kate and Grace,' she said unclipping two panniers from the back and handing them to Michael. 'There's food and some things for the baby from Dublin,' she stated. 'I would like to be able to come back and see her later, if that's all right with you,' she asked, still apologetic. Although she was escaping without giving a reasonable explanation, she wanted to be able to return.

'I suppose,' replied Michael shrugging his shoulders. He did not have much choice in the matter. 'I might be out,' he said, 'I have things to do. But I'll leave the front door open and you can let yourself in. It would be good for Kate to know that she has a friend around,' he added. 'You are welcome any time.'

Elsabeth smiled, thanked him for his help again and reminded him about the invitation the following evening. She took one last look up at the room where Kate was sleeping, steadied herself on her bike and then rode away. Michael watched her for a moment and then went back into the house, wondering what sort of a situation he had become involved in.

Chapter four

Elsabeth cycled as fast as she could the three miles or so that it took to get to the cottage. 'Their Cottage'. The place she and Kate had been using to keep 'their secret'. The place where Grace had been born. Kate had spoken of a fire. She had been careless she said, reading by candlelight. She had fallen asleep and the curtains beside the bed had started the blaze. She was sorry she had said – didn't mean to do it. She did not know how she was going to pay for the damage. Elsabeth found it all hard to believe. Kate was always so careful, and she seemed very scared by the fire. Elsabeth had never known her to be fearful of anything before, and she found it impossible to understand.

'We'll fix it up,' she reassured her friend. 'It can't be that bad. And sure if it is, we'll find somewhere else!' But her friend was more than distracted. When Elsabeth mentioned her brother John, Kate almost had a fit. He had been great when he had originally discovered their secret. She was sure that he would be glad to help them again. Elsabeth had tried to reassure her of John's help, but Kate was adamant.

'You must not tell him!' she begged in tears again. 'Please don't tell him where we are.' She grabbed Elsabeth by the hand and made her promise to keep her whereabouts a secret before Elsabeth had left the priest's house.

Elsabeth arrived at the cottage in less than twenty minutes. It was the fastest she had ever made the journey. What had grown to be her most favourite place in the world now greeted her in a state of ruin and absolute desolation. The white walls were blackened and the thatched roof had caved in. The charred remains of the inside of the house were scattered around the garden. After all of the hard work they had put into it there was nothing left worth salvaging. Elsabeth was appalled. Kate hadn't been exaggerating after all. Her eldest brother Brendan, who had gone off to the war, had once joked that the cottage was so well built that it was hurricane proof. The way it looked now it seemed like the big bad wolf had come to visit. Tears welled up in Elsabeth's eyes at the devastation. As she walked around to the back of the house she thought of Kate and the terrible ordeal she must have been through. She had done such a good job at fixing up the cottage. It was the only place she had had to live. They had been so happy there, she and the baby, with Elsabeth coming to visit every few days. It had been their little piece of heaven.

At the back of the house it was even worse. A thick layer of ash had been blown off the roof and covered the ground, destroying the vegetable garden that Kate had so lovingly nurtured. A cold shiver ran down Elsabeth's spine as she thought about how Kate and Grace could have been caught in the fire. She crossed herself in thanks to God that they were both safe. But if she had been looking more closely she would have seen the impression of the wolf's hobnailed boot marks in the fresh ash. If she had gone inside and searched through the wreckage, she would have found the broken whiskey bottle that still reeked of the petrol that had been used to start the inferno. She would have seen it and she would have been terrified in the same way that Kate had been. She would have understood why her friend now lay sleeping, too miserable to carry the day. As it was, she was full of worry now about what she could do to help. She felt very much responsible.

The cottage had been her idea. It was on the family land, out of the way where no one would disturb them. It had been the perfect solution at the time, but now that it was gone she did not know what she could do to help Kate. Winter was bidding, the school holidays were almost over and she would be busy with her new teaching post. She would have to find a solution quickly if she was to be of any use to her friend. What to do though? The more she thought about it, the fewer options she had, the more she realised that she would have to go back on her promise to Kate and ask John for help. There was no reason why she should not ask him. She could not imagine why Kate had been so hysterical. She put it down to shock and the thought of having to pay for the damage. She was sure that if she went and confided in her brother he would help her come up with a solution. When they had thought of something she would go back to Kate, and everything would be all right. She decided to see him straight away and got back on her bike. He was always at the manor on Fridays to pay the wages and get the farm hands ready for the following week. He would be just as concerned and just as eager to help as she was. She reassured herself that he would probably come up with something straight away and that calmed the echo of Kate's pleading in her mind.

When she reached the manor she was disappointed to find that John was not in his office. One of the workers told her that he was down at the river fixing the damage to a cattle bridge, caused by the recent rains. Afraid that she might miss him, she cycled off as fast as she could, and found him under the bridge in a pair of waders, up to his knees in mud and water. He was swinging a large axe, throwing massive blows at a tree stump that was lodged between the two main uprights supporting the bridge. It might collapse the structure the next time there was a heavy downpour, unless he could free it. His aim was poor, he seemed distracted and he cursed out loud several times in frustration as most of his hits amounted to nothing more than glancing blows. Elsabeth shouted to get his attention.

'What is it?' he shouted back with irritation. She made him stop what he was doing and climb the bank out of earshot of the workers before telling him what had happened. His tone quickly changed when he heard the news.

'That's terrible!' he said turning his back to be sure the workers could not hear them. 'Are they all right? Are they hurt?'

'No, they are not,' she replied. 'You have to come and see it. The whole place is devastated,' she stated without exaggeration. One look would soon change his priorities.

'I can't. I have to get this job done,' he said upon hearing that Kate and the baby were safe. 'I'm short of help and have to be sure the bridge is secure before the cows cross for milking this evening.' Elsabeth grew desperate, frustrated by his seeming lack of concern for the situation. He was dragging his feet when he should have rushed to help.

'What will we do?' she asked, annoyed that she was pleading with him when she should not have to. She wanted to remind him that Kate was practically part of the family, but couldn't, for fear the workers might overhear. 'Something has to be done,' she said finally in exasperation.

'The gatehouse,' John said quietly. 'Tell her she can stay at the gate house.' Elsabeth stood back surprised.

'But it's already occupied by the farm manager!' she said.

'Not that one, ya amadhan. The one on the southern wall,' he replied, noting her confusion. 'You know!' he explained. 'The one with the pointed roof and the cock crow on the gable. Seamus Flaherty used to live in it,' he reminded her.

'Oh. Of course!' Elsabeth finally got it. The farm was so big she seldom got around it. There were three gatehouses altogether on the walls that surrounded the estate. Each one guarded the points on the compass. Besides the main entrance the other two had been vacant for years and served no real purpose. The one that John referred to was furthest away and the most secluded. Elsabeth's heart skipped a beat with excitement when she pictured the small house.

'Oh John, do you really think so?' she said.

'Why not? Sure no one need know and I'll tell these buggers to stay well away from it,' he said nodding to the workers who stood waiting for him under the bridge. 'Give her my regards and tell her I'll be seeing her soon.' He turned and picked up the axe now that the matter was closed. Before he could start up again Elsabeth grabbed him and gave him a hug and kissed his rough face. He had to brush her off with embarrassment.

'You're the best brother in the world,' she said as he slid down the bank to get away from her. She did not care who was listening. She cycled back to the manor, unable to decide what she should do first – tell Kate or just bring her to see her new home as a surprise. Telling John had been the right thing to do. Although he had so much work on with the farm since their brother Brendan had gone away, he was never too busy to help her.

'It's not like we hadn't been close before,' she had once explained to Kate. 'It's just that Brendan and John are different.' She had always spent more time with her elder brother Brendan before he went off to the war. Kate had agreed, remembering her first impressions of John had not been great, but how, more recently, she had changed her opinion. Elsabeth was sure now that Kate would not mind him knowing.

•

Chapter five

Kate had believed in fairy tales. Once upon a time she had believed in princes and princesses and knights in shining armour and castles in the sky and happy endings. She had believed because her mother had told her so in songs and stories as a child.

Kate was born Kathleen Rachel to Patrick and Mary Spillane on the finest day of the year on the island of Inis Beag, off the north-west coast of Ireland. No more than fifty people occupied the island. They all knew each other's business, but were too busy surviving the elements to worry about what the others might be thinking. They worked hard and spoke softly of each other, knowing their very existence depended on the grace of God and their ability to pull together through all of the good and bad that was sent them. Pat and Mary had been childhood sweethearts. When Kate arrived, their world was complete. Mary worked the garden and Pat fished the waters around the island with his father-in-law. Life was hard but ends were always made to meet. They had a roof over their heads, food on the table, and they wanted for nothing save perhaps a bit more of the good weather. 'Even that improved,' her grandfather had said, 'since the day Kate was born.' Then her mother died.

Her father laboured on, doing the best a father could. Through his own actions he taught Kate to become independent and self-determined and after a long while their broken hearts began to heal. Her grandfather picked up with the story telling, admonishing sometimes his daughter 'for not giving all of the facts' as he called it. He went about re-telling for Kate all the stories of her childhood. He was the best in the world, and told the stories with such embellishment that she believed them even more the second time around.

Then one night while they were out fishing, a terrible storm came and took her father and grandfather away, so that all she had left were her stories and her songs. After the tragedy the people on the island did their best to look after Kate and pulled together to share the burden. The authorities on the mainland, however, had different ideas, and in their wisdom decided that they should take action. The government men came and disbanded the islanders altogether saying that after the last storm they were too exposed and too expensive to look after. They sent them north and they sent them south and some of them they even sent off to America. But Kate, because she had no real family, was sent to a children's home, to be 'looked after'.

St Patrick's, on the West Coast of Ireland, stood on a barren piece of granite, void of all humanity except for the hardened souls that ran the place. It was neither a home nor an institution, but a place where the unwanted and bold children of the country were sent to be reared under the watchful eyes of Jesus their saviour. But there was not much of 'Himself' in the place, save for the prayers that the children offered up beseeching Him to save them from the strap that was too often used to invoke His *so-called* Word. Island life may have been hard, but St Patrick's was hell by comparison. Kate would never have survived if she had not had the stories and songs her mother and grandfather had told her. She would never have managed without the independent spirit instilled in her by her father. But survive it she did, by using her brains rather than her brawn to sort out her peers. She was a clever girl and quick to learn, especially from her early punishments. She discovered how to please, not by conforming, but by being smarter than those who would have seen to her undoing if she hadn't been shrewd enough to outwit them.

By the time she turned twelve she was untouchable. She was top of her class, which earned her a certain level of status and respect from her teachers. It had been years since she had had the strap. Her class mates looked up to her because she used her position to help them, especially the smaller ones, and in turn set an example that saved many from regular thrashings. Her greatest gift, however, was her singing. She was the star of the school choir with the voice of an angel. When she sang she lost herself in the music completely. Everyone in the choir was inspired to let go from their hearts, a gift that you cannot beat out of children. This brought the school status and several awards never attained before in local choir competitions, and for the two years before leaving she was celebrated as a hero. That was as good as it got. As good as she could possibly make it.

They invited her to stay on and train to become a teacher, but she could never have called St Patrick's home. It was somewhere you were sent until you were eighteen years of age. A place you lived to see the back of when you finally became old enough to escape. They fed you and clothed you and beat the life out of you when you did not do what you were ordered. The so-called education that was given had nothing to do with the outside world. On your eighteenth birthday you were given a suitcase for your few belongings, a five-pound note and a train ticket to Dublin on the far side of the country. There were no 'farewells' or 'good lucks' or 'call us if you have any problems'. They just dropped you at the station and told you never to return. Many of the past pupils never made it, returning instead to a life of poverty and destitution after the money had run out.

In spite of her excitement at being finally set free the thought of going to the 'Big Smoke' held no attraction for Kate. She no longer felt intimidated by the people who had charge of her and consequently was not going to go some place because someone else said she should do so. During her time in St. Patrick's she had been fortunate enough to travel around the southern part of the country winning competitions. The place that had stuck most in her mind was the town of Tralee in the county of Kerry. There had been something about it. She had liked the people. Of all the places she had visited, they had been the nicest to her. So when they dropped her at the station she had already her mind made up and persuaded the ticket man to change her ticket before setting off on the road to freedom.

Chapter six

Kate boarded the train to Tralee, ordered tea and a ham sandwich to celebrate her freedom and, feeling like royalty, watched the countryside rock slowly by. She was amazed how much she remembered of the previous journey, having gone through it a thousand times in anticipation of leaving St Patrick's. It all seemed so familiar, so reassuring. Hidden in her bag on a scrap of paper, was the address of the accommodation she had stayed in during her last competition. Mrs Cummins was the name of the old landlady. She had been more than kind to Kate and made a special fuss by baking a celebration cake with icing on top when Kate won her last competition. On her arrival in Tralee Kate went to the post office and with a bit of help from the operator, managed to get a call through to speak to the landlady.

'Of course I remember you!' Mrs Cummins replied with delight. 'Are you coming to stay?' Kate could sense a hint of hope in her inquiry. 'I was hoping you could put me up for a while, if it's not too much trouble,' Kate replied with the relief of being recognised. As confident as she felt, she had pinned her hopes of starting her new life on the familiar surroundings of the boarding house and Mrs Cummins' grandmotherly affections. She wasn't to be disappointed.

'It's lovely to see you again,' Mrs Cummins said, with a big smile of welcome when she opened the door. 'Come in, come in.' She ushered Kate into the kitchen at the back of the house. She was short in stature and a little overweight. She walked with a shuffle because of a chronic pain in her hip, but it did nothing to dampen her enthusiasm at seeing Kate again. On the table she had prepared tea and biscuits.

'Where are the nuns?' was the first question she asked of Kate as she poured the tea.

'I'm on my own,' replied Kate. 'I finished at St Pats just this morning and I'm hoping to find a job and live in Tralee,' she explained. Mrs Cummins reminisced about the great thing it had been for Kate to win the singing competition. She asked all sorts of questions about this and that and an hour had passed before they realised. Because it was the quiet season, and she was by herself, Mrs Cummins gave Kate a room of her own. It was like a hotel compared to St Patrick's. You could leave the light on all night if you wanted, and stay out past nine if the fancy took you. In the beginning Kate couldn't imagine doing either.

She spent the next day walking around Tralee wide-eyed with the wonder of getting to know the place. The freedom of it all was intoxicating. In a small park a flock of seagulls were arguing over scraps from an overflowing rubbish bin. When no one was looking, she spread her arms and chased the big white gulls up into the sky in the same way she had chased them off the beach as a child. It took her a week to come down from her ecstatic state. Kate reckoned she had enough money to last her a month if she was careful. She had a good head on her shoulders and spent most of the first week looking around for a job. She had decided to find all the work she could handle in the short term, until she built up a kitty to fend off any disasters she might have to face in the future.

Mrs Cummins watched Kate with a keen eye. Her only son had left many years before and gone to Dublin. Knowing where she had come from and what lay ahead for her made the old lady anxious for the young girl. After two weeks of disappointment, knocking on doors and attending interviews with the greatest of ambition, but the least chance of success, Mrs Cummins finally took a rather disconsolate Kate to her side for a chat.

'No matter how you might feel about yourself,' she said to Kate, 'St Patrick's is a blight on your ambitions. It can't be helped. It's an institution and regardless of your reference it will do you no good to mention that it's where you have come from. It might as well be Mountjoy jail!'

'What will I do?' Kate asked, devastated that her plans had not worked out. She only had a pound left of the fiver she had been given.

'You have a lot to learn about the real world, young lady,' said Mrs Cummins as she handed her a cup of cocoa to comfort her. 'Good intentions are of little use when you live in a place that passes judgment long before you have had a chance to plead your case. Especially in these parts!' She told Kate that if she helped out with the odd jobs around the hostel that she could have room and board for free for as long as it took to get herself established. In the meantime Mrs Cummins promised to trý to help Kate to find a job. For the first time since she was a child Kate began to think that there might be a God after all and that night she said a prayer of thanks for Mrs Cummins.

That was on a Tuesday. By Friday she had found herself gainful employment. A friend of a friend of Mrs Cummins offered Kate a job in a small cottage industry on the outskirts of the town that made specialty cheeses for those who could afford them.

'It isn't much,' Mrs Cummins explained. 'Well below what you are capable of, but it's a start and that's all that matters. If you work hard at it then you'll be fine!'

Her employers, Joseph and Lotty Kramer couldn't help but take a shine to her because she worked like a Trojan and was always a joy to be around.

'You know he is not so grouchy since you started!' Lotty confided to Kate about her husband. 'You are putting us all to shame the way you work. You will have to slow down or we will all be out of a job,' she joked. Mr Kramer agreed. The cheese they made was of the highest quality. Over time the business grew and Kate along with it. She understood the importance of efficiency and what it meant to make a profit and she was quick to point out how things could be improved. Mr Kramer was a traditionalist at heart and reluctant to do anything that was new or different. Kate's enthusiasm and determination usually got the better of him.

'Gott in Himmel, okay, okay ve vill try!' he would say in exasperation at her gentle persistence and cajoling, 'but it better not affect ze taste of ze cheese!' By the time she had turned twenty she had become an indispensable part of their business. She spent long hours at the factory, including weekends and made little time for socialising. She built up her kitty and was kind to those who were near and dear to her. She stayed with Mrs Cummins as a permanent boarder and was forever buying her little presents and taking treats to work for her employers. She came up with the idea for a vegetable garden from which they could sell produce along with the cheese and so half of the Kramer's property was turned into a small holding.

'Ach, Kate, you have already proved yourself. You must slow down and take time for yourself,' Lotty kept saying to her. 'Go out and make some friends and do some things for yourself!' But Kate lacked the confidence and found she was unable to do either.

'You must take ze weekends off!' Mr Kramer insisted at the behest of Lotty, but Kate always found some reason to show up at work and would keep busy by doing something or other. On the outside she was light-hearted and fun to be around, but on the inside she was a mixed-up bag of raging hormones and clashing emotions. She had never gotten over the rejection she had faced during the first two weeks of looking for work.

'Don't be telling folks where you are from when they ask

you for God's sake!' Mrs Cummins said when Kate finally confided her misery to her one day. 'At least not straight away. Tell them you are from Inis Beag and, after that, if you like them and they like you then none of the other will matter.' But Kate couldn't bring herself to do that. She felt it was dishonest and that she would be lying and that when the person found out it would make her look worse than she already was. Her only consolation was the outdoor farmers' market that was hosted every Saturday morning in the car park beside the football stadium. It was there she bought a second-hand guitar from a music stall. She spent long hours teaching herself to play and would return every week for new sheets of music to add to her repertoire. After a while though her business mind took over when she recognised the potential of the market for the Kramers' cheese business. With a flash of inspiration she came up with the idea of having their own stall. As usual, Mr Kramer took some persuading before he would agree to it.

'It has to make sense,' he would say always insisting on seeing the logic before agreeing to doing anything different. 'Ve can't just go doing thinks villy nilly because you think it is a good idea,' he said to dampen her enthusiasm, but Kate had become a master at persuading him otherwise.

'We are making more cheese than ever before,' she stated. 'It's one of the problems with efficiency. Why not take a stall and sell the surplus direct to the public?' she suggested. 'It is a busy market that everybody in the town attends. It will increase cash flow and get rid of the surplus. You could use the money to go home to Holland for Christmas,' she rounded off with a smile as she stood next to Mrs Kramer. It had been years since they had been home and Mrs Kramer missed her family. The idea was too good for the old man to turn down.

'Ve will go,' he smiled, 'and ve vill see,' he said, as he pointed a finger at Kate. 'But on your head vill be it if zis dosen be ze success,' he warned, feeling cornered by the two women he loved most in the world. 'You unzerstant me?' He always said that when he saw that Kate was running his business again. She gave him a hug and Lotty kissed her because she knew they would be home for Christmas.

As usual Kate's ideas and dreams had a way of working out – not quite the way she had expected, but they worked out all the same. They arrived at the market early, full of energy and enthusiasm and she did a fantastic job of dressing up the stall with ribbons and decorations. She was soon to find out selling was a different matter. Kate had thought that if you just set the right price and showed a little generosity when dealing with the customers that they would be happy to buy all she had to offer. What she did not understand were the 'ways of the market'.

It was a day out for a lot of people and so had to be managed in a way that would make it last. If you spent your money early then the purpose for being there went with it. Consequently there was an art in going to the market and rules to be followed if you wanted to make the most of it. Firstly, the real punters, the ones that are most likely to buy the cheese, did not arrive until after breakfast. Why rush when you have all day? The art then is to hover for an hour or so and check out all of the wares, and to see what's new and what's worth buying. None of the stall holders expect to sell much during this period. It's what they like to call the 'quiet time' and see no point in being anxious when nothing is happening. You talk to your neighbour, have a cup of tea yourself and make sure that when the buying does start that you have enough coins for change and hands on deck to cope with the demand. For the new stall holders there is an extra sort of rule. You have to be checked out. Your wares assessed and a mental note made as to whether it is worthwhile coming back later or not at all. The final unwritten rule applies to all customers and that is that you don't buy from a new stall that isn't busy. People go where people go. If they are not seen to be standing in front of your stall and actually buying your produce then no matter what you are selling it is deemed as not worth having.

Not knowing the rules had poor Kate in a thither. By the time the town clock tower struck ten o' clock Mr Kramer's words of warning were ringing in her head. Although she knew he meant none of what he had said, she couldn't help but feel nervous. Lotty had not stopped talking about going home for Christmas since they had started planning their new venture. So Kate was terribly anxious that everything should work out. The disappointment would break Lotty's heart and she would be the one to blame. Several people had stopped by since they had opened and tasted their produce, but then moved on without making a purchase. Twice Kate had to chase away a snotty-nosed kid who kept sneaking up and stealing the samples that she had left out for the serious punters. Even after the market became busy and it was obvious that money was being spent, no one ventured across to their table.

Kate was almost beside herself until at last a well-dressed old man, in a tweed coat and fishing hat came up to the stall and started sniffing around. He didn't say much, just 'hummed' and 'hawed' as if he knew what he was on about and smiled when Kate offered him a sample. Her mouth was as dry as the cheese that he was tasting. She had to hold her hands behind her back to stop them from shaking and she avoided Mr Kramer's amused looks of approbation.

'How much?' the old gentleman finally asked, looking up at her through half-moon glasses as he pointed at a large round Gouda that stood proudly in the middle of the display.

Kate felt intimidated. He might be a doctor or a professor and she had never spoken to either before. 'It's three shillings and two pence ha'penny a pound,' she finally piped up, annoyed with herself for being so nervous.

'No, no, for the whole wheel,' he stated. 'How much for the whole thing?' Kate was too taken aback by his request to give him a straight answer. She did not know how much a whole round was worth.

'Well, it's about five and three-quarter pounds,' she said. Her mind raced to do the calculations.

'Sixteen shillings and ten pence then,' he stated, before she had a chance to finish. He must be a professor, she thought with embarrassment. 'You'd have to sing for that,' he added remarking at the price. And that's how it all started.

'Actually it is sixteen shillings and three pence ha'penny,' Kate corrected with a smile. Checking the calculations twice in her head had delayed her giving an answer, but she knew she was right. The answer brought her confidence and with it she felt that she could handle her first potential customer. 'Of course, if you are buying the whole thing then there'd be a discount,' she stated as she looked to Mr Kramer for approval. She watched the old man re-do his calculations. 'And if you want me to sing I'll do that as well,' she added, meaning every word she said.

The old man looked at her, obviously impressed by her mental agility. He realised he had forgotten to carry the half.

'Can you sing as well as you do mathematics?'

'Even better,' Kate replied, buoyant at the prospect. 'Do you have any particular favourites?' she asked and reached for her guitar behind the trestle to show that she was serious.

'Do you by any chance know "Ever the winds?"' he asked. Kate did not answer. She just smiled and held his gaze for a moment then started to sing. Her voice was sweet and enchanting and as she sang each bar, the notes seemed to linger for longer than it was possible:

> 'As I went to walking down by the green brook
> Down where the ivy and laurels entwine
> I heard a bird singing a sad plaintive love song
> She mourned for her true love as I mourn for mine
>
> Ever the winds keep on changing their journey
> Ever the waves keep on changing of the sea
> Evergreen summer keeps changing to autumn
> Oh my true love has changed but there is no change in me
>
> I bought my love flowers all tied up with ribbons
> But soon the sweet flowers had faded and gone
> Like the flowers my true loves affections have withered

> Which leaves me alone here to pine and to mourn
>
> Ever the winds keep on changing their journey
> Ever the waves keep on changing of the sea
> Evergreen summer keeps changing to autumn
> Oh my true love has changed but there is no change in me
>
> My constant companions are sadness and sorrow
> Oh trouble has never forsaken me yet
> Wherever I wander my days are all numbered
> The love of my soul I will never forget.'

When she had finished the old man had his eyes closed as if he had been savouring every word.

'Wonderful,' he said when he opened them.

'It's a sad song, don't you think?' Kate replied.

'Not the way you sing it,' he said. 'It was my wife's favourite song, believe it or not,' he said, without any sadness, nor did he mention that she had died. The song and the memories of his wife made him truly happy. He pulled out his wallet, fumbled for change and gave Kate the exact amount for her revised calculation.

'No, no, it's too much she said, trying to give him back the discount she had promised, but he refused.

'Young lady, you have given me today a little bit of heaven for which I am truly grateful and it has been worth every single penny of it,' he said with the warmest of thanks.

He tucked the round of cheese under his arm. 'Good day to you,' he nodded, taking off his hat. 'I'll see you again soon.'

That's all it took. With a little bit of daring Kate had managed to sell her first piece of cheese and attract an audience of potential customers into the bargain.

'Do I have to buy a whole one to get a song?' a mother asked half-jokingly with two noisy children in tow. She did not expect that Kate would sing for her at all. But Kate obliged and the children settled down and gave their mother a moment's peace. She was so appreciative that the woman ended up buying more than she really needed.

'Keep singing, keep singing,' Mr Kramer encouraged enthusiastically as the crowd swelled to listen to her voice. Such was her repertoire that she was able to tailor her songs to each customer and the amount of cheese that they were willing to buy. A chorus, a verse, a whole song was sung if they spent enough. Lotty looked on in amazement as Kate worked the crowd. She had them in the palm of her hand and charmed and joked with them like a real entertainer. Every word and movement was measured to bring out the best in her audience. By twelve o'clock they had sold all of their produce.

'We'll be back next week!' Kate called out after giving one last encore and then she disappeared behind the stall. She was exhausted, but exhilarated by the outpouring of nervous energy. Mr Kramer appeared a few moments later, wild with excitement. Several people had already placed orders for the following week. 'Ve are on to ze vinner!' he said and for the first time he grabbed Kate and gave her a crushing bear hug to express his affection. Lotty joined in with a chorus.

Chapter seven

Every success brings its own unique set of problems and for Kate this was no exception. It wasn't the extra work or the fact that she had to sing or that sometimes she would be a little bit hoarse for a day or so afterwards. As the weeks rolled into months she gained a steady following of loyal customers – including a fairly decent bunch of young men. Most of them were her own age, cheerful and good mannered, full of words of encouragement, but it was an unfamiliar situation for her. That in itself though, was not what ailed her.

The problem was that she was a girl and they were boys and the effect they were having on her was starting to lead to confusion. Here she was, the natural entertainer, singing to them and flirting with them and calling them all sorts of names from the safety of her stall, to get them to buy her cheese. But their response to her was starting to affect her in a way that she could not comprehend.

'Stay away from men,' Sister O' Connor, her old dorm

matron had scolded with a tongue so venomous and spiteful you would think all men were poisonous. Kate understood what she was talking about from the wide-eyed stories her classmates had told her. Her seclusion up to now had been part and parcel of following the advice that had been drummed into her.

'Easy when you are a child, because fellahs are ugly,' she remembered one of her more mature classmates say in St. Pats not long before she departed. But the late blossoming of her confidence and youth brought a different story. For as long as she had dreamed, she was going to marry a prince. It had just never occurred to her how she was going to do it. When the right man came along she would know it, just like in the stories her grandfather used to tell her. She really was not on the lookout for anything else. Now, all of a sudden, it seemed she had all of these suitors hanging around and didn't know how to cope. They came looking for cheese, but it was more they wanted, like to talk or to walk or something a little bit extra.

'One thing always leads to another,' Miss O' Connor used to warn. Kate was well aware, but the physical effects they were having on her were starting to drive her to distraction.

'Ach, she is getting very moody,' Mr Kramer commented to Lotty one day. 'I vish zat she vould hurry up and meet ze nice fellow and do something about it.' Kate was used to being in control of herself. Used to being able to handle whatever life threw at her, but now, in spite of it's great success, she found that she was beginning to dread going to the market. That is, until the day she met Brendan.

Chapter eight

'You have fifteen seconds left in the game after I blow this whistle!' the referee informed Brendan. 'Make sure you get that ball over that bar,' he whispered out of earshot of the other team as he stood back to let Brendan take the penalty. 'We don't want those bastards taking the cup home!'

It was neck and neck. Fifteen seconds, and it would all be over. It was the toughest game that Brendan had ever played as captain of the hurling team. He was one player short, with all of his subs used up and most of his team-mates battered and bruised. The other side were in no better shape. There had been several hot-tempered scraps along the way, but the competition had been fair, if not something fearsome. His team had been fouled on the side line at the halfway mark with a penalty awarded in their favour. With hurley in hand and the ball placed on the ground Brendan stood facing the goal posts at a seemingly impossible angle. The entire game now rested on his shoulders and the air was tense with the crowd's excitement. He stood in front of the ball, at right angles to the sideline with his sights set rigidly on the narrowest of gaps between the goal posts. He brought his focus to bear, looked down at the slither again. He was on his way to returning his gaze one last time to the posts before shooting, when he caught the sight of Kate in the middle of the crowd. In an effort to follow the Kramers' advice she had decided to go to the game by herself for a change, but she had never intended such consternation.

'Come on Brendan!' one of his team-mates shouted at him. He was so distracted by her beauty that he had not heard the whistle. Valuable seconds were being wasted. The crowd went crazy, sensing his hesitation and every voice rallied him into action.

'Go on!' She willed him in unison with the crowd and the urgency that was written all over her expression. It was enough to bring him back to his senses. He dropped his gaze and focused on the ball. With a quick scoop of the hurley to get it in the air, he used his entire body to give it an almighty belt and sent it in the direction of its target. There was awestruck silence from the crowd as the slither sailed across the gap to where it had been aimed. Time stood still and breaths were held in anticipation. It was impossible to tell if the ball was going to make it or not. All eyes were on it save for Kate's. Hers were fixed on Brendan's who returned her gaze. She was suddenly embarrassed and blushed at being the cause of his confusion as he had tried to make the shot. They should have been watching the ball, but Kate could tell by his face what was going to happen. The determined look was replaced by a smile and then a broad cheeky grin as the crowd let out a deafening roar. Brendan had timed it perfectly to stall before the posts. Then, aided by the wind, it dropped through the very centre of the gap. In the dying seconds he alone had won the game. There was pandemonium as the spectators invaded the field. Five of his team-mates rushed forward to congratulate him and lifted him up on their shoulders in celebration. Overwhelmed, there was little Brendan could do to save himself. He held onto the sight of Kate for as long as he could, but in the excitement he was swept away. After the final whistle Kate returned to the boarding house and made Mrs Cummins her tea. She told her all about the game and the exciting ending, but in all of her descriptions she failed to mention Brendan and the somersaults her heart had made when he had looked at her. When Mrs Cummins was settled, Kate went off on her evening walk as was her habit. She was floating down a river of happiness when suddenly she was awoken from her dream by the sound of revelry. It was then that she discovered that she had not taken her usual path down by the sea. She found herself instead in the centre of the town. She had stumbled unwittingly across a party that had spilled outside of a pub onto the street in celebration of the big win. Such was the love of the game that the players from both teams had been celebrating together. There were bodies everywhere in various states of merriment, but all stood to salute in admiration as Kate walked past. Further down the street there was a man lying on his back on the path under a street light with his head propped against the railings of a house. He had a half-glass of Guinness balanced on his chest and several full bottles sitting on the ground beside him. Kate could hear him humming quietly to himself as she approached. The tune sounded like 'Molly Malone'. He noticed her and that he was blocking her way. Kate was about to step on to the street to walk around him when he sprang to his feet, surprising her.

'I'm not that bad,' he said, noting the look on her face, but he had to lean against the railings to steady himself. 'I needed the break,' he added nodding in the direction of the party. It was the honesty in his voice that stopped her from walking past him. 'You'd think that we were after winning the All-Ireland Final the way they are carrying on.' But there was a certain sense of triumph in his smile all the same. 'Everybody insists on buying the captain a drink,' he said to justify all of the bottles on the pavement beside him. 'I don't know what I'm going to do with all of this – there's way too much for me.' Then his eyes suddenly came to focus in the dim light. 'It's you!' he gasped and jerked himself upright. 'I was just thinking about you,' he said pointing to where he had been lying. Kate was thrown completely, as if he had been reading her mind. She had been caught off-guard and was too embarrassed to say anything. Her only recourse was to make an escape.

'Don't go,' he said reaching down for a bottle in the hope that she might share a drink with him, but when he straightened up she had faded from his view just as quickly as she had entered.

'I couldn't have done it without you,' he called after her, afraid to give chase in case he might frighten her. His statement made her stop in the darkness. 'The most beautiful thing I have ever seen,' she heard him say. She was not sure if it was her he was talking about or the shot that had won the game. A part of her had the urge to go back and talk to him, but sense prevailed. It might be the drink that was talking and that he would regret what he had said in the morning. She watched him as he slid down the railing and sat back on the pavement. He took a sip from his pint and cleared his throat then started to sing again.

'In Dublin's fair city
Where the girls are so pretty
I first laid my eyes on sweet Molly Malone ....'

His voice followed her all of the way to the end of the street.

Chapter nine

Brendan was born Brendan Francis, to James and Joan Finucane, on a rainy day, typical of the weather in Ireland. He was the first son of the first son of five generations of the Finucane family, and the heir to one of the biggest estates in the southernmost counties. His birth was followed in quick succession by his younger brother John and his little sister Elsabeth. James and Joan had been trying for years to start a family. After two miscarriages and three healthy children they were content that their family was complete.

     The early years were happy. The children had all they wanted and led a privileged life. Their estate house was filled with maids and private tutors – only the best for the Finucane family. As well as the estate they had a town house in Tralee and another in the capital city of Dublin. James Finucane had inherited an ancient title. Behind his back the locals referred to him as the 'Lordy'. It was a hang-back from the olden days when his ancestors, for all intents and purposes, ran the county to their pleasing. He could be a hard man to deal with and even harder to live with because of his impatience and quick temper. Not the most ideal disposition for raising children. But everyone coped, and with their mother to look over and protect them, they were what you might call a united family.

Brendan was lean and agile and loved the outdoor life. Hunting and fishing and climbing the mountains that surrounded their estate were his favourite pastimes. Anything that required a sense of adventure. School, from an early age, had never really suited him. He found it hard to apply himself to what he called the 'intangibles'. It was a struggle for him to study anything that did not have some sort of practical application. His tutors were always reprimanding him for looking out the windows and daydreaming when he should be concentrating on his work. He lost his fishing rights several times over the years, a punishment his father found far more effective in making him concentrate than any other reprimand.

'That boy is too much of a dreamer,' James complained to his wife more than once about their eldest son. 'He has too many grand plans that will never amount to anything.' He was a worry to his father, too soft like his mother, and too full of notions that as far as he was concerned were crazy. 'He's always walking around with his feckin' head in the clouds. Why, last week he was talking about flying across the Atlantic. Can you imagine it? It takes a week by ship for God's sake! Who the hell would pay to travel that far in an aeroplane? It's on the ground he needs to keep his feet, if he is ever going to learn to manage the estate.' James was doing his best to mold the boy, but Brendan was too wayward. He thought too much, asked too many questions, and from an early age had too many ideas that were simply impossible. His father nearly had a fit when Brendan proposed the idea of a co-operative.

'What the hell does a farmer with five-hundred acres need a co-operative for?' James lectured him. 'You'll give your advantage away to too many small holders. Before you know it you won't be making any money. You know it has taken us five generations to build things up to the way they are. Why would you want to be giving it all away when you are set up for the future?' He nearly had a heart attack on the day Brendan qualified as an accountant from university and raised the idea of splitting the farm with John.

'There is more than enough for the two of us,' he had tried to persuade his father. 'What with all of the new machinery that is coming in, and farming methods changing. The estate will become twice as profitable as before. I wouldn't be giving up anything.' It took two large whiskeys for his father to calm down. Joan Finucane took the brunt of his father's frustration.

'Most of my time these days is spent with my eyes raised up to the heavens over that boy,' he complained to her, his underlying tone of disapproval indicating that she was to blame. Her going soft on his children was a terrible frustration to him. If his younger brother had been the first-born, then his father would not have had any problems. John was a different story. He was smart in school and good at his subjects and used it as a way of having one up on his elder brother. By the time they had grown into teenagers it was inevitable that an overblown sense of sibling rivalry had developed between them. It was something that their father encouraged and he was not averse to playing one off against the other. Brendan would win approval by excelling at sport and whatever else he put his mind to. John, on the other hand, achieved the same results, by simply making those around him look worse than he appeared himself. In doing so, he had become cunning and ruthless, not the sort of person you wanted to get on the wrong side of. It was a quality his father wished he could develop in his elder son. In the early years, Joan was well able to handle her husband and shelter the children from his manipulations and ministrations. But as they began to approach adulthood she held far less sway.

'Sure the boys are their own masters!' He became fond of saying that when confronted by his wife over his 'interfering' as she called it. But he was forever in the background pushing and controlling their lives more than a parent should. Eventually Joan gave up arguing with him when she realised that he was no longer listening. He had grown used to having his own way and as a result assumed he was always right.

The Finucane children always gained their father's approval at a price. From an early age there had always been strings attached to his affections. A fishing rod or a bike, their first gun when they could be trusted, the use of the family car when they had grown old enough was his way of getting them to do what he wanted. The ultimate reward, as far as he was concerned, was their inheritance. Nothing else was made to matter, neither their thoughts, nor their dreams, nor their ambitions. The inheritance was the rock to which they were anchored. It could be seen and quantified, planned and built upon. Secured in the knowledge that their position in life was guaranteed. 'Why would they be wanting to do this or that or take any chances when their future is already there and waiting for them?' he would reason. All they had to do was behave themselves and fit in with his plan, and in the end they'd get what they had always wanted.

The inheritance to James was the hub around which his ancestors had revolved. Their compass, their centre, their bearing. By their teenage years James had a firm grip on the helm and their course was very much set for the future. Brendan by birthright would inherit the farm after he had trained as an accountant. He would get married and carry on a tradition that would eventually lead to politics. John would train as a lawyer and be set up in a successful business and he too would marry and be expected to show a profit. Elsabeth was left very much under the tutelage of her mother. James Finucane professed to having very little understanding of women. He did not mind what she did, as long as she grew up a lady and married someone respectable.

What Brendan had in mind was far removed from his fathers ideals, but saying so made no difference. He held little sway with his father and had learnt from an early age that it was better to keep the peace than argue with him. He harboured his discontent quietly, biding his time as his mother advised, in the hope that as he grew older his father might see him in a different light. In the meantime he got on with his life.

He was a keen sportsman and had been the captain of the local Under Twenty-One hurling team for two years. In spite of his position in the community as the Lordy's son, he had proved himself as one of their best players, earning the position of team captain through strong leadership qualities, hard training and a quick fist to any opponent who threatened himself or any of his team-mates on the field – a symptom perhaps of his frustrations with his father. Despite this, the selectors had their eye on him for the senior county team when he turned twenty-one. It was all working out according to his father's plan. Then one afternoon a bi-plane fell out of the sky on top of him and changed his life forever.

Chapter ten

Brendan had been doing fitness training on the beach. If hurling was his first love then swimming was his second. He would swim all year round regardless of the season or weather. A large group of rocks lay about a mile offshore and he would swim out around them and back to the beach again 'just to warm up'. If he had the time he would do two circuits to help strengthen his shoulders and arms and harden him for the more physical games. As a goal to keep him motivated he would enter in to the 'Muglins', an annual endurance race of over eight miles to a small group of islands offshore.

The beach was level, long and compact. Perfect for sprints and distance running and perfect for a runway. Just what the stricken pilot had needed to make an emergency landing in his bi-plane. His engine had overheated, spewing hot oil into his face and goggles. In his struggle to get down safely he had failed to see Brendan, missing his head by a matter of inches as he touched down. He was shocked when Brendan ran up behind him after his plane came to a halt. He thought he was going to receive a thumping for nearly killing the runner. Instead he found the young man out of breath, but exhilarated.

'God, I'm awful sorry,' Victor Beamish said. His embarrassment was genuine as he climbed out of the cockpit. Although he was just under six feet tall he was shorter than Brendan. When he took off his flying cap he had rust-coloured hair, but his thick moustache and face under the outline of his goggles was stained black. He was twice Brendan's age, but agile as he jumped from the wing onto the strand. Brendan had little interest in his apology.

'It's an Avro,' Brendan exclaimed. 'Looks like a 631!'

'Actually it is,' Victor was surprised by Brendan's knowledge. 'You seem to know a bit about aeroplanes.'

'A bit,' said Brendan, his eyes wide with delight. 'I flew in C3 a few years ago at Baldonnel,' he said. He explained how his father had paid for a joyride for himself and his brother while attending an air display when they were younger.

'Do you mind if I take a look?' Brendan asked.

'Delighted!' said Victor. 'Give me a second to clean this bloody oil off me face and I'll be happy to give you the grand tour.' He had a flask of coffee which he pulled out from behind the passenger seat and they shared it as they talked.

'She is a great little plane, but not exactly designed to be flown the way I was throwing her around,' he said, pointing to the oil spray on the fuselage and cockpit windscreen. It was then that he noticed the tide was coming in. He had purposely landed on the firmer sand below the high water mark to prevent the wheels from digging in and causing the plane to nosedive into the ground. Now the sea was threatening to sink him.

'I'll give you a push,' said Brendan, noting his predicament. They struggled with the weight of the aircraft up the slope of the beach to drier sand. With the tide quickly gaining Victor was more than grateful for Brendan's help. 'I have a few tools in the car, spanners and the like,' Brendan offered. When he hung around to help fix the oil leak Victor made an offer.

'Would you be interested in a go?' he asked.

'Are you serious?'

'Absolutely. I'm more than grateful for your help. It's the least I can do in return.' And so began Brendan's first flying lesson. Victor started with the theory of flight, but Brendan already knew it from the books he had read. It was just a matter of getting his hands on the controls. By the time they had fixed the leak and the tide had receded he was more than ready to take to the skies.

'I can only give you about fifteen minutes in the air because the light has almost faded,' Victor apologised. 'I don't suppose you know of a decent paddock inland away from the salt air? There is no way I'll have time enough to make it all the way home.' Brendan's eyes lit up with a sudden inspiration.

'You can use our front garden,' he stated with enthusiasm. Victor laughed at the offer.

'It would have to be the size of a football field to land this thing,' he said.

'It is!' Brendan replied, 'and our house is as big as a hotel. If you give me another flying lesson tomorrow I'll throw in free room and board.' Victor could not help but smile at the method in Brendan's madness.

'Let's get going then,' he said. They worked quickly to get the bi-plane ready for take-off. 'You better not be joking me,' was the last thing he said before they taxied down the beach. With a hop, skip and a jump they were in the air. Brendan was in heaven for the ten minutes it took them to fly to the manor and Victor was more than pleased upon their arrival. The so-called front garden was indeed the size of a football field and perfect for landing. Victor could not get over the size of the house.

'This is something else,' he said as they climbed down from the cockpit.

'It's you Brendan!' Elsabeth called out in surprise. She had run out to greet the strange apparition and did not recognise the visitors until Brendan had taken off his flying helmet and goggles. 'Mam and Dad are staying in Tralee for the night on political business,' she informed him after he introduced her to Victor. He had been anxious that his parents meet his new friend.

'That will have to wait,' he replied. With the promise of some serious flying time the following day, and a joyride for his sister, Brendan and Elsabeth took it upon themselves to turn on the hospitality. Victor was given the 'half acre', the largest guest bedroom in the house named for its voluminous size and reserved usually for bishops and visiting dignitaries. A bath was run, his clothes were freshly laundered and Brendan plundered the cellar for a dozen different bottles to kick off the evening.

'Oh, you're a man after me own heart,' Victor stated as he wiped the dust off a bottle of Johnny Walker scotch whiskey that Brendan had brought back along with some stout, red wine, port and a half-sized bottle of sherry for his sister. Their guest was as good a talker as he was a flier, and regaled Brendan and his sister with adventures of his flying past that included combat in the final days of the First World War.

'No way!' said Brendan with reverence when Victor told him that he had met Mickey Mannock, the great fighter ace. 'What about Albert Ball?'

'Albert and I were good friends,' Victor said surprised yet again by Brendan's knowledge, but he was reluctant to answer the question about the mystery of how Albert had fallen to his death from his own aircraft. He spoke with great animation, using his hands to describe the numerous engagements that they had fought together.

Originally from Dublin, and of independent means, Victor had had wanderlust for years, but decided just recently to settle down outside of Tralee. He was in the process of starting a small flying school. By the end of the night Brendan in his excitement had all but committed to being his first student.

They woke early the following morning with hangovers. For the first time in his life Brendan missed hurling training. The idea of flying was far more appealing and Victor's loose tongue from the drink the previous evening had promised him aerobatics.

Pure, unadulterated, naturally distilled adrenaline would be the best way to describe Brendan's experience the next day. Climbing, falling, twisting, tumbling and rolling until his insides were like jelly and his mind ablaze with the thought of how he was going to get his own aeroplane some day. When Brendan pointed out his parents' car, returning from Tralee, Victor dived on them from behind and made a hair-raising pass overhead as they drove up the tree-lined driveway to the manor.

'He has the touch,' Victor said in all honesty of his young protégé to his family as they lunched together afterwards. Brendan by now was hooked on the idea of earning his very own flying licence. He gave his visitor a tour of the estate by horseback and did not return to the manor until Victor had disappeared over the horizon in the late afternoon. Despite the great day that it had been, Brendan's father had left a summons to see him in the drawing room the very second that he had returned.

'Who do you think you are?' he attacked, the second Brendan entered the room. James Finucane was not amused and made it clear now that Victor had gone. 'That Beamish fellow is loud and crass and not the type we associate with.' Out of good manners James had been sociable towards their visitor which had prevented him from making a scene, but now he got stuck into Brendan for his recklessness.

'And what the hell do you think you are doing, allowing your sister to go up in that contraption and endangering her life?' he demanded. 'As far as I'm concerned that man is a danger to us all and I do not want him near this place,' he stated.

'But Father!' Brendan tried to defend himself in front of his mother and sister but his father quickly cut him off.

'Cop on to yourself for God's sake!' he admonished. The only saving grace had been that his brother John was not there to capitalise on his embarrassment. Brendan had been on a high. He had made a new friend and was having the time of his life until his father shot him down. They had only been having a bit of fun. There was no way he would have let his sister up with Victor if he'd thought for a second she might be in danger. He was sure that if his father had not spent the morning brooding in the background that his mother would have enjoyed a short flight as well.

It was becoming harder and harder to put up with his father. He did all he could to please him, never a cross word, but the man was never satisfied. It might not have been so bad if the flying had not been so good. He could have worn it if his father had held his tongue. He could have put it down to a great day, gone back to his hurling and concentrated on the preparation needed for the county final. Instead he found after that day that he craved the thrill of the air to relieve his stifled existence.

'Will ya ever get on with it!' John said one morning to his brother over breakfast a couple of weeks later when their father was not around.

'What do you mean?' Brendan stopped buttering his toast to hear John's reply.

'Go and get yourself a flying licence for God's sake! These walls have ears,' he pointed with a fork that had a piece of bacon on the end, when he noted Brendan's confusion. 'Don't be telling Elsabeth what you are thinking if you don't want everyone else to know!'

'She told you?'

'Of course, and Mam as well. Sure isn't it obvious and the long face on ya since you landed.'

'What about the old man?' Brendan asked, knowing that there was no way he could do it without his father's support.

'Are you mad?' John replied. 'Article 42, subsection five, of the Brendan Finucane conspiracy to get a pilot's licence clearly states that only those parties who will support said conspiracy are to be notified. The old man is not included!' John stated with legal authority. Brendan was relieved. John had missed Victor's visit and all of the excitement because of his work in Tralee. In spite of this though, he too had received a bollocking from his father on his return home, warning him not to get any similar ideas. Brendan decided to confide in his brother. It was better to do so than run the risk of being discovered later on and have it used against him.

'It is easy for you to say. You have a real job. Victor is not going to teach me for nothing!' Brendan's biggest problem was money. He might have been the manager of one of the biggest farms in the southern counties, but the profits were not going into his pockets. He had a modest expense account, of which he had to justify to his father every penny spent. He had a small cash allowance also, but it simply was not enough to pay for flying lessons.

'Relax will ya,' John said, sensing his brother's desperation. 'I have been doing some thinking on the subject.' He tapped his forehead in an animated gesture. John had always been very clever about his rebellions, and was never short on ideas to defy his father. 'There is money to be made if a body is willing,' he said, and leaned closer to Brendan to let him in on his little secret. 'There is a small business that you might be interested in taking over. It's an old woodworking shop left idle after the owner died last year. I have seen the books, and the old fellah who worked it was into a nice few shillings making children's toys and simple furniture. The opportunity is there,' John winked. 'You can have it for buttons before it goes on the open market.' The fact that John was the executor of the will was purely coincidental. 'All you have to do is grab it!' Brendan argued that he did not live in Tralee, but John, being way ahead of him, reminded him that the disused stables at the end of the courtyard could be used as a workshop.

'It will be good and healthy to have an interest other than the farm,' John suggested in answer to their father's inquiries. 'And you won't have to justify how you spend the money either!' he said to his brother, nodding towards the heavens. Brendan could not help but smile at the simple brilliance of his brother's conspiracy.

In the short term it meant a delay in getting off the ground. Brendan used all of his savings and an extra twenty pounds he had to secretly borrow from his mother because some of the machinery he had bought needed fixing. He employed one of the farm apprentices and an older hand with a bit of experience who was glad of the extra income to support his young family. Brendan talked to retailers and used Elsabeth as an adviser because of her experience as a junior school teacher. He designed a basic line of simple toys that were imaginative and colourful and easy to manufacture.

It sounded easy to begin with, but as it turned out, it wasn't. It was frustrating and heartbreaking and drove Brendan almost to despair. The machines kept breaking down, the paint would not dry, and retailers cancelled orders on a whim, without explanation.

He was on the verge of giving up on the whole idea when he finally got the break he badly needed. The purchasing manager of HP Williams, the biggest store in Tralee, fell sick and was replaced by the daughter of the store owner. Angela Williams was young and pretty and inexperienced in purchasing, but she was keen to make an impression on her father. She took a shine to Brendan, not only because he was handsome, but for his manners, which set him apart from all of the other gobshites she had to deal with. He did not talk down to her as if she was a little girl, but rather treated her as an equal – something she really appreciated. They spent hours together talking about presentation and displays. A deal was done where Brendan supplied merchandise on credit and Angela promoted them with a creative display at the entrance to the store. The toys were a great success and impressed her father, enabling Angela to place a regular order. When she took it one step further and contacted several big stores in the surrounding counties Brendan began to get the cash flow he needed for flying.

For a while his discontent was put on the back burner. So long as he was busy he was happy. Victor was an excellent teacher and Brendan a good pupil. It did not take him long to get through the basic course. After gaining his licence Brendan finally fulfilled his greatest ambition when Victor set about teaching him cross-country flying and aerobatics. He mastered the skills easily, growing more confident with each lesson, and more daring every time he took off.

In spite of his success as a pilot he could not shake his growing feelings of frustration. He was never one for feeling sorry for himself, but he felt trapped, weighted down by the responsibility of five generations and a father who just would not listen to him. He loved the farm and knew that the estate, in many ways, represented a great opportunity. With diversification and the addition of new technology, the old-fashioned methods and gross inefficiencies could be overcome to create great potential for the future. The thought of it held a certain excitement for him. In spite of John's help there remained a sibling rivalry that was divisive. He knew that he could use the farm to redress the imbalance. If he halved the farm with his younger brother they could easily unite to double the output and carry on the tradition of the family. But the way his father talked there was little chance of it.

The more he flew the more detached he became so that he considered giving up the land altogether. Flying gave him a confidence that he had never imagined. There was a whole world out there, waiting to be taken on and Brendan was beginning to think that it might be better than living in the shadow of his father's limited imagination.

Chapter eleven

John could never understand his brother. He was always on about something. Marketing boards and co-ops and raising standards and giving something back to the community. It all seemed like a whole lot of work and that held very little attraction for him. John was nothing like Brendan. He always enjoyed the 'big' lecture their father gave them about their heritage and their position and 'how some things should never change'. He liked the idea of superiority, having the 'moral high ground' to look down from, and used his position to his own advantage when dealing with those he perceived as beneath his standing.

'You either have it or you don't,' he loved saying, revelling in the knowledge that, to his cronies, *he* was one of the privileged. From an early age though, John's problem was that he knew where he had come from and where he was expected to go, and he was not all that pleased about it. His role in life, it seemed, was always to come second. Brendan was getting the farm, that was a foregone conclusion, which meant he, John was going to have to go out and earn an independent living. It was a big comedown from what he had grown used to, and he had every intention of putting it off for as long as possible.

What annoyed him most was Brendan's enthusiasm to share the farm. He could not understand where he had come up with the idea. He had little interest in crop rotations and percentage yields or field irrigation or efficiency. The idea of working with his brother 'in a family business' was beyond his imagination. He knew what he would be doing if he was getting the farm for himself. Sharing it with his brother was not part of the plan. He would put a manager in and have him do the work while he kicked back and enjoyed the status that he had been born into. He liked the idea of being the Lordy and holding court. It irritated him how Brendan always played it down. His father in his wisdom had decided that he should be a lawyer and was prepared to pay for the privilege. He had made arrangements for him to join a long-established law firm in Tralee after his graduation. It was a staid affair run by two old partners in ancient offices overlooking the town centre. John was made partner after only one year. On the face of it he looked like the young up-and-coming lawyer with a promising future and he was shrewd enough to play the part. It suited the old lawyers, for they wanted to retire and he was being groomed as part of the arrangement that had been made long before John had gotten wind of it. If they had one thing in common it was that John's destiny was as pre-ordained as that of his elder brother.

In spite of his father's machinations John managed to have plenty of good times along the way. He enjoyed socialising and drinking and attending parties. With his new success he bought his own car and took up with his cousins in Tralee. There were plenty of them on his mother's side and he got himself invited to all the social occasions. As he matured he began to have ideas about himself and worked hard on perfecting his image. With his background and the contacts, he quickly learnt to use his position to his advantage. He discovered that women were easily attracted to him and 'the right type' were more readily mislead by his cunning. His silvery tongue and persuasiveness made him seem like a good catch. For the 'right women' he would do anything – whatever it took to give them what they wanted, and get what he wanted in return. John was a different breed to his brother altogether, and that was what led him to Kate.

    He was in Tralee one Saturday having lunch with a friend and complaining that he was having a bad day.

    'Some clients are genuinely thick,' he complained as he downed his first pint, 'and the rest are not far behind. I've had better conversations with the priest in confession.'

    'Cheer up,' his friend said, shifting the subject to matters more vital. 'Have you heard about the pretty thing down at the market who sings for her customers?'

    Forever on the lookout, John leaned in closer. They were two of a kind that shared stories of their conquests, and after hearing a lengthy description of the girl, John promised he would go down that very day to form his own opinion. Brendan was 'away with the birds' as John would say about his flying. They had an arrangement to meet down at Fitzgerald's hardware store to pick up some new parts for the threshing machine for the farm. But that was not until two o'clock. He had a half-an-hour to kill after lunch and, armed with a promise and a couple of drinks under his belt, he ventured down to the market to take a quick gander at the girl.

    When he finally laid eyes on Kate he could not believe what he was seeing. The crowd that surrounded her were just as taken by the spell that she wove around them. She was laughing and joking with her customers and flirting with those who had the wit to rib her. It was all harmless fun that the crowd enjoyed, but John saw something different. She was a spirited filly with her big mane of hair. The way that she played to the crowd made him feel that she was looking for a riding. He decided there and then that he would have her. He had done it before, calculating and ruthless, biding his time until his prey lay themselves open to his pleasure. He watched her for a while, making sure that she did not see him – not until he was ready to make his first move. First impressions were always half the battle and he knew this one might be his greatest challenge. At the turn of the clock he had to meet up with Brendan, but he left in better spirits than he had started out that morning. 'Things are looking up,' he said to himself as he departed the market. When he met his brother it turned out that he was in a foul mood with no desire to go to Fitzgerald's.

'Feckin' threshing machine,' Brendan cursed in exasperation. 'I spent the whole morning trying to get that bloody crankcase taken off when I should have been flying. The last thing I want to do is look at more machinery!'

'Fair enough,' John replied with a smile, delighted to be free of the obligation. 'It's your department. Anyway I've got a better idea!' He nodded in the direction of the market. 'Come on, I've got something to show you.' It was not like John to show off the future victims of his less than noble intentions. He liked to talk about his trophies to those that would listen, but seldom brought them out for display, especially in front of his puritan brother. Brendan was too old-fashioned and lacked relish for the hunt that was sport to John and some of his friends. But this time John could not help himself.

'What is it?' Brendan asked, his curiosity now piqued.

'You mean who is it, more like?' John let go a sly wink before grabbing Brendan by the shoulder and steering him towards the market. He seldom rushed anywhere, but now he was almost in a fever, anxious that she might be gone by the time they got there. He could hardly believe himself. He'd had a few drinks over lunch but it was the thought of her that filled him with intoxication. She had gotten *'into him'*. Now as they rushed headlong towards the market he was obsessed by the thought of doing the same to her. Brendan forgot about the crankcase and his oil-stained overalls and took up the chase in obedient pursuit. It was not often he saw his brother get this excited. They turned off the main street and into the market and almost imperceptibly a voice could be heard singing above the hustle and bustle of the crowd. John forged ahead through the throngs of people milling about looking for a bargain. Brendan lost sight of him and it was several minutes before he finally found him standing at the edge of a large gathering. They were surrounding a fruit and vegetable stall with a large display of cheese in the centre. To his surprise there was a beautiful young girl singing.

'What do you think?' John said under his breath and elbowed Brendan in the ribs. 'She's a fine bit of stuff, what?' Her chest heaved with each breath so that she could sing out to the back of the crowd. Brendan realised she had the most beautiful voice he had ever heard. As she lowered her tone and sang softly to the accompaniment of her guitar Brendan felt himself being drawn in by the effort to hear her. He was charmed and enchanted and, in spite of his appearance, half-hoped that she might notice him. For John it was lust at first sight, and seeing her for a second time that day reaffirmed the promise that he had made himself earlier. He was going to have this girl. He did not care how long it took. She would be worth the waiting.

Brendan, on the other hand, was thunderstruck. For him it was love at second sight, for here was the girl from the game who had inspired him to make the winning point. He had been dreaming about her every day since. As he looked at Kate he admired her not just for her beauty or her voice, but also for the very clever way in which she played the crowd. It occurred to him that she was also the best sales person he had ever seen. She finally finished to the approval of the gathering. She had sold all she could. She stepped back to allow the crowd time to disperse so that she could attract a new set of customers.

'Give us another song,' someone called out from the back of the audience.

'Encore, encore!' someone cried out beside him. She smiled, but turned them down.

'You'll have to buy something if you want to hear another tune,' she said boldly, but no one took her up on the offer. She was about to put a bag of apples she had in her hand back on the stall when Brendan piped up, afraid of missing the opportunity.

'I'll take them!' he said, a little self-consciously. He was suddenly aware that he might have called out too eagerly. 'And a bag of pears,' he added to encourage her. She smiled back at him aware that she had been caught by her own devices. She had never demanded that someone buy her produce before she sang, and now she had to oblige for the very first time.

'Do you know "Shannon Bawn"?' he found himself asking as she handed him the fruit. Her eyes were like looking into heaven.

'Of course I do,' she replied as if he thought she was stupid and started to sing. John looked on, taken by surprise. Brendan had gotten in before him. He could have slagged him to embarrass him, but he did not want to attract attention. He decided instead to bide his time. Her singing to his brother meant nothing. Brendan enjoyed himself in the meantime, but was in for a big surprise when, at the end of the very first verse, she stopped singing.

'Is that it?' he said, clearly disappointed. He had expected her to sing the whole song.

'That's all you get for apples and pears,' she shot back with a cheeky grin and the crowd erupted with laughter. They could see that she had indeed gotten one up on him, but he took it well and laughed along with them. Not to be upstaged however, he pointed to a large round of cheese in the centre of the display.

'What if I buy one of those?' he asked, throwing down the gauntlet. The crowd jeered, impressed by his audacity. Despite his oil-stained overalls and greasy face, this time he had gotten her attention. He smiled back at her and those that looked on could see that there was romance flirting around the edges. She eyed him up and down and knew that he was serious. Despite his grubby appearance there was something about him that attracted her.

'Sing "The Day You Left Me",' the older woman behind the stall whispered. Kate sat on a stool and started to sing a sweet lament about two lovers parting. As she did, she wrapped the round of cheese carefully. It was as if she was the girl and the parcel was for the boy that was leaving and she was putting all of her heart in to it for him to take away on his journey. The crowd stood still, captivated. They could see that she *was* the girl in the song. On the second verse she stood up and walked over to Brendan, still singing. She handed him the gift, but caught by his gaze, their hands touched momentarily. It was then that she recognised him from the game a fortnight before. She was startled, but the urge to draw back to a safe distance was matched equally by the desire to linger on the touch of his hands. Brendan was shocked by the surge of passion that flowed between them, and embarrassed in front of the crowd. Those that were gathered could see that he was the boy in the song. It was absolutely magic. No one dared breathe for fear of breaking the spell.

Their hands held together long enough for a secret promise to pass between them – a knowing that they would meet again. The girl retreated then to the safety of the stall and Brendan backed into the crowd, but they didn't take their eyes off each other. Eventually she finished singing and the spell was finally broken. The crowd remained silent for a moment and then erupted into great cheers of laughter and applause.

'Well done, you boyo!' said a stranger, clapping Brendan on the back. 'That was mighty!' The crowd began to disperse.

'Are you right?' John said impatiently. 'We had better be going.' He was not happy about what had unfolded between his brother and the girl. Not happy at all.

'Hang on a second, I haven't paid for the cheese yet!' he said. 'You'll have to lend me a couple of quid.'

'What?' said John exasperated at the thought of having to pay for his brother's pleasure. 'You're not serious!'

'I thought you wanted me to meet her,' Brendan reminded him, happy to have an excuse to introduce himself properly. He stepped up to the stall before John could do anything about it.

'I'm Brendan,' he said to Kate as he struggled to hold the fruit and cheese under his left arm while at the same time reach out to shake hands with his right.

'John's brother,' he added, so as not to seem too forward. He nodded back to John, thinking that she already knew him. She took his hand and shook it politely, but he could see that she was a little bit confused. He opened up the space between himself and his brother so as to include him in the conversation. 'You do know each other?' he asked. John was visibly flustered, but he was quick to recover his composure.

'I'm John,' he introduced with an animated air of self-confidence and stepped forward to offer his hand. 'Don't mind him, he's only a Gombeen,' he stated, dismissing his brother in an effort to shift his own embarrassment. Kate shook his hand apprehensively.

'You said you had someone you wanted me to meet,' Brendan shot back, quick to capitalise on his brother's embarrassment. 'I assumed you already knew her.'

'No,' John replied, cool as punch. 'What I said … and to clarify the matter,' he added smiling at the girl, 'was that I would very much like to meet the young lady.' Brendan decided not to pursue the matter any further. John's embarrassment had helped him to overcome his own shyness. The girl, he noticed, was not as relaxed as before, and he did not take too kindly to the way that John lingered in holding her hand. She looked different when she had been lost in her singing. He sensed in her a certain vulnerability.

'Come Kate, das is time to pack up!' the old man called out from the back of the stall. 'Das is time everybody vas going home,' he added giving her a good excuse to finally free herself of John's hand. John released his grip reluctantly, smiling at her as she retreated. It was suddenly obvious to Brendan why John had brought him to the market.

'Thanks for the fruit and the song,' he said almost apologetically and offered her the money. 'We'll come back and see you another time,' he promised. Gripping his brother's elbow he steered him in the direction of the entrance to the market.

'She's something else, isn't she?' said John with a sly smile as soon as they were out of earshot.

'You're something else,' Brendan retorted. 'Will you put your tongue back in your mouth for God's sake before you trip over it!'

'What are you on about? She's a fine bit of fluff.' John tried to stop his brother from being so serious. 'There is no need to be so puritanical.'

'I'm not!' said Brendan annoyed at John's attitude towards the girl. 'You should not go on about her that way. It's very embarrassing. For all you know she is probably a great person.'

'She is great!' John winked at him, 'and you can fuck off,' he said, amazed at his brother's reaction. 'What about Lady Godiva?' he reminded. 'What about the hunt last winter and that blonde bird from up north that you were so stuck on?'

'I was drunk for Christ's sake!' replied Brendan. 'I didn't even know her,' he justified. He could barely remember who John was talking about and stormed ahead of his brother. At the entrance to the market he passed a dishevelled old man sitting on his hunkers with his cap in hand begging for pennies for the price of a dinner. Brendan was too annoyed to take any notice and passed straight by. John slowed momentarily and reached in to his pocket, but continued past the old man when all he could find was a half-a-crown. He was halfway across the car park before he thought twice about it and then turned back.

'Here, good luck to you,' he said and from a distance flipped the coin straight into the old man's hat who could hardly believe his eyes. For a half-a-crown he'd not only get a decent dinner, but a few pints of stout as well to go with it.

'God bless ya!' he shouted with appreciation after John, but he had already disappeared after his brother.

'You don't know this one either,' John continued the argument as he sat into the driver's seat beside his brother. 'So what are you on about? You wouldn't have met her if it wasn't for me!'

'That's not the point,' Brendan said. He could have explained about seeing her for the first time at the hurling match or singing to her in the street that night, but he fell silent instead, for fear of showing his true feelings.

'Fine!' said John. 'I won't say another word.' He was beginning to regret he had ever shown the girl to his stupid brother. 'God, you can be such a pain sometimes,' he stated as he steered his way out of the park. They drove on in silence, surprised at each other's reaction more than anything else. They had been getting on reasonably well lately and had not had a row like this in ages. After a while Brendan smiled at himself, amused at the effect the girl had made on them.

'Jayzis, I'll have to stop being so serious,' he said.

'You will, ya bollocks,' John agreed and they both broke into howls of laughter.

'Who are ye calling a bollocks?' Brendan demanded, landing a hefty punch into John's left shoulder that caused them to swerve. 'You're only a hoor.'

'And you are an eejit,' John said. 'Christ, for a minute there I thought you were serious,' he shot back catching Brendan off guard with a dig in the ribs. It was a good way of relieving the tension between them.

'You're right ... she was something else. But hardly worth falling out over.'

'Oh, I don't know,' replied John. Brendan punched him again until he said he was joking and that was the end of the row between them. Nothing further was mentioned of the girl after that, but for the entire trip home neither of them could stop thinking about when they might get to see her again.

Chapter twelve

Three days after Brendan met Kate he had arranged to make a large delivery of toys and furniture to a new customer. He was halted in his tracks by a phone call announcing that there had been a terrible fire and that the store had been levelled to the ground. As a consequence the order had to be cancelled and Brendan was left with an enormous surplus on his hands. He tried to offload it to his regular customers, but things were a bit slow. By the time he paid his workers and covered his expenses he was left strapped for the cash to pay Victor for his lessons.

By a sort of divine inspiration though, it suddenly occurred to him that the market might be the solution to his problem. Surplus was overhead, and overhead must be kept at a minimum. The fact that Kate happened to be there, he told himself, was purely coincidental. He made some inquiries, found out who the manager was and, with a bit of negotiation, secured himself a stall.

The decision put Brendan in better form. His work seemed lighter and the days running up to the opening of his stall a little shorter. The two lads in the workshop were delighted at the extra overtime to get organised and went about their jobs a little more relaxed than usual. It was not that Brendan was a hard man to work for, but he tended to be a bit on the serious side. He didn't talk much – just liked to get on with it. They had always felt obliged to do the same. Then he brought in an old wireless so that they could listen to the national station while they worked, and a primus so that they could make a cup of tea. If John had been around the workshop at all during that week he would immediately have grown suspicious. It was not like his brother to be so happy; not like him at all. When he worked he worked, you could not get a word out of him ... 'and he never listened to the feckin' radio!'

Brendan had been meaning to tell him about the market. To let him know. But somehow it had slipped his mind. Sure it was just the market and he'd be too busy looking after the business to be taking note of a girl. It was hardly even worth mentioning. Brendan had done a line with a couple of girls in the past, but none of them had ever made him feel like he wanted to get serious. He found them hard to relate to, especially when they found out who he was and where he was from. It would change them – change the way they would go on and they would always be trying to please him.

He would get married some day, but in the meantime there was work to be done. He had the farm and the workshop, his flying and now the market. There wasn't any room left for romance in his life and what little time he had he did not waste in playing around. John was always teasing him that the only idea he had about 'talent' was his so-called appreciation for classical music. 'Swing was in and he was out,' John would slag him, but it had never really bothered Brendan.

Chapter thirteen

Kate could not believe what she had done. There she was on her routine early morning walk around the market checking out each stall, and all of a sudden she saw Brendan setting up his own stock. Before she knew it and without thinking of the consequences, she had invited him over for a cup of tea. It was the shock, not knowing what to say, and then saying too much. She remembered how nerve-wracking it had been when she had set up for the first time. Kate had only wanted to make him feel welcome.

'What's wrong, Kate?' Lotty asked, after she arrived back from her walk. She knew her well enough to see she was flustered.

'Oh, God, Lotty,' she replied turning pink with embarrassment. 'What have I done, what have I done?' she said. 'What will I do?' she pleaded as she wrung her hands in her apron and hid behind the Kramer's car at the back of the stall.

'What is it, child?' Lotty said, worried something terrible

had happened. 'Heinrich, come quickly,' she called out to her husband who was standing close by.

'I've invited him for tea,' replied Kate, as if she had committed a mortal sin. The Kramers stood there totally confused.

'Who?' said Lotty, still caught up in Kate's anxiety. But Mr Kramer started to laugh.

'Ach, you haf done it now,' he joked and his eyes fixed firmly on Brendan sitting across the way. 'Look, Lotty,' he said nodding his head in Brendan's direction. 'Kate hass de boyfriend.'

'I do not!' Kate shot back. She hid behind Lotty so that her husband would not see her embarrassment.

'Mein Gott!' replied Lotty with pleasant surprise.

'What will I do?' Kate pleaded. 'I was only trying to be friendly.'

'He will come for tea and it will be very nice and we will all have a good time,' Lotty said, taking command. 'And you!' she said to her husband who was chuckling at Kate's predicament. 'You will behave yourself,' she ordered firmly 'or you know what will happen.'

'Ach, I vas only having ze fun,' he said, not put off one little bit by his wife's threats. 'Na na na na na,' he hummed after Kate as he returned to his work. Lotty shook her fist after him without saying a word, but he could tell by the expression on her face that she was also amused.

'Go down to Mrs Collin's stall and get a madeira cake,' Lotty ordered Kate. She reached into her apron for her purse to give her some money. 'And go over and get a new mug from the potter. By the time you get back I'll have the rest organised.' Lotty's command of the situation made Kate feel somewhat calmer. She returned with the cake, a bag of scones and a packet of biscuits, along with a cup the size of a toilet bowl and an expression that she knew she had overdone it.

'I owe the potter for the cup,' she said.

'It is okay,' said Lotty. 'Put them on the table and go and brush your hair and fix your apron. I have the kettle boiled so we are all ready.' She had covered a small camping table with a tablecloth and placed a glass of fresh daises in the centre. 'It will be fine,' she said, gesturing to the great spread of food.

'Thank you,' Kate whispered feeling a little calmer. It wasn't long after that Brendan showed up. He had a packet of biscuits in one hand and his cap in the other. He introduced himself, but for all of the confidence that he aired he still came across as being a little bit nervous. Fortunately for Kate, Mr Kramer liked the look of Brendan so the talk began easily between them. It was one-sided of course, because Brendan was too busy staring at Kate, who made herself busy, pouring tea and serving biscuits to distract herself from returning his gaze. Heinrich mostly talked about the market. He did the best he could with his limited English to dispense worthwhile information, but it was not long before he ran out of conversation. A moment of awkward silence followed, but then suddenly, he had a bright idea.

'Do you sing at all?' he inquired of Brendan, looking levelly at him.

'Excuse me?' Brendan was suddenly aware that Mr Kramer had asked him a direct question that needed an answer.

'Sing, young man. Are you able to sing ze songs?'

'I know one or two,' Brendan stammered. 'I wouldn't say I have a very good voice though.'

'You better start taking ze lessons!' Mr Kramer replied. 'If you can't sing you von't make ze shilling in dis place,' he continued tongue-in-cheek.

'Oh,' Brendan replied slightly crestfallen, as if his pathetic voice might be the difference between success and failure. Kate sat mortified, as she watched Mr Kramer indulge in his favourite pastime of winding a person up to make them look like a fool. There was a moment of silence while Brendan, knowing he could not sing, calculated his loss, but then suddenly he realised that Mr Kramer was pulling his leg.

'You are joking me, right!' he said with a hopeful smile on his face. Mr Kramer let out a burst of laughter. 'You bugger you!'

Brendan exclaimed, flushed with embarrassment, but he managed to laugh along with his tormentor. Everyone laughed then, especially Kate, relieved that the ice had finally been broken between them.

'You are ze gobshite ya,' Mr Kramer replied, laughing with tears in his eyes. There was nothing he liked more than setting up someone to make fun of them.

'I am ze gobshite,' Brendan replied, all the while looking at Kate and laughing at himself and she along with him. The relief was something wonderful. After that they all talked and joked and made fun of each other and the welcome warmth of friendly conversation settled between them as the market slowly began to fill with people. Brendan could have happily stayed there all day, but it wasn't long before Kate saw some potential customers hovering around his products.

'Go on, quick,' she urged him, almost pushing him off of his seat. 'We didn't come here to drink tea and eat biscuits,' she said as she hooshed him with enthusiasm towards his stall.

A lot of people stopped by for a look and were so impressed that Brendan managed to make some sales. He enjoyed the atmosphere and found that selling could be fun if you put a bit of 'energy and enthusiasm into it' as Mr Kramer had so sagely advised him. When it came to the toys the children were the key. Brendan found that if he could grab their imagination then the parents could easily be persuaded to purchase by offering them a discount or a bargain. By lunchtime he had made his first few pounds and by the end of the day he had made a small profit. His success added fuel to his ambitions. Some day he was going to own his own airplane. He was clear in his mind about that. He would build a hangar in one of the flat paddocks on the southern border of the estate where the drainage was good. From there he could fly all over the country. The way his toys and furniture were selling he might have an outlet in each of the major cities. He often daydreamed about flying all over the place checking on his expanding empire. It would be a great way to make a living. Not to mention the benefits of air travel. He knew his plan was in its infancy, but he could foresee a great and exciting future for himself. With bigger and better aircraft being developed, not only the rich or famous, but everybody could afford to fly. He might even have his own airline.

The highlight of his day though had been his time with Kate. He had slipped the market manager an extra five shillings to place his stall across from hers so that he was close enough to hear her sing. It made for a good marketing strategy as well. Her singing attracted the most people in the market and put them in good humour. It made sense to him to capitalise on the situation. The fact that he was in awe of her, was coincidental. But who did he think he was kidding? The crowd had seen it the day she first sang to him. The Kramers had made him welcome and encouraged the young couple's friendship.

'I'll see you next week,' he said when he came over to say goodbye at the end of the day.

'Thanks for all of the tea and cake, Mrs Kramer.' But all of the time he was looking at Kate and she at him and they were both smiling.

'You haf had ze gud day, ya?' Mr Kramer said, nodding in the direction of Brendan's stall.

'I have had ze great day!' he replied. 'I'm not such ze gobshite after all!' he joked, patting his pocket to show that he had made some money. He'd have gladly given it away and do it all over, just to see Kate again.

'You vill be back next veek then?' inquired Heinrich, watching the anticipation and hope on Kate's face.

'I will for sure,' replied Brendan and extended his hand to thank him for his friendship and his advice.

'Das is gut.'

'Thank you, Mrs Kramer,' he said to Lotty and shook her hand as well.

'Kate,' and he lifted the front of his cap to salute goodbye. He made no effort to get close or shake her hand.

'Okay,' she replied. ' Sure, it was no trouble,' she said

making herself busy this time breaking down the stall so that she would not have to come too close to him. Oblivious to the Kramers, she watched him as he walked away. She admired his powerful shoulders and his long stride and she finally allowed herself to think about him. She wanted him to turn and wave back one last time, but in a way she was glad that he did not, because Mr Kramer would never have let her live it down.

Chapter fourteen

As soon as the market became viable, Brendan was supposed to put Sean, the farm apprentice, in to manage the stall. He had flying to do. Hours to build up. Victor had said that the way he was going it would not be long before he could go on to twin engines. But he kept putting it off, saying 'maybe next week' to a disappointed Sean. He would make up excuses like 'it's not ready yet', and 'as soon as it has settled down I'll leave it to you', but at the market he was sitting with Kate, whenever they had a spare moment for drinking tea and eating the great cakes she had started baking, and chatting each other up as if there was no tomorrow.

'It was sheer luck,' he said when she commented on the closeness of his stall. 'Being in the right place at the right time.' He avoided her eyes for fear that she might discover his conniving. She was so beautiful and so light-hearted. He had never laughed so much with any other person before in his life. She had a great sense of humour and a mischievous manner. She in turn found him easy to talk to and was particularly glad when he started joining her on her early morning round of the market. Hitting it off as they did, it was inevitable that they would talk about their past and where they had come from. With Brendan it wasn't long before she felt secure enough to tell him about St Patrick's.

'Where did you learn all of your songs?' he had wanted to know.

'In a prison up on the west coast where they send all of the bold children of Ireland,' she joked, but waited in fearful anticipation to see what his response would be.

'Really!' he said, fascinated and a little curious. 'Tell me more,' he inquired. She gave him the broad picture, holding nothing back about the loneliness and the tyranny.

'I feel as sorry for the poor nuns as for the children they look after,' she said, 'but there was never any God in that place.' Her tone was serious. 'I believe in God,' she said, 'honestly I do, but not that one, and not from any of those sorry bitches who would have it beaten into you. What sort of a government have we that they would do that to small children?' She came down hard on the institution, and the church that supported it. By the time she finished Brendan knew that she was 'anti-establishment' or opposed to any class of people for that matter who saw themselves as being better than anyone else. But in all that she described, she never came across as being sorry for herself. It was a rare consolation to her that St Patrick's was where she had learnt to sing. 'Sure, look where it has all led to,' she smiled, sounding upbeat again. Brendan admired her for her resilience and was grateful for the way in which she had confided in him.

'I had it terrible bad, meself,' he said trying to lighten the subject. 'Barefoot, I had to walk to school uphill both ways and in the snow and the freezing rain. And the beatings,' he added, with great embellishment. 'They were something awful!' For a moment Kate believed him because she could relate to some of what he was saying. Then she realised that he was only joking.

'Go on, ya git,' she pushed him sideways with a laugh. Brendan told her that he lived with his family out on the Dingle Peninsula where he was captain of the local hurling team.

'The brother thinks he's a big shot solicitor in Tralee,' he said, describing John. 'He's harmless enough,' he added when he could see that Kate was not all that impressed. 'We have a younger sister. Her name is Elsabeth. She has just qualified as a teacher. You'd like her,' he said with affection. 'She is very nice and really deserves the new job she got out at the school in Clochan.'

'What about your parents?' she asked when he didn't mention them. She could see that he was self-conscious about her not having any.

'They have a farm,' he said, without going into detail. The way he said it made it sound small. 'My mother is a dote and me father is the opposite!' he smiled, not mentioning the fact that he belonged to the government that had made the rules that had put her in St Pats. 'He thinks I spend too much time with me head in the clouds.' He was very careful with what he revealed. He did not mention his flying, nor anything, for that matter, that might make her think that he was above her station.

'I'm going to have my own farm some day,' Kate stated with conviction. She wasn't joking and looked at Brendan to see if he believed her.

'I don't doubt it,' he said, smiling, which gave her the confidence to continue.

'I'll start with a cheese factory,' she said. She had it all worked out. 'And with the cash flow I'll buy a piece of land. Not big, mind you, but enough to get started. I'll add a few animals to subsidise the income and I'll grow vegetables the same way I do for the Kramers.'

'Really,' said Brendan impressed. 'And what does Mr Kramer think of all of this then?'

'He doesn't mind as long as I don't try to steal his customers,' Kate smiled. 'They have been very kind to me,' she added. 'I wouldn't do anything to harm them.' And so they went on each week, talking about their lives and their futures. With each conversation, their hearts became more entwined. It might have been okay if Brendan had spoken truthfully about himself. She could have liked him for who he really was. But he didn't. He was afraid because of the social boundaries and the family responsibilities and the future that was mapped out that he knew would stand between them. He had never liked somebody so much before in his entire life and without realising it, the fear of losing her was already upon him.

Chapter fifteen

The lead up to each weekend was full of anticipation for Brendan that grew stronger with the longing to see Kate. There was no way he could calm himself beforehand. It was like waking on a Sunday morning with his head already buzzing with aero-noises because he was going flying that day or the sound of the crowd cheering before a game. The butterflies that flapped inside his body would almost shake with the excitement. It was not until he laid his eyes upon Kate that he would find peace.

As his feelings for her grew deeper Brendan began to feel guilty about his lack of honesty. Maintaining a front was getting more complex as the weeks passed by. The game he had played at first was one of wanting to please her. But he came to realise that this wasn't a game anymore. This was for real, and he was playing with her heart. It was the last thing he wanted to be doing. If she had given him a sign that she felt the same way, it might have made it a little easier. For a word, a touch, a small gift of affection he might risk it all, but she didn't. She just made him tea and baked him special cakes and seemed happy. For Brendan though it was an affair that was getting out of hand. Without their realising it, their love had been blooming. He found that he could not help himself any longer. Everything around reminded him of her – the roses at the manor, the setting sun in the evenings. He could feel her presence in every breath that he took. His anticipation turned to dread when he finally realised what it was that had come over him. It wasn't that he did not want to see her any more. He did with all of his heart. She was on his mind every waking hour and lay down beside him in his dreams every night, and yet, he had never even touched her. They were friends. There was nothing more to it. 'She isn't part of the plan. She's a nothing', was how his father would have described her, if he had only known what was going on. One more reason to tell his son to 'cop onto himself'. They were from different worlds – oceans apart. She was from the island of Inis Beag and he was from the manor. How could they possibly be together? He knew something had to be done.

After weeks of soul-searching he finally came to a decision. Sean was beside him in the car as they drove to Tralee. They would open the stall and get things going together. At nine o'clock Brendan would head off for the day and leave him to it. They had rehearsed during the week. Brendan drummed into Sean all of the things that needed to be said and done when dealing with the customers. When the market was over he was to pack up the stall and Brendan would come and pick him up after everyone else had departed. The following week he would just be dropping him off early before anyone arrived and he could set up in his own good time.

It wasn't that he had decided not to see Kate. He was just getting on with his original plan. There was flying to be done, hours to be built up, and he wasn't doing it sitting there drinking tea and talking. He made sense of it all by reasoning that there was nothing going on between them. Only what was in his head and sure that couldn't be trusted. He did not have to explain. He was a busy man. Sure, didn't she have her own plans? She never talked or hinted about including him in them so he wouldn't be letting her down. He ignored the fact that he felt like a traitor. It would be better for them both this way. Give them a chance to cool off. After a while, then, they could really just be friends again.

Chapter sixteen

Kate arrived at the market at her normal time, usually well before Brendan. To her surprise he was already there and with a young chap.

'This is Sean,' Brendan said making a polite introduction. 'He will be managing the stall from now on,' he added. She could tell from his voice he was a little bit on edge.

'Something has come up.' He did not want to say what it was when she inquired other than that he would be tied up for the next few weeks at least. It was unlikely that she would see much of him during that time.

'You'll come over for a cup of tea before you go?' Kate asked expectantly. But her heart sank when he said that he would not have time.

'I've made you lunch,' she said surprised at her own insistence.

'Thanks, Kate,' Brendan replied, but firm that he would not be there. 'I have to go now. I'm already late,' he added. He turned down her offer to keep an eye on Sean as well. It was as if he did not want to be beholden to her. There was an awkward moment between them, and before she knew it he had made his departure. Kate knew then that it was over whatever they had shared. It had been only that morning on the way to the market that she had admitted to herself that she really liked him. That there was something to the teasing Mr Kramer had been giving her. She had denied it, of course, and played the exact opposite. But this morning she had come prepared to show her true feelings.

She returned to her stall down-hearted and shocked at Brendan's rather abrupt departure. She was glad that it turned out to be a very busy day which helped to keep her distracted. But the Kramers could tell that Kate was dragging her feet. She was distant and detached and not the usual chirpy self that they had grown used to since she had first met Brendan. The following week Kate did not see him at all, which was a major disappointment. She had spent the whole week wondering if she had done something wrong, or if Brendan had discovered something about her that he did not like.

As the weeks rolled by and she no longer saw him, her confusion and disappointment turned to a vague kind of acceptance. She did her best to settle into the market as she had done before, but it was no longer the same without him. To top it off poor old Mrs Cummins wasn't well. There had never been a bother on her for as long as Kate had known her, but in the last few months she had suddenly started to decline. So much so that her only son had to come down from Dublin to help look after her. He was a nice man, a bachelor in his early fifties who was very appreciative of all that Kate had done for his mother, but the writing was on the wall. The doctor had diagnosed cancer.

'When the end comes I'll have to put the hostel on the market,' he said to her quietly after Mrs Cummins had had a particularly bad night. 'I'll not do it until she has passed away of course. But you need to be knowing so that it's not a surprise in the future,' he had warned her. It was more than a surprise. It was a shock to her system. Mrs Cummins had been like a second mother to Kate.

Chapter seventeen

It was four weeks before Brendan returned. Half the time that she had known him. His stall was still in the same place as before, but with Sean in charge she had given up looking in that direction. It had become just another vendor.

He had come back because he had forgotten to leave the cash box for Sean. It would only take a minute to sort it out. He hadn't planned on staying for any length of time but, when he heard her singing he couldn't help himself and decided to stop to listen. A minute or two he told himself wouldn't do any harm. The sound of her voice though was like the elixir of life to a dying man and he found himself holding on to every word that she sang. He hadn't been doing well, not at all, and the sight of her now was almost too much for him to bear.

She began her song as she always did with her eyes closed until she had balanced her voice. When she opened them, Brendan had walked over and was standing in front of her. There was a longing in his gaze as he looked at her. Kate's heart soared, her voice grew notably stronger and she smiled back at him like never before. It was so good to see him!

She lost herself then, of course, and sang as if only to Brendan, and in every word her heart went out to him. The change in her tone was so obvious that the Kramers, who had been sitting out the back for a break returned to see what was going on. When they saw Brendan they were a bit taken aback by his dishevelled appearance, but smiled with understanding.

Poor old Brendan looked like some unkempt drunkard. His clothes were a mess, his hair had grown long and he looked like he hadn't shaved in days. When Kate finished her song the Kramers took over the selling and told her to go out the back for her own break. Brendan immediately made his way around after her. Kate's initial surprise and delight at seeing him quickly changed to indifference. She was sore at him. She couldn't help herself, it wasn't like her at all, but he was the one who had ignored her. She didn't want him to think that she had been missing him, so she acted busy for the first few moments that he stood in silence behind her. But on the inside her heart was racing.

'Can I talk to you for a minute, Kate?' he finally asked, when she wouldn't acknowledge him. 'There's something I want to tell you.' He was awkward in himself and she could see that it was hard for him. He looked so terrible that a part of her felt sorry for him, but her heart had hardened towards him over the last few weeks and she wasn't about to make it easy.

'I suppose so,' she finally turned to face him, and stood with her arms crossed to listen to what he had to say for himself.

'Not here, it would take too long,' he said. 'Can we go someplace else? Like maybe tomorrow. Will you meet me? We'll go for a drive or a walk on the beach. I really need to talk to you!' There was desperation in his voice, but she could sense from his pleading that he was genuine. 'I'll bring a picnic and we can spend the day together. I don't mind what we do!' he said. Anything that she might agree.

'Okay,' she finally answered with reluctance, not letting

on that she would have rushed headlong into his arms there and then had he given her half an excuse.

'I'm staying in Tralee for the night,' Brendan said. 'What about I pick you up outside the cathedral after nine o'clock Mass?'

'I'll bring a cake,' Kate said as a peace offering.

'Thanks,' replied Brendan genuinely relieved that she would meet him. 'I'll see you in the morning, then,' he said and cheered up for the first time in weeks as he left the stall.

Chapter eighteen

Brendan spent the night in the family town house in Tralee pacing the floors and trying to think of what he was going to say to Kate the next day. But what could he say that would bridge the gap and right all the wrongs? After a brief, restless sleep he woke up late the next morning and arrived at the cathedral almost a half-an-hour after the appointed time.

'I'm sorry I'm late,' he apologised. He had the good sense to jump out and open the passenger door for Kate, but failed to comment on her dress, or the way she had done her hair especially for the occasion. She looked very beautiful. He had noticed, but he was afraid to tell her. He had finally resolved in his head what he was going to say, but to tell her she looked great with one breath and that he was never going to see her again with the next was hardly a good way to go about it. Kate thought that maybe he had regretted his decision to ask her out. She grew anxious herself, and didn't say a word. As a result, they drove along in silence, until eventually they came to a crossroads. There was a signpost with four arrows pointing in different directions and Brendan stopped for the longest time to study them. The one that pointed left was for the beach where he had suggested they might go for a walk. It was a mile and a half away, but if you were to roll down the windows you could hear the surf crashing in the distance. Straight ahead were the mountains, the peaks of which were in clear view because it was such a fine day. They could be there in half an hour or so if they did not stop at Cadogen's pub halfway for a Guinness. To the right, three and a quarter miles away, lay the entrance to the paddock that hosted the aero club. Brendan knew the exact distance because he had driven it almost every other weekend. In all of the time they had been together, he had never told her about his flying. It was one of many things he had held out on telling her about. She had liked him for all of the wrong reasons, he reminded himself. Trapped by indecision he made no effort to drive on.

'Are you all right?' Kate said, rubbing his shoulder gently to attract his attention. It was the very first time that she had ever touched him. 'Are we going to the beach like you said or did you have something else on your mind?' She had noticed him gaze in the opposite direction. Finally he realised they were still sitting at the crossroads and the dazed look left him. All of a sudden it was clear what he must do. To the left was the illusion. To the right, the truth. He was tired of playing games. He wanted to be up front with her regardless of the consequence.

'I'm fine,' he said, his smile offering her the first reassurance she had had that morning. 'Come on, I have something to show you.' He jerked the wheel to the right, gunned the engine and took off in the opposite direction to the beach. His decision gave him a new source of energy.

'Fine so,' Kate said. She had not the foggiest idea what he was talking about but she could see that he was back to his old self again and she was content. It did not matter what they did. She was no longer sore at him, as she had been at the market. The airfield consisted of a large hangar at one end, and a windsock at the other, with a flock of sheep grazing in between. Brendan hardly slowed down before swerving through the entrance, gouged out of a low hedge that bordered the field. The car bounced hard, making a terrible racket as he drove it across the cattle barrier. Kate had to hold on for dear life for fear of being tossed out. Brendan swung left, then fishtailed hard right again and headed off down the grass strip runway. He pumped hard on the horn and stuck his head out the window shouting to disperse the sheep that grazed lazily in his way. His enthusiasm was so infectious that before she knew it, Kate was leaning out the window on her side too, yelling and joining in the fun. Any second she expected that Brendan would turn tail and zoom off out of the field before the angry farmer came out to get them. She hadn't taken any notice of the big building that Brendan was now racing towards, other than to think that it must be a barn. At pretty much the last second Brendan jammed on the brakes and the car slid to a graceful, but somewhat mucky halt not ten feet from the building.

'Come on, quick,' he said, as he jumped out of the car and took off in a run for the front entrance.

'What are you doing, for God's sake?' Kate was looking around, afraid that someone might have seen them. But she followed him all the same. The hangar was a large semi-circular corrugated iron affair with no walls and a red roof that stretched down to the ground. When she reached the front, Brendan already had one of the large entrance doors open and was swinging it to one side. Kate was surprised to see a bi-plane inside.

'Do you like aeroplanes?' Brendan inquired as he made his way around her to the other door. 'Give us a hand, will ya?' he said, as he wrestled with the bolt at the foot of the door. 'The hinges are bad on this side,' he stated. With a grunt, he finally released the bolt and together they managed to half-lift, half-drag the door open on the opposite side. They stood then for a moment gazing into the shadows of the barn.

'What do you think?' asked Brendan. He had his hands on his hips and stood the proudest and tallest she had ever seen him. Two bi-planes were parked in line before them. In the front was the Avro, behind it the Tiger Moth that Victor used to give flying lessons. It began to dawn on Kate that Brendan might have been here before. She had never seen an aeroplane in real life. She had looked at pictures of them in magazines, but they were so far from her reality that she had never given them a further thought. Up close, the two bi-planes seemed massive and imposing. Their wingspan filled all the available space in the hangar. Brendan could tell that she was impressed. He crawled under the wings of the Avro to get to the tail. The large wings were silvery-gray and the main part, the fuselage, was black. It had beautiful lines, balanced and symmetrical, and Kate was about to say so when he asked her to help him push it out of the way. She lent a hand and to her surprise she found that it was light and did not take much effort. It was the aircraft at the back, the red one, that Brendan seemed intent on getting to, and within a few minutes they had it pushed out into the morning sun.

'Out the back, quick,' Brendan said, not giving her time to think or ask any questions. There was a small room at the rear of the hangar that was used as an office. 'Take off your dress,' he ordered as soon as they were inside. 'Be as quick as you can.' Kate was shocked. 'Put these overalls on and I'll see you out the front when you are ready. We haven't got much time.' He did not explain further, just expected her to comply. It was his sense of urgency that made her do so. It crossed her mind that Brendan had a job to do on one of the aeroplanes and that the overalls were to prevent her from getting her dress dirty. It was a strange way to spend a Sunday morning, she thought, but who was she to argue? Brendan seemed so excited.

While Kate was changing, Brendan quickly donned his own flight overalls. He filled out a flight plan in the club register and then set about preparing the Tiger Moth for take-off. It was shaping up to be a beautiful day with lots of clear sky that would mean very little turbulence. A great way to introduce Kate to the air. He wanted to be away as quickly as possible. Sunday was a popular day for flying and he had not booked the plane. He had made his decision on the spur of the moment. If another member came along they had a right to claim at least part of the day. As it was, Des Walsh had his name on top of the register. Luckily he had not specified which plane he wanted, but he would be along any minute and it could ruin Brendan's plans.

He had just finished his flight checks and was priming the motor to start when Kate stepped out of the office. She was a sight to behold in a suit that was three times too big for her and Brendan would have laughed if he had not been so anxious about getting away. There were two separate cockpits in the aircraft. He reached into the front and pulled out a leather sheepskin jacket.

'We're almost ready,' he said, as he handed her the jacket. 'Put this on and we can get going,' he shuffled her towards the plane. Before she knew it he had her seated in the front cockpit and was strapping her in. It was only then that it finally dawned on her.

'We are not going flying?' she asked, trepidation and excitement in her voice. Brendan gave her a smile and pulled a leather flying hat on over her head.

'You can talk to me through this,' he said and pulled out a funny-looking leather funnel that was attached to a tube which ran to the rear cockpit. He stepped back on the wing, reached into his own cockpit and set the controls and throttle to idle so that he could start the engine. He gave the entrance of the airfield a quick scan to see if Des was coming, then jumped down and made his way to the propeller. The whole afternoon hinged on him getting the next part right. It took a deep breath, a soft touch and a gentle tug on the prop as Victor had taught him that if he got right first time, would start the engine. If he got it wrong the engine would flood and then there was no saying how long it would take before he got off the ground. Brendan let out a deep sigh of relief when the engine fired up first time and settled into a steady hum.

'Are you okay up there?' he shouted into the voice tube above the noise of the engine. Her head strained around to let him know she had heard. 'Put your right hand up in the air if you are okay,' he shouted. When she gave him the thumbs up he knew that they were finally ready. He pushed the throttle forward to the stops and the engine roared. There was a great blast of air from the prop wash and the Tiger leapt forward. Brendan did some fancy footwork with the rudder pedals to point them in the right direction and before Kate knew it, they were in the air. The airfield fell away behind them and she was amazed at how quickly they rose. Brendan let out another sigh of relief when he saw Walsh's car at the crossroads. They had just made it. It would cost him a couple of bottles of whiskey to appease him, but he knew that it would be worth it.

Kate was glad that Brendan had not told her about going flying beforehand. She was not scared at all, but this way was much more exciting. She knew she was safe. Her instincts told her that Brendan would not let her come to any harm.

'How are you doing up there?' she heard him call and this time she remembered the mouthpiece.

'You can keep your beach,' she shouted. 'This is a million times better.' She thrust her arms into the air to feel the slipstream. There was no point in talking. It was too hard to hear above the din of the engine so she just sat back and let him take her where he wanted.

Brendan flew south out to the coast keeping at three hundred feet all the way. When he reached the ocean he banked left and put the bi-plane into a shallow dive. He levelled off above the wave tops and flew parallel to the beach where they were supposed to have taken a walk. The sea was a deep blue and shimmered in the morning light. There were great rows of rolling breakers lining up one behind the other to march their way up onto the beach. They came across a couple on horseback and Kate waved excitedly as they flew close overhead. Brendan was glad that she was enjoying the flight. It would have been a terrible shame if she had been scared. At the end of the beach he climbed steeply and headed out across the bay to the mainland where he picked up the coast road and followed it for several miles.

It wasn't long before they came to Clochan, the first destination on Brendan's intended journey. He flew around the town several times gaining height until, in the distance, the manor came into view. The land that surrounded it was easily defined, five-hundred acres of some of the most fertile soil in the district. Brendan levelled off and flew towards the enormous house. When he reached the boundary he banked to the right and began following the high wall that surrounded the property in an anti-clockwise direction. He completed the circle at the large gatehouse that served as the main entrance to the estate and turning again, he followed the gravel driveway all the way up to the manor.

From the air the manor looked twice the size that it did from the road. He wondered what Kate was thinking. He completed one last turn and dived steeply, this time making a rather daring pass in front of the house. Kate let out a scream of delight at the manoeuvre. Brendan stayed low, just above the tree-tops and flew out across the estate back to the coast, and from there he headed out to sea. Rathlin Island was in the distance, uninhabited, but easily accessible. It had a long beach on the sheltered southern side that Brendan intended landing on if the wind was not too strong. The breeze was crisp as it blew in off the forbidding Atlantic and he could see Kate huddling down in her seat to try and stay out of it's chill. It was a little bumpy, but the trip did not last long. Satisfied that it was safe to land, he made a careful approach and settled the plane gently on the sand just above the water line.

'Are you all right?' he asked, noticing she was pale when he took off her flying hat and goggles. Kate was a little subdued.

'I feel a bit queasy,' she said as Brendan unstrapped her from her seat. He had to help her down from the wing as she was a bit wobbly on her feet.

'Just take a little walk on the beach for a minute and you will be grand!' he instructed. From a small compartment behind his own seat he took a thermos and the small picnic that he had made with all of her favourite treats.

'Brendan Finucane, you have a lot of explaining to do!' Kate said, when she returned.

'I know!' replied Brendan, dreading the thought. 'Come on, we'll go up to the old lighthouse and I'll explain it all there,' he said. They set off on a trail which led to a partial ruin at the top of the highest part of the island. The lighthouse was built of ancient granite. On the inside there was access to the top by a stone stairway that spiralled up inside the westerly wall. Brendan and Kate were out of breath by the time they reached the flat roof at the top. They were rewarded for their efforts with a magnificent 360 degree view of Tralee Bay and the distant south coast of Ireland. It was a different kind of feeling, being this high on solid ground and Kate was delighted by all that she could see.

'The tower was used for centuries as the outer navigation mark for Tralee harbour,' Brendan explained. 'It's nine miles east of here,' he stated and pointed in that direction. 'As long as you leave the island to port when approaching from the Atlantic at night you are guaranteed a safe passage all the way. To the south-east, from where they had just come, Clochan was easily discernable.

'It is amazing how you can still see that big house on the left-hand side of the town,' Kate said. She pointed it out to Brendan who was busy laying out the picnic. He stopped what he was doing and stood beside her.

'It was built that way for a particular reason,' he said. 'Do you remember when we flew over the manor there was a tower at one end of the roof?' Kate nodded.

'Well before the great famine in 1872 and even during it, the owner of the manor was involved in the shipping business. He used to transport immigrants to America and bring back raw materials on the return journey,' he explained. 'When the boat left Tralee with the regulated number of passengers, it would stop at this island and load on another hundred or more that the lord of the manor had brought, out of sight of the authorities. He could watch them leaving and, by a series of secret signals from the captain, he could find out how many passengers were on board going out, and if the cargo coming back had survived the journey. It saved a lot of to-ing and fro-ing from Tralee at a time when the only transport was horseback.'

'That's terrible,' said Kate. She was thinking of the miserable conditions the immigrants had to endure to make it to America. 'They were coffin ships,' she murmured. 'A lot of the passengers died along the way,' she said remembering her history.

'The most important use, however,' Brendan went on, 'was for a smuggling operation he used to conduct from this island to avoid customs duties at Tralee. The island belongs to the manor,' he said, and returned to fixing their lunch. They had been the bleakest years in the annals of Irish history. Dark and sad and dangerous. Brendan's ancestors had made a lot of money out of other people's misery. He wasn't very proud of some of his heritage.

'If the island belongs to the manor,' Kate said, 'should we not have to have permission to be here? Are we trespassing?' She felt giddy at the idea.

'No,' answered Brendan, avoiding her gaze. He suddenly had that troubled look about him again.

'Why not?' she asked indignantly, but there was fun in her tone. 'If it were my island I'd make people ask! They would have to get my permission!' She strutted around the rooftop with her hands on her hips. She did not really care, but was playing it up because Brendan had become so dark and serious all of a sudden and she was trying to lighten him up.

'I don't need permission,' he said with a flat kind of smile. He was standing facing her now. He handed her a cup of tea from the thermos and took a sip of his own without letting go of her gaze. He decided he'd tell her everything now; it was not the way he had planned it, but her questioning had led them there. It was as good a time as any to face the firing squad.

'Why don't you need permission?' Kate asked haltingly. There was something in his look that made her suspicious. A signal. A warning. Something to be revealed. It began to dawn on her that this was what had been disturbing him all along.

'Do you see that island over there?' he pointed north to a smaller island about two miles away. 'And this one here that you are standing on and the two on the way back to Clochan.' She followed his arm as he pointed out the islands he was talking about and then the manor, and all of the land that ran out to the peninsula on the right. 'It all belongs to the manor,' Brendan explained. 'The manor is where I live,' he revealed without any expression. 'I don't need permission to be here, because this is my island.' He stood there and let it sink in. Kate went pale with the realisation. She gave him a such a look of betrayal that was worse than if he had hit her.

'How could you?' she said and then took off down the steep granite stairway.

'Kate, please, I'm sorry.' But she was away before he had a chance to apologise. 'Please let me explain,' his voice echoed off the walls as he chased after her. 'I was afraid it would come between us!'

But she wouldn't stop. She took the steps two at a time and broke out into the dazzling sunshine at the bottom of the tower twenty paces ahead of him. Determined to catch up, Brendan leapt the last five steps in an effort to make up ground. As his luck would have it there was damp moss on the place that he landed and he slipped, twisting his ankle.

'Damn!' he shouted in frustration. The agonising pain stopped him dead in his tracks and he hobbled around in circles, clutching his injured ankle. 'Jesus Christ!' he cursed, but it was himself he was cursing for his stupidity as much as his pain. Kate stopped when she heard him cry out. She walked back slowly to see what was the matter. When she saw the pain he was in she was overcome with guilt and compassion. He wouldn't have hurt himself if she had not taken off like that without at least giving him a chance to explain.

'I was liking you,' she said, with anger in her voice as if he deserved what had happened.

'I was liking you a lot,' she went on and pointed to the top of the tower which had been the happiest place in the world. 'I trusted you and you let on all of this time that you were someone else. How could you do that to me?' Brendan was standing still, facing her, and for the first time he was hearing the words that he had wanted to hear. About her liking him, and liking him a lot, and it gave him the courage to say what he wanted to say.

'You only hurt the ones you love,' he broke in.

'You what?' Kate said confused.

'I was in love with you,' he said. 'I didn't know what to do!' His eyes appealed to her.

'What do you mean, "was"?' Kate replied, less indignant now, her tone softened completely. He had said that he loved her! She realised then for the first time why she was always so miserable when he was not around.

'I'm in love with you,' he said again. They reached out and took hold of each other's hands and the gap closed between them. Words would no longer suffice. He raised his hand and gently touched the side of her face. Kate did the same in return. They held each other's gaze, all the while gathering courage until finally, with a tremendous passion they kissed for a very long time.

Chapter nineteen

The light was fading, and Brendan knew that they should be making a move to get back, but neither wanted to let go of their loving embrace. They had an hour at most to return to the airfield before it was too dangerous to fly, and in the end, it was the danger that got him moving.

'I wish we could stay here forever,' Kate said. 'Stay here, away from the world and all it's evils.' It was impossible of course. They would have to leave, but they held on until the very last minute.

'Seeing that it is your fault that I've hurt myself you can get the picnic stuff off the top of the lighthouse,' Brendan grinned and started to limp his way towards the beach. Without argument and as light as a feather, Kate took off up the granite steps with a spring in her step. From the top she could see her knight in shining armour hobbling down to prepare his trusty steed, and she thought that her heart would almost burst with the enormous joy that she felt. Quickly, she collected all of their belongings, but before she turned to run back to the plane, she faced north for a moment in the direction of where she imagined Inis Beag was located. Breathing out a deep sigh of contentment she said a little prayer in memory of her grandfather to thank him for Brendan.

By the time she reached the plane, Brendan had the engine started and her nose pointed into the wind. He strapped Kate in quickly, with just time to give her one last kiss before climbing into his own compartment. His ankle was not half as bad as it had been earlier on and he found that he had only slight discomfort when he applied pressure to the rudder pedals. He eased the plane forward until he was sure that he was on firm sand and then, with a thumbs-up from Kate, gave the engine full throttle and they raced down the beach and into the air. When they flew out of the lee of the island they were greeted by a strong tailwind that made for a faster passage and a smoother ride and it did not take long before they were over the mainland. Brendan tried not to feel anxious. It was nothing to do with the fact that they had left it so late, or that he would get hell from Des Walsh for stealing his booking for the plane. He knew in his heart that he had crossed the invisible line – broken the unwritten agreement. Kate had no idea of how complicated the whole thing was, or how difficult it would be with his father. He had tried to explain to her about their way of life and all that was expected of him, but how could a girl with so much freedom possibly understand?

Kate was a little more dreamy. She thought of their first kiss and the way that he had held her. It had been perfect in every way. She smiled to herself at each tender moment. It had all been such a surprise and it took some getting used to. That and trying to fathom the undercurrents that ran through everything Brendan had talked about. He seemed so bogged down when it came to his family. She decided to concentrate on the fact that their feelings were mutual. 'Let's just take it one step at a time and see how we get on,' she had said, to try and relieve his anxiety. On reaching the airfield Brendan circled once to get used to the light and disperse the sheep that had settled back on the runway. It was not as bad as he thought it was going to be and with a sigh of relief he made a perfect three-point landing and then taxied up to the hangar. He cut the engine and they sat there momentarily in silence. Whatever the outcome might be, it had been a perfect day in every way and he decided not to let his worries spoil the ending. He undid his harness and stepped forward to help Kate. Smiling at her, he jumped down from the wing, but instead of helping her down he lifted her up in the air and twisted around several times with delight.

'Put me down, Brendan,' she cried, 'You'll twist your ankle again, you twit,' but she laughed at his exuberance. He released his grip slightly and let her slide down along his body until they were at eye level. Then he embraced her again and they kissed each other joyfully until he could no longer hold her. It was pitch dark by the time they had the bi-plane tucked away in the hangar. Before leaving Kate went over and patted her gently on the side of the fuselage.

'I christen you Molly,' she said and kissed the cockpit where Brendan had been sitting as a 'thank you' for bringing them safely through a wonderful day. 'And this one is Malone,' she said to Brendan as she went over and kissed the Avro.

'Why those names?' asked Brendan.

'Don't you remember?' she asked. 'It was the first love song you ever sang to me,' she said.

Sunday night was strictly a family affair at the Finucane house. It had been a tradition since Brendan was a child, and all were expected to attend. It was originally intended by his mother as a time when the family gathered to talk about their weekend, but had been commandeered by James Finucane as a platform for pontificating and giving orders for the week ahead. By the time Brendan got home not only had he missed dinner but everyone had gone to bed. Everyone, that is, except John.

'Car trouble,' Brendan said, as an excuse for being late. 'That's the second time it has broken down,' he added without a hint of annoyance in his voice. 'It took me ages to fix it.' John watched as his brother hummed to himself and danced around the kitchen looking for dinner scraps.

'And you the genius and not a drop of oil on your hands?' replied John.

'Electrics,' Brendan said simply and disappeared into the pantry in search of something to eat. He'd had the entire journey home to think of an excuse and he wasn't about to let his brother have one up on him.

'Maybe you should have prayed harder in the church this morning,' John said, knowing that Brendan had not attended. There was a touch of sarcasm in his voice. By coincidence he had met Des Walsh in Cadogan's pub at lunchtime and had to spend half-an-hour being ear-bashed about Brendan and some girl called Kate whom he had taken for a joyride in the plane that Des claimed to have booked for the day.

'Her name is written in the flight log at the club,' he said when John had pressed him as to how he knew of Brendan's passenger. 'What he wouldn't do,' he had said to John, when he got his hands on his brother.

'The old man wasn't too happy about you missing dinner,' John claimed. 'I'd say you are going to get it over breakfast by the sounds of it. He said that next week is an important week!'

'Next week is always an important week when it comes to Da,' Brendan replied with little concern. 'You'll get it worse when he finds out that you did not stay at the town house last night.' He winked knowingly at his brother as he walked by him out of the kitchen to go to his bedroom. 'It's confession you should be going to,' he shot back as he mounted the stairs and that put an end to their jousting. It had not been much of a victory. Brendan would
need John on his side now more than ever before. He wanted to tell him, confide in him the love he felt for Kate, but they had never been much for talking in that kind of way. In spite of how well they had been getting on there was always the rivalry, the

dividing line between them that left Brendan feeling exposed and vulnerable. His brother was still in the habit of putting him down when the need served him and, as a result, he was unsure if he could ever trust him. If John sided with his father against him over Kate the obstacles would be insurmountable.

'Being your own man', usually meant you were on your own when you failed to agree with James Finucane. Brendan had spent a long time worrying about the consequences of his actions, but now that it was done he would take his chances. He drifted off to sleep with the thought of Kate in his arms.

John, on the other hand, was raging. He'd spent sleepless nights thinking about Kate after their first meeting. He had prepared a plan that included a night in the grand suite of a very expensive hotel in Tralee. Like a hound to the hunt he had decided that he would not let up. He would do whatever it took to bed her. Unbeknownst to Brendan, he had been to the market to set the bait a few weeks after they had first met Kate. To his shock, however, he had found that his brother had beaten him to it. He tried to forget about her after that and used the hotel room instead for another of his distractions, but thinking of Kate with his brother vexed him. When he heard from Walsh that Brendan had taken her up flying he knew that they were serious. 'The idiot,' he thought to himself. She was good for one thing, and one thing only. Love had nothing to do with it.

Chapter twenty

The Kramers waited a whole week to tell Kate their news. A week after the letter that had arrived unexpectedly that would change all of their lives forever. It was great news and would have suited them all perfectly if Kate hadn't fallen for Brendan.

'We have received an inheritance,' Lotty announced from the letter she held in her hand that evening. Kate was in the habit of sharing dinner with them at least twice a week after work and they were just finishing off with a cup of tea.

'God, that's great news,' Kate replied, genuinely pleased for their good fortune. She was totally unaware of the gravity of the situation.

'It is from my uncle in Holland. You remember we were planning on staying with him at Christmas,' Lotty explained, looking all the time at her husband so that he might break the bad news.

'Oh, I'm sorry,' Kate apologised, realising that she had forgotten to express her condolences.

'It's okay,' replied Mr Kramer. 'He vas very old and he had a good life so we are happy for him,' he shrugged his shoulders, 'but this is not ze problem,' he said, growing impatient with his wife. Lotty held on to the letter, but stared at the table without saying anything. Kate was suddenly shocked when Mrs Kramer produced a handkerchief to wipe her eyes.

'What's wrong?' Kate inquired, growing pale at the realisation that whatever was in the letter was still a cause for sadness. In spite of their agreement, Mr Kramer knew that it was now up to him to explain the consequences of the letter.

'Ach, vomen,' he admonished Lotty, before turning to face Kate. 'Ve have to leave and go back to Holland,' he stated. 'It's quite a big farm,' he said, explaining the nature of the inheritance. 'Ve had intended moving back zer in a few years anyway, but now ve must move the time forvard.'

'We want you to come with us,' Lotty piped up. 'It would be so good – it is such a beautiful place.' She reached out and took Heinrich's hand to show that they were in agreement. They thought of Kate as part of their family now, and they were anxious that she should share in their good fortune. 'It would be that new start you had talked about,' Lotty said, referring to the previous weeks when Kate had thought that she had lost Brendan.

'I can't,' said Kate, thinking about her landlady. 'There is no way that I can leave her.' Mrs Cummins was old and frail now and needed constant attention. In spite of her son's return to care for her, Kate felt it her duty to be there until the end, however long that might take.

'We understand,' said Lotty. 'We wouldn't expect you to come straightaway. But maybe after, when you are free?' she said gently.

It was with a sadness that Kate watched the Kramers sell off what they could, pack up their cottage and factory and make their farewells. Brendan was helpful and arranged for a lot of their belongings to be put into storage until such time as it could be transported to them. It was only a matter of weeks after receiving the letter that they departed, with the hope that Kate might join them some time in the future. Without the Kramers Kate was at a loose end. She was fortunate enough when Mrs Cummins' son offered for her stay on at the boarding house expenses free and gave her a bit of pocket-money in return for helping to look after his mother. But she knew in her heart that it was time for a change. The life to which she had become anchored was quickly fading. She had been lucky from the day she left St. Pat's, but when Mrs Cummins passed away she wasn't sure if there was any reason why she should not be moving on herself.

Those were her thoughts when Brendan met her at the market a week after the Kramers departed. He was full of energy and excitement with news he couldn't wait to tell her.

'Guess what?' he said, like a child with a big secret that he was bursting to reveal. 'My parents are moving to Dublin in two weeks,' he blurted out, not giving Kate a chance to question him. 'My father has just been elected a member of Government!' James Finucane had been involved in politics for more than twenty years at various levels, and had finally won himself a place on the front bench due to a cabinet reshuffle.

'He's delighted with himself,' Brendan said, 'he's finally got his chance to run the country. He'll be out of the way for the rest of the year and that means two things!' he said.

'Go on,' said Kate, not too sure of where he was going, but certainly interested in knowing.

'Well, for one, I'm going to be running the farm myself,' he said, proudly. He waited until curiosity got the better of Kate before he revealed anything else.

'Brendan Finucane!' she said in exasperation, giving him an impatient dig in the ribs with her elbow. 'What's number two?' she demanded, sensing that he had left the best until last.

'Freedom!' he said. Finally free from his father's shadow, the coming year would give him the liberation he'd dreamed about. An aura of confidence descended upon Brendan that Kate had never seen in him before. With his father gone he became a different person. The first thing he did after his parents had departed for the big smoke was to throw a massive party at the manor. It was John's idea, of course, but it had not taken much for him to persuade Brendan and Elsabeth to follow suit.

Brendan had decided to tell his brother and sister about Kate. It was better to confide in them now than to be discovered later. He wanted their support and approval. The time would come when he would have to tell his parents, and he wanted John and Elsabeth on his side. Brendan confided in his brother about his relationship with Kate two days before the party. It was hard for him to gauge how John really felt. He never let on that he already knew. Instead John gave him the teasing that was expected and inquired about their parents knowing, and nodded thoughtfully when Brendan told him that he was taking things one step at a time. The fact that he was playing along, however, meant everything to Brendan. The party would be a great way for Kate to meet all of the people that they knew. Elsabeth was delighted to hear about Brendan's romance.

'It's about time you had yourself a girlfriend,' she said. 'You are always working too much for your own good.' She had a romantic streak that had transcended the barriers of class that they had grown up with. The notion that Kate came from a 'different place', as she called it, only served to make her that much more exotic and attractive. She didn't say this to Brendan directly of course, but wrote it in her diary the night that Brendan had confided in her. As far as she was concerned, and she had told him so, she and Kate were already good friends.

On the day of the party, the young couple flew down in Molly in the early afternoon with Victor flying beside them in formation, in Malone. Brendan had told him that he could bring a friend if he wanted to. Instead, he had a keg of Guinness strapped in the passenger seat in front of him. When they arrived, there was a large crowd gathered on the lawn in front of the big house. For ten minutes or so they were entertained with daring aerobatics by the two planes. A dogfight ensued with some low-level treetop hopping, then loops and turns as they chased each other in front of the crowd. Brendan eventually had to concede the fight because he had Kate on board, so he broke away to join the party. Victor climbed to 300 feet for a safe margin and performed a series of victory rolls while Brendan landed.

'My kind of party,' Victor announced loudly, when John handed a glass of stout to each of the aviators as they stepped down from their aircraft. Those who gathered around cheered him on with their approval. Victor was introduced as 'Baron Von Nutcase' and Elsabeth took Kate in hand and introduced her to everyone as her friend. The two pilots started taking volunteers up for a quick joyride, and the party quite literally got off to a flying start. As the evening progressed to nightfall, most of the rooms downstairs began to overflow as the house filled with cousins, friends and acquaintances from all over. Brendan had invited the entire hurling team, girlfriends included, and John did the same with any member of the hunt under twenty-five years of age.

At one stage Victor organised thirty-four people to play musical chairs with anything they could find to sit on in the ballroom. It was a great success until somebody got knocked out temporarily in the melée for a seat. Then it had to be called off altogether when a huntsman took exception to a member of the hurling team over a 'bloody good drink' that was spilt during the foray and asked him to step outside. Luckily for the huntsman Brendan intervened with two fresh drinks and a cigar each as a reward for being so spirited. John announced that the food was served and the dancing started shortly afterwards to a five-piece band that played jigs and reels and all sorts of lively music.

'Are you all right?' Brendan shouted to Kate. He held her hips from behind and followed her in a conga line of cheering people with John at the front leading them merrily around the house.

'I'm grand, I'm grand!' she shouted back to him as they picked up speed, but they were going too fast to have any sort of conversation. Brendan had been too busy playing the host with John and trying to keep Victor's party antics under control to show her much attention. Kate, however, was having a good time. She and Elsabeth had genuinely hit it off and she had been introduced to more people than she could ever possibly remember.

'Ladies and gentlemen,' John announced, bringing silence to the band. 'It's time for some real music.' He pulled a cotton sheet off a piece of furniture at the side of the room to reveal a gramophone. He wound it vigorously, placed the needle on the record, and a great cheer went up to the sound of Glen Miller. Brendan did the best he could to join in the swing with Kate, but he had two left feet when it came to modern dancing. He was finally relieved of his embarrassment when a slow set was played that began with a love song by Jimmy Dorsey.

'Tangerine...she is all they claim...,' the gramophone sang out, and Brendan and Kate embraced lovingly as they slow-stepped around the room.

'I like this one,' he said to Kate, knowing how much she enjoyed modern music.

'Me too,' she replied

'You are my Tangerine,' he said with a flash of inspiration. 'Let's make this our song,' he was looking into her eyes. She smiled her assent and was about to welcome his kiss when the music changed from a slow step back to swing. A female voice took over and boomed out the remaining part of the song, and with it Kate stepped back into the rhythm.

'Ah, for God's sakes,' he cried out. The moment had been spoiled.

'You can kiss me later,' she promised laughing. The last of the revellers were finally farewelled just after five am. By this time Kate and Elsabeth had long since departed and were fast asleep.

'That was the best party we have ever had!' John said triumphantly to Brendan as they sipped on a brandy nightcap beside the smouldering fire in the living room. 'I have been waiting to do that for twenty years, you old bastard!' he said to a very large portrait on the far side of the room of their great grandfather who stood stern-faced, looking down on them with a condescending gaze.

'Couldn't have gone better!' Brendan added.

Victor let out a snort of approval. He'd fallen asleep on the chaise longue in the corner of the room and, by the look of him, he'd had the best time of the lot of them. They would all be rough as guts in the morning.

'Thanks,' Brendan said. 'I really appreciate the way you have welcomed Kate and Victor.' He chinked his brother's glass in a toast.

'What are you on about?' John avoided Brendan's gaze, letting on he had no idea what his brother was talking about. 'I'll tell you what, those planes are great!' He changed the subject quickly. For most of his friends who had attended the party it was the first time they had ever flown. He had made a great impression.

'You know what I mean!' Brendan said, knowing that his brother would never admit to supporting the friends that he had chosen for fear of their father's backlash. He finished off the last of his drink and, in an extravagant gesture, he smashed the expensive crystal glass in the fireplace. 'Great party!' he said, smiling, and with one final flourish and a slight wobble he turned and went off to bed.

John stood by the fireplace a little bit longer, thinking about all that had happened that day. As he considered himself in the ornate gilded mirror that sat on top of the fireplace his mind settled on the highlight of the evening. Kate hadn't been expecting a party. When she arrived in Molly she was wearing a pair of flying overalls and had a change of clothes in an overnight bag that Brendan had told her to bring along. But the party was a complete surprise. Elsabeth had lent her one of her favourite outfits, with a plunging neckline in a style that really suited Kate's figure. She didn't want to wear it. She felt like she would be showing herself off, which was something she wasn't used to. Elsabeth had to reassure her that she didn't look risqué, and reminded her how much Brendan would like the outfit, before she could be finally persuaded. John could hardly keep his eyes off her. He found himself shadowing her wherever she went. After musical chairs they danced the conga line through the house with Kate leading Brendan, then Brendan leading Kate. John couldn't help himself. Seeing his opportunity he jumped the line and bumped the person behind Kate out of the way so that he could hold onto her. When they danced through a narrow passage way and became momentarily compressed at a dead end he was overcome by the urge to follow the curve of her perfect hips to cup her breasts in his hands, but she was saved by the instruction to 'turn about face'. Thinking he knew the type Kate was, he assumed that he would have gotten away with it without any embarrassment.

Chapter twenty two

The great start to their summer together was nearly ruined a couple of weeks later when Mrs Cummins died unexpectedly. Kate had known that she was sick and been prepared for the inevitable, but it still came as a shock when it happened so soon. A service was held, and her estate settled. The hostel was put up for sale. As soon as it sold, Kate would find herself not only jobless, but homeless as well. It was John though, who resolved the dilemma.

Father Flaherty, the parish priest at Clochan needed a part-time housekeeper, but couldn't get anyone to work for him. He was grumpy and mean, always complaining about this or that. The last housekeeper had left him and no one in the community was desperate enough to take up the position.

'If I just had someone to cook for me,' he complained forlornly to John. Most of his food came from the estate, and by chance it was John who had made the delivery that day. John had little sympathy for the priest, but it occurred to him though, in a flash of inspiration, that Kate might just be the solution to Flaherty's problem. He didn't say it there and then, other than promising to give it some thought, but when he left the priest's house he drove immediately to find Brendan.

'She'd have a job and somewhere to stay. It would be the perfect cover,' he reasoned. In spite of Kate's situation, Brendan was reluctant to consider the idea. 'Flaherty's passion is the church choir,' John persisted. 'If Kate joins it and sings the way that she does at the market then I'm sure the old man will be nice to her. Think about it, man, the summer is coming, it's the best part of the year. The two of you could have endless time together!'

Brendan began to warm to the idea, but for another reason. If he could persuade her to take the position, even on a temporary basis, then she might give up her talk about going to live in Holland with the Kramers.

'Just for the summer,' he said to her. 'We will make it a holiday in spite of the work. We can go to the market together, and fly on weekends. If you are not happy then we will find you something else.' It didn't take long for him to persuade her. Once she had agreed, Elsabeth was recruited to make the introduction. She was the junior teacher at the local school and had a lot to do with Father Flaherty. It was her job to present Kate as a visiting friend who had come to live in a rural community and improve her Irish language.

'It just so happens,' she said 'that she is looking for a bit of part-time work over the spring and summer while she is here, and I heard that you are looking for staff.' Flaherty was reluctant at first because Kate was young, until Elsabeth mentioned how beautifully Kate could sing. It was most unusual for a priest to have a young woman for his housekeeper, especially a live-in, but he had tried to fill the position with a more mature woman.

'They've had their chance,' he finally decided. 'If they are going to 'tut tut' behind my back then let them. The matter is none of their business!' The priest ruled his parish with an iron fist. It was they who had to answer to him. Kate, however, hit it off with him from the very beginning. The experience of living in an orphanage run by nuns had given her an extra quality that none of the other housekeepers possessed. She knew that all that he needed was a little laughter to stop him from getting too serious and, with her kind and friendly nature, Kate quickly found a way around him. Being a friend of the daughter of the biggest benefactor to his church coffers also added to her status, and meant that he never questioned her, or asked where she was going in her spare time.

So summer turned out to be bliss in every way. It was as if Mrs Cummins had gone to heaven, pulled God to one side and asked him to do her a favour. And He did. There was more sunshine that year than ever before in recorded history. Spring was on the land and love was in the air. All that Kate and Brendan shared between them made it feel like it could last forever. There was an old workers' cottage on the estate at the end of the peninsula that was no longer in use. It was about three miles out of town in the wrong direction which meant that only those who were invited would ever come and visit. Brendan and Kate set about tidying it up and making it somewhat liveable. They needed a place, somewhere they could spend time alone without having to worry about who would see them. Kate had been introduced as Elsabeth's friend, and Brendan did not want the news getting back to his parents about their relationship before he was ready.

When Brendan told John about the cottage he wanted to throw another party, but was quickly persuaded otherwise. It was Brendan's place. John and Elsabeth were welcome to visit whenever they wanted, but it was out of bounds to everyone else. Brendan taught Kate how to ride a horse and showed her all over the estate. They had picnics and long walks on the beaches and endless talks about anything and everything. It was not long before they had the world that was at war put to rights. Elsabeth spent a lot of time with them and often came to the cottage for picnics with Kate, especially when Brendan was busy. Kate volunteered to help at the school part-time with singing and music. She had a passion for literature and was great at reading stories to the children who were having any difficulties.

Even Father Flaherty couldn't have been happier. She did a good job around the house, minded her own business and sang like a lark on Sundays. She was kind to him which took away some of his hardness, something that was noted by the gossipy members of the community. Maybe it was old age, and because of it he was letting his guard down. There were one or two of the opinion that he had gone soft in the head since Kate had arrived. Certainly there seemed a little less fire and brimstone in his sermons on Sundays.

Father Flaherty thought that Kate had the voice of an angel – a rare find in the most desolate of places to which he had been banished from the capital city by his superiors over twenty years before. He had been over-ambitious, and was made to pay the price for trying to climb above his station. If he had learnt his lesson and bided his time they would have eventually allowed him back into the fold. But he was a stubborn man, conceited and righteous. Instead of serving his penance he kicked up a storm, the ripples of which almost made it back to the Vatican. As a result, he was left there, forgotten. It was his hell on Earth, if ever there was one. The last thing he wanted to be doing was looking after a bunch of rurals. As a consequence he made sure at every opportunity, that those whom he served paid the price and would go on doing so until his retirement. With Kate, on the other hand, he was keen to see her rewarded. When the final term before summer holidays came around he persuaded the school committee to pay for her volunteer work in the hope that she might be attracted to staying on in a permanent capacity.

As for Kate, things couldn't have worked out better. On the Saturday morning of the week that school finally closed for the holidays Brendan collected her as usual to go to the market. She had a week's holiday because Father Flaherty was going away. It was also her twenty-first birthday. It was a surprise to her then when he didn't take her to the market, but drove on instead to the airfield. He wouldn't explain where they were going, but stowed away a small tent inside Molly with a couple of sleeping bags and enough provisions for a few days. Victor was there to help him. He talked seriously with Brendan about compass headings and contingencies and phone calls that could be made in the event of an emergency. He also made several references to a map of Ireland on the wall of the hangar. Kate had learnt to trust Brendan and his surprises, and knew that the only way to find out what was going to happen was to have patience and let it all unfold.

They took off shortly afterwards and headed north up the jagged west coast of Ireland, flying for almost two hours solid before putting down in a small airfield just outside Galway to refuel. Within half-an-hour they were airborne again. This time Brendan headed west until suddenly they left the coastline altogether and flew out into the Atlantic. He put Molly into a steady climb so that Kate wouldn't see where they were finally headed. The last thing he wanted her to realise was where they were going. Kate had the worst sense of direction in the world and if he had told her they were somewhere off the east coast instead of the west she probably would have believed him. He wasn't taking any chances though on spoiling his surprise as Inis Beag loomed over the horizon.

'Look down below you,' he shouted, as he put Molly into a steep bank and flew them in a long lazy spiral down to the island. The ocean sparkled like newly cut crystal and the land shone emerald green. The heather was purple like the velvet of a royal gown. Kate could hardly believe her eyes when it finally dawned on her where they were. It was as she had always imagined. All the years she had been away she had spent dreaming of her island as if from the wings of a gull. Now her dream was real. As they came in to land she put her arms out either side of the cockpit as if she was a bird and watched with delight as a flock of gulls took off from the beach to make room for her arrival. She knew at once that she was home. Kate didn't climb down off the wing of the airplane like she usually did. She jumped and landed in Brendan's arms and they both ended up sprawled on the beach in laughter. Before he knew it she was up and away with her arms outspread chasing the seagulls that had landed and willing them to take off again. She whooped with laughter and swooped back on Brendan who began playing along with his own set of wings. They ran down the beach until they were out of breath.

'I love you, Brendan Finucane!' She stood close to him, tears in her eyes. 'I love you with all of my heart.' She hugged him with all of her might and then they kissed as never before.

It was well into the evening by the time they had walked the length of the island and back to the ruins of the village beside the beach. The summer sun was bidding farewell from the west while a crescent moon chased from the opposite direction with the first stars in sight bringing up the rear.

They set up camp and built a fire from driftwood and sat side by side on a large rock with their sleeping bags wrapped over their shoulders to ward off the cold from the Atlantic dew. They were done in, all talk spent, at the end of another perfect day together. Kate had re-lived her childhood with all sorts of memories, and taught Brendan songs she had forgotten about, but now remembered. She told him of her grandfather and the stories he used to tell her, and then she began talking about St Patrick's. She was no longer unhappy about it, but rather more relieved that she could finally let the memories go. The person she most wanted to share her past with was beside her.

'My grandfather said I must hold onto my dreams. That eventually they would come true,' Kate explained. 'There were times when I found it hard to believe in what he said, but now look at me,' she paused and took Brendan by the hand. 'I'm in the place of my dreams with you!' she said. 'This is *my* island!'

'Happy Birthday,' Brendan said and with a gentle shove he half knocked her off her perch. 'Stop being so bloody sentimental,' he laughed.

'I am not,' she shot back, surprised and half-hurt that he would mock her special moment. She threw her sleeping bag down and shoved him back and then proceeded to tickle him.

'Okay, okay,' he cried out. 'I'm sorry,' he blurted, for he was very ticklish. He finally stopped her by wrapping his sleeping bag over their heads and pinning her arms by her side in a bear hug.

'Do you give in?' Kate demanded, in spite of the fact that she was powerless to continue torturing him.

'I do,' he said, softly and released his grip to a gentle hug.

'And do you love me?' she asked. She seized her chance by digging her claws in to his ribs to punish him further if he gave her the wrong answer.

'With all of my heart,' Brendan replied in submission. With that Kate melted and they kissed again for the one hundredth time that day. Unawares, a heavy rain cloud had crept over the island and suddenly began a torrential downpour.

'The tent, quick!' Brendan said and they ran into it to escape the rain. It was then that Kate realised that she had forgotten her sleeping bag on the ground beside the rock. She dashed out again before Brendan could stop her, but it took an age to find it because the light from the fire had been dampened by the downpour. She was saturated when she finally made it back to the tent. She changed her sodden top and they settled down for the night beside each other. Exhausted from all of the day's excitement they fell asleep almost immediately, but Brendan awoke a short time later to the sound of Kate shivering.

'Ah, God, I'm sorry. I had no idea,' he said, mortified that he had been the cause of her suffering by losing her sleeping bag. 'You should have told me how wet you were.'

'I'm very prone to the cold,' Kate replied.

'Here, put this on over your top,' he said, pulling off his jersey and handing it to her. 'You'd better get in here,' he said thinking the pullover might not be enough and that he would be responsible for her catching pneumonia. He opened his bag and Kate climbed in beside him. It took a while, but Kate finally warmed up and eventually, they dozed off in each other's arms. The warmth they shared led to dreams and their dreams became entwined and led to kisses and without knowing it, they were locked in the sweetness of a lovers' embrace.

'Stop!' cried a voice. It was the deep-seated memory of Sister Hannigan from St. Pat's who brought Kate to her senses. 'You must never allow a man to do such things,' she had warned a thousand times if not more when the girls were growing up. 'It is dirty and it's evil and you will go to hell,' she admonished. Kate awoke to find herself under the weight of Brendan's body.

'No, we mustn't,' she cried and pushed him away from her.

'What's wrong?' Brendan responded, suddenly startled from his sleep.

'We mustn't do it!' Kate repeated again.

'Oh, Kate, I never meant to!' Brendan replied in shame when he realised what had been happening between them. He made an attempt to climb out of the sleeping bag so that she would know that he meant her no harm, but she stopped him.

'It's okay,' she said, for she was equally discomfited. 'It's just that we shouldn't do anything like that,' she said. 'We should just cuddle. Is that okay?' she asked hoping that he would agree.

'Yes, of course,' Brendan replied, relieved that she trusted him. 'That's all I ever meant to do,' he said and had her turn, so that her back was snuggled against the warmth of his body and her head lay on his arm.

'Are you comfortable?' he asked as he cuddled her in his arms and drifted back to sleep again.

They woke the next morning to the barking of a pair of seals, playing in the water close by. Nothing was mentioned of the previous night nor was there any awkwardness between them. Brendan packed their gear into Molly while Kate took one last walk through the remains of her small village.

She felt at peace. It was as if the last fifteen years and all that she had been through were finally worthwhile. She said a prayer for her family and all of those she had known, realising that they had always been with her in her heart.

'Thank you,' she said, with heartfelt gratitude to Brendan when she returned to the plane.

'It isn't over yet,' he smiled as he handed her a large paper bag of flour and several smaller, empty bags which he instructed her to fill before they took off.

Chapter twenty three

Brendan strapped Kate into her seat in the plane and placed the half-dozen smaller bags of flour that they had just wrapped on her lap.

'When I give you the signal, hand one of these back to me and I'll show you what to do with it,' he instructed. He took off and headed east, back to the mainland. On reaching the coast he veered south and followed the shore line for thirty miles or so, comparing landmarks to references that Victor had helped him pick out on the map. He turned inland then and flew at low level, snaking his way through a series of valleys and between several high peaks. His navigation was spot on, and his eventual target appeared on an escarpment directly in front of them.

'Can you see it?' he shouted through the voice tube above the din of the engine. Kate had no idea what he was referring to until Brendan flew a low-level pass across the grounds in front of the large granite building.

'Oh, my God!' she cried out when it dawned on her where

they were. A cold shudder ran down the back of her spine.

'It's St. Patrick's.'

'Hand me back one of the bags,' he instructed, but she failed to hear him because she was so mesmerised by the view.

'Kate,' he shouted again and wobbled the wings to attract her attention.

'Give me one of the bags,' he called out again as he turned to line up on his target. This time she responded.

'Watch this,' he said as he flew low and fast at ground level directly at the front entrance of the building. To her shock and disbelief he launched the bag down towards the ground and then pulled in to a gut-wrenching steep climb while banking tight to the right in preparation for another run. On their next approach Kate could clearly see where the first flour bomb had exploded leaving a massive white mark on the porch. She was horrified. She strained in her harness to look around at Brendan and when she caught sight of him she could see that he was laughing.

'Give me another bag,' he called out and brought Molly on to a different heading across the top of the roof. He took them into a slow steady turn so that they could watch the trajectory of the second bag after he released it. Within seconds it exploded harmlessly on the slate roof, leaving another massive white stain that looked devastating from the air.

'Your turn,' he called out to her as he maintained height and circled so that she could drop another bomb on the roof. By now several people were running out into the front garden and pointing up to the bi-plane. 'Go on!' he shouted to encourage her. Kate could not believe what they were doing, or rather what they should not be doing.

'Throw it,' he shouted again and before she knew it, she had launched the third bomb out of the plane. Wide-eyed, Kate covered her mouth as she watched the bag of flour sail down to her target. There was another big explosion, this time on a parapet wall beside the gutter. The flour burst out sideways and showered some of the people on the ground below.

'Oh, my God! Oh, my God!' she cried out, but before she knew it she had the fourth bomb in her hands. 'Over there, over there,' Kate pointed. Brendan could see a large glasshouse come in to view.

'No, no, no, no!' Brendan shouted back as he shook his head, but she insisted that he take her over. 'It's glass,' he called out. 'You'll break it.'

'I know,' she yelled.

'You're mad,' he shouted at her.

'You're the one who started it,' she shouted back at him.

'Okay,' he said. 'Make sure you don't kill anyone,' he warned as he dived directly for their new target. Kate remembered how the students hated that glasshouse. It was known that when the season was upon them, the best tomatoes and strawberries were grown there, but the children never got to taste them. Kate let out a scream rather like a war cry as she released the fourth bomb. At the same time Brendan pulled up sharply and banked hard again to watch as the bag hit home. The entire glass house seemed to shudder as the force of the exploding flour rippled through every window pane. It had been a lucky shot though; no glass had been broken because the bag had hit one of the rafters carrying the glass, but the effect was the most spectacular of all.

'We better get out of here before they call the police,' Brendan shouted as Kate clapped her hands in delight at the sight.

'Pass me another bomb,' he said and turned once more to approach the school. 'We'll make the last drop together.' By now there were at least a dozen nuns on the ground running and pointing and screaming and shouting; two were on their knees praying for their salvation.

'Hold it, hold it,' Brendan ordered Kate to prevent her from dropping too early. He wanted to be sure that their last two bombs hit their intended target.

'Now!' he shouted and they let go their bombs in unison. The big black car standing outside the entranceway did not stand a chance, and was completely covered. Brendan circled one last time to survey the damage that they had done and then beat a retreat back over the mountains.

The remaining part of the trip was a relaxed affair. They were in Galway within thirty minutes where they stopped for a couple of hours to refuel and have breakfast. From there they flew south along the coast of County Clare for a look at the cliffs of Moher that towered six-hundred feet above the Atlantic Ocean. It was another clear blue day with a stillness in the air that was seldom found on the ragged and usually storm-swept shores of south-west Ireland. Brendan took his time and circled several spots that caught their interest and, to Kate's delight, landed in a field beside a shop just to buy her an ice-cream and the largest bag of liquorice allsorts that she had ever seen. It was well after dark by the time they had arrived back at the airfield and driven out to Clochan.

Chapter twenty four

'Dad wants to see you in Dublin,' John told Brendan the following morning over breakfast. His mother had called to speak to him the previous day. 'I have no idea what he wants! I just said you had gone away on a dirty weekend with Kate when she asked me where you were,' he spoke with all of the honesty he could muster. For a second Brendan panicked, until he realised his brother was only joking. John had to duck to avoid the sausage that Brendan hurled at him, and he laughed as he left the kitchen.

Brendan called his father in Dublin, but he was out at his government office. He just managed to catch his mother on the way out the door. She reassured him there was nothing wrong, but that he should come to Dublin the following weekend.

'It's important,' she said, 'he has lots he wants to talk to you about. It's all to do with your future.' She explained that she was late and had to go. It wasn't unusual for Brendan to be summoned like this. It was how his father had always dealt with his children. He wouldn't call them directly. He'd send a message through their mother or perhaps one of the house staff and then a meeting would take place in his office. A summons only ever meant two things, and no indicators were ever given beforehand. You were either in luck and would be given a small reward of some kind, or you were going to be given a long lecture. As a consequence, a summons always had the affect of unnerving the receiver. It had to be important, Brendan thought to himself, if he was to go all the way up to Dublin.

It occurred to him with a certain sense of guilt that word had gotten back to his father about St Patrick's, but he quickly persuaded himself there was nothing to worry about. His parents knew nothing of his flying. His father had been on at him several times about coming to the big city to see how the country was run. He had lectured him about going into politics and how he should be taking advantage of their present position to 'meet the right people'. The idea held very little appeal for Brendan. However, a summons was a summons and he knew that he would have to go.

He decided to make it an adventure. He called Victor and suggested that they fly to the big smoke on a cross-country training exercise. Victor was all for the idea, but he was busy and unavailable for at least a week. There was no reason why Brendan could not go on his own, but, after the great success of their last trip together, Victor suggested that as Kate had never been to Dublin before he should take her along instead. Brendan decided that if he stalled his father they could fly up in Molly a day or two early and have a good look around the city. When he suggested it to Kate she was thrilled. After their trip to Inis Beag, Dublin would be amazing. Victor asked Brendan to deliver a parcel to his brother in the capital and for doing that, he said his brother would organise their accommodation.

'A friend of mine will meet you at the airport,' he explained the following morning as they were about to depart. 'Give him the parcel and he'll give you a lift into the city. Everything else has been arranged!' Brendan and Kate flew north again through the middle of the country and landed in Dublin in the late afternoon. They were surprised and a little confused when they were greeted at the airfield by a man wearing a chauffeur's uniform. He was very officious in his welcome, and introduced himself as Albert.

'Please follow me,' he said with the poshest of accents. Albert took their bags and led them out of the small airport building and, to their even greater surprise, there was a shiny black Rolls Royce waiting. Brendan and Kate were lost for words. 'Victor said that you would like it,' Albert smiled as he helped Kate into the back seat. When Brendan was seated beside her a tartan rug was placed on their laps and then the man disappeared to the back of the car to stow away their bags. There was a sudden 'pop' and when he returned he had an ice bucket in one hand and two champagne glasses in the other.

'Welcome to Dublin,' he said with great ceremony. He poured them a glass and offered them smoked salmon on crackers from a silver tray that he took out of a small picnic basket. When they were settled he drove them at a very relaxed pace into the city. They pulled up outside the Shelbourne on St. Stephen's Green, the grandest hotel in all of Ireland. Two doormen ran down to help them from the car and take their bags while a third impeccably dressed gentleman introduced himself to Brendan.

'I'm Francis Beamish,' he smiled at the young couple's surprise. 'Victor's brother. I also happen to be manager of this hotel.' He led them across the opulent foyer to a private elevator, and took them straight up to the top floor.

'The Presidential Suite,' he announced, as he opened the door to their room. It had two bedrooms with en suite bathrooms and a grand piano in a massive living room that overlooked the park. Kate was entranced. She walked around and smelled all of the freshly cut flowers that had been especially laid out for their arrival. She played several notes on the piano to see if she was dreaming. Even Brendan was taken by surprise. Brendan had not known what to expect when Victor had winked at him and said that he had organised the accommodation before their departure. He had imagined a bed-and-breakfast in some town house by the river. A phone began ringing somewhere in the room. It was hard to be sure where, because there was so much furniture. Francis answered the call and while it was obvious that he knew the person on the other end of the line, he motioned to Brendan.

'It's for you,' he said and handed him the phone.

'Hello.'

'Well, have you shagged her yet?' It was Victor on the other end of the line. Brendan was mortified and turned his back to Kate for fear that she might overhear the conversation.

'Eh, hello, Victor,' he stammered, as he tried to recover from the shock of his question. 'Yes, yes we had a great flight,' he replied in an effort to make it sound like a normal conversation 'It's all going well. Aren't you the lad?' he said, as he tried to extend the phone cord across the room away from Kate. 'We had no idea.' He was babbling to cover his embarrassment. He was relieved when Francis took Kate on a tour of the suite while he finished his call.

'You are all set now. You know what I mean,' Victor stated encouragingly. He was neither gruff nor crude. 'I had to pull a few strings to make it happen so don't waste the opportunity. Do you hear me?'

'Yes, yes, I'm very grateful,' Brendan replied, as if receiving sage advice, still afraid that Kate might overhear them. 'We will do our best to have a good time,' he said, but living up to Victor's particular suggestion was the last thing that he had had on his mind.

'If there is anything you need just call room service,' Victor's brother said to Kate when they returned from their tour. 'And please let me know if you are not happy. I have told them you are royalty, so you shouldn't have any problems. If you do, and I don't care how small, just call me on this number,' he instructed and handed Kate a beautifully embossed business card. 'It's good to keep them on their toes!'

'I'll tell her you said "hello", okay,' Brendan finally said to to put an end to his embarrassing conversation with his mentor.

'Good luck, then,' Victor replied and rang off. Francis thanked them both for delivering a parcel that Victor had sent and departed by wishing them a pleasant stay. Before they had a chance to recover from their surprise there was a knock at the door. When Brendan answered a waiter from room service handed him their second bottle of champagne for the day and two tickets for the theatre the following evening. Finally alone, Kate and Brendan kicked off their shoes, put their feet up on the sofa and Brendan poured them a glass of bubbly. After a while he snuggled up to Kate and they kissed.

'Would you like to have a bath?' he asked softly. She knew that she looked a bit windswept from all of their travelling, but she could hardly believe herself when she smiled over the top of her glass with a coy look. She remembered how she had felt the previous week in his embrace on the Inis Beag. The timing was right now. She wanted to be with him. Brendan gulped his drink, almost in shock, when he realised what she was thinking. It wasn't what he had meant, but he was every bit as keen now that all of a sudden their feelings were out in the open. The champagne bubbled up his nose and backfired into his lungs and for a minute, he could hardly breathe. They both rolled around in hysterical laughter when he recovered and then for a moment, things became very quiet and serious between them.

'I feel like I should say something,' Brendan said. 'You know…,' he paused, trying to think of the words.

'Yes,' Kate replied. It was a big step for them both.

'There's only one thing for it!' he said, as he reached for the bottle of champagne.

'Brendan Finucane!' Kate screamed. 'Don't you dare!' she cried as she tried desperately to escape him, but she was too late to save herself from what she knew he intended. He had his thumb over the top and was shaking the bottle violently and began spraying and chasing her around the room.

'If we are going to have a bath we might as well have a shower as well,' he shouted and managed to corner her by jumping over the sofa.

'Stop or I'll shoot,' said Kate grabbing up a vase of flowers. She couldn't believe what they were doing. But there was no way he could hold back, the bubbles were too strong and they ended up both drenching each other and half the room. It was easier after that. They took their time, and had their bath together, and made love by soft candlelight while the rest of the world lay sleeping.

Chapter twenty five

On Friday mornings the city was busy. Everybody seemed to be pushing and shoving to see who could make it first to the weekend. There were trams and buses, horses and carts, and throngs of people hurrying to and fro. On the street corners news vendors were plying a brisk trade with stories of the war. Above them pigeons and sparrows were making a racket with their own gossip. Brendan and Kate, oblivious to the hustle and bustle, wandered arm-in-arm to wherever the mood took them.

The first stop was Bewleys, the oldest café in the city, renowned for its cream buns and coffee. The pair were famished from their previous night's exertions and stuffed themselves greedily to build up their energy. They crossed the city twice sightseeing and looking at all of the historical places that Brendan thought Kate should see while she led him astray every now and then with window-shopping. By mid-afternoon they had covered so much ground that the legs were worn off them.

'What's that smell?' Kate asked, sniffing the air as they dragged themselves back towards the hotel. At first Brendan thought that it might be coming from the river Liffey that ran through the centre of the city and was renowned for stinking at low tide. But this was different. It had more of an aroma, like something roasting. It was sweet and pungent with a warmth to it that stirred your very soul.

'That,' Brendan said, inhaling slowly, 'is what makes you thank God for being born Irish!'

'What do you mean?' Kate asked.

'Guinness,' replied Brendan with a smile. 'They must be roasting a new batch of barley down at the brewery.'

'It smells divine,' Kate replied as she too filled her lungs. 'Does it taste as good as it smells?'

'What do you mean?' Brendan quizzed as if she should already know the answer. 'Don't tell me you you've never had one?' he said with a look of incredulity

'I've never been to a pub,' Kate replied innocently.

'Ah, Jayzis!' Brendan said, with genuine sympathy. 'Saint Patrick's has a lot to answer for. Sure you haven't lived until you've had a Guinness! C'mon,' he said and grabbed her by the hand.

'Where are we going?'

'It's an emergency,' Brendan replied as he half-led, half-dragged her. At the end of the street was a granite building with a Toucan on a sign outside. 'Here's me spending the whole day trying to give you an education on your first visit to Dublin and you have never had a Guinness. Sure nothing could be more important. The day will be ruined,' he stated in an animated tone, 'if we don't remedy the situation immediately!' Kate had little choice but to follow as he weaved and ducked his way between the oncoming pedestrians. It did not take them long to reach the pub at the pace he had set.

'Sit down over there and make yourself comfortable,' he said, and pointed to a corner booth by a large frosted window when they stepped inside the pub. As luck would have it the place was almost empty save for a few early birds propping up the bar. Kate was a little self-conscious that she was the only woman in the place, but her unease was pleasantly distracted by the surroundings while Brendan made his way to the counter. The air was heavy with the ancient smells of a thousand nights of revelry combined with a light waft of cigarette smoke and mahogany that had been freshly polished. The ceilings were high with ornate fixtures that were dimly lit and, to her surprise, in the shadows, Kate was amused by the sight of cherubs dancing around the walls and the ceilings with little bows and arrows.

'The day is saved,' Brendan declared as he returned from the bar with a pint of stout in each hand. He placed the two large glasses on a small low table between himself and Kate and then sat down regarding her with a look of anticipation. 'What do you think?' he said, referring to the creamy brown liquid that swirled around the glasses. Thinking that he meant for her to have a taste, she reached out to take one of the drinks, but he stopped her before she had a chance. 'What are you doing?' he questioned as if she was about to commit sacrilege.

'I was going to have a sip,' Kate replied confused by his tone.

'No, no. Good things come to those who wait!' he patiently explained. 'Watch,' he instructed and leaning forward with his elbows on his knees, he fixed his eyes firmly upon his own glass. Slowly but surely, as if by some mental exertion known only to himself, the fomenting liquid started to change. The bottom of his glass turned to a dark treacle, the colour gradually began to ascend and obliterate the brown swirl above. By the time he was finished both glasses were filled with a black liquid that was topped with a distinct and thick pure cream head.

'It's ready now,' he announced, and sat back nodding with reverence.

'Are you sure?' Kate questioned, making fun of his behaviour.

'It's all part of the ritual,' Brendan smiled, confident that she would soon change her mind. 'Go on, have a try.' He lifted his glass and waited for Kate to do the same. 'Slainte,' he toasted when they touched rims and then he closed his eyes and proceeded to take a long luxurious sip of his drink. 'Ahhh. Pure magic!' he sighed, deeply satisfied and licked the excess cream from his lips as he placed his half-empty glass back on the table.

'Well, what do you think?' he questioned after Kate had taken a tiny sip.

'It tastes a bit like velvet licorice,' she replied.

'I know,' he smiled, impressed by her description. 'But do you like it?'

'It's strong,' she said, not wanting to disappoint him.

'Did you know that they give it to the new mothers in the Rotunda Hospital to help build up their strength after they have delivered their babies?' Brendan said, but pointed to his mouth to show that she still had some of the cream on her upper lip. Conscious that she might look a little foolish, Kate used her bottom lip to try and clean the excess, but still left a tiny ring around the uppermost part.

'Did I get it?'

'No, there's still a little bit there,' he replied. She tried again, this time using the tip of her tongue, but still missed the outer rim.

'Here let me do that for you,' Brendan offered and without warning he leaned across and kissed her full on the lips.

'Brendan!' Kate drew back, mortified that the other customers might have seen them in such a public display, but Brendan only laughed.

'It's good stuff, isn't it?' He excused himself then, stood up and walked over to the bar. A short conversation ensued with the bar man and two of the customers followed by a further laugh before Brendan returned with a bottle of dark wine-coloured liquid. 'Black-currant,' he explained and poured a generous serving into Kate's glass. 'It takes a bit of getting used to,' he acknowledged. 'Try it now and see what you think.' Kate took another sip and was surprised by the difference in flavour. Without saying anything, Brendan again pointed to his lips, but Kate played as if she had no idea what he was saying.

'I'll do it again,' he threatened.

'I dare you,' she replied.

Without hesitation, Brendan leaned across, but this time she grabbed him by his coat and encouraged him to linger. There was uproar and jeering from the men at the bar.

'I think I like it better that way,' Kate said, as Brendan sat down red-faced from the mocking. 'The cherubs have a lot to answer for around here!' she added and held her glass in the air to toast the angels dancing around the walls.

When they finished their drinks Brendan insisted that Kate have her hair done for the theatre that night while he went off and made other arrangements. When she returned to the hotel there was a large box waiting for her on the bed as well as a dozen roses and a card that brought tears to her eyes. In the box was a magnificent wine-velvet floral evening gown that fitted her perfectly. Kate was a vision to behold. Brendan had hired a tuxedo for the evening to complement her style. With all their dressing and messing around in front of the mirror with bow-ties and floral corsages, they only just managed to get to the theatre in time. Brendan handed their tickets to an usher in the entrance foyer and they were directed to a private box overlooking the stage. Kate was in awe of the opulence and scanned the theatre to see if any other couples were dressed so grandly. When Brendan handed her a box of chocolates wrapped in a red ribbon the night was complete. The play was 'The Importance of being Earnest', a comedy by Oscar Wilde that made them laugh all of the way through and had them in high spirits by the time it was over.

'That was a tremendous performance,' Brendan said as they left the theatre arm in arm.

'What now?' Kate inquired, smiling as they stepped out onto the pavement. It was just after eleven o'clock.

'I wouldn't have a clue!' Brendan replied with a mischievous smile. 'Why don't we ask Albert!' It was then she discovered Albert waiting for them with a horse and buggy.

'My lady,' he said, tipping his driver's hat. He helped them to climb aboard, tucked a blanket around their knees, and offered them hot port from a thermos.

'Flanagan's, Ma'am,' answered Albert, when Kate pressed him about where they were going. 'The best Guinness, the best music and the best kept secret in Dublin,' he explained as he climbed into the driver's seat. 'You haven't been to Dublin until you have been to Flanagan's. I'll have a pint for myself while I'm waiting if you don't mind and one for the horse,' he joked, 'if I can find a big enough bucket!' And so they snuggled together for the twenty minutes that it took for the horse to clippity-clop to the north side of the city. They could hear the music and laughter long before they came to the pub. Flanagan's was an oasis for all of the tenement houses that surrounded it – a haven for those in need of sustenance. In spite of the late hour there were plenty of children outside. The boys played football and chasing while a group of girls danced a 'ring a rosie' in the light of a gas lamp. It was a stark contrast to the affluence that they had left behind and many of the kids stopped playing to watch Brendan and Kate as they made their way to the entrance of the pub while Albert tied up the horse. It all looked very promising until a young man in a faded suit with the air of authority about him confronted them at the front door, and told them that they could not enter.

'There's a wedding on. It's a private function,' he said in a strong city slang. 'If ye haven got an invitation yis can't come in.' He was abrupt to the point of being rude. They were unprepared for such a reception. When Albert stepped into the porch he was rubbing his lips in anticipation of his pint and almost ran into Brendan and Kate who were on their way out again.

'Where are you going?' he asked, afraid that they had been put off by the noise. If they left, he was not going to get his glass of stout. Brendan explained about the wedding. They were obviously disappointed.

'Come on,' said Albert. His tone changed dramatically and there was an inner-city ring to his voice. 'Some eejit in a suit isn't going to stop us from having a drink!'

'Come here you!' he said pointing to the doorman. 'Who do you think you are?' he demanded in a loud voice, 'turning these people away. Have you any idea who you are dealing with?'

'I've got me orders,' replied the doorman, taken aback by the threat in Albert's tone.

'Orders?' said Albert with exasperation. 'Look!' He pointed to Brendan and Kate, standing there slightly embarrassed in all their finery. 'This is Royalty! Orders don't count with these people. This is the King and Queen of Sheba!' Albert announced, but the doorman still stood firm, adamant about not letting them in. 'Wait till Victor Beamish hears about this!' Albert mentioned as if conceding defeat. He winked at Brendan, and turned as if he was about to make his way back outside.

'Victor sent you?' the doorman asked. He grabbed Albert's coat to stop him turning away. 'These people are friends of Victor's?' His voice was suddenly full of concern that they might leave.

'Friends? Friends?' Albert repeated for affect. 'Sure they are practically bleedin' Family!' Excuse the language your Highness,' he winked at Kate, and with that, the doorman stood out of the way.

'Ah, Jayzis, why didn't you say so in the first place,' he apologised. He pulled the door open as wide as he was able, and half-bowed as he let them inside. The place was jammed with bodies and the thick fog of smoke and laughter. Everybody was having a good time. Albert waded across the packed lounge to the bar which was three layers deep with people all trying to order at the same time. Somehow he managed to make it to the middle, dragging Brendan and Kate in beside him.

'Sean,' he shouted to a fat man with a moustache behind the bar who was busy pulling pints and giving orders. Albert had to call him twice before he got his attention.

'Howya Albert,' the barman said when he finally noticed him. He wiped his hand in his apron before extending it to shake the hand of his friend. All the while he had his eyes on Brendan and Kate who stood out like two sore thumbs.

'These are friends of Victor's,' he shouted above the din.

'Cead mile failte,' Sean shouted back in a welcome. 'Is that lunatic still flying them string-bags?' Brendan nodded. 'He's a nutter he is. His brains are in his arse!' Sean said with affection. 'But any friend of Victor Beamish is a friend of mine!' He smiled warmly to Brendan and Kate and handed them both a pint of Guinness on the house. 'Slainte,' he said and then excused himself and went back to serving the wedding party. Albert found them a space at a table and introductions were made all around. He was kin to a lot of the people there, so it wasn't long before they were accepted as part of the gang.

As the party progressed it was time to sing and, as is the tradition, the bride and groom were the first to start. Each table took their turn singing after them, with hoarse and ragged voices. There was hardly a sober enough person in the room that could do justice to the words. It did not take long for Albert's table to make their contribution and, before she knew it, Brendan had volunteered Kate for the part.

'You're in for a treat now, Albert!' Brendan said as Kate stood up. Albert was about to make a renewed call for 'quiet' to give her a decent chance of being heard, but Brendan would not allow him. 'You'll see!' he said knowingly. Within a few notes, sure enough, as if by magic, the pub fell silent to hear the love song. A few noisy children that were running around were quieted by their parents and the jostle for drink at the bar ceased to be important. Some even left it completely to get a better view.

'Jayzis, Brendan,' Albert whispered, with the greatest of respect. 'She's gorgeous, I'll tell ya!'

'She's not bad, is she?' Brendan replied smiling as he watched the effect of Kate's singing draw couples closer together in cuddles of affection.

'Not bad?' said Albert, taken aback that Brendan might not adore Kate in the same way that he and most of the other men in the pub did at that moment.

'Not bad?' he repeated, stressing his point. 'She's an absolute stunner ... I'm telling ya!' Brendan laughed and nodded. There was rapturous applause and whistling after Kate had finished her performance and the cries for an encore were made all around for a second song.

'Would ye like another love song?' Kate inquired of the gathering. Brendan knew from her mischievous smile that she had a treat in store for them. There were great cheers when she agreed to sing again. The beat was different for she had upped the tempo, but all ears strained to listen.

'Well Johnny be fine and Johnny be fair he wants for me to wed
And I would marry Johnny but me father up and said
I'm going to tell you daughter what your mother never knew
That Johnny is a son of mine and so is Kin to you.

Well Seamus be fine and Seamus be fair he wants for me to wed
And I would marry Seamus but me father up and said
I'm going to tell you daughter what your mother never knew
That Seamus is a son of mine and so is also kin to you.

Well Michael be fine and Michael be fair he wants for me to wed
And I would marry Michael but me father up and said
I'm going to tell you daughter what your mother never knew
That Michael is another son of mine and so is Kin to you.

Well you never saw a girl so sad and lonely as I was
The boys are all me brothers and me father is the cause
Well if this should continue I will die a single Miss
I think I'll go to my mother and complain to her of this.

Well didn't I tell you daughter to forgive and to forget
Your father sowed his wild oats but still you must not fret
Your father may be father to all the boys but still ...
He's not the man who sired you so marry who you will!'

The crowd erupted into cheers of laughter and clapping and it took two more encores before Kate was allowed to sit down. Before they knew it an abundance of drinks arrived at the table in thanks and they settled in for a night of celebration. At closing time the wedding party spilled out onto the street, full of merriment. The party was still in full swing. They were just changing venue and Brendan and Kate were invited to join them. In return, the bride and groom were offered the use of Albert's horse and carriage while everybody walked behind them, singing.

They soon arrived at a row of terraced houses ending in a cul-de-sac, and there on the street, the party was continued. There were tables and trestles laid out with food and more drink and a band in place at the closed end. Flags and streamers hung from every lamppost and the weather above was kind. The band started playing as the crowd approached. With more room to manoeuvre than there had been in the pub everyone, except for the very old and those too feeble with drink got up and danced. Somewhere along the way a gang of small girls latched onto Brendan in his dapper suit and from then on they competed for the attentions of their handsome prince. One in particular, a four-year-old named Peggy had to be carried around several times because he was afraid she might get trampled on. She had curly hair and big brown eyes and would take sips from Brendan's Guinness when he wasn't looking.

At three in the morning the band was silenced and the party was brought to order by the father of the bride. He gave a rather soulful speech about his firstborn and how she was now leaving home and how he would 'bleedin well' kill the groom if he didn't look after her. This brought a great roar of cheering and slagging between the two families involved, and it was a minute or two before silence was restored. The father kept on talking, but Brendan was distracted by a faint droning sound overhead. Kate was on the far side of the street helping some of the children get food from one of the trestle tables. When she looked across to find Brendan gazing up into the sky it was the sudden fear in his eyes that made Kate go pale.

'Three cheers for the bride and groom!' the father shouted and the crowd roared out an approval that drowned out

Brendan's cries of warning.

'Hip hip...Horaay!' They called the first time.

'Hip hip...Horaay!' They called the second time.

With the third cheer there was an earth-shattering explosion followed closely by another and the cheering for joy was demolished into screams of terror. German bombers, lost over a neutral territory, had let loose their deadly cargo, thinking it was Liverpool or Birmingham. Four of the houses on one side of the street were completely destroyed by a bomb that had fallen in a back garden. It was the closest hit, but half the terrace was destroyed throwing most of the debris out on top of the revellers. There was smoke and dust everywhere and fires had started. The attack lasted only seconds, but the carnage would stay in the guests' minds forever. Brendan, lucky to be unscathed, was quick to recover from the shock of the blast, but when he looked across to see where Kate had been standing he was horrified to find her lying motionless on the ground with little Peggy beside her.

Chapter twenty six

'Kate!' he cried out, racing over to where the two bodies lay. One of the trestle tables had been destroyed by a blast of bricks and mortar that had been flung across the street from the bombing. She was covered in debris. He quickly removed the wreckage and was somewhat relieved to find her conscious. 'Are you okay?' he asked. He was afraid to move her in case something was broken, but she sat up and acknowledged him. His attention then was drawn to the little girl. She lay motionless, a few feet from Kate, her body twisted in an unnatural position, a pool of blood slowly forming around her head.

'Dear God!' Brendan cried out. He abandoned Kate and ran over to Peggy. She was lying face down. She let out a cry of agony when he turned her over to find the source of the blood. There was a large wooden splinter from the trestle-table lodged in her neck. Blood spurted all over his hands and arms from an artery that had been severed.

'Help me, Kate,' he cried. He reached into his pocket and

drew out a clean handkerchief to stem the flow. The sight of the blood-soaked handkerchief brought Kate to her senses and she was quick to respond.

'Find Albert,' Brendan ordered as he blocked the artery. 'We have to get her to a hospital as quickly as possible.' Kate wobbled as she stood up to search for Albert. Her ears were ringing and her head pounded from the force of the explosion. As far as she could see, the entire street was covered in wreckage. There were fires burning and the stench of cordite smoke made it difficult to breathe. All along the street she could see groups of people gathering around the badly injured. She hoped that Albert was not one of them. She was relieved then to find him searching in her direction and when he spotted her he broke into a run.

'Are you all right?' he asked when he reached her.

'I'm all right,' Kate replied, not noticing the mess that she was in. 'It's Peggy,' she said. 'She has been badly injured.' She pointed to where Brendan was cradling the little girl in his arms.

'Oh good Jesus.' Albert dashed over to help them. Brendan had managed to stem the flow of blood, but Albert could see that he was struggling.

'We have got to get her to a hospital,' he shouted. 'Is the horse still alive?'

'Yes,' Albert replied. The horse had been tied to a railings further down the street.

'What about her parents?' he questioned.

'I'll take a quick look, but we don't have much time.' Brendan stood up with Peggy in his arms. She let out another wail of agony, her shattered arm dangling down by her side. Brendan handed the girl to Albert and showed Kate how to keep the bleeding under control. Kate did her best to comfort the child as they made their way to the carriage. Brendan went off to try to find someone related to her. Within minutes he returned with a small group of people carrying two more badly injured victims that he had helped to pull from the wreckage of a burning house. One of them was the girl's mother.

'How is she?' he asked Kate as the group quickly loaded

the two other victims on board the carriage.

'Not good,' she replied. 'She has quietened down a bit, but there is a horrible sound coming from her lungs.'

'You can't come,' said Brendan when several relatives tried to climb on board the carriage. 'We can't afford to be slowed down.' There was consternation among the group and objections, but Brendan was adamant.

'They'll be all right,' Albert said. 'Walk on.' He flicked the reins hard several times to make the horse move. Nothing happened.

'Hurry, Albert for God's sake or we will never make it,' Brendan cried out afraid that the crowd might change their mind and try to board the carriage. Albert was already doing his best.

'Go on,' he roared and lashed the horse's rear with a long whip, but she still would not respond.

'She's been stunned,' Albert said in frustration. 'She won't budge.' One of the crowd grabbed the horse by the halter to lead it forward, but it reared back, flinging him to the ground.

'It's the fire,' Albert stated pointing to burning debris that blocked the road fifty yards in front of where they stood.

'Leave her!' Brendan shouted as he leapt from the carriage. He took the animal by the reins and spoke words of kind reassurance to her as he took off his jacket and gently placed it over her head. The horse calmed down almost immediately. He tried to lead her forward then, but in spite of his efforts and every trick he could possibly think of she still resisted.

'Dam you to hell,' he whispered and let go of her reins. 'Stay clear,' he ordered the crowd as he backed away from the stubborn animal. He ran across the street and disappeared into one of the burning buildings. When he returned moments later, he had a burning ember in his hand.

'Are you ready?' He motioned with the ember to Albert as he grabbed the horse's mane. Albert could see the determination on Brendan's face and told Kate to brace herself for what was to come.

'Go on,' Brendan screamed as he drove the burning ember in to the flank of the animal. The horse attempted to rear, but Brendan was having none of it. He held her down by mounting her. He stabbed the burning stake in to her flank on the opposite side and with that, the animal took off.

'Ha!' he roared, spurring the animal forward with his heels. In seconds they were past the burning obstacle. The terrified animal settled down then, but Brendan remained on her back and following Albert's directions, he continued to push hard for the hospital. Kate hung on as best she could across the cobblestones as Brendan cut corners to make the trip as quickly as possible. Every second felt like an hour, but she knew that they must suffer the discomfort if they were to have any chance of saving the child. The streets were clear. By the time they reached the hospital the animal was breathing heavily and covered in a lather of sweat. Brendan leapt down from the horse.

'Hurry,' Kate said as she handed Peggy into his arms. He took off up the granite steps to the entrance of the hospital. The child was deathly pale and barely breathing. Inside the hospital lay sleeping, oblivious to the destruction that had rained down only a short distance away. The wards were quiet, the lights turned down and the sisters went about their business in whispers. The senior sister in St Jude's ward was busy filling out the night report when a commotion in the outside hallway distracted her attention. She was about to get up from her desk to investigate the disturbance when Brendan burst through the door with the night porter in tow.

'What's going on?' she demanded in a loud whisper as she confronted Brendan to prevent him from disturbing her ward. She was halted by the shocking site of the blood-caked child in his arms.

'She needs a doctor,' Brendan demanded, every fibre in his body wracked from the exertion of getting them to the hospital. He was physically and mentally shattered. The matron moved quickly to examine the girl. Albert appeared behind them carrying Peggy's mother with the help of Kate. One of the nurses ran as fast as she could for a doctor.

'There is one more down in the carriage,' Albert said as they lifted Peggy's mother on to a vacant bed. Two of the nurses attended to the her while a third followed Albert and Kate out to the front entrance.

'For God's sake, what's taking him so long?' Brendan demanded out loud when the doctor had not appeared after a few minutes.

'She's gone,' the matron said softly to Brendan. She placed her hand on the little girl's upturned face and closed her eyes as she made the sign of the cross. 'Why don't you give her to me and I will lay her on the bed over here,' said the matron. She reached out to take the dead child, but Brendan refused to let her go. When Kate returned with the third victim she found Brendan sitting on a chair with Peggy in his arms.

'I'm sorry, I'm sorry,' he kept repeating in a wretched whisper and cried openly as he rocked her gently back and forth in his arms.

Chapter twenty seven

It was daylight before Brendan and Kate stumbled into their hotel, completely shattered and smeared in blood. Their valiant efforts had saved the lives of Peggy's mother and her neighbour, but they found it difficult to come to terms with the loss of the child. Albert had returned to the blast site to inform the father.

They spent an hour, showering, scrubbing and bathing in an attempt to wash away the terror that had spent itself on them. At last they succumbed to a fitful sleep that brought only nightmares. Kate awoke after midday to find a note from Brendan telling her that he would be back later and to meet him in the lobby. He wanted to go for a walk in the park across the road before his appointment for lunch with his parents at one thirty. She had almost forgotten about it, and had to drag herself out of bed. Her ears were still ringing and her bones ached terribly from the shock of the two explosions the night before.

She hurried to get ready as best she could. On the bathroom floor her beautiful gown lay crumpled, a stark and bloody reminder of the tragedy that had befallen them.

Brendan was waiting for her as arranged. He looked pale. He'd just had his hair cut to take away the singe marks from the fire. The bandages that the nurse had applied to his shoulder and upper back were covered by his shirt and jacket, and except for a slight stiffness when he moved there were no visible signs that he had been injured. They walked arm-in-arm slowly through the park for a while, with barely a word between them. Kate found his silence unsettling. She thought he might be anxious about seeing his parents. Before leaving Tralee he had told her in a light-hearted way about the summons and its meaning. Perhaps now that they were here, he was a little more worried. After a while they reached a fountain at the centre of the park. To her great surprise he stopped to face her and got down on one knee.

'I want you to be my wife,' he said. For a moment she was stunned. In his hand was an open box with a ring.

'I don't know what to say!' Kate blushed in reply. 'I mean, are you sure it's what you really want?' she asked.

'Say "yes",' he said, 'and yes I'm sure!' She tried to make him stand up so that she could put her arms around him, but he wouldn't let her because of the burns on his back.

'Yes will do!' he said smiling.

'Yes, I will,' she replied. The ring was a single diamond with a bright red ruby either side. It looked magnificent when he placed it on her finger.

'I want you to come and meet my parents,' he said surprising her again. 'Not now of course.' He could see the shock on her face.

'I'll make the arrangements with them.' He was already late, so they bid each other farewell at the park with a kiss and Kate jokingly wished him good luck with his summons. Brendan took off as briskly as he could on the ten-minute walk it would take to get to his parents' town house. When he reached the railings at the far end of the park he looked back, and Kate returned the hearty wave he gave her as he disappeared out of view. She would have liked to have had more time to talk to him about meeting his parents – to talk about the many things that had happened between them in the last week or so. Especially the last two days. Everything was moving so quickly, almost in spite of them. It was different now, more serious, and Kate wondered if they had any idea of what they were getting themselves into. She had no regrets about loving him. She was sure of that. But what would his family say? She tried to reassure herself that the sense of foreboding she felt was just the affects of the night before and that everything would be all right in the future.

Brendan reached his parent's house later than planned. He'd bumped into an old neighbour who had always been kind to him as a child, and he had felt obliged to stop and talk with him for precious minutes about the bombings the previous night. Punctuality was one of the foundations on which James Finucane had built his great life. He seldom made exceptions. Brendan knew, however, by the way his mother made a fuss over him in the hallway, that he might be in for a lot more trouble than just being late. When they entered the dining-room his father was already seated at the head of the table, looking stern enough to be a high court judge about to make a ruling. His greeting was brief and made no reference to Brendan's trip or the bombings. He tapped his fingers impatiently on the table while the house staff served lunch. Brendan sat opposite his mother who couldn't stop talking. He hadn't seen her so tense in years. The room fell into silence after the staff departed. Conversation was useless and Joan Finucane knew it.

'You didn't tell us!' his father finally said as he buttered a piece of bread. To Brendan's surprise his father sounded almost cheerfully disappointed, as if he had held back news he should have told them that they would have welcomed.

'Tell you what?' Brendan tried to sound offhand but, inside alarm bells began ringing.

'The flying you've been doing. Why didn't you tell us?' James sounded as if his son had won an award and they had not been invited to the ceremony. Pride and disappointment at the same time.

'How long has this been going on?' From his tone Brendan could tell his father already knew the facts. He was being baited for something more serious. He felt a trickle down his spine. He was not sure if it was a cold sweat or his wounds weeping, but he braced himself either way for what was coming.

'Are you doing anything else behind our backs that we should know about?' his father finally asked him. Brendan knew by the look on his mother's face that he had been discovered.

'No, Father,' he replied, flushed with shame and embarrassment. He had been trapped and there was no way he could hide it.

'Really!' James was taking his time. 'What about this girl you have been seeing? I believe her name is Kate?' Brendan looked at his father in shocked disbelief. Somebody had informed on him. He had been going to tell them; he had it all planned. This, though, was not how he had wanted it to happen.

'Actually I was going to bring her here to meet you today,' he said. He had given it serious thought, but was glad now for Kate's sake that he had decided against it.

'What,' his father fired back in an acid tone, 'as an interview for a job?'

'James,' Brendan's mother cried out in shock. It was the first time she had said anything.

'She is not that kind of person!' Brendan said. He struggled to maintain some sort of dignity.

'Cop onto yourself man!' said James, slamming his fork down. 'How serious is all of this?' He stood up and began pacing the room.

'I have asked her to marry me!' Brendan said.

'You what?' James shouted in disbelief.

'I have asked her to marry me,' Brendan stated more firmly.

'Don't be bloody ridiculous!' his father glared at him.

'Calm down, James,' Brendan's mother said. 'Go easy on the boy. You promised you weren't going to get like this.' He sat down again, but his anger was evident.

'You can't do this,' he said coldly. 'You had a duty to come and discuss it with us beforehand.'

Brendan sat in silence. There was little that he could say to defend himself. He knew from experience that his father would already have a plan in mind. He waited to hear what he had to say.

'How serious is this flying business?' James finally asked, changing the subject and adopting a reasonable tone. The knowledge of his flying paled in significance to Brendan's declaration of love for Kate.

'I flew up here,' he said, surprising both of his parents. He nearly said 'we' but for the sake of peace decided against it. 'I will be starting on twin engines later on in the year as soon as Victor can arrange it.' They might as well have the truth. There was silence again while the servants cleared the table. Dessert was left on a tray stand by the window.

'I have a proposition to make to you,' James said, when the staff departed the dining-room. 'Do not answer me until you have heard what it is I have to say.' Brendan remained silent, knowing that the true purpose of his summons was about to be revealed. 'If you give up on the girl,' James said slowly, 'you can continue flying.' Brendan was about to protest at his father's attempt at bribery, but his father stopped him by putting his hand in the air. 'Listen,' he almost whispered. 'We will see what we can do about getting you an aeroplane. There's bound to be one somewhere that will suit you. I'm sure Victor Beamish could be persuaded to assist. He seems like the helpful sort to have around.' His suggestion of using Victor in his conspiracy was a measure of the length he was prepared to go to make a compromise.

'You haven't even met her,' Brendan replied not wanting to hear any more. 'How can you possibly know what she is like?' He looked to his mother for some sign of support.

'We know the kind she is,' James said, as if his wife and himself were already in agreement. 'We don't have to meet her. We have heard enough to know what we are talking about!'

'Please meet her,' Brendan pleaded. He appealed to his mother again, hoping that she at least might consider his request. He knew there was little point in arguing with his father. His mother was his only hope. She, however, sat in silence. Joan Finucane had given up on rebellion a long time ago, crushed by the force of her husband's personality.

'Give her up, Brendan,' James said, in a softer tone when he saw that his wife was behind him. As long as she stood firm Brendan would listen, even if it was his father who was doing the talking.

'Be patient, son!' he said, his tone soothing. 'Let it pass. You have it all ahead of you. Sure isn't that why we are here today? To talk about the future.' As if now they were all in agreement. Brendan fought hard to hold back his tears from the pain of the previous night and all of the worlds that were colliding around him. Kate had become a part of him that he would never have the freedom to realise, as long as his father had any say in the matter. If he thought that he could sway him with the promise of an aeroplane he was wrong. But to his surprise, his father hadn't finished.

'It's time for you to be really taking command of the estate,' James said. 'You are so close to owning it now, sure you might as well have it. With myself and your mother spending all of our time in Dublin, running the country, it's only proper that you should take over.' There was a ring of triumph in his voice, as if all the years of waiting had been worth it. 'Signed, sealed and delivered,' he told his son. 'Provided this nonsense about marriage stops now. The papers are being drawn up, and we will have them in a week. From this day on, though, you can practically consider it your own.' There were a couple of clauses he neglected to mention at this stage, about his retiring, and profit-sharing, but for the most part he was giving Brendan control of the farm. The bait was set. All he had to do was give up Kate.

'Have a holiday while you are here with us,' James went on. 'Take a break and go back when you are ready. We'll be back at the end of the month, and we can finalise everything.' He talked as if his proposal had been accepted. Brendan knew from the beginning that there had been no point in arguing. He could see why his mother sat so quietly. How could she argue with such a man? For the first time in his life he wanted to hit his father. To cause him pain to the very bone.

'I'm not going back,' he said. There was a madness in his eyes. A determination that left no doubt when his mother looked up and saw his expression. He stood up, and she knew that what he was going to say next would break her heart. 'I'm going to the war,' he said. 'To fight the Germans.' A thunderbolt might as well have struck the room.

'Are you out of your mind?' James roared, losing his temper again. He'd had the whole thing wrapped up – everything organised. It never occurred to him that his son might rebel against him. He had been helping himself to some dessert from the tray-stand when Brendan made his announcement. As he turned to face him, he dropped the silver-serving spoon which fell on the polished wooden floor with a loud clatter.

'Get out, get out! he raged, at the top of his voice when one of the servants came into the dining-room to see what had happened. He threw his dessert bowl after her and it exploded on the closing door behind her.

'Repeat yourself!' he demanded standing face to face with Brendan, his fists clenched.

'I'm going to join the RAF.' Brendan glared at his father, ready to defend himself if James made any attempt to strike him.

'Fighting for those bastards,' James said. 'You are a traitor to the cause,' he pointed his finger accusingly into Brendan's face. 'Look what they did to us.' James Finucane hated the British for the eight-hundred years of tyranny that they had wrought on his country. He had lost relatives and friends in the great rising of 1916 to finally evict the British from Ireland. It would not have been possible without the support of guns and ammunition at the time from Germany. His government had taken a neutral position in the war as a consequence. What Brendan was proposing was tantamount to treason and would be of great embarrassment for him as a member of the government.

'If you stand beside them against our allies, I'll disown you and take away your inheritance,' he said.

'What about the bombings last night?' Brendan shot back in defiance. 'What are you going to do about that?'

'It was a mistake,' James said. 'The German Consulate apologised this morning. There will be compensation given shortly,' he added, as if somehow it made everything all right. 'Mark my words,' his voice was cold. 'If you cross those waters, then don't come back. I'll give it all to your brother!' He turned away and stormed out of the room. Brendan's mother sat silently weeping. He regarded her for a moment with frustration and anger for not speaking her mind, but knew in his heart that she had given up the fight years before.

'Goodbye, Mother,' he said. He bent down and kissed her on her forehead. She didn't answer, just stared out the window, shaking her head.

Chapter twenty eight

They had arranged to meet again at the park. Kate was feeding the ducks and didn't notice Brendan's approach until he was very close. When she saw him she held out her arms for joy and ran the few steps it took to reach and embrace him. He put his hands in the air to brush her off. She realised something was wrong. It wasn't his wounds he was concerned about. He had the look of betrayal that for as long as she lived she would never forget. He could hardly face or speak to her. In the few short hours they had been apart Brendan had changed completely.

'What is it?' she implored. The foreboding she had banished from her mind earlier on hit her with a vengeance. She was suddenly afraid of what he might have to tell her.

'I'm going to the war,' he said. His eyes were wild and there was a hardness in his voice.

'What's happened?' she asked.

'They already knew.' He didn't have to elaborate.

Their response was written all over him. It wasn't that they knew. It was what they thought. The scourged look in his eyes was all the explanation she needed.

'Don't let them do this to you!' Kate shouted in anger. 'You're taking revenge for all of the wrong reasons.' But Brendan was blind to what she was saying.

'What about us?' Kate pleaded. 'Have you forgotten so quickly the last few days? And this?' she said, pointing to her ring. Kate tried to talk with him as they walked to their hotel, but he had locked her out behind a wall of anger.

'I'll be back later,' he said to Kate when they reached the entrance of the Shelbourne. Without any further discussion he abandoned her and took off on a walk. The city was not big enough for him that evening as he covered every corner, brooding and rehashing each word that his father had said. His mind was wild and his memory ran deep, raging through a life of discontent at the manipulation and interference that had gone before it. He was determined to no longer be a pawn in his father's games. Kate was asleep by the time he returned to the hotel. He slept on the sofa in the lounge until dawn. They were supposed to have returned to the bomb site the following morning to see Albert and his family, but Brendan ordered a taxi that took them straight to the aerodrome.

The weather had changed and it started to rain; enough to make their trip home miserable. They were grounded halfway and spent the night in separate rooms of a bed-and-breakfast with hardly a word between them before venturing out again early the next morning. It was a testimony to Brendan's skill despite his fury, that they managed to reach Tralee at all the following evening. Kate was sick twice along the way. When they arrived Victor was at the hangar.

'Well, how did you get on?' he asked when they finally landed.

'Did you hear about the bombings?' was Brendan's only reply. There was no mention of thanks for all his kindness, only talk of the bombings and the destruction. Twelve people had

175

been killed with a dozen or more in critical condition in hospital. Kate had flown enough times with Brendan to know what to do after they landed and she helped them to put Molly away in the hangar. It was obvious to Victor however, that something was very wrong between the couple as he watched Brendan through the window of the small office, filling out his flying log.

'You're both acting very much out of sorts. Is it over between you or something?' he asked her straight, never being one for tact.

'He's going to the war!' she told him. She dried the rain off Molly with a cloth, and the tears from her eyes when she thought he wasn't looking.

'It doesn't surprise me. Albert called me,' he said by way of explanation. 'He had been anxious to thank you for your help. It was very brave what you both did!'

'You have got to stop him,' she pleaded.

'I can't,' he replied.

'Why not?' she demanded. 'He will get himself killed.'

'I'm going as well,' he said.

'No,' Kate said in anguish. Victor had been her last hope of talking sense into Brendan. His going would only strengthen Brendan's resolve.

'I have been grounded,' Victor explained.

'What do you mean?' asked Kate shocked at the news.

'Who knows?' he said still looking in Brendan's direction. 'Supposedly some directive from the government about a state of emergency. They are afraid of spies or something. The police came over yesterday especially to tell me,' he said without noting how strange it was that of all the private aircraft owners in the country, he was the very first to receive the order.

'Oh, I'm so sorry,' Kate said for she knew that beneath his bravado flying was everything to Victor and that without it his life had little meaning.

'Do his parents know yet?' he asked.

'Yes, they know everything. It's because of them that he's going!' Kate tried to stop herself from crying, but the strain was too much and she could no longer hide it. 'I'm sorry. I can't help it!' Victor stepped over to her and took her in his arms and rocked her gently.

'Are you on the rampage?' he said to Brendan when he came out of the office. 'Look at the state of the girl.'

'It's something I've got to do.' Brendan's tone was full of righteousness.

'Well don't be taking it out on her,' Victor replied. 'It's not her fault you and your father don't get on!' he said cutting him down to size. 'If you want to go off to war then that's your business, but save your anger for the real enemy.' It was the first time since Victor had known Brendan that he had spoken his mind. He made them sit in the office and drink a cup of hot Bovril to warm them up after their arduous trip, and relate all that had happened to them in Dublin. The terrible events of the latter part of their visit had overshadowed all the great things that Victor had organised. It was hard to be excited or grateful after all the sadness. Kate apologised for not bringing him a present. Victor brushed the fact aside, saying he hadn't expected anything. He apologised in turn about the bombs and said they weren't his idea, which made them laugh. But when Brendan tried to talk about what had happened between his parents and himself Victor did not want to know.

'You have to grow up sometime!' he commented. As much as he liked him, he had come to know Brendan as being a bit strong headed. He had no interest in hearing his protégé justify himself. 'If this is how you want to go about doing it, that's up to you. I can't be telling you what you should be doing. You have to work that one out for yourself!' Victor was required by law to deliver the two bi-planes to the air-corp base in Dublin for impoundment until the end of the war. They made arrangements to leave together two days later and go on from there to England where Victor had a contact in the R.A.F. he hoped he might be able to use to short cut their enlistment. 'He will be all right, Kate,' he said. She was about to climb into Brendan's car after locking up the hangar. 'He won't come to any harm, as long as he uses this!' he said and pointed to his own head. Brendan drove the entire distance home in silence.

'Please talk to me,' Kate begged as he pulled up outside the priest's house. 'I have changed my whole life for you. The least you could do is talk to me!' But Brendan stonewalled her by saying nothing more than that he would come and see her before he left. Despite her exhaustion from their arduous trip Kate didn't sleep that night. She tossed and turned for hours on end and then rose and walked the floors to try to wear the anxiety out of her. It was lucky Father Flaherty was still away. Brendan had become the centre of her world and her reason for living. They had been so happy only days before. Soon it seemed he would be gone and she might never see him again.

The two days passed and she didn't hear from him. Two lonely days of praying to God to beseech him to change Brendan's mind. Two days of vain effort to contact Elsabeth in the hope that she might persuade him differently. Two days to finally resolve that she would tell him that she would wait for him, no matter what. On the morning of the third day she thought she heard an aeroplane overhead, but when she rushed outside to see, it was gone. The sound was confirmed by a letter, hand delivered by one of the house staff, later that afternoon. It was only then she learned that he was gone.

Dear Kate,

What right have I to see you? You deserve better than I who would steal your heart and break it without any real thought as to what I was doing. I hope that some day you will be able to forgive me.
    Forever sorry

        Brendan.

Chapter twenty nine

John learned what had happened long before Brendan arrived back from Dublin.
'You made the right decision telling me,' his father had said, and after a long conversation he rang off with specific instructions. John was flabbergasted at the outcome of his scheming. Informing on his brother had been an act of malice, the consequences of which were beyond his wildest imagination. A week before, he had been feeling miserable. The novelty of being the big shot lawyer in a little town had worn off. The work, he discovered, was hard. Getting paid even harder. He was beginning to realise that he was never going to amount to much if he continued with the drudgery. He had been half-thinking of going to America to try his luck, but changed his mind when the phone call from his father suddenly placed him in charge of the family fortune. When he had told his father about Brendan and Kate he had never imagined that this would be the outcome. It

had been a 'quiet word', something that he thought that his father should know, but enough to get his brother summoned to Dublin. Pay back for Brendan taking what was not his.

The toy business was never supposed to have been a success. When he had proposed the original idea he had expected it to end in bankruptcy. Instead, Brendan had made a go of it, and in doing so had launched his flying career. What galled John most was the fact that the business had also given his brother an excuse to go to the market. When John had shown Kate to Brendan he had only been staking his claim. Brendan should have known better than to interfere in his business. He had never planned that anything should happen between them. It was one thing to be bringing her out to Clochan to visit the manor while their parents were away, but when they started playing house in the run-down cottage out on the peninsula he knew that things were getting too serious.

'Having her' and having her in the family were two different things. Brendan would want to marry her, and make a decent woman out of her. Make her *part* of the family. The latter was never John's intention. If he had gotten to her first he would have taken her for the ride he thought she really wanted and be done with her by now. It occurred to him, after speaking to his father, that if he played his cards right he still might get the opportunity.

His father had told him that the key to a safe that he never knew existed was hidden behind a loose brick in the back wall of the tack room. The safe itself was in the floor of his office under the big oak writing table. John was to hide the contents along with the key thus preventing Brendan from taking what did not belong to him. To his astonishment there was several thousand pounds in cash among the paperwork and some very expensive jewellery that he had never seen his mother wear. In a small leather satchel he was further surprised to find an old Webley service revolver wrapped in an oil cloth. His father had used it during the uprising and subsequent civil war to mete out justice to those who had wronged Mother Ireland.

James Finucane had been brave and fiercely nationalistic and had been feared and respected throughout the area.

'He has betrayed us,' he told John. 'You are not to give him any assistance.' By the time his brother had reached the manor though, John had given the matter a great deal of thought. He did what his father had instructed him to do, but confided in Brendan afterwards. He wanted his brother to think that he had his support.

'I don't blame you!' he said when Brendan told him about what had happened in Dublin, and that he was going to go off to the war. 'I was half-thinking the same myself. I'll see what he's like when he comes back, but I might just be following you on afterwards,' he said taking Brendan by surprise. 'There are more important things in life than to be pleasing the old man,' he said. Brendan, however, made him promise he would stay. Someone had to look after the farm. He had been counting on his brother to do it.

'This is something that I have to do,' he said. 'I appreciate your support, but I have got to fight my own battles.' John was surprised when Brendan handed him a large manual that he had been writing in, with all of the changes that he had planned for the farm. 'If you read through this, you will see all of the ideas that I have had. It will make your job easier and more than make up for the fact that I'm not here to help you.' John humbly accepted the manual saying that he would do the best he could, but that he doubted he would ever be able to do as good a job as his brother. Brendan packed a duffle bag with the bare essentials and put the rest of his belongings in a number of boxes that Elsabeth was to give to charity when she returned from her holidays. John surprised him by saying that he would keep the toy business going and look in on Kate to make sure that she was all right.

'Sure you will be home by Christmas with a chest full of medals and you will be a force to be reckoned with!' he joked. 'By the time you get back I'll have the old man sorted out and you'll receive a hero's welcome!' It was a relief to Brendan that his brother was being so supportive. Elsabeth arrived home unexpectedly. She had been away up north on a camping holiday with her Girl Guides. She cut short her trip when she had heard the news while talking to her mother on the phone. Their father had forbidden his wife to contact their son, but he couldn't stop Elsabeth. Joan had begged her to go home and see Brendan and prevent him from leaving. She arrived at the manor just as Brendan and Victor were about to take off. In desperation she tried to stop Brendan from getting into the plane.

'What about Kate?' she demanded. 'You can't just walk out on her like this!' She was crying, but Brendan ignored her. It was only John's persuasion and the strong arm he used to hold her back that kept her clear of the propeller. The last thing he needed was her interfering in his plans. He was by no means yet lord of the manor. John knew that there was a very good chance that he might be gambling away his own future if he did not play his cards right. But if the deck stacked against him in the end then there was always America. Brendan's acceptance into the Air Force would make this unlikely. He knew that the average fighter pilot had a three-week life expectancy – if they were good. Many didn't last their first mission. With a bit of luck, John thought to himself, the game would be over by Christmas.

His parents arrived home the weekend after Brendan's departure. The papers that Brendan had been meant to sign were given to John instead and he readily agreed to the clauses that were stipulated within. His father was further infuriated when he discovered that there was three-hundred pounds missing from the safe. In taking the money for himself John had driven the wedge deeper between Brendan and his father and robbed his brother of any small chance that might have remained for future reconciliation. He added fuel to the fire by misleading his father about his elder brother's loyalty.

'I don't like being the one to have to say these things,' said John with a tone of sincere honesty, as if it was better that the truth be revealed. Persuasion wasn't difficult. James had already become a believer. When John waved his parents good -

bye as they headed back to Dublin the scene was set. Brendan just had to complete it by playing his part. The postman delivered the ace three weeks later with a letter from Brendan stating that he had been accepted for Spitfire training.

John was a happy man. The biggest gambles are always fraught with anxiety and potential disaster. For John, anything could have gone wrong. Brendan might have been turned down, or even worse, seen the light and returned as the prodigal son begging forgiveness. But he didn't. On hearing the joyous news it occurred to John that maybe someday, he too might become a politician.

Chapter thirty

By twelve-thirty, it had already been a long day. Father Michael was heading home, tired and hungry. He'd had little sleep the previous night and the day had brought too many challenges. He'd got lost twice, been abused by a hostile dog whose owner thought it was funny, and got a puncture that took him well over an hour to change. His only consolation was that it had not rained.

    He had a lot on his mind. Catching up with the stacks of correspondence in his office and confession would take an inordinate amount of time. There was Mass during the weekday mornings at seven-thirty that few would attend and now there was talk of a hurling match he had to officiate over on the Sunday after next. He wouldn't mind, but he did not have a clue how to play the game!

When he pulled into his driveway he saw Kate and Elsabeth on the steps to the house. He was heartened to see that they were talking again. That is, until he pulled up beside them and got out of his car.

'You shouldn't have told him!' Kate said to Elsabeth in accusation. 'You promised you wouldn't tell him where I was. You promised!' she said bitterly. Elsabeth was visibly shaken by Kate's anger. She had come to give her the good news about the gatehouse that she had organised with John's approval. Instead of rejoicing, however, they were arguing.

'I had to tell him,' she shot back. 'Who else could I turn to? I was trying to help my best friend, that's all. There was no alternative!' Elsabeth glared at Kate in frustration. 'John of all people has been the most helpful in the past. Now he is coming to our rescue again. Why do you always have to be so bloody independent? All my family want to do is help you.' But Kate turned her back on her and walked into the house, slamming the front door behind her.

'Leave her,' said Father Murphy gently. 'She's had a hard time. Whatever it is you're on about will just have to wait.'

'But Father Murphy, please!' Elsabeth pleaded. 'I have just organised a place for her to stay. She would no longer be a burden to you.'

'She isn't a burden,' he said. 'She is a great help to me, and she can stay as long as she pleases. Stop worrying. Give things time to settle. She has only been here for a day,' he reminded her. 'She needs time to get things straight in her head. Then I'm sure she will talk to you and you can both make any decisions that need making.' His words were comforting. Elsabeth took a deep breath and let out a sigh.

'I just wish she would tell me what happened,' she said. 'I'm beginning to think that her story about the candle burning the curtains isn't the truth. I only want her to be settled. She was having a hard enough time without having to cope with all of this.' Kate's predicament weighed heavily on Elsabeth's shoulders.

'Give her the space that she needs and I'm sure you will be rewarded,' Father Michael was reassuring. 'Come back in a couple of days, or better again, I'll give you a call when the time is right,' he promised. 'Sure I'll see you for tea at the end of the week!' He gave her a friendly smile and the matter was settled.

'Thank you again for your help,' Elsabeth said as they shook hands. He bid her goodbye and went in to get his lunch, which Kate had left on the kitchen table. She was nowhere to be seen and he made no attempt to find her. When he finished his meal, he sat down in the office to catch up with the pile of correspondence that lay waiting on his desk. After a few minutes, however, he started to get a headache. He just couldn't face it. The last thing he wanted to be doing was paperwork.

There was more pressing work to be done. He wouldn't be able to put off saying Mass so easily the next morning, and decided he had better check that everything was ready in the church. It was a short walk, across the plot of land on which the priest's house stood. Behind it was the playing field where hurling and football matches took place after church on a Sunday. He reminded himself that he would have to look up the rules. St. Malachy's church was a cold affair. A sad and lonely testimony to the man who had been in charge before him. With great effort he opened all of the doors and let the church breathe deep gulps of the fresh air that blasted through – probably for the first time in years. With a few flowers and some paint, he knew he could transform the place. All he needed was a little co-operation.

The sacristy was next, and it was while rummaging around to find the keys to the tabernacle on the alter that held the chalice that he came across two leather-bound notebooks. Surprise led to curiosity. The first one had a thick, well-worn pad of foolscap paper. It contained over three-hundred pages. Each page had, in alphabetical order, the names of two families and contained a list of all of the items that each family had given to the church over the years. Every donation was dated. Some of the lists were quite extensive recording everything from money to furniture and even food. One or two included a cow or a pig that had been given on occasion and their value recorded after being sold at the market. Slips of paper, and even whole pages, had been added to account for the more generous of Father Flaherty's benefactors. He noted that Elsabeth's father was by far the biggest contributor.

If the first ledger was a surprise the second was a shock. It took several moments for Father Murphy to comprehend its meaning. It was the same size book, but had far fewer pages. Most were blank, save for a name on top, and various comments recorded underneath. 'Stingy'. 'Mean'. 'Wouldn't give when asked'. Halfway through the book he found the name of Micilin Og the man who had confronted him at the square. Below his name were two lines. The first read 'wife deceased' and the date three years before. The second line read 'Too many children'. Beside it in brackets was written 'not a good enough excuse'. There was a vindictiveness to every word. The first book was Flaherty's bank account through which, as God's representative, deposits could be made in heaven. It was just a matter of a fee. The second book, on the other hand, contained all those who could go to hell as far as he was concerned. That was what it all boiled down to. Staying on the right side of the old bastard!

'Kate. Kate!' he called out as he walked back to the house. He didn't care who might hear him. When he got closer he could see her in the kitchen.

'Do you know a Tom O'Gorman and his family?' he asked as he walked in. She was busy making bread.

'I do. What about him?' she replied in a curious tone. She could see he was vexed about something. She folded the bread mix into a baking tin.

'When was the last time you saw him at Mass?' he asked flicking impatiently through the pages of the second ledger. Kate was embarrassed by the question.

'What's wrong?' Michael questioned, sensing her discomfort.

'It's been a while since I was at church myself,' she confessed.

'That doesn't surprise me,' he replied. She could see he had returned his attention to the ledger and that something was bothering him.

'So what about Tom and his family?' he asked again.

'I don't think they have been for a long time,' she said, placing the dough in the oven. 'Why are you asking?'

'And Paide O'Shea or Dermot Kavanagh and his wife and five children?' he said, but he already knew the answer. Kate put down the dishcloth on which she had been wiping her hands, intent on where this conversation was taking them. Michael listed off several more names to which she nodded the same answer.

'But if they are not coming here for Mass and Holy Communion, then where are they going?' He threw the book down on the table.

'Nowhere, Father,' she said with embarrassment, as if it had been her fault. 'It's too far to go anywhere else. The pass makes it too hard a journey!' The Connor Pass connected the northern bay of Brandon to the southern bay of Dingle over a two-thousand foot rise across the mountains. It was twelve miles to the closest town.

'It's a trip you make only in good weather and preferably in a motor car if you have one,' she explained. 'Otherwise it takes all day.' He gave her a look that made her feel guilty, as if they should all have been making the weekly pilgrimage. But then he began to look slowly around the kitchen as if searching for something.

'What are you looking for, Father?' Kate asked, curious at his odd expression. He had a look of calculation, as if he was seeing his surroundings for the first time, and was comparing them to a mental picture in his head. Without answering Kate, he left the kitchen. She followed him as he walked methodically around the downstairs of the house.

'Did he have any family?' he asked as he stopped in the living-room and regarded an expensive looking piece of furniture that stood out as a showcase.

'Not that I know of,' Kate replied. 'He was pretty old and no one ever visited while I was here. He never did much of what you might call entertaining.' Michael walked back into the hallway and through the office that was furnished with equal grandeur, then he disappeared out into the back garden. Kate followed. He stopped at the side door of a large shed-like garage and found that it was padlocked. Stepping sideways over a small rock garden, he pressed his face against a window, using his hand to shield his eyes from the glare outside. To his frustration he found that the window was painted black on the inside. He could see nothing.

'What did he keep in this shed?' Michael stepped back to face the doorway.

'I don't know,' Kate answered. 'He always kept it locked, and he never went near it while I was around. It probably hasn't been opened since he died.'

'Why do you think that is?' Michael was sizing up the hinges that held the door to the frame. He had a calculating look.

'I don't know,' she replied, 'I suppose people were afraid,' she reckoned. 'They might have been accused of trespassing or something. Do you know what I mean?'

'I think I do,' he said and gave a tremendous kick to the door. Kate was startled by his violence and stepped back. She was scared, but excited at the same time, her curiosity silently willing Michael on with every boot. When the door crashed off its hinges Michael disappeared into the darkness. A moment later the side window exploded outwards as he used a stick he had found inside to let in more light.

'Come in here, Kate,' he shouted. 'The Bastard!' She could hear the disgust in his voice as he looked around. Kate was amazed by the contents.

'Holy Mother of God,' she exclaimed. 'Where did all of this stuff come from?'

'He's been collecting it all of these years,' Michael said. 'It's all listed in the books on the kitchen table,' he added.

'Look at it, Father, some of this stuff is awfully expensive. There are not many in this district that could afford to have it in their homes.' She lifted up a large sheet to reveal more of the booty.

'I doubt if any of it came from this area.' He made his way to the back of the garage. Most of what they had found had been covered in large sheets of calico. But it was the smell of gasoline that attracted his attention. He stopped beside the main door and lifted a heavy tarpaulin to find eight jerry cans standing in a row. He lifted the first one and found it to be full and so were the others. With the war on and petrol rationing what he had discovered was equivalent to a gold mine.

'Did he travel much, Kate? I mean out of the district? Did he ever tow a trailer? Dingle, Tralee, one of those places. Was he ever gone for more than a day?'

'Actually he was Father. At least once a month or so. He used to say he was going off to Dingle to help with the missions, but I remember Dessie Hurley saying he saw him in the opposite direction once on the road to Tralee. Strange now that you mention it. But why, what has he been doing?'

'I'll bet he was trading,' Michael said. 'Several small items for a larger one. Or money maybe. That's how he'd have got all of this expensive stuff,' He pointed to a very ornate piece of antique furniture that she had uncovered. 'It wouldn't surprise me if half of it is stolen,' he added. Kate was shocked. 'He was supposed to retire next year,' he reminded her. 'I'd say he had plans. I wonder has he got another stash someplace else?' he mused and his eyes searched the roof for a secret location. Kate sensed that the hunt might not be over.

'Actually,' she said. 'What about the room upstairs that's locked? I have heard him up in the attic once or twice when he thought I wasn't around.'

Michael smiled. His instincts told him that the best was yet to come. 'Let's go up and take a look, shall we?' There was mischief in his eyes and Kate had trouble keeping up with him as he took the stairs three at a time. He made enough noise to wake the baby when he kicked in the door to the room at the top of the landing. It gave in more easily than the shed, and Kate followed with Grace in one arm, and the two books off the kitchen table in the other. Michael was disappointed as he looked around the room. It wasn't what he had expected to find. The room was dark and bare. There was no bedroom furniture except for a free-standing wardrobe against one of the walls, and a pair of matching chests of drawers standing on either side.

'Hardly Aladdin's Cave,' he said to Kate until his eyes adjusted to the darkness of the room. He looked up at the ceiling then, and saw one of the most spectacular chandeliers he had ever seen in his life.

'Now that must be worth a few quid,' Kate said, as he reached up and tinkled a few of the crystals together. They glistened in the little light that entered from the landing, but positively sparkled when he drew back the curtains to let the afternoon sun into the room. Grace gurgled with delight at the sight and Kate, to amuse her, ran her fingers once more through the crystals as Michael had done. The furniture, which in the dark room had looked drab and inconsequential, now shone as the light picked out the beautiful grains and lacquered finish. The wardrobe standing against the wall looked a little more hopeful, but no matter how hard he tried, Michael couldn't open it. He shook the chest of drawers and found them just as stubborn. Everything had been locked and he had no keys. He was just about to deal with them the same way as he had with the doors when Kate intervened.

'Here, hold these,' she handed him Grace and the books and disappeared out of the room. Michael was agitated by the delay and wanted to take it out on the lock that impeded him. He had no other choice, but to wait and see what Kate had in mind as an alternative. She returned with a set of keys in her hands. 'I found these the other day in Father Flaherty's old overcoat down by the front door,' she said. 'Might save you breaking any more doors down,' she smirked and exchanged the keys for the baby and the books. He tried the first key on the wardrobe door, then the second and third. More frustration. He was strongly considering his original approach when the last one unlatched the door. He opened it slowly and let out a whistle when he saw the contents.

The interior of the wardrobe was in shelves. Laid out on each, as if on display in a shop, were ornaments, jewellery and miniature antiques of every description. There were several gold carriage clocks and pocket watches and fobs of every kind, and, in one corner, a crystal decanter of exquisite proportions glistened with the joy of release from the darkness.

'Bingo,' Michael said, as he held a heavy gold wrist chain up to the sunlight. 'This guy was a crook!'

'That belonged to Mary McKeon,' Kate said with surprise as she took it from him and turned it over to show him the inscription on the back. 'To Mary, Happy 25th – Sean' she read out. 'She died of T.B. last year,' Kate was horrified at the thought of how the priest must have stolen it from her on her deathbed. It took an hour and a half before they had worked their way through the contents of the wardrobe and the two chest of drawers.

'I need a drink,' Michael said. He was sitting on the floor beside some of the stolen treasure. He wasn't too sure what to do next. The last drawer he opened had been the biggest surprise of all. It contained a thousand pounds in crisp new bank notes and another ledger, a detailed inventory of all that was in the room and the garage outside. There was a brief description of each item, whether bought or traded, and its value at the time it was acquired. There were several items per page that had no purchase or trade price and Michael assumed that these were the articles that had been stolen. The book dated back fifteen years and contained over two hundred and seventeen pages; all of which were full except the last two. Every ten pages or so there was a summary of the contents and a total value of the items there-in. Eight thousand three hundred and seventeen pounds was the grand total on page two hundred and four. What they had discovered amounted to about a quarter of the total. The rest was on cash deposit with a finance company in Tralee. There were still twelve pages to go. Michael was absolutely astounded at his discovery and relieved that Kate had missed the last two drawers when she had gone to feed the baby. 'What am I going to do with all of this stuff?' he wondered aloud. There was enough there to build them a brand new church. His final discovery however, was like a gift from the gods. Just as he was about to leave the room he found a small wooden case with the lid lying loosely on top. When he lifted it off he was astonished to find eleven bottles of Bushmills Black Label whiskey inside. It was his favourite beyond all measure which he took as a sign of heavenly approval for breaking into the room in the first place.

Michael made his way downstairs with a bottle in hand. 'Will you have a drink, Kate?' he said putting the bottle on the kitchen table. She was just about to begin making their tea.

'I will, but not that stuff,' she said with a laugh.

'I'll make you something special then as a celebration,' Michael said and then went into a flurry of activity as he sought out the ingredients he needed. They included fresh cream, brown sugar, cold coffee left over from breakfast and among other things, a small bottle of vanilla essence.

'What sort of drink is that?' Kate inquired as he measured the correct proportions. He reminded her of Merlin mixing a magic potion. She was enjoying the display until he reached the last step and then her mouth dropped when she saw him add a generous sup of the Bushmills into the concoction. 'You don't seriously think I'm going to drink that, do you?' she declared when he finally placed a half-filled glass in front of her.

'To our good health and fortune,' Michael said after pouring himself a large Bushmills, but Kate made no attempt to lift her glass. 'Go on, try it,' he said. 'My grandmother used to make it for us at Christmas.' He took a long swig of his whiskey. Trusting that he was telling the truth Kate finally raised the glass to her lips and her taste buds were surprised and delighted by the flavour.

'God, that's lovely!' Kate replied and immediately took a second sip. 'What do you call it?' as she discreetly licked her lips.

'My mother used to call it a Bailey. I don't know if it will ever catch on, but it is delicious over a lump of ice when you can get it.' This was a strange priest. She hadn't quite worked out what kind of man he was, but she appreciated what he had done for her. 'Things are looking up,' he said and to her great shock handed her a ten-pound note. 'Go and get yourself and the baby some new clothes,' he said, 'and if there's any comment from anyone,' he stated, 'just say that the money came from the father!' He winked.

'I'll pay you back...I promise,' she said, too proud to accept it as a gift. He dismissed her protests with the wave of his hand. They were just finishing their drinks when there was a knock at the front door.

'I'll get it,' said Michael springing out of his chair with an enthusiasm inspired by their new-found treasure. When he answered the door there was no one there. At least not standing in front of him. He heard instead the footsteps of a horse and when he stepped outside that's what he found. A man on a horse. A big man on a big horse! One of the finest he had ever seen.

'Good day to you, Father!' the man said, as he steadied the animal. Michael stood on the porch way three steps above the ground, but the man on the horse still towered above him.

'Welcome to Clochan,' he said and handed him a long weighty parcel wrapped in newspaper. There was the distinctive smell of a freshly caught salmon inside. 'I'm John Finucane,' he introduced himself and held out his hand. 'That's my place over there,' he nodded referring to the manor. 'I thought I'd drop by and say hello.' His grip was very strong. Michael had difficulty holding the salmon and shaking his hand at the same time.

'I'm pleased to make your acquaintance,' he said, thinking it strange that the man had gotten back on his horse after knocking at the front door. 'Come inside, won't you and have a drink?' he invited, but John Finucane declined. Then Michael made the connection. 'Of course,' he said 'you must be Elsabeth's brother,' he smiled.

'I can't stop. I just wanted to say hello,' John said, but his eyes were shifty. He kept looking past the priest into the house, as if he was trying to find something, or someone. He didn't seem very interested in conversation. 'We are having you up for tea on Friday,' he reminded the priest of the invitation and then gave the horse a nudge to send them on their way. 'I'll be seeing you then,' he called out. He had made no attempt to shake hands before departing. The whole meeting was bizarre, Michael thought, as he went inside to the kitchen to show Kate his catch. Fresh salmon would do them nicely for tea. But she wasn't there.

'Kate,' he called out but there was no response. He eventually found her hiding in the pantry. She was terrified, and for the first time since he had met her some of the puzzle started to fall into place.

Chapter thirty one

When Kate discovered that she was pregnant, she didn't know whether to be happy or sad. Her reaction would have been one of delight if Brendan had been around, for they could have worked it out between them. But now that he was gone, she wasn't so sure. She remembered back to the island and the warnings of Sister Hannigan that had stopped them in their tracks. But Sister Hannigan had never known the love that Kate and Brendan had shared that much later in the hotel. It had made Kate feel like anything was possible. It was only now that she found herself in such a predicament that the warnings seemed real.

    Though they had been so close, they were now worlds apart. Kate didn't know which way to turn. She prayed for Brendan's safe return, hoping that she might not be pregnant. Then the tiredness came and the nausea. She began to experience days when she couldn't get out of bed without vomiting. When she felt the small bump after three months she finally realised that there was no way that she could avoid what lay ahead. She had been waiting and praying that Brendan might return, or at least send some word that he had heard from her. She had written to him several times and given Elsabeth the letters, who in turn, had sent them on through John. Kate hadn't told him she was pregnant. She just wanted him to know that she loved him and would wait for him. She asked him to send her a reply.

Kate thought that if she dressed in loose clothes she might reach five months without being discovered. But then her luck ran out. She had been suffering from a severe bout of morning sickness one day when Father Flaherty came home sooner than she had expected and found her asleep on the couch. She had removed her apron and her dress revealed her bump. He had been suspicious for a while for the place had lacked the lustre he had become used to. He feared that she might be getting too comfortable, or lazy, or worse still, that she had the drink on her. Seeing her pregnant though was totally unexpected. He didn't confront her straightaway, but decided instead to take a few days to think about it. A few days to get used to being without her. He had liked Kate for she had brought a sweetness to his otherwise bitter existence. Having to get rid of her would leave a hole in his world. If it had been anyone else he would have driven her out right away, but Kate he would sorely miss.

'I'm sorry, Kate,' he said two nights later when he sat her down in the kitchen and told her that he knew. 'I'm afraid I can't keep you on – what with the town's people and my position. The whole thing would cause a scandal.' He was genuinely apologetic. 'Have you some place to go?' he inquired with concern.

'I'll be okay,' Kate lied through tears of shame and guilt and the terrible feeling of having let him down. Despite his reputation he had always been decent to her and she was grateful for his concern.

'Here,' he said and handed her an extra five-pound note along with her wages. 'To help tide you over. You will have to be gone by the end of the week.' From anyone else he would have demanded to know who the father was, but with Kate it was a gentle inquiry. 'There are ways of helping – if I know who the father is,' he said. Kate did not doubt him, but declined to reveal

Brendan's identity. The priest was going to Tralee at the end of the week and offered to give her a lift, but she turned him down. She wanted to say goodbye to some people. It was Elsabeth, mostly, that she wanted to see. She hoped that through Elsabeth she would eventually make contact with Brendan. She made arrangements to meet her in the coffee shop in the village before leaving on the pretence of visiting a sick aunt. The meeting didn't go as she had expected.

'I thought you said you didn't have any relatives in Ireland,' Elsabeth commented. Kate, in her honesty, was unprepared for the question. She was not very good at telling lies and when she stumbled over a made-up reply, Elsabeth suddenly grew suspicious. 'He hasn't fired you, has he?' she suddenly said with a mix of anger and concern in her voice. Kate's silence was enough to give her an answer. 'Oh, the old bastard,' she spat. 'Why, for God's sake? I thought you two always got on so well!' She reached across the table and took her friend's hand to comfort her. Kate was unable to speak as tears ran down her cheeks. 'What's wrong, Kate? What's happened?' Elsabeth asked. 'He didn't try to do anything bad, did he?' she asked when she saw the terrible look of shame that appeared on Kate's face. She still failed to answer, but looked instead like she might break down completely. Elsabeth held on to her hand and led her outside and down to the square where they had a little more privacy.

'Tell me,' she said, sitting them down on the step at the foot of the large granite cross. Kate refused to face her. She sat hunched over with her elbows on her knees and stared vacantly in the direction of the ocean.

'I'm pregnant,' she said at last. Tears streamed down her cheeks and her head dropped slowly, shaking from side to side in defeat.

'That bastard,' Elsabeth exclaimed, assuming the worst. 'How could he do such a terrible thing?'

'No, no! It wasn't the priest,' Kate said, finally facing her, but giving no clue as to who the father was. By now Elsabeth was crying in sympathy for her friend. She took out a handkerchief and wiped her eyes, then handed it to Kate so that she might do the same. Being pregnant out of wedlock was a terrible situation. There were one or two girls that Elsabeth had heard of over the years who had gotten themselves into the same condition. It always ended up badly. Whatever happened, the men always got away with it, for in the end, it was the girl who was left holding the baby. All of these things raced through Elsabeth's mind along with the stigma and the shame and the loss. Kate would have to go away. There was no other way she thought.

'But who else could...?' Elsabeth asked, then failed to finish the question because she had suddenly realised. There was really only one other person in the world who could possibly be responsible.

'No!' she said wide-eyed. 'You're not serious!' 'But of course!' She was suddenly embarrassed, as she looked at Kate, that her friend might think she had doubted her. 'Oh my God, oh my God, oh my God! I'm going to be an aunty! Oh Kate!' In her excitement, she pulled Kate off the step and hugged her, and made her dance around. 'I'm going to be an aunty!' she squealed. 'Look, everything will be all right. You can stay at the cottage,' she said, suddenly inspired. 'I'll have my holidays soon and I can look after you. We will fix it up nicely, and you can make it your home. No one has to know,' she gabbled on. 'It won't matter anyway, Brendan will be home soon,' she reassured her. Her mind was racing with plans and preparations. Kate refused at first. There was no way she could stay. But the more Elsabeth talked about it, the more the whole thing made sense. Or at least it was a softer option. It was better than going all the way to Dublin. With Elsabeth's support she could do it. She would not have to leave. She could stay and have the baby and wait for Brendan.

'What about John?' Kate asked with concern. 'He is in charge of the farm. The cottage is part of the property?'

'What about him!' Elsabeth replied offhandedly. 'He doesn't have to know. John's always away and too busy to be noticing what's going on at the cottage. It doesn't matter anyway, he's Brendan's brother,' she said. 'He'll do the right thing by him. With a baby nothing else matters!' Kate believed her because she wanted to. If only half of it turned out to be true, she and her baby would be fine.

Chapter thirty two

Later that day Elsabeth arrived with two bicycles and the girls set off on the road out to the cottage. They wobbled and giggled all the way, and with the sun streaming down on them, it was wonderful – the best that Kate had felt in a long time. Elsabeth chattered and sang the whole way.

'It's my nerves,' she said, making a twisted face. They both laughed so much that Elsabeth nearly crashed which made them laugh even more. The relief for the two of them was enormous. They understood the consequences of what they were doing. Laughter was the only way to quell the fear in their hearts. The cottage, up to then, had been a shelter for spending a few quiet hours out of the bad weather, but not the sort of thing you would want to be living in.

'Don't worry,' Elsabeth reassured Kate. 'We'll soon have it right.' With great gusto they set about cleaning and fixing the cottage up. By the end of the day, after much scrubbing and puffing they had the little dwelling looking a bit more cheerful. Elsabeth made a list of the things that they would need. Paint and curtains, proper bedclothes and kitchenware. Kate was thinking she could never afford it. 'Who said anything about buying it?' Elsabeth asked. 'There are lots of other ways of acquiring it,' she gave a wink. 'The manor for instance!'

'Wouldn't that be stealing?' Kate said mortified.

'Borrowing more like. Sure isn't it still on the farm? Borrowing is definitely an option!' Elsabeth insisted and they laughed at the thought of pillaging Brendan's home. 'It will be easy,' she said. 'There's no one there to miss it, and you might as well stay there with me until this place is fixed up. My bed is big enough for two!' Elsabeth was true to her word. They started that very night with a torch in one hand and the list in the other, going around all of the unused rooms, selecting furniture. From the kitchen to the attic they pillaged crockery and curtains, and generally helped themselves to anything that took their fancy and would not be missed. At the cottage the following day they painted and polished, stopping only briefly to lunch on a leg of ham that Elsabeth had stolen from the pantry. It took two weeks in all, but the cottage was transformed and, with it, a new hope for the future. Kate looked around her new home on her first night, awed at how her life had been turned upside down and inside out once again. She said a prayer for Brendan and his safe return and thanked God for His intervention. She said a special prayer for Elsabeth who was truly her best friend. She was completely exhausted after the two weeks' work on the cottage and before she knew it she was fast asleep.

The big manor was a lonely old place for Elsabeth with her parents and Brendan away. With his legal work and the estate John was too busy to be around so, from then on, she spent most of her days and nights with Kate in their secret sanctuary. They built a chicken coup out the back, dug up the garden to make a vegetable patch, and white-washed the front of the cottage to brighten it up. The time flew by unnoticed. It was a surprise to them both then, when Kate was seven months pregnant, that John appeared one morning, unannounced. It had been ages since Kate had seen him, but she could tell by the way that he got out of his car and approached them that something was wrong. She was suddenly afraid that they might be in trouble over the cottage. He was carrying a brown envelope in his hand which she had seen him take off the dashboard and it struck her that the matter was something more serious.

'I have some terrible news,' he said. He seemed oblivious to what they were doing, or the difference that they had made to the cottage. 'Brendan's been shot down – over France, three weeks ago,' he waved the envelope from the Ministry as proof. 'Missing in action,' he said. 'I have made some enquiries, but there's little hope. They say his plane was seen hitting the ground.' He never mentioned the medals that his brother had won for bravery, or the fact that he had become famous throughout England as a fighter ace.

Kate collapsed, the life suddenly drained out of her. Her face was deathly pale. Elsabeth caught her and hugged her as they both broke down in tears for each knew the consequences of Brendan's failure to return. John put his arms around them in a show of comfort. He had known from the beginning through his farm manager that they were there. It had been a surprise to him because the priest had informed him that Kate had left the district, supposedly to attend a family matter. He had said nothing though, and decided instead to let them play house until his plan had unfolded. Sooner or later Brendan would get himself killed. Now that he finally had it in writing, he could make his move. He'd stayed away, bided his time, but on arrival now had discovered something wholly unexpected. Kate was different. She had put on weight. A lot of weight, he realised. He noticed the changes that they had made to the cottage. Kate was so distraught that Elsabeth had to make her lie down.

'What's going on here?' he asked, when she returned. Elsabeth had no choice but to tell John their secret. There was no other way to explain what had been happening behind his back.

'Why didn't you tell me?' he admonished her quietly. His

voice full of concern. 'Does anyone else know you are here?'

'We were going to...when the time was right,' Elsabeth hesitated. 'We were waiting for Brendan to come back, hoping that it might be any day now. The last thing we expected was that he'd be killed. What are we going to do?' she asked, as tears welled in her eyes again. John took her in his arms. She was not asking John for his help. She was just talking out loud. 'We' was Kate and her, together.

'You'll need turf and firewood and some sort of better arrangement with the water,' was his answer. 'Kate can't be expected to draw water from the river in the middle of winter.' She looked at him in surprise. 'Brendan is lost in action, but that doesn't mean that he's dead.' His tone was resolute, as if he believed his brother would come back. It suddenly occurred to Elsabeth that there might still be some hope. She ran back inside and told Kate how John was going to help. Kate appeared a few minutes later, dry-eyed and slightly embarrassed. John pretended he didn't notice, making himself busy drawing up a list of the things he thought they would need. If Kate had any reservations, she kept them to herself. She thanked him for his generosity and understanding. She wanted to believe that everything would be all right, but since the very first day she had met him, there had always been something about John that made her feel uneasy. In her present situation, however, she did not have any other option but to trust him. Elsabeth boiled the kettle and made tea.

'Brendan will come home,' she declared bravely. 'Maybe sooner than we expect,' she added, patting Kate on the arm. With John helping them now, she believed everything would turn out fine.

The days turned into weeks. Elsabeth came by every day after school and stayed as much as she could. John remained attentive. He dropped by on a regular basis, always with something for Kate. Mutton or butter or extra eggs off the farm. He would stay a while and they would chat over tea. To impress her he would talk about all of the great things he was doing and how the big changes he was making on the farm were working out. He neglected to tell her that all of the credit was due to the plans that his brother had left him. He would talk about Brendan and how he was making inquiries all the time through his law firm in Tralee, but that the Ministry in England was slow to respond. He carried on as though he and Kate had always been old friends.

As Kate's pregnancy advanced she glowed with the life that was forming inside her, and radiated a wonderful softness. Her breasts were full, her cheeks were red and her eyes shone like diamonds. Each day grew longer as she had less to do on the cottage. Each day became a little lonelier, so that she began to look forward to John's visits, even to anticipate them. She would set the table and bake fresh bread on Tuesdays and Fridays. It had become a little routine. He would arrive at ten and stay for an hour, but then it stretched more to midday. They would walk and talk and sit and chat. She began to feel relaxed in his company. He would make her laugh, cheer her up, and leave her feeling guilty after he had departed because she began to think that she might have misjudged him. Then one day he brought her flowers – a big bunch with magnificent colours, with pink carnations at the centre of the arrangement. Without thinking, she kissed him on the cheek to thank him for his lovely thought. Before she knew it he had her in an embrace. It was an embarrassing moment. They both knew that he should not have done it – at least not in the way that he did.

'I'm sorry, Kate,' he said as she drew back. 'I hadn't been expecting you to kiss me! I was just giving you a hug to go with the flowers. It was a reaction. That's all, you'll have to excuse me!' he begged. She offered him his food and some tea. But no matter how hot her drink was, she could not get rid of the chill that had coursed through her veins when he had taken her in his arms. It had not been a hug. A hug would have been okay. It had been more like a clutch, a grab. The animal inside him that he had been hiding for so long had pounced ... and given the game away.

Chapter thirty three

John had given Elsabeth driving lessons and the loan of Brendan's old car as a contingency in the event of an emergency. They'd had great fun pretending, with Kate lying on the back seat screaming and shouting as if in terrible pain, while Elsabeth wrestled with the vagaries of 'the stupid clutch' as she practised her hill starts. They had made a first aid kit and all sorts of preparations to be sure that they were ready, and the local midwife had been engaged in the utmost secrecy. But the baby was not having any of it.

'Is it kicking?' Elsabeth inquired when she saw Kate suddenly put her hand to her stomach. It was now two weeks before the due date, and they were sitting outside the cottage watching the sun go down.

'No,' replied Kate suddenly alarmed by the unexpected contraction. 'It's coming,' she stated. She stood up and pointed to a wet patch on her skirt.

'Oh, dear God,' Elsabeth cried in a kind of terrified excitement. 'I'll go and get the midwife. I won't be long. Don't do anything until we get back.' She raced to the car. To her horror the engine would not start. The battery had gone flat after they had forgotten to turn off an inside light after one of their rehearsals. Elsabeth's confidence about the birth had been founded on the knowledge that the midwife would be present. The thought of her not being there spun her into a panic.

'What will we do?' she cried, her excitement turning to alarm. Without the car she knew that they were too far out on the peninsula to get help in time. The second contraction arrived shortly after the first. Kate was calm.

'It will be all right,' she stated, quietly. She knew what to do. She made Elsabeth sit down and read to her from a book of Shakespeare's sonnets, which helped them both to concentrate. She got very hot later on in the night so she went outside to the cool air and paddled in the stream up to her knees. The relief was just what she needed. When the time was right Kate went back inside to find that not only had Elsabeth come to her senses, but that she was busy preparing for the big event. She had the fire going with a kettle and two pots simmering. Beside the fireplace was a chair with a stack of sheets and towels on top and a large tin bath in the corner of the room standing ready. The contractions were getting stronger now, and Kate stood with her hands against the wall to brace herself until the moment passed.

'Here, take this,' Elsabeth said to Kate when the contraction subsided. She handed her a large spoonful of honey and a cup of warm milky tea to wash it down. 'It will help to keep your strength up,' she said remembering all of the little tips the midwife had given them about the delivery. Kate nodded and did as she was told. 'Do you want to lie down?' Elsabeth asked. She could see beads of perspiration on Kate's face that signalled another contraction.

'No,' Kate grimaced as the spasm took hold.

'I've got you,' Elsabeth said and grabbed her under her arms to take her weight. Kate was greatly relieved not to have to support herself, and to be able to focus instead on relaxing with the contraction. 'That's it,' Elsabeth said as she felt Kate letting her body go. With the routine established they worked together for another hour or so. Between contractions Elsabeth wiped the sweat from Kate's brow and gave her hot compresses to comfort her.

'We are almost there,' Elsabeth said. The contractions became more rapid and the head began to show. 'Don't be afraid to cry out. Now push! push!' Kate changed her position to a squat with an armchair behind her for support. Elsabeth knelt between her legs with a fresh new towel to catch the baby.

'One last time now; that's it!' she instructed and then the baby dropped gently into Elsabeth's arms. 'It's a girl,' she said and handed her to Kate. The baby let out a couple of good lusty roars to convince them she was healthy, and then settled down quietly on Kate's breast.

'What a clever girl you are,' Elsabeth said to an exhausted Kate as she wrapped her in a blanket to keep mother and baby warm.

'No, you are the clever one,' Kate said in reply and squeezed her hand to thank her.

'I'm glad it wasn't twins,' Elsabeth sighed. 'God, that was amazing. *You* were amazing!' Though physically shattered, it was the proudest moment of Kate's young life. She forgot all of her troubles the moment she laid eyes on her new baby. She chose the name Grace, after Grace O'Malley, the fearless Pirate Queen of the west coast of Ireland who featured in many of the stories that her grandfather had told her as a child. In her arms she held a part of Brendan to whom she had given all of her love. She knew that no matter what happened in the future, he would always be with her.

John showed up the following morning. Kate had not seen him since he had given her the flowers over a week ago. This time he arrived with gifts like never before, unaware that the baby had already been born. He was delighted with the news. A girl posed little threat to his plans for the future. In the back of his car he had a cradle that the workers in the toy factory had built from a picture he had found in a book on mediaeval history. It was made from the best Irish oak and polished to the most wonderful finish. Inside was the softest of mattresses and a patchwork quilt made from the finest of white cottons and lace. It's beauty surprised even Kate. He carried it inside and set it down, and from under the quilt pulled out a bottle of French champagne. He made a great ceremony about opening the bottle, saying it was high time for a celebration. He had cheese, crackers, real champagne glasses and a big fruitcake covered in icing.

'There's nothing like a surprise party,' he said, as he poured the champagne and gave them each a glass. Elsabeth and Kate were too busy being matronly and motherly to notice any difference in him, but a glint was in his eyes. He looked greedily at Kate, noticing that her belly was less swollen. The cogs of his imagination were running overtime. He had coveted her from that first day that he had seen her at the fair. Now he had her where he wanted her. It was only a matter of time before she would have to begin paying for his indulgence. He had been patient so far and he could wait a little longer. It would make the 'having' of her that much sweeter.

Chapter thirty four

'What do you mean you didn't go to see her?' Victor said. They were standing on the platform of the railway station in Birmingham waiting to catch the train.

'I didn't have time,' Brendan lied, weakly.

'Blazes, man. Of all the people! Why didn't you go and say goodbye to her properly?'

'I couldn't face her,' was Brendan's reply. He was already ashamed of the note that he had sent to Kate.

'You'll have worse to face in the coming months,' Victor admonished. 'I told you to go and see her and end it before we left. It was the least you could have done, man!'

Although firm in his own decision to go to the war, Victor had called at the manor the following day to dissuade Brendan from doing anything rash. He was never one for meddling in other people's business and had always kept quiet when Brendan complained about his father. This time, however, he'd felt responsible for Brendan's situation. 'Once you are in, there is no turning back,' he had said. 'There is a bloody good chance of you getting killed.' When Brendan had shown him the shirt that was covered in Peggy's blood, Victor knew then that his mind was made up.

Their acceptance into the Royal Air Force had been based on a flying test. The instructor had declared that he couldn't have done any better himself. Brendan was selected as a fighter pilot, and was to go to Scotland for advanced training in Spitfires. Victor, on the other hand, was deemed too old for the rigours of constant combat. His superior knowledge represented a greater asset and he was sent to Wales for training as an Air Force instructor in Hurricanes.

'I'm sorry that you were not selected,' Brendan said after Victor had cooled down.

'Don't be,' Victor replied. 'The more of the likes of you I can get my hands on and train, the more Germans will get shot down and the sooner this madness will end. Don't forget to use this every now and then,' he added, pointing to his head as Brendan's train pulled in to the platform. 'It's not a game any longer. It's the real thing, with real bullets.' He knew that there was every possibility that he might never see his young friend again. 'There's more than me wants to see you coming home,' he said.

When Brendan got his hands on the controls of a Spitfire they made perfect sense to him. From the position of the throttle to the grips for his feet on the rudder pedals, the reflector gunsight and the button on the joy stick that fired a deadly hail from the machine guns and cannons on the wings. They all felt like an extension of his body. It was as if the aircraft had been designed with him specifically in mind. The supercharged engine was almost six times more powerful than that of Molly and Malone combined. In the months that followed, Brendan worked the hardest of all of the recruits in his conversion group. It was all he could do to keep himself from thinking of Kate and his family and what had happened between them. John had promised to keep in touch. He was the only one who knew of Brendan's location. But he always seemed slow to respond to his letters.

'The postal service is being hampered by the war,' John wrote. It seemed that not all of their letters to each other were getting through. On top of that, he said, he was very busy with the farm. In spite of Brendan's experience, the training was rigorous and filled with challenges. One of the recruits whom he had befriended early on was killed when his neck was snapped by a vicious crash landing. His aircraft somersaulted, landed upside down and shattered the cockpit. Another was so badly burned in an accident that he was virtually unrecognisable after his discharge from hospital. Neither incident acted to deter him from the single-minded desire that had been forged by the scorch of the bombs in Dublin. Some of his fellow recruits flew for adventure. Others flew for status. Brendan's only reason was to seek vengeance for the little girl and all of the others who had been killed by the German bombers in Dublin. He never got close enough to anyone to mention the spite he held for his father or how much it drove him once he got into the air.

When he received his 'Wings' he was immediately posted to a squadron in the south beside the English Channel. His task was to help protect the shipping convoys that were the lifeline between Britain and America. His personal troubles were soon forgotten. Staying alive had suddenly become more important. There was plenty of action, with lots of scrapping, and they always seemed to be outnumbered. The early days were grim, with heavy losses among the new and inexperienced recruits in his squadron. He adapted quickly though and, after making his first kill from fifty yards, he shot down a second fighter a day later. He soon gained a reputation for getting in among the action. Unlike other fighter pilots in his squadron it was rare for Brendan to come home from a mission with any ammunition left to spare.

To Brendan the job at hand was to shoot the enemy. He was a ruthless and efficient killer to the point that he often scared his own pilots as much as he did the Germans. When he latched on to the tail of the enemy he would not let go until the other pilot was dead. It was nothing for him to dive after one of his victims and follow him in a vertical plunge at over four hundred miles an hour to make sure that he hit the ground.

There wasn't a week went by that he did not have a lengthy discussion with Victor by phone about their latest scrap or lucky escape. Victor had managed to get himself promoted and transferred to an active combat unit as a station commander. Although he was not supposed to fly, he was ever the rebel and managed to lead his men from the front on a regular basis to score several kills for himself. He kept his focus on his student and a full analysis would take place of how Brendan as a fighter pilot and leader could be doing a better job. While Brendan's success was mostly a product of his natural skill, it was the maturity gained by Victor's mentoring that kept him alive.

Within three months he had racked up fourteen kills and earned himself a Distinguished Flying Cross with two Bars. His aerial swagger though was contrasted by his modesty on the ground. He forbade his ground crew to paint his 'kills' in the form of swastikas on the side of his aircraft. As an alternative they came up with the idea of a Shamrock Crest and emblazoned it with the initials BF on the side of his cockpit. For propaganda purposes none of this was lost on the British press, and Brendan's reputation quickly spread throughout England. Model airplanes of his Spitfire with vivid green shamrocks were sold along Piccadilly Circus and The Strand. Small boys robbed their mother's purses to have a treasured reminder that their greatest flying ace was winging his way across the murky Channel to protect England. His reputation travelled as far as Germany and it wasn't long before word was spread to 'get Finucane of the Shamrock'. Despite his spreading fame the reality of promotion was that it was accelerated by death, and soon Brendan was given his own squadron. They were an exuberant bunch of New Zealanders and Australians with a brilliant record on Spitfires and a rather casual approach to King's regulations and 'Pommy Bastard' wing leaders. They were a different kind of breed, unlike any he had flown with before – a band of brothers to whom he had greater affinity than any of his British counterparts. Every one of them had a nickname. Bluey for his eyes, Frizz for his hair and Hoppy for the way he landed. It wasn't long before they started calling Brendan "Paddy."

'Couldn't they think of anything more original?' Brendan inquired of the most stereotypical name ever given to an Irishman.

'The alternative was Spud!' his wingman replied.

'Spud?'

'You know – as in potato!'

Brendan was appalled at the thought.

'All right, Paddy it is,' he said realising that there were worse names to be called. Brendan soon settled in and instructed his men in the deadly game of aerial combat in the same way that he had led his team in the hurling championships. He pushed them on the ground as well as in the air, and was always working on team tactics. When under attack he had the uncanny ability to look after his pilots as well as himself. If he wasn't directly engaged in combat, he was busy shouting instructions from the cockpit that cost the enemy dearly and saved his men on countless occasions. He was cool under fire and there was many a time he managed to turn the tables to outwit an overzealous enemy, too eager to press home their advantage.

The only respite they had for their weary bones was when the weather turned bad. But even then, it had to be atrocious. To keep morale high, Brendan allowed a gramophone to be played in the dispersal area as the men lounged in readiness for orders to scramble. When they discovered that 'Tangerine' was Brendan's favourite song, they played it to honour their chief. Despite the bitter sweet memories that it brought of Kate, Brendan allowed it, and soon it became the squadron song, to be played as a lucky talisman every time they went into action.

Before every mission Brendan usually had a funny feeling in his stomach, not unlike the one he used to experience before a big match. Once in his aircraft, though, he settled down and his mind began to work like a clockwork motor; accepting this, rejecting that, sizing up this, remembering that for later, nerves on edge, not from fear, but from the excitement and intensity of the mental effort. On return, he would find that, although dog-tired, he was unable to sleep, as his brain struggled to remember all that had happened to him that day. He might have a clear impression of three or four incidents that stood out like illuminated lantern slides in his mind's eye – perhaps a picture of two Messerschmitt fighters belting down on his tail, or another of his cannon shells striking at the belly of his foe, the aircraft spraying debris all around. But for the life of him he would be unable to recall what exactly had happened.

Later, when just asleep, some forgotten link in the chain of events would suddenly come back. Instantly he would be wide awake and aware; then the whole story of the operation would piece itself together and he would lie there, reliving every moment of combat. Everything happened so quickly in the air, such a tremendous amount of thinking had been squeezed into such a short space of time, that he often suffered from mental indigestion.

Within a few months, however, Brendan's earlier sense of jubilation and relief after making it home from a mission was replaced by a morbid sense of his ability to kill the enemy. He had always enjoyed hunting, hurling, clay shooting and boxing, but the energy he brought to battle was different. To understand it, you had to have walked through the doors of the Mater hospital with the shattered and bloodied body of an innocent child in your arms. It was the vow that he had made to avenge all of those who had been killed in the atrocity that set Brendan apart from his fellow fighters. But revenge is a double-edged sword, and Brendan was beginning to feel that he had cursed himself as much as he had cursed the enemy. 'I'm beginning to feel like a walking graveyard!' he confided to his armourer the day that he had destroyed three Messerschmitt fighters in less than ten minutes on one mission. The life expectancy was so low and attrition rate so high that a fighter ace was any pilot who had shot down more than five enemy aircraft. It was nothing for Brendan to do so within a week. The pressures of combat were relentless and unending and gave little time for recovery. His face was drawn, his skin grey from the physical exhaustion of continuous combat and the killing that he had done.

Twice he had put in for leave in the hope of travelling back to Ireland to see Kate. Both times he had been cut short at the last minute by a combination of bad weather and the heavy losses among his men that left the remainder of his squadron vulnerable without his leadership. In some ways his New Zealand and Australian comrades had a heavier cross to bear because they were so far from home. He was torn between his new loyalty to those who would so readily follow him into mortal combat and his eternal love for Kate who might as well have been on the far side of the world. There was no time though, to question the doubts that began to spring to mind about the decisions that he had made or the regrets that were slowly seeping into his veins. The following day he cheated death yet again by shooting down two more of the enemy to bring his tally to thirty-two kills. He was awarded the Distinguished Service Order shortly after, the second highest order for bravery in the United Kingdom.

The day that Brendan was shot down was like any other day. He had received a long awaited letter from John. It was not, however, what he had expected. He had written to John for news of home in the vain hope of some sort of reconciliation. He'd had time to think about all that had happened. The war had given him a different perspective. He had hoped for some sort of understanding. Most of all, though, he had wanted to know about Kate. He felt like such a fool for leaving without saying goodbye. His mind was wracked with guilt. How would she ever know how much he loved her? In desperation he had written to Elsabeth on several occasions and enclosed a special letter for Kate, but neither had replied.

John's letter left him in no doubt as to where he stood.

Dear Brendan,

This is in reply to your recent letter. I have spoken with Father several times in an attempt to bring about a resolution to our family situation. However, after a great deal of discussion and thought, I am persuaded that your version of events is misleading and untruthful and leaves me torn as to the true nature of your integrity.

In short I am convinced by Father that you are in the wrong and that I can no longer support your position. By going off to fight in a war that has nothing to do with our country, you have shirked your duties and responsibilities, and in doing so, you have turned your back on us as a nation and a family. I speak as our father's representative. Your position in this family is no longer tenable. Please refrain from contacting us in the future.

I wish it could be different, but you only have yourself to blame.

John

Brendan was devastated. John had been his lifeline. His only means of contact with home. He was sure that they had parted on good terms. John had spoken as if he understood and supported him. In the days before leaving Brendan had felt the closest to his brother that they had ever been. This was the last thing he could ever have expected.

'What the hell was I thinking?' he asked himself as he read the letter over and over. He spent the entire morning trying to telephone his home in Ireland to demand an explanation from his brother, but before the operator was able to make a connection the claxon sounded for his squadron to scramble. A small fleet of coasters was being attacked by German bombers off the coast of France and needed immediate assistance. Within minutes they were airborne and Operations gave them a heading as they charged towards the coast. Brendan's wingman had trouble keeping up with him as they raced at full speed to engage the enemy.

By the time they arrived at the battle scene one of the ships was already sinking, two more were ablaze and a third one was being badly mauled by a flight of Stuka dive bombers that were having it all their own way. The two vessels that remained untouched were returning fire valiantly, but it was only a matter of time before they succumbed to the same sort of punishment. High overhead was a squadron of Messerschmitt fighter escorts waiting to pounce on anyone who tried to intervene. The odds were heavily stacked against Brendan and his men as usual, but that just made them more determined.

'Ignore the fighters and attack the bombers!' he ordered as he dove into the pack. The bombers always took priority. The Stukas were slow and cumbersome compared to the faster and more nimble Spitfires. He was in among them in a flash and the first casualty was sent spinning into the sea. The Messerschmitts were quick to enter into the foray and the whole scene turned into a shooting frenzy. There were fighters everywhere dodging and weaving, climbing and diving in an attempt to shoot each other into the sea.

Within a matter of minutes, two more Stukas became casualties and the bombers were forced to break off their attack. They dropped down to sea level and scurried for home with their escorts following quickly behind them. Brendan's flight did not hesitate for a second. They had plenty of fuel and lots of ammunition and gave chase across the French coast after them. A running battle ensued and within a matter of minutes they were twenty miles or so inland. Three more Stukas were shot down and a Messerschmitt exploded when caught in the united crossfire of Brendan and his wingman. The Germans managed to score a few hits before breaking off the engagement, but miraculously, none of Brendan's men were hurt. It was a great victory which no doubt would have to be celebrated back at the base, but Brendan decided that he would not be there to share the glory. In the heat of battle he had spent his fury. As he turned for home he knew what to do. When he landed at the base he would put in for immediate leave. If he was refused he would contact Victor and find some way to have himself grounded. He would go home to Ireland and sort out his brother and his family once and for all and bring Kate back to England, if she would have him. Victor was right. He had been a bloody fool and treated her badly. She had deserved better. If she decided not to see him then he would take it like a man. She had her life to live. It was not his to use as a pawn in the battle against his father. The thought of seeing Kate again cheered him immensely. Whatever the outcome the decision seemed to calm him, and for the first time in a long time he felt like he was back in control until his thoughts were interrupted by the voice of his wingman.

'Blue leader, this is Blue One. I can see a trail of white smoke coming from the back of your plane. What is your status?' Brendan's wingman inquired. Brendan looked at his instrument panel for the first time since the dogfight and, to his horror, found that his engine was in the red and overheating. The wingman knew by the way that Brendan said 'Christ' that his situation was critical. He drew up alongside him for a closer look. The side of Brendan's fuselage was peppered with holes that had just missed the fuel tank, but had scored a direct hit on his radiator.

'How much time have you got?' he asked again, with a hint of hope in his voice, but it quickly faded when a belch of smoke came from the underside of the fuselage and Brendan's prop stopped turning.

'I'm buggered!' he said. Brendan adjusted his controls to glide. At ten-thousand feet he could just make out the cliffs of Dover on the horizon but there was no way he was ever going to be able to make it back to England. The French coast loomed below him several miles away. He was going through his options when a cry of warning suddenly screamed out over the radio.

'Break, break, break!' shouted one of his pilots and with it, all hell broke loose. They had been bounced from above by a squadron of attacking Focke Wulf fighters, intent on balancing the score from the recent engagement. Without any power Brendan was a sitting duck. He rolled his Spitfire into a vertical dive in an attempt to put as much distance as he could between himself and his attackers. Tracer bullets flashed past him on every side followed by his wingman who shot by him with two of the German fighters in deadly pursuit. Instinctively Brendan pressed hard on the firing button on his joystick, but with no ammo left from the previous scrap, there was nothing that he could do to help him.

His own luck finally ran out when he felt several hard punches into his starboard wing. In his rear-view mirror he could see that another fighter had made his range with cannon fire. There was a sudden explosion which tore off the outer part of the wing, and then a second which almost knocked the wind out of him as it exploded directly behind his seat, against the armour plating. In spite of the destruction to his aircraft, his attacker held on, intent on seeing him into the ground. Brendan knew that he would have to bail out, but to do so there and then would have put him in the line of fire or even worse, being pulverised by the propeller of his attacker. He knew from experience that the German could only follow him as far as fifteen-hundred feet before having to pull out of the deadly dive to save himself. The few seconds remaining before his Spitfire was obliterated by the earth would be his only opportunity if he was to have any chance of getting out. None of the enemy pilots that he had chased to the ground had ever parachuted to safety from their aircraft in time. It took every ounce of Brendan's concentration to prevent him from panicking. He undid his safety harness and cleared his lines as he watched his altimeter spin backwards, eating up the distance to the ground at an almost unreadable speed.

'Too fast, too fast!' a voice screamed in his head. The German was still there, blasting away at him, determined to hang on until the very last second. Brendan suddenly thought to lower his undercarriage and in doing so bought the extra seconds of height that he desperately needed. The drag slowed his aircraft down sufficiently to make his aggressor overshoot and Brendan bailed out into a bullet-free sky. His parachute jerked open with a bang and he had just seconds to remember the drill for landing when he came down in a heavy roll into a field not far from where his Spitfire had disintegrated.

His tunic and flight jacket were soaked through with perspiration, but he was not injured. Anxious to put some distance between the crash site and himself he took off in a steady jog in the opposite direction. The further away he could get before it got dark the better chance he had of not being captured by the Germans. It all depended on who had seen the plane come down. After an hour of crossing fields, skirting hedges and ditches, he felt it was safe enough to go to ground. He was suddenly exhausted. From the time he had bailed out he had been berating himself for being careless in battle. He knew that it was his fault. It had been a reaction to John's letter – a wilful act of self-destruction that had caused his plane to be shot up. Victor had warned him about losing his head, but John had truly outwitted him and Brendan's fate had been sealed before he knew it.

Now he was stuck in a ditch in France, further away from Kate than ever before, with little hope of seeing her again. He had been crazy all along to think that John was on his side. The only thing that had kept him going was the hope of returning to Ireland. He began to realise that John had taken advantage of the fallout between he and his father and had manipulated the situation to his own favour. He finally understood that it was not the Germans, but his brother who was his worst enemy.

Overcome by the release from battle he fell into a deep sleep and into a terrible nightmare: he was back in his plane. His guns were jammed. There was a German fighter ace on his tail. He tried to out fly him, but no matter what he did, the ace got the better of him. He could not shake him. There was gunfire and tracer, smoke and danger. His aircraft started to disintegrate, burning around him. Everything slowed down. He had lots of time to escape and parachute to safety, but the canopy on his cockpit was jammed shut. His terror was real, his life suddenly finite, but as his stricken aircraft plummeted towards the ground with him trapped inside, the only sounds he could hear were those of laughter. When he looked behind him at the attacking aircraft he recognised John as his adversary. His face was twisted in a mocking rage, his laughter drowning out the sound of his machine guns as he chased Brendan all of the way into the ground. It was only on impact that he woke up, covered in sweat.

Having killed thirty-two men in battle, it was hard for him to feel that he had any right to ask God for help. But there he lay on his back in a ditch in France with his eyes to the heavens, praying with all of his might for divine intervention. As the decider of death he lay powerless to act. His rapier had been struck from him in a moment of madness and the chariot that carried him through the heavens destroyed. He had come to realise that he had been fighting the wrong war and, in doing so, had left the one he loved the most in peril. He had been a fool, playing the fool's game thinking that somehow he would be victorious. But there are no winners in a fool's game and no end to a war that had already cost millions of souls.

Brendan realised he had abandoned Kate when she had needed him the most. Given reign over her life to the devil. He felt a sick certainty that Kate was in danger from John and that somehow he had to get home to her as quickly as possible. In his hour of need he confessed to God the terrible thing that he had done and asked Him to somehow watch over and protect Kate until he could return to beg for her forgiveness.

Chapter thirty five

Hauptmann Rolf Kudelka of the advanced light-armoured division silently cursed the war as he took a break from the men in his half-track unit to smoke a cigarette. A professional soldier and a veteran of the Spanish Civil War, he had led the Blitzkreig into France and earned an Iron Cross for his 'duty' to the Fatherland. At twenty-four years he already felt like an old man. The early days had been exciting. He had been a First Class officer, dedicated to the cause, but the recent turn of events had started him thinking. His fellow officer and friend Willy Webber in D company had been assigned to a special unit for rounding up undesirables that took the form of mostly gypsies and Jews. The stories he had been hearing from Willy had nothing to do with bravery.

'What to do?' Willy shrugged. 'I must follow my orders.'

'Keep quiet about it and don't let anybody else know what you are thinking,' Rolf warned. 'When the time is right put in for a transfer,' he advised. Three days later Willy went missing. Since then Rolf was no longer convinced by the reasons that his great leader had used to wage war on the rest of the world.

'Hauptmann, Hauptmann!' one of his men shouted as he ran towards him. 'A parachute!' he pointed. In the distance Rolf caught a glimpse of a white plume of silk with a tiny figure suspended beneath it sinking to the ground.

'Round up the men,' he ordered without enthusiasm. He stubbed his cigarette out slowly and made his way back to the half-track where his men were already waiting. It was inevitable, when Brendan bailed out of his stricken fighter, that someone would see him. Kudelka's unit was a roving patrol that spent a week at a time touring the countryside and the coast line, looking for signs of resistance. His job would have been easier if Brendan had bailed out from a greater height. In the half-track they could have raced in time to meet him as he landed. As it was, they only had a rough idea where he had come down. With a bit of luck they still had a chance of finding him. It was bad luck for Brendan that by sheer coincidence, Kudelka stopped on the road on the far side of the ditch two-hundred metres down from where he lay. He instructed his men to search the field and the surrounding area while he stood on the bonnet of the half-track and scanned the scene with his binoculars.

Brendan was surprised that they had come across him so easily. It had been the noise of the approaching half-track that had brought him to his senses. The presence of the German soldiers made his need to see Kate that much more urgent. From the roadside he was hidden, but from the field he could be seen. It was only a matter of minutes before he would be discovered by one of the soldiers searching along the ditch in his direction. Spurred on by the thought of being captured, Brendan took off on the opposite track. The ditch was clear for several hundred metres and he made some ground before his escape route ended abruptly at the corner of the field. From the opposite side another soldier was working towards him in a pincer movement.

With no other option he scaled the ditch out onto the road and
followed by his bad luck, he was spotted by Kudelka's binoculars.

'Achtung!' he shouted to alert his men and pointed to Brendan as he disappeared into the ditch on the far side of the road. He jumped from the bonnet into the front seat of the half-track. 'Quickly,' he ordered the driver. He pulled a Luger pistol out of his holster and took off the safety catch. The engine of the half-track roared as it sped down the road. The soldiers and the vehicle converged at the opening in the hedge where Brendan had disappeared, but he had made it to the opposite side of the field before Kudelka caught sight of him again.

'Damn!' he said as he watched Brendan vanish behind a thick set of bushes. The half-track was useless. Because of the ditch there was no way they could get it into the field to use it's superior speed to catch the fugitive. They would have to go after him on foot.

'Find a gate and follow us,' he ordered the driver, as he jumped down to give chase. 'The rest of you spread out fifty metres apart.' They formed a line across and took off after Brendan like hounds in pursuit of the fox. Brendan knew from his hunting days that pace was very important. If he set it right he would wear out most of his pursuers and that would even up the odds against him. The training manuals said that he should go to ground if he got the opportunity, but he knew that was often when the fox got shot.

'Keep up!' Rolf commanded. Some of his men were falling behind because of their weapons and the heavy ammunition kits they had to carry. Before long he was down to just three men. When it was obvious that Brendan was getting away, Kudelka called his men to halt.

'Take off your equipment, your jackets and helmets,' he commanded, as he threw his own jacket on the ground. 'Knives only,' he said. 'Schmelling,' he called to a rather portly soldier who had fallen behind and was no use at all. 'Gather all of this stuff and put it in the half-track and follow us. Watch out in case he doubles back,' he said, as he set off with the rest of his men after Brendan. The going was lighter and they caught their second wind and with it they began to match Brendan's pace. When they crossed the next field the scenery started to change. The flat grass gave way as the paddocks suddenly ended in hillocks and tussocks of wild grass that ran all the way out to the coast. The air was salty. Brendan tried hard to keep out of sight, but he knew that they could see him every time he had to cross a hillock. His heart was bursting and his legs were burning – even more when the terrain underfoot changed to sand.

As he crested the last dune he was sure he could see the white cliffs of Dover, but his heart sank when the half-track came into sight. The driver had found his way through the dunes and overtaken him somehow. He crouched down out of view to see which way it would turn and, to his great relief, it headed off in the opposite direction, giving him an opportunity to make it to the water. Having to stop though had cost him valuable seconds. By the time he reached the sea, two of Kudelka's men were almost upon him with their knives, while Rolf brought up the rear with his Luger.

'Take him alive,' Rolf said. The two soldiers pounced on Brendan and all three crashed into the water. A desperate struggle ensued. Brendan flailed and punched and kicked and screamed and, despite their knives, almost had the better of the two men before Rolf put the Luger to his head.

'Stop Englander or I will shoot,' he commanded. Brendan had no other choice but to obey.

'I am not English, I am Irish,' he retorted, as they dragged him out of the sea. In spite of the gun, it took all of their strength to subdue him.

'You are captured, Irishman. Surrender and make it easy on yourself!'

'I have to get back to Kate,' Brendan shouted and struggled as if they should somehow understand his pleading.

'What were you going to do, Irishman? Swim across the Channel?' Rolf said, mockingly. 'The Irish, they are crazy,' he turned to his two men. 'One minute they are busy trying to kill the British. Then the next it is "God Save the King"!'

'Fuck the King! All I want to do is get back to Kate,' Brendan said. He was almost delirious from the physical exertion and the thought of being captured.

'Get some rope and tie his hands behind his back,' Rolf commanded as the half-track pulled up beside them. 'And be careful of him,' he said to the other men. 'He is a madman.' He searched his pockets for a cigarette to calm himself and offered one each to the two soldiers who had caught Brendan. Never before had they run so hard. Not even in basic training. As they smoked they acknowledged a grudging respect for Brendan's stamina and determination.

'Set up camp in the dunes,' Rolf commanded. It would be dark in less than an hour. 'We will take him in for questioning in the morning.' The capture of the airman was more a reflection of reaction and training than a desire to do him harm. In his dilemma about 'duty', Brendan's desperation to get back to his woman had struck the chord of discontent that was simmering in Rolf's conscience. Later that evening when the camp was settled and the sentry posted, Rolf went over and crouched down beside his prisoner who sat tied to the back of the half-track.

'My name is Rolf,' he introduced himself.

'Brendan,' he replied with a certain resignation in his voice. He had stopped resisting his captors after they'd had the decency to feed and give him water. Rolf offered him a cigarette as a gesture of friendliness.

'I don't smoke,' Brendan waved it away. He avoided eye contact as Rolf sat down beside him. He preferred instead to stare straight ahead.

'That is probably why we had such a hard time catching you,' Rolf said with a slight hint at humour. 'Never before have I run so hard.' Brendan said nothing.

'Who is Kate?' Rolf asked. Brendan was surprised that the German remembered her name. 'On the beach today, you said that you had to get back to Kate. I was wondering if you would tell me who she is?' Rolf enquired sympathetically.

'She is the only thing that matters,' Brendan replied, his voice desolate. He sighed deeply at the thought of his own stupidity.

'Would you really have swum the Channel to be with her?'

'Whatever it takes,' replied Brendan.

'I understand,' Rolf said quietly.

'Do you really?' Brendan said looking him straight in the eye for the first time. Rolf did not reply, but walked away instead and left him with his thoughts. Later that night the sentry came over to wake Rolf, but he was already sitting up drinking from a cup of cold coffee.

'The prisoner wants to go to the toilet,' he said.

'I will take care of it,' Rolf replied.

'Do you want me to help?' the man inquired.

'No, it won't be necessary. Make a fire instead so that I can have some warm coffee when I come back.' Rolf walked over to the prisoner. He ignored him and stretched into a box in the back of the vehicle and pulled out a small container. He untied Brendan from the back of the truck and, with his hands still bound behind his back, led him over the dunes and down to the beach. They walked in silence until they reached the water. Rolf took the can and stood in front of Brendan.

'Hold this,' he instructed and placed the can under Brendan's chin. He had to compress it against his chest to stop it falling. Up close he could smell the odour of grease.

'Now listen carefully,' Rolf said. 'I am going to untie you. If you make any attempt to challenge me I will shoot you,' he showed Brendan his Luger. He scanned the beach back towards the camp to make sure the sentry had not followed them as he released the prisoners bonds.

'I had a girlfriend in Berlin,' he said. 'Her name was Helga. She died from T. B. last year. I did not get to say goodbye.'

'I'm sorry for your loss,' said Brendan, with genuine sympathy.

'When you say that Kate is all that matters I understand what you mean. I used to be a long-distance swimmer before the war,' Rolf explained as he undid the lid of the can of grease. 'Strip off your clothes down to your underwear and spread the grease all over your body,' he instructed as the ropes fell from Brendan's hands. 'Especially under your arms and between your legs.' Brendan did as he was told, hardly able to believe what was happening. 'England is that way,' Rolf pointed. 'If you can swim as well as you run, then you may even make it!' he said. Slim as it was, he was offering Brendan a genuine shot at freedom. He had been crazy enough earlier in the day to take his chances without the slightest hesitation. The danger was more real now that he had time to think about it, but it was his only hope of getting home. He looked beyond the horizon where the south-east coast of England lay, and without saying anything, made his way into the water. He was waist-deep and almost out of view when Rolf was surprised to see him turn around and head back towards him. For a moment he thought that Brendan might have finally come to his senses.

'Thank you,' Brendan said simply, extending his hand.

'Good luck,' Rolf said and shook it firmly. Brendan headed back into the water and Rolf watched as this time he was swallowed up by the night.

Chapter thirty six

John showed up uninvited late one evening not long after Grace was born. He had never done that before. He had taken a drink, not a lot, but enough that it was noticeable.

'Have you had your tea, Kate?' he asked, when she opened the door. He had a large basket in his hand, full of treats. He beamed at her as he invited himself in. They made tea together and it was very satisfying. He had a couple of bottles of porter which he finished as they chatted by the fire afterwards. The lovely food he had brought was a pleasant surprise and he could not have been nicer.

Kate accepted out of duty to her benefactor, but the rules of the game had changed. She cooked for him and she talked to him and listened to all he had to say. But she kept her distance and offered no encouragement. The chill that had crossed her the day he gave her the flowers had never left her. Kate knew that a storm was brewing. It was only a matter of time before it struck. They could not go on playing this charade forever. He left that night at a reasonable hour, and never faltered as the perfect gentleman. 'I'll see you again,' he said and thanked her for the lovely meal. It was as if it had been her idea all along. Kate felt lonelier and more vulnerable than ever. She wanted to tell Elsabeth about her suspicions but she knew Elsabeth would never see through her brother. He had been too nice by far – too generous for her to think that he might have an ulterior motive. Kate's waiting for Brendan had grown more desperate. Her hours of loneliness made her certain that if he did not return soon all might be lost.

John returned again and again, staying a little longer each time; the porter was followed by a bottle of Poteen, a traditional alcoholic spirit made from an illicit still that he claimed as a business interest. He tried to get her to join in, have a good time. But she wouldn't be part of any drinking session. He was the big man now, with big plans and big ideas about himself and the future. Nothing was going to stop him. The more she resisted him the more desperate he became until finally one night he could contain himself no longer and dragged her to the bedroom.

'I've been nice about it,' he told her. 'You haven't responded. I've done all I could to make you want me! So now I'm taking what's due, what should have been mine all along!'

Kate screamed, and Grace screamed. She hit him and flailed at him and she tried her hardest to prevent him from doing what he wanted to do. But he was too strong, too enraged by the alcohol and desperation and waiting for what he felt was his. He flung her on the bed, pinning her down with one arm, and began to tear at her clothes with the other. Her fear and terror turned to anger and then hatred. With no other way to reason with him she reached out for the carving knife she kept under her pillow for her own security. She struck out and tried to gut him. In her anger, her aim was poor, and she only slashed him in the arm. Not badly, but enough to bring him to his senses, so that he sprang back off her just in time to prevent her from stabbing him. He knew by the rage in her eyes and the curse on her tongue and the blood that flowed freely from the knife that had wounded him that he would die before she gave him satisfaction.

'Damn you!' he shouted as he retreated from the small bedroom, careful not to give her another opportunity to have a go at him. 'Damn you both to the fires of hell!' he raged as he stumbled from the cottage, drunk and shaking from his defeat. Kate slammed and locked the door behind him. Grace's cot had been knocked in the tussle and she was screaming. Kate went to pick her up and comfort her. She held her daughter and tried to soothe her. Then with all of the courage she could muster she went out to the back of the house and bolted the door as well. When she was sure John was gone she collapsed on the old sofa in front of the fire. Grace's screams slowly subsided. It was late and she was exhausted. She wanted to sleep to relieve the pain and the suffering that John had inflicted on her, but she knew that she must get out in case he returned. She comforted Grace until she fell asleep and then placed her on a sheepskin on the sofa. She went to the bedroom and started packing a bag with some clothes and belongings – whatever she could carry. It was a long way to the safety of Tralee.

She cursed herself for allowing herself to become so vulnerable. She cursed Elsabeth for being her best friend. She cried from the pain where John had hurt her and the thought of losing her little home. Grace cried out, but Kate was too set on packing the bag to pay attention. She would be finished in a moment, then could hold her. Grace cried out again, and this time in a high wail so that Kate could no longer ignore her. She put down the bag and went out to comfort her baby. She was hardly out of the room when the window behind her exploded and a shower of flame enveloped the small bedroom. Kate was horrified. For a moment she was torn between the bag with their belongings and money and Grace's screams from the other side of the room. Instinct took over. Getting to safety was more important than retrieving the bag which was already on fire. She gathered up Grace in her sheepskin and a blanket and headed for the back door. She was just in time to avoid the crash of another bomb as it came exploding through the front window and set the sofa on fire. Kate ran, possessed by a terror, the likes of which she had never experienced before. A hand reached out from the night and grabbed at her by the arm that held Grace. She could make out neither face nor body. But her anger found his eyes and with her rage she clawed and tore at them so that she drew more blood. She ran with John's screams cursing her as she disappeared into the night, pursued only by the light of the flames that now engulfed the little cottage and the crackle that sounded its imminent destruction. She ran until she could run no more; until she was sure that she had escaped him. Safe at last she turned at the top of the hill to face desolation and ruin as the thatch roof gave way to the fire and with it any hope she might have had for the future.

Kate sat down and cried, clutching Grace for a very long time until her terror died down. They were safe for the time being. John had made no attempt to chase them. In the distance she could see his car weaving its way slowly back along the peninsula towards the town. There was nothing she could do until daybreak. The road to safety lay beyond the cottage, but she could not risk it. He might be waiting for her. She decided to stay put and wait it out. Grace fell asleep. Kate settled down in a large clump of heather for comfort and covered them both with the blanket to keep out the cold. In the morning she would search the ruins of the house and see if there was anything worth salvaging. Then she would make her way to Tralee somehow when it was safe to travel.

Kate awoke at daybreak to the sound of the birds and a cloudy black sky that threatened rain. She was tired and aching from sleeping on the ground. The first thing she did was take herself and Grace further up the mountain to greater safety. She was sure that John would return to survey the damage. She could not risk being seen, and Grace might cry out at the wrong time. She wanted a good head start if he decided to come after her. She found a spot about a mile away, and they were not long settled when a car pulled up at the cottage. It was John, and he was by himself. He walked around the back, surveying the damage, then made his way inside the walls of the cottage that were left standing, kicking through the debris and destruction. Again he came out the back of the ruins, but this time he looked up in the direction of her escape, as if he was in two minds to come after her. Kate was relieved when he finally went back to the car. To her horror though, he returned a couple of minutes later with two of his best hunting dogs. She had felt safe, sure that she could outwait any searching John might do. It never occurred to her though that he might hunt her like an animal.

Kate felt sick at the thought of the dogs catching up with her and what they might do to her and Grace before their master would be able to subdue them. She had heard terrible stories about what happened when they caught up with the fox. She did not know if she could outwit them. It would not take long for them to pick up on the scent that her fear had left behind the previous night. It would not take long to close the distance between them. She began to move, but every step felt like lead, as if she was being held back by invisible chains. The barking in the distance grew more frantic and excited. The dogs were keen for the chase. The lead she had would quickly diminish if she did not find some way to throw them off her trail. Grace was awake, but not making a sound, almost as if she knew the consequences it would bring.

Kate's ear honed in on the sound of running water and spurred her into overcoming her fear. A stream lay ahead and she remembered clearly. It was the one that ran down by the cottage. In happier days she had walked to its source high in the mountains with Brendan. Now it offered her only hope of escape. If she could get to it in time and cross it she could lose her trail. The dogs were closing quickly.

'God help me,' she prayed, as she struggled across a ridge. As if in answer, the stream gurgled in front of her. The dogs by now were almost upon her. With what little time she had left she found the shallowest place to cross, but still sank up to her waist when she entered the water. It was absolutely freezing and she had to hold Grace above her head for fear of her squealing if she got soaked. It was hard to find her footing and she stumbled a few times, unable to see the bottom in the brackish water. With a sigh of relief she made it downstream a hundred yards or so to the other side and just managed to get out of view before the water halted the dogs. They barked and yelped and sniffed around to pick up the lost scent while waiting for their master who had fallen well behind. From the distance he knew by their sound that they had lost the trail, and cursed himself for not bringing a horse. Kate had managed to outfox him.

She worked her way quickly over familiar ground making sure to keep herself low and out of view. She doubled back and headed for the cottage, hoping that it would be the last place he would think to look for her. John was out of breath and frustrated when he reached the dogs. He crossed them over hoping to pick up her trail on the far side, but his efforts were a waste of time. It had started to rain, big heavy drops that would dampen the most determined of spirits. Finally he gave up, gathered the dogs and headed back for the car. He was soaked by the time he reached it, cold and tired and hungry. The dogs barked madly at a new scent they had picked up, but John shut them up quickly and loaded them into the boot. He took one last look up the mountain and then back at the cottage before he drove away.

When she was sure he was gone, Kate stepped out of the shadows. Some corrugated iron had fallen from the roof against the inside wall of the cottage, and it was behind this that she had managed to conceal herself and Grace. The dogs had almost given the game away. She was thankful for the rain that had driven away her pursuers. Despite her searching there was nothing left in the cottage worth taking. Her bag and her money had been completely destroyed along with everything else. She realised that there was not much time left in the day. If they were to have somewhere safe to stay she was going to have to try to make it to Tralee. God only knew what lay ahead of her. The rain stopped and she sat down on the remains of a garden chair and gave her full attention to Grace, who had not been fed all morning. She was hungry herself and cold and weary, but her own comfort would have to wait until later. When Grace was satisfied she wrapped her in the driest part of the blanket and they set off on the road. It was there, in answer to Brendan's prayers, that Father Michael came upon her.

Chapter thirty seven

It was time for Michael to say Mass. He had prepared a midweek sermon, but apart from his altar boy there were only seven people in attendance. Michael thought that it was hardly worth the effort and decided on the spur of the moment to take a different approach.

'Gather around,' he instructed. He stepped down from the altar and waved his arm at the three parishioners who were sitting separately at a safe distance halfway down the church.

'Please come and join the rest of us up the front,' he said. They looked at each other inquisitively, but did as they were directed. 'No, no, here,' he said gently, and pointed to the front pew when they tried to sit two rows back. 'I want everybody to sit up here.' He smiled to alleviate their discomfort. He took off his robes and gave them to the altar boy along with other instructions and then he found a chair and sat down in front of the small gathering.

'I'm Michael Murphy,' he said and leaning forward he introduced himself to each individual by shaking their hand. It was all very strange. Everyone called him Father. Nothing like this had ever happened to them before. 'I was thinking to myself that we could have a chat instead of Mass, if it's all the same to you. Just so that we can begin to get to know each other.' He started off by asking each person to introduce themselves and say where they were from. They were slow to warm to the idea. At one stage he thought that it might have been better to have just laboured through Mass, but then he finally came up with an idea.

'I have a confession to make,' he stated. All ears perked up because it was usually the other way around. He knew that he had caught their attention. 'I believe I'm supposed to officiate over a hurling game in the next few weeks,' he confided. 'And to be honest with you, I don't know the rules.'

'Are you serious?' James Darcy, one of two men in the congregation, asked with incredulity. For a Catholic priest this was unthinkable, but it was enough to kick-start the conversation. Hurling was neutral territory in which they were all well versed, and it was not long before they were trying to outdo each other with their well-meaning advice. Michael just sat back and listened. Things were going well until Kate walked in with the altar boy. They were carrying two trays with tea and some cake. Her presence brought the conversation to an abrupt silence. All eyes followed her as she put the trays down and started to pour the tea. She tried not to take any notice of those who looked on, but you could tell by the way that they stared that she was making them feel uncomfortable.

'What's wrong?' Michael asked. The group remained silent. The affect that Kate's presence was having on them was obvious. No one would answer though, at least not while she was present. They were more used to talking behind her back.

'Well, what is it?' Michael asked again a little more assertively when Kate left the church. It did not take long for someone to speak up after she had gone.

'It's not right!' said Mary, the old woman who lived in the terrace house with the half-door on the main street. The one who had watched Michael chase after Kate when he first arrived in town. 'Having her in the house with that child is not right,' she stated. 'The Bishop would never agree to it!' The rest of the group nodded in agreement.

'What about this?' Michael asked, pointing at the trays that Kate had brought.

'What would the Bishop say about me inviting you into God's house for tea and cake that Kate had made,' he asked making sure to refer to her by name. 'Is there anything wrong with that?'

'No,' was the collective answer.

'What if she was my sister?' he asked James Darcy, a stooped octogenarian with a walking stick, who not five minutes before had been all animated by chat about hurling. 'What if she was my sister and had come to stay with her baby and help me out for a while. Would that be all right?'

'Well of course Father – she would be your sister, wouldn't she?' James said. 'That would be a different matter!'

'Well, let me ask you a simple question then,' he said turning back to Mary. 'Doesn't the bible say we are all God's children?'

'It does,' she said glad to be able to agree with him. She, like the rest of the group, had never actually read the bible, but she had heard the statement used enough times before to know that it must be in there somewhere.

'Right then,' he said, 'if we are all God's children doesn't that make her my sister?' he asked, 'and yours as well, all of you here.' He nodded at the small gathering. There was little they could say to deny his reasoning. 'And that makes me your brother, doesn't it, Mary!' he said, and he could see that although she was slightly guarded, she was left with no choice but to agree with him.

'I suppose it does,' she said.

'So would you put me out of your house if I was sick and

had no place to go?' he asked.

'No.'

'Well, there you go,' he smiled, 'it's all right then, isn't it?' He shrugged his shoulders, lifting his hands in question. 'There is nothing to worry about, is there?'

'No, Father, I suppose there isn't,' she said not sure of his logic. He was being nice to her and on the surface she did not want to be disagreeable. Deep down she had actually felt the beginnings of liking the young priest before Kate had walked in, and she was anxious to preserve the good feeling he intended.

'Thanks, Mary,' he said and took her by the hand and squeezed it with affection. It was something that she was not used to.

'What for, Father?' she asked, still not quite in tune with his thinking.

'For being my sister, of course,' he told her. Everyone laughed, clearing the air between them and it left the mood that much lighter. Michael wished that the church had been full to witness the effect that this one simple act of kindness had upon them, when the unexpected sound of stomping hooves and the mooing of cows outside distracted him. There was whistling to be heard, and a dog barking madly, the echoes of which filled the church. The commotion outside the church suddenly put an end to their conversation.

'We might as well find out,' he said to the group, whom he could see were looking just as curious. There was a quick shuffle as Michael lead them to the side entrance closest to where all the noise was coming from. He was almost out the door when Kate came running in. Behind her was a man by the name of Paide O'Shea.

'Father, you have to help me,' he pleaded, without giving Kate a chance to explain what was happening. He had a look of desperation about him. 'They are going to kill my herd, Father,' he stated. A stranger came in and stood beside them.

'Come on, Paide, take it easy now. This is none of the priest's business,' he said. He placed his hand on the farmer's shoulder to try to lead him back out of the church. 'I'm only doing my job,' he insisted. 'If you had called me before buying them this would never have happened!' His words were of little consolation to the farmer as he brushed the vet's hand off his shoulder.

'What's going on here?' Michael asked with concern. The entire churchyard was full of cows.

'They have got T.B.' the vet declared. 'I'm sorry, I really am, but I'm under Department orders to destroy them.'

'Yes,' the farmer shot back bitterly, 'and me along with them. It's everything I have ever worked for.' His eyes were full of anguish. Coming to the church was his last resort.

'They have to go, Father,' the vet said flatly. 'There is nothing that you or I or anyone else can do about it,' he said. 'I'm bound by the State to do my job.' Michael asked Kate to take care of the gathering while he talked to the vet out of earshot. He suggested they take a walk across the yard.

'What about one more day?' he suggested, not too sure what he could do. He knew the first thing he needed was to buy some time. 'If I was to keep them here on the church grounds until tomorrow afternoon, let's say. That wouldn't do any harm would it?' He was using all the sincerity and trust that his position afforded him. 'A stay of execution for all concerned. Even if it means only reasoning with Paide and trying to help him with his loss. And it might make it easier for you to do your job.' Without the vet realising it, Michael had steered him to his car. His soft words and kind reasoning had left little desire to chase after Paide again. 'I give you my word,' Michael promised before the vet had to ask him. It was enough to get him into his car.

'As long as you keep them in the church grounds it will be all right,' he instructed. 'Give me a call when you're ready,' he was grateful to be off the hook for a while at least. He shook Father Murphy's hand and drove away. Back at the church a different scene was unfolding. Out of concern for Paide and the state that he was in, Kate had suggested that everybody should leave. To her surprise old Mary was the first to agree with her and she quickly took charge. She thanked Kate on behalf of the group for the tea and lovely cake that she had served them, and the small gathering was ushered out of the front door of the church and away to their homes before they knew it. She returned then and fussed over Paide in the way that only an old woman can do. It was not long before she had him calmed down and taking the last of the tea and cake.

'The priest is a good man!' she said convincingly. 'I'm sure that something can be done.'

'I hope you are right,' said Paide as Michael walked back into the room.

'Come on, we will leave them to it,' Mary said. To Kate's surprise she picked up a tray. 'I'll help you to do the dishes.' The two of them walked back to the house.

Later that day Michael and Kate sat down to eat. He was not as surprised to see Mary helping Kate as she was.

'She told me that I was a good girl,' Kate said self-consciously when he pressed her to tell him. She had a beam in her eyes that was like a ray of hope rekindled.

'She offered to look after Grace any time I liked and not to be afraid to ask if there was anything we needed. What in the world did you say to her?' Kate asked as she served their lunch. She had baked him a meat pie as a special treat.

'I told her the truth,' he answered simply. 'That usually does the trick. As long as those who are listening want to hear it,' he added. 'There is goodness in most people, Kate, if you treat them right. However, Paide and his cows are a different story!'

The old man had been a subsistence farmer all of his life; hard-working and honest, with a block of land that ran along part of the eastern boundaries of the manor. He'd always subsidised his living with lobster pots and fishing, but now that he was getting older he wanted to stay more on the land. The Lordy, now John, had offered to sell him some cattle at a very cheap price. He also offered to lend him the money to help him get started. It had sounded like a good deal at the time. They had always been good neighbours, he and John's father. There was no reason not to trust his son, the lawyer. The deeds of his property were to be used as collateral. He told Michael that John had reassured him it was just a matter of course, and convinced him that there was nothing to worry about. In two short years he would own the cattle and get the deeds back after paying off the loan.

'Why didn't he have the vet check them out before he took them?' Kate asked, remembering how the vet had made a point of it earlier that day.

'John convinced him it wasn't necessary,' Michael explained. 'He told Paide that they were healthy, that they had just been tested and passed. He said that he would only be wasting his money. Apparently he can be very persuasive!' Michael watched Kate to see her reaction, but she only nodded vaguely in agreement.

'What do you think will happen to Paide?' Kate asked, steering away from talking about John. She did not want him to think that they had any connection.

'I don't know,' said Michael. 'I have an invitation for tea tonight at the manor and I'll see what I can do. It all depends on the type he is I suppose. Going by Paide today I'm not holding much hope for it!'

When Michael arrived at the manor later that night he was greeted by Elsabeth who was full of concern for her friend. He reassured her that Kate and Grace were doing well and not to worry.

'She said to say hello,' he passed on as they made their way to the drawing-room and chatted easily by themselves for a while.

'John is busy in his office,' Elsabeth informed the priest. 'He shouldn't be long.' When he finally made an entrance John was all huff and puff about how sorry he was for being late. Something important had come up at the last minute, which had demanded his immediate attention. He hadn't expected it to detain him so long. He admonished Elsabeth who had been too busy talking about Kate to think of offering Michael a welcome drink and after a few minutes dispatched her to the kitchen to to get some ice and see how the cook was getting on with the tea.

'Now, how is it all going?' he inquired when he finally sat down with a large whiskey in hand. Michael never got a chance to answer. 'It's hard settling in when you are new to the job.' John's voice was full of sympathy. 'Sure I'm still trying to get the hang of this place myself,' he paused only long enough for a good swig of his drink, 'and it's almost a year since the brother took off.' He went on talking about the great responsibilities he had, holding the fort and running his legal practice while his father ran the country. 'Sure, it's all about looking after people, isn't it?' he said. 'Now, is there anything I can do for you?'

Michael was surprised. He had not been able to get a word in edgeways, and now suddenly, his host presented him with the opening he had been hoping for.

'Well, there is something I'd like the opportunity to discuss with you,' he said broaching the subject carefully. 'It's about a man named Paide O'Shea, a neighbour of yours. He's in a great deal of trouble.'

'I'm all ears.' John feigned concern, but there was a hesitation in his voice. The mention of his neighbour put a slight edge on his good humour. Michael went on to explain the drama that had unfolded in the churchyard that morning, and how he was trying to help Paide as best he could.

'Did he send you to see me?' John asked, suspicious. Michael sensed that he was not too happy about him knowing the details of their arrangement. 'Look, it was supposed to be kept quiet,' John went on. 'I was just doing him a special deal, which I didn't want getting out. We loan a lot of money through our finance company, but this was at a very special rate, because Paide is our neighbour. There would be trouble if the rest of our customers found out about it.'

'Is there anything can be done to help him out now?' Michael asked directly. He was never one for beating about the bush.

'Not really,' John lied. 'I gave him enough warning in the first place. Any time we loan money we always give as much advice as we can to protect our interests and that of our client,' John sighed. 'Paide did not listen when I warned him about stress farming. Sure that's the reason the animals got sick in the first place,' he waved a dismissive hand. 'You can't treat cattle like that and expect them *not* to get sick. If you ask me, he defied the laws of nature by being greedy.' He took another sip of his drink and shrugged. 'Look, with all due respect, Paide had it coming to him. If I give in to him I'll end up having to listen to a lot of sad stories from the rest of our customers. They'd start using it against me.' With one long last swig of his drink he put an end to the subject.

'Come on, I've got something to show you.' He stood up. 'We will have just enough time before we eat.' Michael followed him out of the drawing-room. John pointed out portraits and paintings and rambled on about his family's history as they walked. A long hallway led towards an ornate stairway. At the top a very large window overlooked the rear of the estate. John brought him up the short flight to have a look from the landing. It had been especially designed by the original architect for the purposes of watching the setting sun. The view out across the land was magnificent. There were fields of wheat in almost every direction and Michael could tell by the way John pointed them out that they were important to him.

'The biggest yet,' he said. 'It will be three times the size of any harvest that we have ever grown before in the history of the estate. If all goes well I reckon it will take three days to bring it in. That's why I wanted to show it to you. We'll have to start getting organised now and give the community plenty of warning. They will need to be ready when the word goes out.'

Michael was confused. He had no idea of what John was on about, but he guessed that the church must in some way be involved.

'It's a tradition in the area that everybody helps with the harvest,' John explained noting the priest's expression. 'It was born of necessity, as a means of survival in the years of the Great Famine. Saved hundreds of families from starvation!' he claimed.

'There had never been a bank in the area so everybody at one stage or another has borrowed money from the manor ever since to keep them going. Part of the interest to be paid is an obligation to help out with the harvest as long as you are in debt. Those that have no debt make sure to help out so that they can get a loan in the future.

'So what has the church got to do with it?' Father Michael inquired.

'Because the church is a meeting place – the priest always announces when the harvest is ready,' John explained making the arrangement sound normal as they walked back down the stairs to the dining-room. 'In spite of the underlying obligation, there is a great deal of goodwill on both sides, and it does help to bind the community. It's the priest's job to give his blessing to all who gather for the work.'

Because of the great saving it made for the Lordy he always looked after the workers, providing a great spread of food and porter for their lunch. One year someone had brought a football and a game ensued after the harvest was finished. It was great fun and all of the women and children joined in. It was the highlight of the day, and had been repeated each year ever since. By late evening the women would leave with the children to go home and make the tea while the men finished what was left of the porter. With the right frame of mind the harvest could be seen as one of the social events of the year. However, what John was planning this time was altogether different.

'The world is at war and needs feeding. This year's harvest will be in big demand,' he said. 'It will take most of the week to bring in what I have sown, and that's as long as the weather holds. I'm talking about community spirit here and helping the world,' he smiled. 'The few extra days it will take to bring in the harvest will be greatly appreciated and taken into account thereafter.' He spoke as if he was the one making the announcement from the pulpit, hinting at the words that he thought Michael might want to use. 'Everybody benefits from the harvest,' he went on. He eyed Michael speculatively. All the priest had to do was get up on the pulpit like his predecessor before him and talk about 'scratching each other's backs' and the benefits of co-operation. In return he would be handsomely rewarded. Michael realised why he had been invited for tea. He would like to have believed in John's goodwill, but he still had Paide on his mind. As they sat down for their meal with Elsabeth, the priest understood that John had only one thing on his mind and feeding the world was the least of his aspirations.

Michael decided that he did not like his host. It was not often that he put a man in this category. It had been his first impression, despite the fine salmon he'd received the other day. Having been given a second chance to form an opinion he was now sure. The man spent too much time talking, which might not have been so bad if he had something worth saying, but it was always about himself. Michael doubted if he had any other interests, and was taken aback when John excused himself unexpectedly.

'Sorry, Father, but I have other important business to attend to!' he stated. 'I'll catch up with you during the week to finalise the details,' he added, as he left the room, intimating that they now had an 'understanding' about the harvest. Elsabeth apologised for her brother after he had gone.

'He is really taking himself very seriously since he took over the running of the estate after Brendan went to the war,' she explained. 'He is very clever, and he's made some wonderful changes,' she added, not knowing that they were inspired by the notebook that her older brother had given to John. It had been Brendan's plan, originally, that the extra days of free labour would be compensated for by a new machine that he planned on buying with the profits. The rest of the community could then use the machine at a nominal charge to harvest their own fields. The following year the efficiency of the machine would release all of those under obligation, thus rendering greater independence to all concerned. It was to be the beginnings of the co-op that Brendan had envisioned for the future. John had no intention of pursuing it. When Michael broached the subject about her brother, Elsabeth became downhearted and melancholy.

'There has been a family rift,' she explained quietly. 'My father has disowned him because he went to fight for the British. He's in the RAF. I have written to him secretly on several occasions, but I have never received any reply.' She never mentioned the connection between her brother and Kate. 'He was shot down over France some time ago,' she went on. 'The only news we have is that he is missing in action. It has been so long now that I'm beginning give up any hope of his safe return.' She stared out the window of the drawing room and tears ran down her cheeks.

Later that night when Michael arrived back at his house the lights were still on. He had not expected Kate to be up so late. He got an even bigger surprise when he went inside and discovered Mary in the kitchen drinking tea.

'How did you get on with the Lordy?' she inquired. 'Will he help Paide?'

'I don't think so,' he replied, noting the cynicism in her voice. He wondered what she was doing visiting so late. 'I doubt if there is anything can be done, not the way John was talking anyway. Nothing short of a miracle will save Paide now,' Michael sighed. 'I suppose I'll have to go down and tell the poor man in the morning.'

'No, you won't,' Kate replied. There was a hint of mischief in her voice. 'I've got an idea. Go up and get changed into your old clothes and when you come down I'll tell you,' she ordered him. Five minutes later Michael found her outside, herding the cows from the church yard into the field behind. She had them halfway across and into the next paddock before he caught up with her. 'Trust me!' was all the explanation she would give him.

Chapter thirty eight

Kate woke the next morning tired and stiff all over. It had been a long night, trying to keep the cows moving, especially over the more difficult terrain. At one stage she had thought that they were not going to make it.

She dragged herself out of bed and tended to Grace, who had been well behaved for Mary while her mother was out gallivanting around the mountains. Kate wondered how Michael was getting on. He had twisted his ankle badly on the way back and had to use a branch to help him to walk the last of the journey. It reminded her of Brendan and their first day out together. She felt so sorry for Michael that she almost confided in him about Grace's father. He had trusted her with her idea about the cows, and Kate wanted to return that trust. But in the end she decided it was best to keep the secret to herself. She was halfway through making the breakfast when there was a bang at the door. It was Paide.

'I'm looking for the priest.' He was very contrite and wanted to know where his cows were. The only animal that remained in the grounds of the church was the one that the vet had tested positive for T.B. Kate told him to go and look in the church. Michael was kneeling before the alter when Paide walked in behind him.

'Where are my cows?' Paide demanded.

'We have just been talking about you,' Michael replied. 'Everything is under control.' His tone was reassuring as he walked Paide out of the church, telling him of God's plan 'which was divine inspiration'. Paide should act upon it immediately. 'Don't worry about the cows,' he said. 'The cows are gone, and it's all been sorted out with the vet. Take your boat and go fishing,' he said. Paide looked at him in disbelief, as if he was out of his mind.

'It's the fishing I'm trying to get away from,' he exclaimed. 'It's too much work for too little money. How's that going to get me out of trouble with the manor?'

'Trust me, God has a plan for you,' Michael intoned gravely. He had his fingers crossed behind his back in the hope that Kate's idea would work. Paide had little faith in his reassurances, but with no other choice, he promised to do whatever God had bid him. Paide got organised and went down to the harbour and launched his boat, heading for the place that the priest had told him to go. It was just as he had expected. Hard work for little return. At the end of the day he had barely enough to cover his expenses.

'Is it a miracle you want?' Michael admonished him later that evening when he came around to complain. 'You'll go back out there tomorrow, and the day after, and the day after that,' he ordered, 'until God knows by your persistence that you are sincere. Then I think you will get your miracle!'

Paide's fishing had become the talk of the town and so had Michael's promise of divine intervention. People were starting to gather on the pier at the end of the day to see what Paide brought back after a day of back breaking work, but the little that he had caught was hardly worth mentioning.

'Tomorrow is the last time I am going out,' he said bitterly to the priest the following Thursday. 'It's becoming an embarrassment. I've been trying now for more than a week and I'm no better off than when I started.'

'I'll go with you,' Michael said, 'to see what you are doing wrong,' he laughed, comfortable in the knowledge that he could use the money from the cash stash he had found in the upstairs bedroom if the fishing did not work out in the end. He was not going to let Paide down. Paide however, did not appreciate his humour. He was a good fisherman, respected for his ability by all in the community. Following Michael's advice would only add to the loss of his land if things did not work out for him.

Clear blue skies and sunshine are always a good start to the day, and the fine weather made up for Michael's late arrival the following morning.

'Sorry, Paide, I was delayed with Mass,' he said, as he climbed on board. Attendance had quadrupled since Michael had introduced his own version of midweek Mass. Paide said little, other than to tell him where he could sit, and that if he was going to be sick he should 'throw up downwind'. Kate had made up a basket with sandwiches, cake and two thermos flasks of tea. Michael handed it to Paide's young crew man, Rory, who received it with a smile, but Paide remained unimpressed. 'To keep up our morale,' Michael shouted, over the puttering of the diesel engine. It took them an hour to make their way around the peninsula to the place that 'God had said they were to go fishing'. It was opposite a cliff face that was over three-hundred feet high.

'This is it,' Paide said, as he slowed down the engine and told Rory to prepare the nets.

'No, it's not,' said Michael. 'Wait for a minute. This is not the place that I was talking about.' An argument broke out between the two of them about who was the better fisherman.

'I know these waters like the back of my hand,' Paide said. 'I have been living here all of my life. What could you know, Father, after only living in the place for a few weeks?'

'You might be living here all of your life,' argued Michael, 'but the man who put the fish in the water has been around for an awful lot longer than you, and if he tells me it's not the place then it's not the place,' he insisted. 'Now hold on to your horses and wait till I show you.' He was growing tired of the old man's grumbling. He kept staring up along the cliff line high above.

'Looking for divine inspiration, are ya?' Paide snapped. He was usually good natured, but the last couple of weeks of stress had taken it out of him, and left him bitter and ill-used. Michael ignored him and kept concentrating on the cliff line. Suddenly it came into view. There was the particular outcrop with a stone cairn on top that Kate and himself had built the previous week. It was the sign he had been searching for.

'Which side of the boat did you cast your nets out on?' he asked.

'Starboard!' came the gruff reply.

'Ah, Jayzis, Paide no wonder you weren't catching anything,' Michael said, 'it's the wrong side of the boat,' he smiled at him, unable to contain his excitement. 'Throw them out to port,' he ordered, and steered him in closer to the mark. It was the conviction in the priest's voice that told Paide not to argue. He went quickly about the boat, setting his nets in the spot where Michael pointed. When he had finished they worked their way in closer to the bottom of the cliffs near the rocks and set a dozen lobster pots. After that there was nothing left to do but wait. They anchored a safe distance off the shore.

'I'm sorry, Father,' Paide said, after he had set the anchor and shut down the engine. 'The last few weeks has me worn ragged. I'm very grateful for all you are trying to do for me. Even if it comes to nothing I know you have tried your best, what with going to the manor and all of that. Not like the other gobshite!' He gave a grimace as he thought of the recently deceased Fuhrer Flaherty. 'That fellah was a good for nothing unless there was something in it for him, I tell ya! A terrible grabber.' He spat over the side of the boat. 'There isn't many that liked him and few have had much faith ever since. You'll have to excuse me for speaking my mind. Mary says you are a decent sort, and I'm tending to agree with her, so it's important that you know what you are up against,' he continued. 'They would just as soon have no priest at all as one the like of him. I don't care much, myself, either way. I hadn't been to the church in years when I came knocking the other day. That in itself was an act of desperation,' he sighed. 'To be honest I don't know what possessed me, but you have tried to help me out and I owe you a favour so it's by speaking my mind that I'll return it to you.' He shook his head. 'You have a hard road ahead of you if you think you are going to get them to follow you. Scones and tea are a nice idea, but eaten bread is soon forgotten around here. Restoring their faith is going to take a bloody miracle!'

It was the most he had spoken in all the time Michael had known him, but there was truth in every word that he had said. He was the first man in the community to speak out against the old priest in terms that left no doubt about his true feelings towards him. It was probably the same view they were waiting to form of himself, he thought. Kate had been very open, but she was too forgiving of the old priest to give a clear impression. Paide had hit the nail on the head.

'God works in strange ways,' Michael replied quietly and left it at that. He was too busy silently praying that God would come through for him.

A couple of hours later they started to haul in the nets and that's when the trouble started.

'It's stuck!' Paide said angrily, reverting back to his bad mood. He had been praying just as hard as Michael that this time the catch would be good and all would be right. Now he stood the risk of hauling nothing on board, and losing his valuable net in the process. 'I bloody told you, didn't I?' he said harshly. Rory helped as best he could, but stayed well clear of his skipper, afraid he might lash out and give him a right telling off. They tried the opposite end of the net but found it held fast as well. Michael joined in and put his back into it, and for a minute at least, nothing seemed to be happening. Then it gave way.

'It's coming!' said Rory with excitement. He changed his stance to get a better view. Slowly but surely the bottom began to yield up that which they had wanted so badly. The sea beneath them started to shimmer, and then boil with the silvery shapes of salmon as they thrashed around to free themselves from being hauled to the surface.

'Holy Mother of the divine God,' Paide said as the first of the fish fell from the overflowing net and landed in the bottom of the boat. 'It has to be over twenty pounds!' he exclaimed excitedly as if it was the first fish he had ever caught in his life. There were over a hundred more to follow. The net was not caught in the bottom at all. Rather, it had been weighed down by all the fish struggling to get free. It was not long before they were hauling the second one on board. Slightly smaller, but just as full. They lost track of how many fish they had caught. The last count was one hundred and eighty. There was almost a ton of fish in the bottom of the boat, which was now sitting significantly lower in the waterline.

'Well, you old sea dog, you were looking for a miracle.' Michael laughed with relief and slapped Paide on the shoulder when they had finished hauling in their catch. 'Looks like you have got yourself one.' Paide took his cap off and wiped the sweat from his brow. He had never seen anything like it before in his life. He was speechless for a while until the significance of what had happened had finally dawned on him. Then a broad smile replaced the look of shock on his face. 'God bless you,' he said.

'What about the lobster pots?' Rory asked. The boat was already overloaded as it was. He had always been lectured by Paide to never take chances. Now here they were considering being foolhardy.

'What do you think?' Paide asked looking to the priest for directions. 'You seem to have all of the answers.' Michael looked out to the clear horizon and at the sea that was running calm.

'I think that God is on our side today,' he said with such conviction that Rory went to the bow without further question, and prepared to haul in the first pot. By the time they motored back around the peninsula and came in sight of the pier the two of them were well on their way to marking the occasion with one of the bottles of Bushmills that Michael had taken from the stash at home. He had brought it in the event that they might need to drown their sorrows, but now they were using it instead to celebrate their victory. In the distance the pier was lined with more people than ever before. They had heard that it was Paide's last day and that the priest in desperation had gone out to help him. Bets had already been laid on the fate of the priest, the consensus being that this adventure with Paide would put him on the rocks. The crowd never considered that the fishermen would arrive back at the quay other than empty-handed.

But the boat was sitting low in the water. Nothing was revealed as Paide and his crew motored close to the pier, eyes ahead, ignoring the gathering. There were curious mutterings from the crowd as to why Paide had covered the inside of the boat with a large tarpaulin. No one believed that there might be anything worth hiding. Paide brought his craft to a halt on the beach, inside the little harbour, and cut the engine. He and Michael jumped into the water and pushed the vessel as far up on the sand as they could. Offloading it there would be easier than on the pier. It would also make it more difficult for all of those who were curious to know what was going on. Paide was intent on having the last laugh. He sent Rory up to the pub to call Alan Moran to lend them his truck. They would be needing it to transport the catch into Tralee.

'Be smart,' he told him. 'And tell him to bring as much ice as you can!' A couple of the curious onlookers on the pier with heavy bets could not hold back any longer. They began to make their way down towards the boat in a casual sort of manner. They were undone, however, by the crowd that suddenly emptied out of the pub. The phone line had been bad and Rory had to shout to tell Alan Moran of their good fortune and why they would be needing the truck. He couldn't help but be overheard by all that were present. The crowd grew around them, but Michael, directed by a wink from Paide, said nothing. They sat smiling and sharing the last of the hip flask. Finally somebody had to ask them.

'Go on Paide, give us a look for God's sakes,' he said, the anxiety of the crowd showing in his voice. 'We are dying to know what you have caught.' With a flourish, Paide and the priest pulled back the tarpaulin and revealed its contents. There was not one person standing that did not let out an exclamation at the sight before them, and a few had to ask forgiveness from the priest for their choice of words in the process. The entire bottom of the boat was covered in the finest of wild salmon, and over two dozen of the biggest lobsters they had ever seen crawling all over them. Every fish box that could be borrowed and found was used and the entire crowd helped to stack the catch at the foot of the pier in readiness for the truck.

'Take it easy, Father,' Paide said, taking a large fish box out of his hands and replacing it with a pint of Guinness that Rory had fetched him from the bar. 'You've done your bit as it is. Have a sup of this instead!'

'It's an awful pity you didn't get to see it,' Michael said to Kate later on that evening, as he regaled the details of his adventure to her over a hearty dinner of fresh lobster. He was in high spirits and very close to being drunk from all of the porter that he and Paide had taken in celebration. 'When the nets seemed like they were caught in the bottom I was sure your plan was done for,' he said. 'Then it was like pennies from Heaven, the first sign of all those fish coming up from the bottom. Well, not pennies. It was pounds more like. There was a fortune in those nets!'

Kate's idea for the fishing had been inspired from memories of her childhood. Most of the families on the island had kept a few cows in stock, which they replenished from the mainland on an irregular basis. The method for transporting the cows from the mainland could be described as precarious. There was no harbour or pier on the island, so the coaster that delivered the animal had to be anchored in deep water offshore.

The quality of the animal's breeding and the farmer's eye that picked it, were soon found out when it was time to get the animal onto *terra firma*. The method was simple. Dump the poor unfortunate cow overboard and make it swim. If it made it to shore then it was considered to be of good stock and the purchaser kept hold of his dignity. If it did not make it, then the fishing was always good for at least a month afterwards while the farmer in question, resorted to capturing all of the fish that fed off the dead carcass on the bottom and, in doing so, he recouped his losses. Either way there was a profit to be made. Kate had applied the same theory to Paide's herd. Alive they were worthless, but in the ocean at the bottom of the cliffs they were a hidden treasure. What better way to help Paide get his money back than for God to send the poor man fishing? For six solid weeks after the first catch he worked the water at the foot of the cliffs where, unbeknownst to him, his herd gave up their gold.

John Finucane was not at all happy about being paid back his money. It took him two weeks before he could bring himself to return the deeds, and that was not before he had tried to find some legal loophole or other that would get him out of doing so. He damned the priest for being so clever. Father Michael's intervention had spoiled his plans for expanding the farm. Without his help, Paide would not have had a leg to stand on. John had to be careful though; the harvest was coming up and he needed the priest and the community on his side. The way things were going, in the few short weeks that he had been around, Father Michael was making a good impression that would count when it came time to getting everyone organised. If he came through with the harvest, and everything worked out, then all would be forgiven. After this year, John had decided, he would no longer lend any of the farmers the money they needed to get by. He would persuade the bank in Tralee to do the same. It would not take long before the rest of the small holders would have to start selling out. Then he would own the entire peninsula.

Chapter thirty nine

Michael, afflicted by a slight hangover from the previous day's success, decided to make a second stab at wading through the pile of neglected correspondence that clogged his predecessor's writing desk. There were twenty-three letters in total, some of which had postmarks that dated back before Father Flaherty had died. He was deliberating whether he should start with the earliest dates and work forward, or go backwards from the most recent letter received when his attention was caught by a British postage stamp. It was the only foreign correspondence in the pile.

'Will you have a cup of tea while you work?' Kate asked as she passed the door with a load of washing.

'That would be great, thanks and maybe one of those fresh scones,' he called after her. She disappeared into the kitchen where there was a great smell of baking coming from the oven. The back of the letter was addressed West Minster Hospital located in Bath, in the south of England. He recalled that there were natural hot springs there that had been used as far back as Roman times for medicinal purposes. He was just about to open the envelope when the phone beside him rang. It was the operator, with a long distance call from Dublin. Kate found the door of Michael's office closed when she brought his tea. She knocked and waited, but there was no answer.

'I'm on the phone,' he called out impatiently when she knocked again. She retreated to the kitchen until he was ready.

'Sorry, Kate,' he said, when he finally came in a few minutes later. 'A bit of an emergency,' he said gravely. 'That was Elsabeth's mother on the phone. She called me because there's something wrong with the connection to the manor.'

'What is it?' Kate asked. There might be news of Brendan, anything at all to let her know how he was.

'I'm afraid Elsabeth's father is very sick. It appears that he might have had a stroke.' Michael said.

'Oh, no!' Kate was filled with concern. 'Is he all right?'

'I think so. But she has asked me to go up and inform the family, and get them to contact Dublin so that they can make plans to bring him home. I'll have to go up straight away.'

By the end of the week James Finucane had returned to the manor. Michael paid his first social call to see him and was brought to the drawing-room where James sat alone staring into a lifeless fireplace. The stroke had left him with paralysis down one side. His speech was still slurred, but he was coherent.

'Forgive me, Father,' James apologised after a short time 'but I'm not much for small talk just now.'

'I understand,' said Michael. He finished with a passage from the bible and then went to the drawing-room where he had been invited for tea.

'The depression was there before he got sick,' Joan Finucane explained. 'It started not long after our eldest son Brendan went off to fight for the British. They had a falling out you see. James saw him as a renegade, a traitor to his country.' She explained how her husband had fought the British in Dublin during the 1916 rising with guns that had been smuggled from Germany. 'They were our allies at the time. He felt that Brendan was an embarrassment to him in political circles – that he had let his country down. But a month after the bombing, a stranger came to our house in Dublin asking for Brendan. He said that he had come on behalf of his family and the people in his street. That he wanted to thank Brendan for everything that he had done. It was through him that we found out about what had happened. We'd had no idea of Brendan's injuries, or the people that he had saved. Then James discovered through the American Ambassador what the Germans were doing in their concentration camps, how evil they have become, and that maybe the bombing in Dublin was not a mistake after all.'

Michael was surprised by the revelation. 'There's an awful lot goes on that we don't hear about,' Joan confided. 'That poor little girl.' Her eyes filled with tears. 'After the man called to the house, James used to listen to the BBC every night in his study for news of the war. You can imagine his shock when Brendan came on and talked about his experience as a fighter pilot. He is a big hero over there. He has received three different awards for bravery,' her voice faltered. 'And now he is gone,' she said. 'I think that was what brought the stroke on in the end. James is full of regret – we all are. He was only a boy. It is such a terrible waste.' She had been so desperate to have someone to talk to and now it was a relief to confide her sorrows to Michael.

'There's hope yet, surely?' Michael said, in an effort to cheer her. 'Missing in action doesn't mean that he is dead.' But he knew from experience that ultimately it was up to God.

'No.' Joan shook her head forlornly. 'A fortune-teller once told me that my eldest son would die when he was twenty-one, and she has been right about so many things up to now that I have no reason not to believe her.'

Michael put a hand on her shoulder. 'Whatever about the dead, you mustn't give up on the living. Try to focus your attention on the people that surround you, and leave your problems up to God,' he said. 'Situations like this are always a test of our faith. I'm confident that you will all make your way through it.' Joan apologised for crying in front of him. She thanked him for his kindness and invited him back again later on in the week, promising to be in better form the next time he visited. And she was. And so was her husband. Every time Michael visited on his rounds over the next few weeks, both showed signs of improvement.

'It is nice to be home,' Joan told him. They had gotten into the habit of walking in the garden after his visit with James. 'Dublin is such a strange place. Not at all what I expected. Living there was different to visiting.' She stopped to deadhead a rose. 'The members of the government are always fighting over something,' she said. 'So it's been just as much a relief for James to be home as for me.'

'Why don't you come to Mass at the church this Sunday?' Michael suggested. He had been visiting the manor each week to hear confession and bring communion to the family, but Elsabeth was worried that her parents were turning into hermits. 'We haven't seen yourself and James there since you came back,' he reminded her. 'Lots of people are asking for you.' He knew that they had not encouraged any visitors other than himself. 'It might be nice to get out for a while.' Joan made excuses about James's condition and his lack of mobility and the loss of his pride as a consequence.

'There is nothing to be ashamed of,' Michael said. 'I have already spoken to him about it. He said he misses the occasion more than he had imagined. We've just started the choir again and they'll be singing for the first time next Sunday. I'm sure he would go if you were to encourage him. My housekeeper sings like a lark,' he added. 'I've not heard her yet so it will be a treat for the first time. You get him down to the church and I'll organise the pall bearers to help him,' he said jokingly. 'If he has any problems they will know what to do with him.'

'Father Michael!' Joan exclaimed, shocked.

'It's time to start living again,' Michael laughed.

Chapter forty

Michael had never heard Kate sing, at least not the way she did at church. He had heard her humming around the house or in the back garden at the clothesline. He'd had no idea that she had the voice of an angel. It had been Mary's idea. She had mentioned it as a way of introducing Kate back into the community.

'The Mass is not the same without her,' she stated simply. 'They had always enjoyed her singing on Sundays before all of the problems with the Fuhrer Flaherty and the baby,' Mary said. 'What with all of the changes that have taken place since you've arrived. I think it would be a good opportunity to smooth things over between themselves and herself.' Mary had become more maternal towards Kate and reminded her of Mrs Cummins.

'I'll give it some thought,' said Michael.

'Sure there is nothing to think about. I have already discussed it with her,' Mary said, with a wink. 'It is just a matter of yourself giving herself the nod.' The following Sunday the congregation gathered, with James Finucane sitting in the front row. Joan sat on the one side of him, Elsabeth on the other. They had come down early in the horse and trap. He entered through the side door with the help of a stick. He was making a good recovery and they were all glad to have made the effort. John was nowhere to be seen. Three rows back sat Micilin Og with his six children. He had come to Michael a couple of weeks before when he had heard how he had helped Paide O'Shea. He said that Paide was a friend and he was very grateful.

'I'm a proud man, Father,' he said. 'I don't easily admit I'm wrong, but I want to apologise for the way I stood up to you in the square, on your first day in the town.' He stuck out his big hand and they had a laugh about it. Michael was invited for tea, which he gladly accepted. The first Sunday he had celebrated Mass only half the congregation attended. The second week, the church was two-thirds full. This was his fourth Sunday and the church was now packed. There was standing-room only at the back. Michael took his time preparing for the liturgy, and it was only when he was good and ready that he silenced the gathering by raising his hands in the air.

'Mary McCracken said to me the other day that the Mass is not the same without the singing,' he began. He smiled down at Mary as she blushed with pride. 'In particular,' he went on, 'there has been one person missing for quite some time and I think it is appropriate today that we show our appreciation.' Mary had pre-empted Michael's announcement by spreading the word during the week that Kate would be singing.

'So I'd like to start the Mass with one of my favourite hymns from the choir.' He looked up to the balcony at the back of the church. On queue the organ started to play. For the first verse the choir sang. You could tell that they were a little out of practice. On the second verse, however, Kate took over. She was everything and more than Mary had promised. The choir joined in for the chorus and they were transformed. Michael saw James Finucane close his eyes and breathe in each note from the music. He knew then that he had made the right decision. During the communion Kate sang solo. Not one person left early at the end for the want of listening to her sweet voice. When Mass was over Michael made his way to the main door and was a good half-hour chatting to the congregation before they finally departed. As he went back into the church he had to massage his sore hand. All of the firm handshakes and well wishes from the many people who had never met him before had left him aching.

'I'm sorry for keeping you for so long,' he apologised to the Finucanes, who had been waiting for him to finish. He had been invited during the week to go to the hurling game in the pony and trap after Mass. He had accepted on the condition that when they dropped him home that they would all stay for lunch and allow him to return some of the hospitality that they had shown him. To his pleasant surprise he found that Kate was with them. James had sent Elsabeth up to fetch her from the balcony so that he could compliment her on her singing. The two girls looked awkward, especially Kate. Father Murphy noted her uneasiness with Elsabeth's parents. It seemed more than shyness. But James Finucane was in such high spirits he didn't notice.

'Kate has promised us that she will sing for us after the lunch,' he said, his speech now well recovered. He had taken a shine to the girl, which Joan interpreted as a good sign of recovery. Elsabeth stayed behind with Kate to prepare the lunch.

'You'll be fine,' she said. 'Stop worrying for God's sake. Sure, it's only lunch we are having!' When Michael had first told her, Kate was horrified by the idea of Brendan's family dining with them, but there was nothing that she could do to stop it. She had contacted Elsabeth all in a tizzy to try and have her cancel it, but Elsabeth thought it was a good idea. 'Sure, isn't it a great way to meet them,' she had teased. Kate was not so sure. Having hit it off well with the Finucanes, Michael had confided in Kate the personal joy he felt in helping to restore a person's health through their faith. He had heard enough stories about the 'Lordy' before meeting him to be biased in favour of disliking him. Certainly his first impressions of John had done nothing to soften the image of his father.

'I would not have believed it myself if I had not seen his

transformation with my own eyes,' he said. 'Inviting them to lunch was just a natural progression.'

'What about Grace?' Kate had said still looking for an excuse to sabotage the idea.

'What about her?' Elsabeth had replied without a bother. 'They know about Grace. Michael has already spoken about you to my mother, so there is nothing to worry about.'

'He has? What did she say?' Kate asked.

'Nothing, other than it was the Christian thing to accept and welcome you, and that if you needed anything to let her know. I told her we are best friends,' Elsabeth added, her tone reassuring. Kate felt very touched by how her friend had described them. She wished that there was some way she could tell her about what had happened with John, but Elsabeth's loyalty to her family would never allow her to believe it. It would more likely spoil things between them if she informed on him. At one o'clock Mary McCracken came to fetch Grace to mind her for the afternoon.

'You were a star in there this morning,' she said to Kate, nodding towards the church. 'A bright light!' Elsabeth nodded in agreement. 'You'd want to hear the lovely things that they were saying about you,' Mary went on. 'It would do your heart no end of good.' She gathered up Grace and all that she needed and reassured Kate that her daughter would be well looked after. By two-thirty the pony and trap had not arrived back with its passengers. Elsabeth was afraid that there might have been an accident. Suddenly the phone rang and Kate ran to answer it.

'It was Madigan's pub,' she said with a strange expression on her face when she put down the receiver. 'They are on their way.' Shortly afterwards they could hear the hooves of the pony, interspersed with the sounds of laughter. Joan steered the trap to the bottom of the steps at the front porch way, where the passengers attempted to dismount. However, one look at the scene told Kate that they were going to need help. She dashed to the back of the trap to see if she could be of assistance.

'It's all right, Kate,' Michael reassured her, as he climbed down. 'Sure we have it under control.' But the slur in his voice told her a different story. James Finucane let out a slight snigger as he shuffled his way to the back of the cart.

'A great game. A great game,' he stated solemnly, then lost his footing and fell into the arms of Michael who was just able to save him. There was a sudden commotion as Elsabeth let go of the pony's rein and ran to the aid of her father. Kate was already there trying to prop him up on one side. The two men held on to each other, and every time they lost their footing they howled with laughter. Joan was mortified. She did not know which way to look.

'What am I going to do with the pair of you?' she asked as she climbed down and secured the pony to the branch of a tree before going to help them.

'What are you saying, woman? Sure it was a great game altogether!' her husband said, belligerently. They struggled up the front steps and into the dining-room where the lunch had been laid out. 'Wait till you hear about what Father Michael did,' he said.

'Hush up now, James, it was a tactical manoeuvre,' Michael wagged a fork at him. 'The girls wouldn't be interested in such things!'

'Interested?' James exclaimed. 'Interested? Sure isn't it their God-given right that they should know.' Over lunch he regaled them with the entire story. 'We were late. We'd stopped for a pint on the way. Just one, mind you, so that I could go over the rules of the game once more with the Father. You know of course that he was supposed to be officiating?' he nodded at Michael. 'Anyway, by the time we got there they had started without us, and when the first half was over we were down six points. They were terrible rough, the other side, punching and kicking and all sorts of carry on,' he said. 'The ref was on their side. You could tell by the crowd. Sure even one of the opposition said to me that what was going on wasn't fair and that they should just play the game, but they were awful determined to win. Then Donal Treherty, on our side, was sent off for foul play, which was only in response to what they were doing, so we were down a man going into the second half. Just before they go onto the field, however, your man here,' he said nodding again to Michael, 'has divine inspiration. "Gather around," he says, and they all kneel around him as if saying a prayer. When they finished you could see that some sort of an arrangement had been made and, by God, I have never seen a team go into a second half with greater resolve. Sure enough, within a minute or two the other side were up to their old tricks again when, lo and behold, your man here puts his fingers between his lips and lets out a whistle, the sound of which could be heard all the way up to Dublin.' He took a sip of porter from his glass to catch his breath, and let the story so far settle in.

'Well? What happened then?' asked Elsabeth.

'They leapt on them,' her father answered.

'Who leapt on who?' demanded Kate. Joan sat at the end of the table shaking her head.

'Our side,' James said. 'They leapt on their side, every one of them, and started beating the hell out of them.' He threw a couple of punches in the air to mimic the commotion that ensued. 'Sure, I have never seen anything like it in all me life. It was inspirational!' he howled with laughter. 'The whole crowd went crazy. It took the ref ages to settle them!' he said.

'And what happened then?' Elsabeth asked.

'Well, what else could happen?' he answered. 'He couldn't send the whole team off now could he? He had stern words with the two captains to get their teams under control and then made them start the second half again from scratch.'

'Are you serious?' Elsabeth exclaimed in disbelief.

'He had no other choice,' her father answered. 'The crowd was ready to riot. There was no other way to settle them down. I think he was afraid of his life that they would go after him,' James explained. Michael with an innocent smile on his face only shrugged his shoulders when the two girls looked at him for confirmation.

'Who won?' Kate thought to ask when they had gotten

over the shock of it all. James hadn't mentioned the final score.

'They did. But only by a point,' he said with great disappointment. 'It would never have happened if Brendan had been their captain,' he added quietly. It was the first time he had acknowledged his eldest son in public since he had gone to the war. The excitement of the day and the drink had gotten the better of him and he struggled to hold back his true feelings. He stared out the window and grieved for his son. There wasn't a dry eye in the room after that. Joan comforted her husband while Kate excused herself to the kitchen under the pretence of clearing the table.

'Are you all right, Kate?' Michael had entered the kitchen with more plates. She was sobbing quietly over the kitchen sink. She nodded that she was fine, afraid that if she opened her mouth her feelings would come out in a terrible bawl. Michael retreated back to the dining-room.

'We'll go into the sitting-room and have some tea before you set off for home,' Michael said. The women set to clearing the last of the dishes off the table, glad of something to keep them occupied. Joan went to join the men when the bulk of the work was done. There was a knock then at the kitchen door. Time had flown and there was Mary, back with Grace as had been arranged.

'I came in the back door,' said Mary. 'I did not want to disturb you. Will I go away and come back later on?' she asked. But on seeing her mother, Grace started crying which put a stop to any notion of taking her away again. It was the first time that Kate had known her to take strange and her screams grew even louder when Elsabeth's mother reappeared in the kitchen. Kate was embarrassed at first, unsure what to say, until Joan asked if she could hold the baby.

'Go on,' Elsabeth's voice was a whisper.

'Ah, would ya look?' said Mary as Kate handed her baby to Joan. Grace went quiet in an instant.

'I'd like to show her to James. Is that all right?' What could Kate do, but bow to her wishes. They went into the sitting-room.

Joan interrupted the conversation and before James knew it, he had Grace in his arms. 'Isn't she beautiful?' said Joan. Everyone agreed. Elsabeth beamed at the thought of her parents unknowingly holding their first grandchild.

'Don't be getting any ideas now, do you hear me!' he said to Joan who was doting over him and the baby. They all laughed, especially when he would not give her back to Joan. Kate did not know how she should act.

'You'll give us a song before we go Kate, like you promised early on,' James reminded her. 'It would be a nice way to finish off the day.' Accompanied by Elsabeth, Kate sang 'The Mountains of Mourne' and, when asked for an encore, she followed it with a gentle lullaby as she slowly took a sleeping Grace out of James's arms.

'Good night,' she said softly, and went upstairs to settle Grace into her cot. The Finucanes lingered on for almost an hour afterwards talking quietly, reluctant to let go of such a perfect day. When they departed, Michael put the last of the glasses into the kitchen sink and it was there, that he had a revelation. He had come into the kitchen earlier to find Kate crying and he remembered thinking it unusual that she should be so affected by the loss of someone else's son. Then suddenly, as if a thunderbolt had struck him, his mind latched onto the letter from the hospital in Britain.

Chapter forty one

Brendan was tired of being poked and prodded. He'd had it with being a good patient. He had played the role of being compliant and agreeable, because the doctors, in their wisdom, had him convinced that his recovery was imminent.

But the weeks had passed by, turning into months and the chances began to seem less likely. His bandages were off, his broken bones had mended and the bright red scars from the stitches over his body were slowly starting to fade. He showed no signs of disfigurement, save for a large scar on top of his head, but that was well hidden by his hair. His eyesight however, still remained the problem. Brendan had done the rounds with the specialists, receiving differing opinions. But it was all to no avail. He could discern light, and the faint outline of shadows, but it was as if he still had the bandages in front of his eyes. His greatest pain though was closer to his heart and incurable, for Brendan had lost his best friend. Victor had been killed in action on the same day that Brendan was shot down. He was returning to base after scoring two kills in a desperate dogfight over the Channel when he responded to a call for help from a village near his airfield that was being pummelled by a wayward bomber. Low on fuel and out of ammunition he made the supreme sacrifice by ramming the enemy. Brendan was devastated and fell into a deep depression upon hearing the news. In this world of madness where life hung by a thread, Victor had been the voice of reason that had kept him alive. His impossible loss now magnified his isolation.

When the doctor changed his tune from recovery to rehabilitation and had him measured for a long white stick Brendan began to lose hope for the future. Without his eyesight he was useless. What chance did he have of returning to Ireland when he could barely make it to the bathroom at the end of his ward? Swimming across the Channel had seemed a far less complicated matter.

The water had been icy at first, until he got himself going and the rhythm of his body helped to ward off hypothermia. His confidence was shaken very early on when he was struck by a severe cramp in his right leg. The pain was so sudden and so brutal that he thought at first that he had been attacked by a shark. It took every ounce of willpower and determination to relax through the pain and stop himself from panicking. Somehow he had managed to stay afloat. When the cramp had subsided he gave himself a bloody good talking to. 'You got yourself into this mess so it's up to you to get yourself out of it! Pace,' he had to remind himself, 'keep a steady pace!' Depending on the winds and tides, the distance he had to swim was at least twice as much as he had ever done before.

His greatest comfort were the stars. Offshore that night the heavens were clear and he was able to take a fix on Pleiades and follow them as they descended into the western sky over Dover. To his left he could see Acheron, further south in the direction of home. When he finally settled down he felt so good at one stage that he imagined he could swim all the way to

Ireland, over a hundred miles to the west. This helped to restore his confidence. The early morning sun came as a comfort for it began to reflect off the white cliffs of Dover, just discernible on the distant horizon. For twelve hours he fought the urge, the hope, the desperate need to be discovered by some passing plane or ship. But dwelling on the remote possibility that he might be plucked from the jaws of death was too dangerous. To rely on false hope would have sapped his willpower. He focused instead on a constant rhythm and feeding a steady flow of energy to his powerful shoulders and arms so that they might drag him across the Channel. He allowed no other thought to enter into his head. Not even Kate. To do so would have caused the horror of his predicament to crash in on his shoulders, and he knew it would surely sink him.

He could not recall the moment of his discovery, or the hours and days that it had taken him to find some sort of coherence. They told him much later at the hospital that he had been found by a child searching for crabs between the rocks on the beach. His body had been so badly beaten by the thundering surf that had washed him ashore that it had seemed unlikely that he would survive. In spite of this, the medical team had fought for his life long after he had lost his own ability. When pneumonia set in, Brendan's stubborn refusal to die had just made them work harder. His blindness was a mystery to all of the hospital staff. Lots of theories were presented and lots of remedies tried, but in the end there was no resolution.

'Don't you want to go home?' Matron had asked him, on more than one occasion, when sensing his despondency. 'You'd be much better off than stuck in this old place.' At the beginning of his war Brendan had never imagined that he would not go home. When John had said originally that 'it would be to a hero's welcome', he had been naïve enough to believe him. He realised now that he had been crazy to think that his leaving home would be enough to change those he had left behind. That somehow, on his return, things would be different and that he could live the life he wanted to lead, rather than conform to his father's way of thinking. Now he felt like a bloody fool. The truth was, and still remained, by going off to war he had turned his back on everyone, especially Kate. Had John betrayed him? He did not know for sure, but it was evident that in spite of writing home continuously, he had never received a reply from his family. He was too ashamed to admit that he no longer had a home or anyone to return to. Without his eyesight and no one to turn to, he felt desperate and alone. It was a long distance phone call in the middle of the night that finally saved him.

'Is this Brendan Finucane?' a voice shouted from the far end of the line through the crackle of static. He could hardly make out what was said, but the sound of his name certainly made him wake up and listen.

'This is Father Michael Murphy in Clochan!' Brendan had no idea who Father Murphy was, but the mention of Clochan made his spirits soar.

'Yes! he shouted. 'This is Brendan. What happened to Father Flaherty?' He was still filled with the wonder at how he had been found.

'Don't worry about Flaherty,' came the reply. The line was so bad that conversation was impossible. Through barks and stutters they made an arrangement to try again in the morning. Brendan spent a restless night, his mind ablaze with all of the infinite possibilities of being contacted by home.

'How did they find me?' he asked the sister on duty. She said that she had no idea. The following morning the line wasn't any better.

'Can you make it to Dublin?' An address was given. Everything else would be arranged.

Chapter forty two

John did not like the new priest. He'd been too clever by far in the way that he had helped Paide O'Shea with his problems. Father Flaherty would not have been so kind. He'd have told him that it was his own fault and that he must suffer the consequences. For a donation to the church the Fuhrer would do anything. The new priest, on the other hand, was not affected by the status of the Finucanes. John wasn't too happy about the good impression that Father Michael was making around the parish either, especially the way that he had taken Kate in and how the village had accepted it. This action alone caused him the greatest anxiety. But he had to be careful. For John, everything was riding on the harvest. He had to stay on the right side of the priest, at least until the crop was in. After that it would be to hell with the lot of them.

      He had followed Brendan's manual and he'd made change after change. The success of each one made him more confident, so that he had grown cocky and decided to accelerate the plans. The great harvest had originally been designed over a three-year period with the increase of acreage made as each year yielded greater income. By reinvesting the profit, there would be no need to involve the bank and the risk was spread in such a way that if the harvest was to fail, the manor could absorb the losses. Brendan had foreseen that the war would incur shortages which would increase demand and prices as a consequence. The market predictions for the season though had made Brendan's calculations seem conservative by comparison. As a consequence John had reasoned that with a higher yield in profit than expected, the plan could be made to work over a one-year period instead of three, if he borrowed money from the bank to kick-start the operation.

 John had always thought that Brendan was conservative so without telling his father, he had borrowed heavily against the deeds of the manor in a gamble that would yield him a fortune with the very first harvest. The Farmers' Almanac was favourable, even better for the next year, and if all went well and the war lasted he would very quickly become a rich man. He had calculated the risk of course. Failure of the crop might see the loss of the farm to the bank, but with his confidence on a high and the way things were going he was prepared to take the gamble.

 At the same time he had given up on the idea of being with Kate. In one of his more sober moments he realised that he had been lucky that she had not reported him. Not that anyone would have believed her, but he did not need that sort of pressure. When the stress was on he found the drink was a comfort to him. It always had been. He thought better and felt better about himself when he'd had a few. Lately he had taken a lot more, which was to be expected. When the harvest was over he'd be able to relax.

Chapter forty three

Kate was woken from a deep slumber by the ringing of the phone downstairs in the hallway. Before she had a chance to respond she heard the footfall of Father Michael on the stairs. It was Mary at the post office. She was full of apologies for waking him so early.

'Could you hold for a call from the manor?' When the connection was made it was Elsabeth at the end of the line.

'We can't get Daddy out of bed!' she said in exasperation. In spite of his progress, James experienced bouts of deep depression from time to time and would lie around in apathy for several days until the dark clouds lifted.

'Remind him that the doctor will only be here for one day. He won't be back for another six weeks,' Michael said. He had made arrangements the previous week for James to travel to Tralee to see the visiting stroke specialist who came from Dublin. It had been difficult to get the appointment, but he said the specialist had agreed when Michael took the liberty of offering him the hospitality of the Finucane town house in Tralee. James had seemed more than happy with the arrangements at the time, and even went so far as to compliment him on taking the initiative. When he suggested that they collect the specialist from the train station, the die was cast.

'I'll do my best to get him moving,' Elsabeth said. 'But I can't guarantee anything.'

'Don't forget, the train arrives at the station at four,' Michael reminded her. He put down the phone. By this time Kate was up and dressed. She had been included in the plan by Father Michael suggesting she do some shopping with her friend and have some fun. That now seemed unlikely. Elsabeth would be fully occupied with her father. The day instead turned out to be a struggle. Without her friend's support, she was melancholy, for carrying the weight of Grace around was nothing compared to the weight of her own conflicting emotions.

It had been almost two months since Father Michael had taken her in. She had originally intended to stay only for a few days until she got herself sorted, but events had once again overtaken her. The ten pounds that she had in her pocket, plus the wage she had earned from housekeeping, would be just about enough for her to break out on her own and make a go of it. She knew that she was more than welcome to stay, but the longer she remained with Father Michael the harder it would be to leave.

Elsabeth had been the best friend that she had ever had. There was no way she would be ever able to thank her for her support. But the problem of John stood between them. The worst of all was seeing Grace being held by Brendan's parents. If they only knew. She cried herself to sleep over their son most nights. It had been over a year now since she had last seen or heard from Brendan, and four months since he had been reported missing in action. Holding out for his love was getting harder and harder. She had seen nothing of John, since that last terrible night, but that did not make it any easier. The thought of him alone was enough to put her heart sideways. He was like a dark cloud, always threatening a storm.

By lunchtime she had decided that she had grown too dependent on Elsabeth and Father Michael. In spite of all of the support that she had been given she was still just as vulnerable. She had made a half-hearted effort at shopping, but decided that what she really needed was fresh air. As she sat in the park watching the seagulls, Kate finally came to the realisation that Brendan was never coming home. It was better, she decided, to face the harsh reality and get on with her life rather than continue living in silent desperation and false hope. If nothing else, it put her back in charge of her own destiny and strengthened her resolve for the future. She decided that instead of buying a dress she would go and buy a decent bag for her few belongings, and leave for Dublin the following weekend. The thought of having to say goodbye was enough to put her on the train there and then. She knew that in their well-meaning way Father Michael and Elsabeth would try to make her stay and she was afraid that her newfound determination might not be enough to resist them. But to leave without saying goodbye would be most ungrateful. She would have to strengthen her resolve if she was to stick to her decision.

It was late then when she arrived at the station. Father Michael's car was parked outside, but there was no sign of the Finucane's big green Ford. It was a relief to her that they were not there. Now that she had made her decision, she wanted to remain as detached as possible. She took a couple of deep breaths to steady her resolve. Father Michael would be her biggest hurdle. The platforms were busy with people coming and going, and it took her a few minutes to find the priest. He stood where the passengers from the first-class carriage would dismount. He was smoking a cigarette and seemed slightly agitated. The train was late.

'Where's the new dress, Kate?' he asked, as she walked towards him. He sounded like he had been expecting her to be wearing it.

'I didn't get one Father. I bought a new bag instead,' she said trying to sound upbeat, as if that's what she had wanted all along.

'Are you going somewhere?' Father Michael asked catching her off guard as if seeing right through her intentions.

'I was thinking about it,' she found herself admitting as her face flushed with the embarrassment of being discovered.

'We will talk about it after we get this lot sorted. All right?' he said kindly. 'Here let me take her,' he offered, as Kate shifted Grace from one hip to the other. He could tell that she was tired from carrying her around.

'I'm all right.' Kate replied, but Grace had responded to the priest reaching out for her and before Kate knew it he had the baby in his arms. It was in fact a relief and Kate had a chance to relax for the first time that day as Michael snuggled the child.

'There you are!' a voice called from behind, and Elsabeth and her parents appeared. Greetings were made, but there was no time for apologies or mention of their delay as the shrill whistle of the arriving train interrupted the gathering.

'Would you mind holding this bundle?' Michael said to Joan as the Dublin train pulled into the station.

'Delighted,' she replied looking to Kate for her approval. 'Would that be all right?' she asked.

'Of course,' Kate replied, at a loss for what else she could say. It would have been rude to refuse. There was a hiss of steam and a billow of smoke as the big engine passed them and came to a halt at the end of the platform. The doors on each carriage opened in unison and a sudden mad rush as passengers began disembarking. A swirling tide of people soon filled the platform.

'How will we recognise him?' James asked on behalf of their little group. Picking out a stranger would be impossible in the crowd.

'I have no idea,' replied Michael. 'I have never met the man before. I was hoping that maybe you could help me!'

'Sure, how would I know him?' James replied with a confused look on his face. 'Isn't it yourself has made all of the arrangements for the man to come down and visit us!'

'Why don't we wait and see?' Michael smiled. His manner only served to pique the curiosity of the group. Grace was momentarily ignored as all eyes scanned the train and the crowd from front to back. The platform soon emptied save for a few stragglers, wrestling with heavy suitcases and awkward luggage. In all of this time, Michael seemed certain of the arrangements that had been made, even as the last passenger left the platform.

Impatient from the waiting, James was just about to suggest leaving, when a carriage door at the end of the train rattled open. In the distance, a nurse in a Red Cross uniform stepped down from the compartment. It became apparent that she knew that she was expected when she raised her hand in their direction, and Michael returned her wave. The nurse paused. She reached back into the compartment and then they could see that she was helping someone to step down from the carriage. A man. His movements were unsteady, like that of someone old. He was hard to make out because he was facing in the opposite direction, and the steam from the train still hung in the air.

'He looks in worse shape than me,' James remarked, thinking that this was the specialist for whom they had been waiting. The nurse stepped back into the carriage and reappeared with a bag. When she had steadied her charge, the two of them started walking in the direction of the gathering.

'Oh, dear God!' Joan exclaimed suddenly, placing her hand over her mouth. Tears welled in her eyes.

'What is it, Mam?' Elsabeth said, concerned that her mother had suddenly grown so pale.

'Father, she's fainting,' James suddenly called out. He grabbed his wife by one arm and did his best to steady her. Michael responded by grabbing Grace out of her hands and passed her to Kate. He took Joan by the other arm and they shifted her to a bench and made her sit down. All the while Joan was trying to look back at the man.

'What is it, woman? You look as though you've seen a ghost!' stated James full of deep concern. Joan was speechless. Elsabeth had been halfway through helping her mother to sit down when her attention became transfixed on the man walking towards them with the aid of the nurse. She stopped, motionless in the centre of the platform, her mind racing to make sense of what was going on. He was wearing dark glasses, but his features in the uncertain light were familiar. She stared at the man, then back at her mother. When she looked again at the man, it finally dawned on her.

'Brendan,' she cried out. 'It's Brendan!' she shouted to her parents and Kate. Her concern for her mother was suddenly swept away by a great sense of joy and excitement and she ran to close the gap between herself and her brother.

'Steady on!' Brendan cried out as his sister collided with him, nearly bowling him over. It was only then, in his fumbling to remain standing, that she realised that he was blind.

'Oh, Brendan, Brendan we thought you were dead!' She hugged him and kissed him, ignoring the nurse as she dragged her brother to her parents. Joan was momentarily shocked at the sight of Elsabeth leading her unseeing son – then she was holding him in her arms.

'We thought we had lost you,' she cried, clinging on to him for what seemed like an eternity. James stood firm and proud beside them. His old-fashioned reserve prevented him from showing any expression, and this was reflected by the hand that he presented to welcome his son when Joan finally let go of him. Brendan did not respond. At first James mistook it as a slight until he realised that his son could not see it. Then all reserve departed him. He stepped forward, took his son in his arms and hugged him and kissed him and clapped him on the back. Brendan responded with equal affection.

'Oh, my boy, it is so good to see you,' he said. He opened one arm and drew Joan in beside him and Elsabeth joined in as they all hugged and kissed each other. There wasn't a dry eye on the platform.

'So much for the fortune-teller!' said Father Michael as he handed Joan a handkerchief to dry her eyes.

'You are a miracle worker,' she replied hugging and kissing him on the cheek. It was only when Grace cried out that the group came to their senses and realised that Kate had been standing there all the time on her own.

'Kate is here,' Joan said.

'Where?' Brendan cried out, electrified by the mention of Kate's name. His hand reached out in search of her.

'She is in front of you,' his mother said. 'Just a few steps.' Kate had been standing a discreet distance from the group, torn and confused by the scene that had unfolded. All her ideas and notions about remaining detached and independent had deserted her the moment she had laid eyes on Brendan. She had just come to the belief that Brendan was dead, and now she was totally unprepared for the sight of him – *alive* – walking down the platform. Father Michael's plan had left her feeling numbed and confused and now she did not know which way to turn. She looked to the priest in a silent appeal. He returned her gaze, smiling, and nodded reassurance that she should go to him. Now, as Brendan reached out she took his hand tentatively, still disbelieving, and lifted it slowly to her cheek, afraid she was dreaming. Grace cried out again and startled him. Kate moved his hand down to stroke her hair.

'A baby,' he exclaimed.

'A daughter,' Kate whispered. They finally fell together in a passionate embrace, kissing and laughing and crying with relief and all the while trying to find a way to hold each other without crushing Grace. He was taller. He was harder. The lines that were etched on his face radiated a wisdom and strength she had not seen in him before. She knew then that he loved her and that all of the waiting and the agony had not been in vain. Kate understood for the first time then what Mrs Cummins had said about 'waiting for the man'.

'How did you know, Mam?' Elsabeth asked as they left the station for the car.

'Know what?' her mother replied.
'About Brendan and Kate,' she said.
'Your father might be the boss of this family,' she declared, 'but I know love when I see it.'

Chapter forty four

'If you come home I think you'll find that you are a lot more welcome than you realise,' Michael had reassured Brendan when they spoke long distance before his return. He had finally arrived back in Dublin, but it had been harder for the priest to convince him to make the rest of the journey. At best he hoped to talk to Kate and wanted to get word to her that she might consider coming to Dublin.

'That's if she'll have you,' the priest replied. 'After all she has been through since you left she'd not be the one to blame if she was to refuse to see you.' He silently asked God's forgiveness for the lie. But he was set on Brendan coming to Tralee for the sake of all concerned and refused to elaborate on what had been happening. 'Look,' Michael said, careful to choose his words, 'for whatever reason – you are the one who took off. You owe it to this girl to at least front up to her. Whatever happens after that, who knows, but a real hero is one who faces up to his true responsibilities and duty.' He made a point of not mentioning the baby.

It was with great reluctance and trepidation that Brendan boarded the train for home a few days later. His loss of sight had robbed him of his confidence and his earlier resolve to confront his family. He'd sooner face a hundred German fighters.

But the priest's words had reached their mark and, regardless of the outcome, he knew what he must do. His war and disability pension was frugal by comparison to his upbringing, but it would be sufficient for he and Kate to live off, if she would have him. After all that he had been through himself he realised that being blind was not the end of the world and that they could make ends meet if she was prepared to forgive him and make a go of it.

The unexpected reception he received at the station was overwhelming – his parents, Kate and the fact that he was a father. It was a tidal wave of emotion that still had not receded by the time the party had retired to the Finucane's town house in Tralee later that evening. As luck would have it, John was away up north on business for a client and not expected back until the following evening.

If ever there was a doubt in Kate's mind after their reunion at the station, it had been washed away and her spirit cleansed by their first proper kiss in the privacy of the drawing-room when they had been left alone. They had both cried tears of joy and laughed with relief. Brendan refused to let go of Grace ever since he had been handed her for the first time at the station. It filled Kate's heart with joy to see them getting on so well. Brendan apologised for the way in which he had left her and promised to never do so again, but there were unspoken questions on both sides. Why there had been no replies to letters sent? The time they spent alone was far too short for all the answers and Kate held back on telling Brendan about John's behaviour. However, Elsabeth could not help but ask the same question about the post that night over dinner, and when it became obvious that her mother had written in secret as well, they began to question the source from which all correspondence was supposed to have been distributed. The question that was left to hang in the air concerned the integrity of the person to whom the task had been entrusted.

It was in the small hours of the following morning before the gathering dispersed to go to bed. James asked Brendan for a private word, and invited Father Michael to join them in his study. He was deeply concerned and he wanted to solve the mystery of the letters that had been raised over dinner.

'I want to begin by saying that I have made a mistake,' he said to Brendan. 'Father Michael knows how I feel, and I want him to be here to witness my apology.'

'It's not necessary,' Brendan replied. He was sore at himself and knew that if he had stood up to his father in the past in the same way that he had stood up to the Germans that their relationship would have been vastly different.

'Well, in my books it is, and I want it known. I have been a fool and I must pay the price for my vanity.'

'I think that it is important that you should listen,' Father Michael interjected, when Brendan tried to speak over his father to save him face in front of the priest.

'Thank you,' James said. Brendan sat silent. 'I fought for this country once so that we might all have our freedom. I killed men who stood in the way of democracy and the right to one's own voice. When I put down the gun I thought I'd stopped,' he paused. 'But sometimes a man gets into the habit of seeing things his own way. I was blinded by thinking that I knew best. Being right all of the time carries its own misfortunes. I gave control of the estate to John after you left. Lock, stock and barrel!' he said to emphasise the enormity of his folly. 'It had suited me because I was up in Dublin,' he said to Father Michael. He made no bones about how he had, in part, done it for spite, as a reaction to Brendan going off to the war. 'The land has always been set up to be easily managed. All that John had to do was keep it going. It never occurred to me at the time that my younger son would have had a mind to do anything else.'

'What do you mean?' Brendan asked, recognising the concern in his father's voice.

'I had no idea that you had given him your manual on managing the estate,' he said. I discovered it in the old oak table in the office when I began to grow suspicious of how John was managing the farm. It's an in-depth study of the estate based on records that had been kept for well over a hundred years,' James explained to the priest. Brendan's first reaction was surprise, but he was defensive at the revelation.

'That should not have been a problem,' he said, confident of the value of the manual. 'I gave it to him before I left. I thought it would help him with the management of the farm.'

'You were right,' his father acknowledged with admiration. 'Following it made the greatest of sense and would have made life very easy for everybody concerned, until we get down to the harvest.'

'What harvest?'

'The one in the back of the book,' James replied. Brendan paused to consider before answering and searched his memory for the harvest that his father had mentioned. The manual was over one hundred and fifty pages long. It had been almost two years since he had last made an entry. Most of the book was dedicated to the day-to-day running of the farm, and divided into four sections, one for each season. The back of the manual was separate and contained in detail several of the innovative ideas Brendan had for increasing productivity and establishing a co-op with the other farmers in the county. The harvest had been one such plan. He recalled the calculations and how he had minimised the risk by spreading the plan over a three-year time frame.

'It's an idea I thought would work,' he said carefully, 'so long as you stuck to the entire plan!'

'Is he following the plan?' Michael voiced all their concerns. 'In most of our conversations he has been very adamant about the importance of the community's involvement.'

'I know,' said James, 'that's why I wanted you to share in

what has been happening.'

'What has he done?' Brendan inquired with concern.

'It's my own fault,' James said. 'To be honest I lost touch with what was going on after my stroke until I received a call from the bank here in Tralee. The manager was an old friend of mine, but he died unexpectedly just after I got sick. John has been dealing with his replacement.'

'And?' said Brendan, fearing the worst.

'We are up to our eyeballs,' his father said. 'He has been using the deeds of the estate to secure loans against the harvest and two new businesses that he has gone into partnership in town. One of them has turned out to be a bad deal and not worth half of what he invested while the other is unlikely to show a profit for at least a year. If at all!' he added. When he found that all of the cash and valuables were missing from the safe he knew that they were in serious trouble. Brendan shook his head in disbelief. When neither James nor Brendan spoke again, Father Michael's curiosity got the better of him.

'How does the co-op work?' he asked, intrigued by the manual, and the basis of the plan that Brendan had devised.

'It has to do with the combining of community resources to reduce overheads and increase efficiency,' James answered before Brendan had a chance to reply. 'Greater profit for anyone involved,' he said rubbing the thumb and fingers of his right hand.

'It is the way of the future,' said Brendan and went on to explain the intricacies of the arrangement and the greater benefit to all concerned in terms of cash flow, security and lighter work load. 'The biggest problem is the money that's needed to get it started!'

'What about the banks?' Father Michael inquired. 'Surely they would be interested in a share of the profit?'

'The banks are difficult enough, but it's the farmers themselves who are the greatest challenge. There is a risk involved and a lot of them would be hard pressed to see it as worth taking.'

'A lot of them are just scraping by as it is,' Brendan added.

'So how much is needed?' the priest inquired. An indirect question, but loaded with infinite possibility.

'Thousands,' Brendan replied. Father Michael smiled the smile of the benevolent. Now it was his turn to let Brendan and his father into a little secret.

'I think that there is something that you both should know!'

Chapter forty five

'You're not serious!' was Brendan's first reaction. 'God, I've seen it all now,' he said as he pushed his dark glasses back on the bridge of his nose to accentuate the irony of his statement. 'Does anyone else know?' he asked of the priest.

'Only Kate,' Father Michael replied. 'She was there when I made the discovery.'

'There will be another bloody war if the community finds out!' Brendan stated.

'It doesn't surprise me,' said James. 'I never met a man so keen to accept a few quid or a bottle of something as that one. Your mother never liked him you know. She always felt that he was up to no good. There's a certain justice at least that he never lived to spend it!' If the harvest failed it would not ruin the estate altogether, but James Finucane at his age and physical condition did not have the energy needed to claw back to a level footing. He would have to sell the manor to cover the debt that had been incurred by John. When it was explained to Brendan the extent to which John had deviated from his plans it was clear to him how likely his brother was to fail. The weather for one thing was a serious issue. A few bad weeks at the wrong time would be enough to cause disaster. There was also the question of his ability to rally the community to support the extra days needed to complete the harvest.

'From what I have heard I couldn't be sure if they will back him or not,' said Father Michael. 'I understand there is a tradition attached to the harvest, but he is not offering them any sort of real incentive for the extra effort he is asking of them. There is only so much that I can do to encourage them to show up on the day. After the way he treated Paide over his herd I don't think they are inclined to trust him!'

If worse came to worst Brendan had the ability to turn things around, even without his eyesight, but in spite of their emotional reunion the question still remained where he stood. Should the harvest fail, Brendan's idea for the co-op would make the land more profitable and provide for the saving of the estate in the future. But it would take a long-term commitment from Brendan to work the solution. It was obvious to all concerned that his heart was with Kate, and that she was the reason that he had come home. Father Michael's revelation about the cash he had found in Aladdin's cave, however, threw a curve ball into the equation. A catalyst that might bring them all together with a new hope for the future.

'It's their money,' he said referring to the community. 'It does not belong to the Church, but it would be a nice way to give it back to them without the real truth having to be known. God works in strange ways, but it is exactly what they'd need to start the co-op. The banks would not have to be involved so they'd be more easily persuaded.'

'I don't have much right to ask you,' James said, knowing full well where Brendan's heart lay. 'We'd be all right either way. We wouldn't be totally ruined. We can always retire on my pension from the government and live here in town,' he said.

'I'll have to talk it over with Kate,' was Brendan's reply.

'I understand,' replied James, 'but I was thinking that it would be a terrible shame for the community if you didn't get a chance at least to try out your idea for the co-op.' The anxiety that Brendan had experienced on his way down on the train had been lifted by the reunion with his family. Now it had been replaced by the dilemma that faced him as he climbed the stairs in the early hours of the morning to the bedroom where Kate and Grace lay sleeping. It had been a long day and he was tired. From what his father had told him there was every chance the harvest would not succeed. However, the possibility still remained that John might just pull it off.

The successful farmer abides by the saying 'that one should always farm for a drought,' but there is many a farmer has had regrets after a good summer that he did not plant just a little more, or take a slightly bigger risk on the weather. Brendan had seen his brother wangle himself out of tight spots before. In a few short weeks, if the weather held, he might just succeed. The possibility alone made Brendan reluctant to become involved. In spite of the months of convalescence and rest in the nursing home in England, he was still suffering the after-effects of head injury. He was war weary and tired of the world and all its machinations. It bothered him little now that his brother had taken advantage of his situation. The whole world was at war over vanities. If he had lost his inheritance to deception it was nothing compared to those he had known who had lost their lives for the very same reason. He almost felt sorry for his brother. He had everything, but he had nothing. For Brendan, in his darkest days of combat when it seemed that he could die at any moment, his dream of heaven had been a cottage by the sea with Kate and a baby. By a strange twist of fate that dream had come true. All that he wanted now was peace for them to spend a little time together.

While Grace slept Kate paced the floor in the light of the fire and waited for Brendan to finish his meeting with his father. Her relief at being reunited with Brendan was quickly overshadowed by the thought of John and what would happen when he found out that his brother was home. She was so caught up in her thoughts that she failed to hear the bedroom door open. Brendan fumbled his way into the room as best he could from memory, but tripped over a chair and gave his head a terrible wallop against a chest of drawers as he crashed to the floor.

'Sorry, sorry!' he whispered out loud when Kate rushed across to help him stand up, but it only accentuated her concern for how vulnerable they really were. 'I didn't mean to wake you,' he said as he tried to rub the soreness out of his head. 'Sorry,' he repeated as she led him across the room to sit on a small sofa beside the bed. They sat for a moment in silence holding hands; a comfort for both of them.

'We have to talk,' Kate blurted out, unable to allay her fears any longer.

'I know,' Brendan replied. He squeezed her hand to comfort her in response to the anxiety in her voice.

'It's about John,' Kate said.

'I know,' Brendan replied. 'I know what he has done.' Kate sat stunned. How could he know when she had not told a soul? The keeping of it inside had her almost shredded. 'He kept the letters Kate. I'm sure of it. My father has told me about the harvest and the terrible risks he has taken. God knows what else he has done.'

'The cottage is gone,' Kate said simply trying to stifle her emotions. 'He burnt it. Everything.'

'What do you mean?' Brendan asked in disbelief for he'd had plans in his head that they would use it.

'I tried so hard,' she said. 'To get on with him and please him and make him welcome so that he would not mind me staying.' The shame and the suffering that Kate had felt for so long were too much to bear and she finally broke down as she told him about all that had happened. For Brendan, the nightmare that had woken him in the ditch in France had been real all along and he relived it with the tears and words from Kate. 'It's the drink, Brendan. He's lost control and it's got the

293

better of him,' Kate said when she finally settled down. 'He was all right to begin with. He was kind and helpful,' she stated in an effort to be grateful for how he had looked after her. 'But it's like dealing with two completely different people. Drink turns him into a monster!'

Whatever reservations Brendan might have had about re-involving himself in his family's affairs vanished when the truth finally came out about how John had treated the mother of his child. Before going to the war Brendan would have cornered his brother and beaten him to a pulp with his hurling stick for all that he had done. But he was a different man now. The following morning, with a resolute heart and a new vision for the future, he struck a deal with his father and the priest and plans were made to move out to the manor.

Chapter forty six

It was the sight of all of the vehicles parked in the driveway that caught John's attention when the manor finally came into view. In spite of his tiredness from the long journey up north he thought it strange, until he remembered his mother mentioning something about the possibility of having some doctor to stay. Even so, it did not justify the number of vehicles in the driveway and the fact that the manor was lit up like a Christmas tree.

He parked around the back of the house and made his way wearily towards the kitchen entrance. The last thing he felt like doing was socialising. The pressure of the pending harvest had been mounting for some weeks and the follies of his business acumen were becoming more apparent. His cash flow had dried up and the reserve from the safe was almost exhausted. When he had approached the new bank manager for the possibility of an extension on his overdraft he was politely refused. When John tried to bully him with talk of going to head office the manager became adamant and threatened to expose him after finding out that he had falsified some of the loan documents. If John failed to service his debt the manager would face a reprimand and possible dismissal. He was not prepared to dig a hole any deeper than the one he had already gotten himself into.

In an attempt to get money through the doors John was working extended hours at his law practice and offering discounts to clients who settled their accounts immediately in cash. The gamble was still set to pay off, but not without the agonies of going to the wire. When he entered the kitchen it was a flurry of activity. John walked through as if unseen. He made his way up the stairway to the main part of the house with every intention of going straight to bed but the noise of voices from the drawing-room and a sudden burst of laughter stopped him in his tracks. He could in a heartbeat miss a 'drool get together' with some specialist doctor, but the atmosphere that resonated from the drawing-room felt like the makings of a real party. There was laughter again and then somebody started singing. It was just what he needed to cheer himself up after the mounting stresses he had endured over the last few weeks. He pushed through the doors and, to his great surprise, the large room was jammed to capacity. The first person he bumped into was his Aunty Norah.

'You're back!' she said with great delight. 'Isn't it a great surprise altogether?' she beamed. 'Look everybody, John is back,' she shouted, before John had a chance to question her. The noise in the room drowned out her announcement.

'Look,' she shouted again. Taking John by the arm, she pushed their way further into the room. She ignored his questions and tugged at anyone she could, to attract their attention. John had little choice but to follow. As the gathering began to take notice of the old woman with John at her side, the room fell silent. It was obvious from his face that he did not have a clue what was happening. People began to laugh and cheer him on. Wherever his Auntie was leading him would soon reveal the secret. In his vanity, John began to suspect that this might be a surprise party thrown in his honour. The crowd moved apart, and he was struck suddenly with absolute horror. Sitting on a sofa at the far end of the room, between his mother and father, was the vision of a ghost.

'Brendan!' he blurted out. It was all he could manage. He went pale at the sight of his elder brother, returned as if to haunt him. The people gathered around mistook the look of shock on his face for one of great surprise and burst into spontaneous cheering and laughter. Someone patted him on the back and handed him a stiff drink, which he gulped down in one large mouthful. Anything to delay the effects of the shock that gripped him, vice-like, and threatened to strangle the very breath from his lungs. It was lucky for John that the atmosphere of the crowded room overshadowed his initial reaction. He felt as if he had slipped off a precipice and that there was no way that he could save himself. His future flashed before him. All of the plans he had made lay in ruins. Now that Brendan was home, the truth would surely be revealed. He had no choice however, but to act as if he was happy to see his long-lost brother.

'Brendan!' he said again, this time with outstretched arms as he made his way towards him. It took every ounce of effort he could muster to appear genuinely pleased. And then, the miracle of miracles occurred. From the second that John had laid eyes on his brother sitting at the far side of the room something in his subconscious had questioned his appearance. The anxiety of knowing that something was amiss was suddenly a great comfort to him when he realised that Brendan was blind! It was as if God had answered his prayers. Blind he could handle. Blind, in fact, was good. If Brendan could not see, then John possessed a distinct advantage.

'You are alive!' he said, grabbing Brendan by the shoulders when he stood up to greet him. 'God, man, it's great to see you.' He gave Brendan a hug.

'I wish I could say the same,' Brendan replied with a hint of regret as he returned his embrace. For a second John thought that his brother might be serious, until he realised that he was referring to his eyesight.

'Sure, you are alive and well,' John said, and shook him stiffly by the shoulders as if to make his point. 'Isn't that all that matters?' Everyone cheered. He made Brendan sit down again, but he himself remained standing. 'All's well, all's well,' he kept on saying, and truly meant it. Once again life had dealt him the upper hand. 'Get the prodigal son a drink,' he commanded to great cheers, 'so we can all toast his good health!' Feeling less threatened, he was getting into the swing of things now. A party would shift the focus from himself back to Brendan and give him time to think. There would be hurdles to overcome, of course, but they would not be insurmountable. His brother was alive, but no longer represented a threat. In fact, if anything, his dependency would require him to row in behind his brother's plans, and bolster the harvest. 'All good things come to those who wait,' he said to himself. From the corner of the room the piano sang out. Someone else started playing the violin. Now that John was there, the celebration could begin in earnest and there was no better man for throwing a party.

Chapter forty seven

The party lasted into the small hours of the morning, the crowd dwindling away, one by one, until Brendan and John were finally left alone in the drawing-room. They'd had little time to talk because of the number of relations and friends who wanted to welcome Brendan home. During the course of the night Brendan asked John to wait up until everyone had departed so that they could catch up. The talk between them was easy because they'd had a lot to drink. At least that was the way Brendan professed to be as John insisted on fixing him another whiskey.

'It's good to be home,' Brendan said, 'I was heartened by the welcome I received from Dad and Mam. Cheers!' he added after John took extra care to place a drink in his hand.

'When I saw you sitting there, and the two of them beside you,' John said, 'I knew bygones were bygones.'

Brendan skirted around his experience of the war, adding that losing his sight had been more than he had bargained for, but that he had to be thankful at least for making it through.

'This blindness is a curse,' he said 'but I'm going to make the best of it. A lot of fellahs have come off an awful lot worse than me,' he added a little forlornly. 'I have spoken to the School for the Blind in Dublin where you can take a one-year course and then they place you in a suitable job. I'm anxious not to be a dependant.'

'Sure, stay here as long as you want,' John said. 'You're making the right decision, but don't be rushing into it.' His tone lacked honesty. Then he brought up the subject of Kate.

'Did you know that Kate has a baby?'

'That's what Elsabeth told me,' Brendan's voice dropped to a whispered surprise, as if it was the latest gossip. His tone acknowledged the past, but gave no hint that there might still be a connection between them. 'Jayzis, that didn't take her long.'

John was thrown by Brendan's reply. He was even more surprised when Brendan made reference to the question mark over the father.

'There's mention of it belonging to the Fuhrer!'

'I heard it belonged to you,' John stated unyielding.

'That's what she told Elsabeth,' Brendan replied, the possibility of deceit hanging in the air. 'Chance would have been a fine thing,' he added. 'All I was interested in was having a little bit of fun. The closer I got, though, the more she talked of getting married.' He made it sound as if, by a stroke of luck, he had somehow made the narrowest of escapes by going off to the war. It served his brother's purpose better that Brendan profess no interest between himself and the girl. His answer was more than John could have hoped for. Now that the matter of himself and Kate were settled, Brendan changed the subject to one of greater mutual importance.

'Dad tells me you have big plans for the harvest.'

'I have,' John replied cheered at the turn of events, but at the same time playing down his ambitions. 'I thought I'd give that book of yours a try and see how it goes, I made a few alterations, mind you, but it's going pretty much to plan.' He quickly launched into an explanation. Their father's worst fears were soon acknowledged as Brendan listened. His manner was impartial, acknowledging that John was in control, but he probed in depth as best he could to try to find the true extent to which his brother had committed the family estate. John in turn played down the risks by building up the figures. By the time he finished he had the air of healthy profit about him.

'That's some money,' Brendan said, whistling in appreciation.

'The weather is the only thing out of my control,' John said, as if nothing else could go wrong 'So far it has been a good summer so with a bit of luck it will co-operate when the time is right.'

'I wouldn't worry so much about the weather as I would getting the help you need to show up on the days that you want them,' Brendan said referring to the community. His words cast the first shadow of doubt on the arrangement. 'It's one thing to get them out there for a day, but a whole week is a lot to ask. I'm not saying that they are not trustworthy, but if the weather plays havoc, then they'll all be trying to get their own harvests in at the same time. You'll be hard pressed to get them to co-operate after the first day if that's the case,' Brendan had pinpointed the true weakness in John's plan, and at the same time cast a blight on his ill-found certainty. John's lack of response confirmed his indecision. The intoxication from the promise of massive profit had made him overextend himself in the first place. But having pointed out his weakness Brendan was quick to offer his brother a solution.

'I won't be much good to you on the day,' he said. 'But that will be of little matter if we can get enough hands out there in the first place. I could go around and talk to them. Explain to them what's needed and why they should co-operate. I'll bring the priest with me for reinforcements. He seems like the handy sort.' Brendan recounted how Father Michael had literally moved mountains in order to help him to get back from England. 'If we can get their commitment to lend a hand and put a bit of extra effort into it, then the weather shouldn't be that big a problem.'

When they finally parted company after staggering arm in arm to the top of the stairs John went to bed feeling that God had finally smiled upon him. His first vision of Brendan had made his heart sink. Now his offer to help to 'rouse the troops' as he had called the locals was probably going to save the day. They were united in purpose. Comrades-in-arms. John could remain focused on his law practice and maintain the cash flow while Brendan made the final preparations on the estate. He slept soundly that night for the first time in weeks.

Chapter forty eight

To maintain the front, and to ensure Brendan's reunion with Kate would not be found out, they lived separately with Kate staying at the priest's house. Brendan confided in her that it had taken every ounce of his willpower to prevent him from grabbing his brother by the scruff of the neck and wringing the very life out of him for all that he had done.

'It would have been easy,' he said, 'eyesight or no eyesight.' No one in the family would have blamed him for giving John the punishment that he so richly deserved. But no one knew, for he had not confided in his parents or his sister about the burning of the cottage and the terrible attack that John had committed against Kate. He kept his head, as Victor had taught him to do so many times in combat. He focused his anger on the solution that was to be the destruction of the enemy. Saving the manor and the estate was vital. There was no escaping the fact that they were all dependant on the success of the harvest. If

Brendan was to keep up his side of the deal that he had struck with his father and the priest then he would need his brother as much as John needed him.

As luck would have it the weather closed in and became overcast and dull with regular showers for the next three weeks, which set back the date for the harvest to begin. This gave Brendan the vital time that he needed to get organised. He spent every hour of every day with the priest, visiting all of those who would be involved in the new co-op to make sure that when the time was right he could rely on their support. When he wasn't with the locals he was in Tralee negotiating new machinery and equipment, and when he was not in Tralee he was in his woodwork shop that he had reactivated since his return.

As hard as she tried, and as much as she understood the seriousness of the situation, Kate took small consolation in the little snippets of time that they were able to spend together after being so long apart. Their meetings consisted of an occasional breakfast or sometimes dinner late at night after a long hard day, but Brendan was always in a rush or with Father Michael. They never had any time alone. She would have minded less if she'd had Elsabeth to keep her company, but she had seen even less of her since Brendan's return. Her normally reserved emotions finally got the better of her one day when Brendan showed up unexpectedly at the priest's house in the late afternoon.

'I need to talk to you,' she demanded in front of the priest. 'We haven't talked properly since the day you returned. You are never around, and when you are you are obsessed with the harvest. It is like we don't exist to you.' She was cradling Grace in her arms. She realised that she was being overly dramatic as the words tumbled out of her mouth, but she could not help herself. She had been too long without him, and since his return, she had found his constant comings and goings harder than when he had been away at the war.

'It will have to wait,' Brendan replied. He took Grace from her. 'Go and pack your bags. The harvest is tomorrow and we haven't got much time. We have a load of stuff to do beforehand.'

'Why do I have to pack?' Kate asked, suddenly feeling threatened by the thought that she might have to move from the one place where she felt secure.

'You can't keep staying here,' Brendan replied. 'It isn't right. And it's not fair on the priest to be such a bind,' he stated.

'You're not being a bind,' Father Michael said in quiet reassurance. 'It has been great having you here. But this fellah has other plans.'

'Go on now with you, woman, we are in an awful hurry,' Brendan said to stir her. 'There's more important things to be doing than sitting around talking!'

Kate picked up a tea towel that was lying on the kitchen table, throwing it at Brendan in exasperation. She was sick of being told what to do without first being given an explanation.

'And make it quick,' he called after her as she stormed out of the kitchen. She shot him a look that would turn milk sour and could be heard pounding impatiently up the stairs to her room to do as she had been ordered.

'You are in for it now,' Father Michael said as he led Brendan and the baby out to his car.

'She is in for it more like,' Brendan said with a smile. He had only just told the priest of his surprise plans the previous day. It did not take Kate long to pack her few belongings. At short notice, however, it was a difficult task to uproot, especially when she did not have a clue to where she was going. When she reached the car Brendan was sitting in the back seat with Grace.

'Thank you for having me all this time,' she said to the priest, as she sat in the front beside him.

'You have been more than welcome,' he answered. 'Thank you for looking after me for all of these months. I'm going to miss you.' He started the car, released the handbrake and they drove down the road in silence. He followed the road that ran alongside a winding wall surrounding the estate. It did not take them long to reach their destination.

'Here we are,' he said bringing the car to a halt. 'Here' was in fact nowhere, with a long stretch of road in front of them and nothing behind. Kate looked to the priest for an explanation.

'I've a surprise for you,' Brendan whispered softly into her ear. 'Go on, Father. Nice and slow now,' he added. Putting the car in first gear the priest drove as instructed. For a good minute nothing changed, but then the estate wall suddenly veered away from the road about twenty yards before running parallel to a grass verge. A hidden view opened up, lined by freshly planted flowers that ran the length of the margin. Ahead of them the wall ran into a turret with an archway that spanned the entrance to the back of the estate. The archway was connected on the far side to a large gate lodge. It was solid granite with a slate roof and a second turret that combined with the first to give the impression of a small castle. It had narrow windows, diamond-leaded with bright red frames. Someone had put a lot of thought and energy into recently restoring it. There was smoke coming from the chimney. Michael turned off the road and drove under the archway. As he did, he pressed hard on the horn, three long blasts, before coming to a halt outside the lodge. Elsabeth appeared in the doorway, wearing a large apron that was covered in flour. She tried to wipe her hands and wave at the same time. She was smiling broadly and she was very excited.

'The big bad wolf won't blow this one down so easily,' Brendan whispered in Kate's ear and gently squeezed her shoulder. 'It's our new home,' he added. Elsabeth ran to the car and opened her door.

'Come on,' she said. She reached in and grabbed Kate's hand, and practically dragged her from the car. 'Have we got a surprise for you!' She hurried Kate into the house. From the doorway came the aroma of freshly baked bread combined with the smell of new paint. They entered a decent-sized kitchen with a large pine table and chairs and several other items of furniture that had just been newly made at the manor workshop. The large wood stove threw off a great amount of heat, and a stew in a cast-iron pot bubbled away on top.

'Guess where these came from?' Elsabeth said as she waved her hand across a dresser fully laden with crockery.

'No,' Kate replied, mortified at the thought that Elsabeth had raided the manor again.

'Yes, and these!' she laughed and pointed to the heavy curtains that hung over the windows.

'Oh, my God,' Kate said, laughing with her. Elsabeth led her on a tour of the rest of the house. There were two rooms off the kitchen. One was a furnished sitting-room with a fireplace. The other was a small bedroom that was made up like a nursery with a cot covered in a canopy of white cotton. In the corner there was a rocking horse that stood out among a large pile of wooden toys in a wicker basket. The scullery at the back of the house had a porcelain sink with fresh water from a large hand pump and in the corner behind a curtain stood a cast-iron bath. Both were fed from an ingenious system of hot water that was piped from the wood stove.

'What do you think?' Elsabeth asked Kate as she led her back into the kitchen.

'It's like a dream,' Kate replied in amazement.

'Well, wake up,' Brendan replied as Michael led him into the kitchen and sat him on a chair with Grace on his lap.

'I've saved the best till last,' Elsabeth said and pointed to a stairway. Taking Kate's hand once again she led her upstairs through a door into a large attic bedroom. It had a low ceiling with a dormer window which had diamond-shaped glass that matched the rest of the house. The view over the estate was spectacular. A large solid pine double-bed stood in the centre of the room against the far gable wall. It had been freshly made up with an abundance of pillows and cotton lace covers. There was a dressing table, a free-standing wardrobe and two bed-side lockers to match.

'We're hungry down here,' Brendan called out with playful impatience. 'What's taking ye so long?'

'Be quiet down there, you,' Elsabeth shouted back. 'Let her look as long as she wants. It's her new house now, so you had better watch your manners. Don't mind him,' she said to Kate. She sat down on the edge of the bed, smiling at the wonder in her eyes. 'He wouldn't let me tell you. He wanted it to be a surprise!'

'It's too much,' Kate replied and sat down beside her.

'No, it's not,' Elsabeth put her arm around Kate and gave her a hug. 'Mam is going to come down and visit after the harvest and help you to do it up. It's perfect, isn't it?'

'Yes. It's perfect in every way. Thank you,' Kate returned the hug that Elsabeth had given her. When they made their way downstairs they found Brendan and Michael sitting at the table with two bottles of Guinness already opened and half drunk.

'Where's me dinner, woman?' Brendan demanded trying to hide his embarrassment when Kate bent to kiss him on the cheek. 'And our guest is half-starved into the bargain. Is this any way to treat the two men that's been working hard to make the perfect home?' Everyone laughed when she kissed him again in spite of his shyness. The table was set, the stew quickly served and they all sat down together. Brendan was just about to start to eat when Kate interrupted.

'Will you say grace please, Father?' she asked. Brendan apologised for forgetting his manners and they bowed their heads in prayer.

'Lord, bless this house and all that's in it. For what we are about to eat may we truly be thankful, especially myself, because it is probably the last decent meal I'm going to have now that I no longer have Kate to look after me!' he smiled at everyone. 'Thank you for bringing Brendan back to us safely, and please grant us all the strength and wisdom to do what is right in the days ahead.'

'Thank you, Father,' Brendan said with sincerity. 'Could we eat now, do you think?'

'Brendan Finucane,' Kate chided him. 'Please forgive him, Father. He must have had all of his manners knocked out of him when he got that bang on the head.' They all laughed and a lively conversation ensued regarding the conspiracy that had led to Kate's big surprise. The gate lodge had been Elsabeth's idea. She had told Brendan the day after he had come back from England and they had worked on it every day to make it into a home.

'We had four of the farm labourers here, painting and plastering!' Elsabeth said, laughing at the memory of the recent chaos.

'It was madness!' Brendan agreed. It did not take long for the conversation to come around to the harvest that was to start the next day, but it was Father Michael who came up with the surprise announcement.

'I think we should start the day with a christening,' he said, looking across the table at Kate. She went quiet. 'It's a time for celebration after a long wait and a lot of hard work. Time for a new beginning, wouldn't you think?' Brendan nodded his head in agreement.

'Not tomorrow,' Kate replied, concerned at the thought of all of the attention of the village being focused on her and Grace. 'And what about the harvest? Surely you'll be wanting to start the day early. Couldn't we do it on a different day, when things are a bit quieter?'

'No,' Brendan replied. 'That would be impossible.'

'Why?' demanded Kate.

'Because I have already invited everybody,' he smiled.

'Everybody?' Kate asked.

'The whole village,' Father Michael confirmed. 'That was my idea,' he confessed. 'You'll remember I told them from the very first day I arrived in Clochan that they would have to attend. So now they are doing it,' he stated.

'Oh, my God!' Kate said again for the second time that day.

'Don't worry, I did not have to use my fists this time,' Michael laughed.

'They are happy to attend,' Brendan said softly and gave Kate his napkin to wipe her tears.

'Do they know that you are Grace's father?' she asked.

'Of course,' he replied. 'I told Mary at the post office.'

'What do you mean?' Kate looked at him, puzzled.

'Well, now you can be sure the rest of the village knows!' he smiled and everyone laughed.

'I have it all organised and a few bits and pieces to go with it,' Elsabeth reassured Kate, knowing she would be worried about having nothing decent to wear.

'Have you any more surprises?' she asked the gathering.

'One or two,' Brendan said. 'You'll have to wait until tomorrow to find out.'

Chapter forty nine

Kate woke the following morning to the warmth of the sun beaming through the dormer window. She reached over to where Brendan lay, but found the bed empty. Then she remembered that Father Michael had collected him before sunrise. Lying back on the pillows, she basked in the glow of finally being reunited with her lover.

After Grace had fallen asleep and Father Murphy and Elsabeth had departed, Brendan took her on a tour of the outside of the house before it got too dark. There were stables big enough for four horses or a cheese factory. 'Whatever you want,' he told her. There was a henhouse beside a large open space that would be the vegetable garden. On their way back into the house through the scullery he explained how the hot water worked. Before they knew it they found themselves by candle light in the bath. It had all been serious and a little awkward until they discovered that their new bed creaked rather loudly. Then through howls of laughter they finally found each other again.

The following morning Grace cried out from her bedroom downstairs and Kate made her way down to tend to her and give her breakfast. There was an unexpected knock at the front door and when she answered Elsabeth was standing in the porch with an arm full of boxes stacked right up under her chin.

'We are early!' she said. 'I hope you don't mind.' Behind her stood Helen McGovern, the local hairdresser.

'It's not like we haven't been waiting for this for over a year now,' Elsabeth stated as she shuffled past into the sitting-room. 'Today is the big day,' she said. 'Here, try this for size,' she said to a surprised Kate, exchanging the largest box for Grace. When Kate opened the box she let out a gasp. She lifted out a stunningly beautiful cream-coloured outfit.

'What's going on here?' she whispered with wide-eyed amazement. She had assumed this was to be an ordinary day. Brendan had told her not to expect too much. After the big surprise of the house, she was more than happy with the simple plans that he said he had made. 'I thought it was supposed to be only a brief ceremony before the harvest!' Kate gazed at the dress and Elsabeth could see that she was affected by the beauty of it and the sense of occasion it brought to the day.

'Nonsense,' she said. 'It's important you look your best. Sure look at what I have brought for Grace.' She opened another box. It contained a glorious outfit that was the same colour as Elsabeth's. 'As the self-appointed godmother on this occasion I have to match my baby. Here,' she said and handed Kate another box. 'Mam sent this down especially for Grace.' When Kate opened the last box she found a soft bundle wrapped in tissue paper. 'It was Brendan's when he was christened. Our grandmother made it,' Elsabeth explained. Inside the careful wrapping was a delicate white lambs wool shawl of intricate lacework.' Kate lifted it to her cheek and luxuriated in its softness.

'It's beautiful,' she said.

'Come on, quick, we haven't much time. Brendan is sending someone to pick us up at half-past six,' Elsabeth reminded her, and they flew into a flurry of activity. Hair was done, dresses put on, a hem had to be stitched because it was a fraction too long. At six-thirty exactly, while they were putting on the last of their makeup, the sound of a horse and carriage could be heard outside.

'I wonder who that is?' Elsabeth said in a conspiratorial tone.

'You,' Kate was smiling as she pointed her finger at her friend. 'You are such a sneak!' They made their way outside. The open carriage was from the manor. A remnant from days gone by that had become a family heirloom, but it was still in serviceable condition. It was covered in a cream velvet sash and there were bunches of flowers decorating the sides, but it was the driver wearing a top hat and tails that grabbed Kate's attention.

'Albert!' she cried out.

'Howya, Kate,' he said in the strongest of Dublin accents as he climbed down from his seat. 'Jayzis, you are looking as magnificent as ever.' He tipped his hat in a bow of appreciation. Kate ran forward to embrace him and kissed him on the cheek.

'Oh, Albert, I can't believe you are here!' she said, for it had been over a year since she had last seen him in Dublin. 'What is going on here Elsabeth Finucane?!'

'Brendan told me that you'd be needing a lift!' Albert explained before Elsabeth had a chance to answer. 'I just got in on the train last night!' he said.

'Are we going to the church in this?' Kate turned to Elsabeth.

'Of course,' she replied. 'There's a war on you know. Petrol rationing and all that. Another one of Brendan's ideas!' she smiled without any further explanation.

'Are you ready for the big day then?' Albert asked.

'With you here I think I'm ready for anything,' she said.

'Right then, all aboard,' he said, opening the door. He helped the girls to climb into the carriage with the baby. When everyone was settled he took off at a gentle pace, chatting with Kate as they made their way to the church. The morning was marked by clear blue skies and a gentle breeze which was perfect for bringing in the harvest. In spite of the seriousness of the day that lay ahead there was still plenty of joking and laughter along the way, but when they arrived at the church Kate became anxious.

'Don't worry about it,' Elsabeth said and stopped her from rushing up the steps to the main door of the church when Kate suddenly realised that they were late. 'You have waited a long time for this, so let them wait a few minutes longer. It won't do them the one bit of harm!' Nothing could have surprised her more when she walked through the main door and found the church overflowing into the aisles with people. Everyone was dressed in their Sunday best and looked as though they were there for a proper Mass and not a harvest. At the far end of the church she could see Brendan and Father Michael, standing at the altar. The priest motioned silently for her to come and join them. She made her way down the aisle, feeling very self-conscious at the attention she was attracting in her beautiful cream outfit. Elsabeth carried Grace and walked beside her.

'Hello, Kate,' Father Michael said, when she reached the altar. 'You look a little bit surprised,' he smiled.

'It has been an interesting morning, Father,' Kate replied and with that Elsabeth led her and Brendan to the front pew and everyone in the church sat down.

'I would like to say a few words about the harvest before beginning this ceremony,' Father Michael announced, 'so that from here on in, there will be no doubt as to where everybody stands.' He paused for a moment. After the recent meetings that Brendan and he had held with the community they already knew what lay ahead, but this was the first time that he would speak to the entire congregation as one. He was about to continue when a loud bang came from the back of the church and John crashed through the door at the main entrance.

'What's going on here?' he shouted, and started up the

aisle. He had been drinking and was in a terrible rage. 'Why aren't you out at the harvest,' he demanded. He made an attempt to try and pull one or two people from their seats, but in his condition he was easily resisted. Spotting Father Michael on the altar he ignored the rest of the congregation and marched up the aisle to confront him. 'You were supposed to be holding this service at the farm to bless the harvest,' he fumed. 'What about our arrangement?'

'That will do!' a familiar voice commanded from behind. When John turned around, Brendan was standing at his seat with Kate beside him, looking terrified and trying to hold him back. She already knew what John was capable of doing.

'I was wondering where you had gotten to,' John said bitterly. 'You'd better not have anything to do with this,' he staggered slightly trying to maintain his balance and pointed a warning finger. The evil look he gave Kate sent a shiver down her spine. He turned again to face Father Michael. 'Tell them all to get out there and get on with the harvest,' he ordered. 'Tell them it's for their own good,' he said with a voice that was mean and threatening, but he did not have time to finish.

'I said that will do!' John felt the grasp of a hand on his shoulder and was spun around. This time Brendan was standing on the altar in front of him. 'So the cripple is involved after all,' said John. 'Get out of my way.' He lunged to push his brother off the altar, but the drink had made him reckless and over-confident and, before he knew it, he found himself sprawled on the floor. Astonished, he looked up to see for the first time that Brendan was no longer wearing his dark glasses. Kate let out a gasp. Brendan's parents were amazed, along with the congregation. But there was no one more shocked than John. 'You can see!' he said in a sudden panic.

'That's right. I can see better than I have ever done before. I'm no longer blind to you and your madness,' Brendan said, his voice cold and deliberate.

'But what about the harvest?' John demanded, as he struggled to stand. 'If I don't get it in before the weather changes,

I'll end up losing the estate.' He grabbed Brendan's arm in desperation. 'We'll all be ruined!' he declared. Brendan flung him off for a second time.

'You cannot lose what you did not have in the first place!' Brendan said. 'Now get out of this church, you are not fit to be in it. Get out before I lose my temper!'

'You can't do this,' John shouted. 'The estate is mine! I have worked for it. You can't just come back like this and take it off me!'

'Leave this place!' Father Michael commanded stepping between the two brothers and pointing at the main entrance. Then John saw his father walk forward and stand beside the priest and Brendan and he knew that they were united against him. Facing humiliation and defeat he had no choice but to retreat. He did so in an outburst of rage.

'I'll get you for this!' he threatened, as he walked past Danny Kelleher, who was sitting halfway down with his wife and three of his four young children. 'And you too Vincent Maguire – you traitor!' He stopped just under the balcony and turned to face the congregation. By now he was seething with fury. 'You think this is over?' he shouted at Brendan. 'You think you can get the better of me? You'll pay for this,' he shouted waving his fist. 'The whole lot of you will pay for this,' he swore. Seamus Kelleher, the youngest of the four Kelleher children was standing in the front row of the balcony above John. He'd been sent up by his mother to fetch her bible, and was leaning forward to see what all of the commotion was about. Frightened by John's threats he turned to escape his wrath, but in doing so let the bible slip from his hands. In full view of the congregation it struck John squarely on the head at the exact moment that he had finished his tirade. In an instant it changed the atmosphere of the church from one of great tension to cheers and loud roars of laughter at John as he staggered out the door.

'Right,' said Father Murphy, trying not to laugh, as he attempted to bring the church back to order. 'Settle down, settle down now,' he waved his hands in the air. Brendan's father assisted by relaying the message to everyone down the church.

'I had been going to talk to you, how shall I say, about the business at hand and what you all might have to prepare for in the future. However, I think now we all know where we stand. My advice for you is not to worry. We have made a commitment as a community and with the leadership of this young man, "Brendan the all-seeing," he made a gesture of surprise, which brought a cheer from the congregation, 'we shall see it through to a successful outcome. But before we start the work at hand let's get back to the real reason why we are here today!' Smiling, he stepped over to the altar and picked up his prayer book. 'Now, you all know that we are here for a christening, but before we start, I want all those involved to step up here on the altar so that I can say a few words to them,' he paused, 'then we shall proceed to the font to complete the ceremony.' Brendan led the way, tall and confident, with everyone, including Kate, following behind, still recovering from the big surprise.

'Will all of those people at the back of the church please come forward and gather around,' Father Murphy said. 'Come on, I want everyone to see and witness what I have to say.' While the congregation were moving forward Father Murphy instructed Brendan to stand opposite Kate, then assembled family and friends around them. It took a couple of minutes, but soon everyone had gathered amiably and squeezed into whatever space they could find at the front of the church so that they all could get a good view.

'Right, I have an announcement to make,' Father Michael said. 'As I said a few minutes ago, we are supposed to be here today for the christening of little Grace. Well,' he paused, 'I can't allow it.' After all of the threats that he had originally made on his first day in the town square, there were surprised murmurs among the congregation as they looked at each other and wondered what was going to happen next. 'In fact I won't allow it under the roof of this church until such time as the parents of this child are joined in holy matrimony!' he finished.

'Here, here!' chimed Brendan's father and several voices

joined in behind him in support of the idea. Kate stood silent as if in a daydream, feeling dazed by all that had happened that morning.

'Do you understand me?' Father Michael said, leaning forward and eyeballing Brendan.

'I do, Father,' he replied.

'Malachy, have you the ring?' Father Michael said impatiently to the altar boy, as if it was he who was holding up the proceedings.

'I have, Father,' he replied.

'Right then, you had better be getting on with it, Brendan,' he said. 'We haven't all day. We still have to bring in the harvest!' Before Kate knew what was happening, Brendan took the ring from Malachy and got down on one knee in front of her. The entire congregation looked on with baited breath. Taking her hand he offered the ring, and after what seemed like an eternity he spoke...

'I am down on my knees praying that you will do me the honour?'

Kate took her time in giving her reply. She had recovered sufficiently from all of the surprises that day to know that this was the one thing she wanted more than anything else in the world, but she was not going to let the man of her dreams away that easily. A look of mischief came across her. She kept him on his knees waiting, while in silence, she surveyed all of those who surrounded them. There was disbelief on some of their faces, that she would make him wait, but after all that she had been through there were also those that understood.

'He has been awfully bold,' she said finally, and with her hands on her hips she stood over him as if describing a wayward child. 'Do you think I should?'

'Yes,' young Seamus Keleher shouted out, enthusiastically, breaking the silence that had held the congregation enraptured. He had come down from the balcony and squeezed in between the legs of the crowd to witness the proceedings.

'What do you think, Micilin Og? Do you think he might stay around long enough this time?' Kate asked.

'Ah, go on now,' he replied. 'Put him out of his misery, before you break his heart. Have you no pity for the man, and he on his knees a-begging?'

She had it in mind to rub it in that little bit longer, to punish him for one too many surprises, but it was the heartfelt sympathy in Micilin's voice that caught her off guard, and her own heart let her down by melting.

'I will,' she nodded, her eyes suddenly full of tears. She leaned forward and took Brendan by the hands and dragged him to his feet. The church filled with cheers of release and joy.

'That's fine, now. Let's make it official,' said Father Michael. A simple ceremony followed in which they were joined together under the eyes of God so that no man would ever pull them asunder. When they finished, Brendan kissed the bride to more cheers from the gathering, and then Michael led everyone over to the font for the christening. It never occurred to Grace to do anything else but smile when she was with Father Michael, and today was no exception. Her cooing and gurgling heightened the happy atmosphere that prevailed among all those that looked on, and her going easy in his arms made him seem like a natural. Pausing for a moment, he said, 'I feel, as I'm sure you all do, a great sense of contentedness and completion today, as we perform this ceremony,' he smiled. 'As you all know, the good things in life are worth waiting for.' With his usual penchant for doing things differently, he stepped up to the font and began the ceremony.

>'This child is an angel from heaven,' he said.
>'Sent here to our safe keeping.
>A child of God we do not own
>Nor is she here for our own pleasing.
>Lord give us the strength and the wisdom
>To raise her with love
>And not crush her with our thinking.

So that she may blossom like the flower of her choosing
We give thanks as the ones you have chosen.'

Taking the water from the font, he poured it over Grace's forehead and then began to cast it about, splashing all those who were present.

'I baptise thee Grace,
Your parents and your family
And charge you *all*,' he said looking at the gathering.
'With her safe-keeping.
Do your best ... that's all that God asks.
It is the way of Peace.
Amen.'

'Amen!' The reply echoed through the church, and hugs and kisses were given all around. When the formalities were over, the organ played, the choir broke into song, and Brendan led Kate down the aisle and out the main doorway. Outside, they found the hurling team assembled to form an archway with their hurlies. To much gaiety and laughter, they ran the gauntlet of confetti and rice that was thrown the entire length of the archway in their honour. It was at the end, however, that the excitement suddenly ended.

John was standing there with a hip flask in one hand and a gun in the other with a frightening look of vengeance. It was the assassin's revolver from the safe at the manor. The crowd drew back in horror as he pointed it directly at Brendan's heart.

'She was mine!' he said. 'I saw her first and you took her away, just like you stole the farm.'

Slowly, so as not to alarm John, Brendan's team-mates began to move forward to defend him.

'Get back!' John shouted, threatening one and all with the gun. Brendan raised his hand to stop them from doing anything foolish.

'Put the gun down,' he said calmly, as he pushed Kate and

Grace behind him and stepped forward to offer himself as a better target. Elsabeth grabbed Kate and pulled her and the child out of harm's way.

'You weren't supposed to come back,' John stated. 'You should have stayed away. You should have died in the war!' he cried.

'Give me the gun,' Brendan said, 'Give it to me before you get hurt!'

'Hurt is it,' John laughed, grimly. 'I'm the one holding the gun!'

'Give it to me, for God's sake!' Brendan pleaded, ' You don't want to do this. You don't want to pull that trigger!'

'I'm the one making the rules now,' John waved the gun. *'I'm* the one who wins in the end.' His whole body stiffened to withstand the recoil as he squeezed the trigger. He laughed as Brendan raised his arms in a feeble attempt to defend himself from the bullet. To his horror Kate suddenly rushed between them as the gun let loose a terrible explosion. A muffled cry of agony could be heard and Kate was thrown back into Brendan's arms from the blast of the revolver. There were screams of terror as people ran for cover. Brendan's teammates charged forward with a war cry on their lips, their hurlies raised for battle regardless of the consequences. Albert came from behind and with a brutal tackle, he knocked John to the ground with the intention of disarming him. But just as quickly they all stopped.

On his knees in front of them, in a state of shock, John struggled to understand the agonizing pain that coursed through his body, and the sight of his shattered and bloodied right hand. The gun lay on the ground in front of him, mangled from the booby-trapped explosion designed to protect the true owner from ever having his own weapon used against him.

'I'm all right,' Kate whispered. 'I'm not hurt,' she reached out to touch Brendan on the cheek, as he held her, frantic about the blood stains on her dress. When he realised that she was uninjured, his concern turned to fury and he stood up to finally vent his anger upon his brother.

'Leave him,' Micilin Og intervened and had to wrestle him to hold him back.

'I'll kill him,' Brendan raged.

'He is already finished!' said Micilin. He managed to restrain Brendan with the help of his father. When it was obvious that John was no longer a threat, the feeling in the churchyard settled to one of relief. The only thing that John had managed to kill was the joy that had been shared inside the church just moments before. The local Garda sergeant who was there as a guest took a handkerchief from his pocket, and fashioned a crude tourniquet to stem the flow of blood from John's hand. He dragged John to his feet, and took him down the road to the station, where a doctor could be called to tend to his wounds.

'Why didn't you tell us you could see?' Kate asked Brendan, after John had been arrested and taken away.

'I wasn't sure if it was going to last. I think it happened when I banged my head. Remember? When I tripped in the bedroom that night. That's how I must have lost it in the first place when I was washed ashore on the rocks,' he said. He rubbed the top of his head where the scar was covered by his hair. 'And then, there was this thing with John. As long as I was blind to him, I was the underdog. It gave me a freer hand to get around and reorganise the harvest. I'm sorry, but I couldn't say anything. It would have been impossible for us to keep up appearances if anyone else had known.'

'You and your surprises,' Kate admonished him for not trusting her, but she was just as quick to forgive him, for she understood who they had been up against.

'Some of them have gone on ahead to the harvest,' said Father Michael. 'The members of your newly formed co-op are already at work. We should be going too!'

'Are you sure you aren't hurt, Mrs Finucane?' Brendan asked Kate one last time.

'I'm fine,' she said smiling at the significance of the title. They looked into each other's eyes and she squeezed his hands in reassurance.

'I have to be going,' he said and nodded in the direction of the harvest. He bent down and kissed Grace.

'No more surprises,' Kate said, as she kissed him goodbye.

'I hope not' Brendan kissed her back.

'I'll see you so,' she said.

Chapter fifty

'Foul!'
'What do you mean foul?!' Micilin Og cried out as Brendan stopped the game with his whistle. Forty-eight men, women and children on each team came to a halt on a freshly harvested meadow to watch Brendan castigate Micilin for tripping one of the younger players in a tackle.
'It was a foul,' repeated Brendan. 'You tripped him up on purpose!'
'I did not!' stated Micilin. 'Sure I was only going for the ball!'
'Do I look like I'm blind or something?' said Brendan as he confronted Micilin and pointed to his eyes as they faced off against each other. The field erupted in laughter and Brendan had to turn away from Micilin to hide his own smile at the irony of his statement. 'Are you all right, Sean?' he asked and distracted the attention of Micilin to the player that was on the ground

making a big show of massaging his leg as if it had been broken.

'It's me ankle,' he said. 'I think it's broke!' he replied with a twisted face of pain.

'Right, you are off!' his composure restored, Brendan turned back to Micilin and with a determined look he pointed to the side lines. There was a good natured roar of approval from all of the players.

'Ah, for God's sakes I barely touched him!' Micilin said as he made his way to the sidelines. 'He's only messing!' Micilin stated. In truth however he was relieved to be sent off for he was all puffed out from trying to keep up with his younger opponents.

'And I'm not deaf either!' Brendan called after him when he overheard him cursing his decision. 'It will be confession and Father Murphy you will have to deal with if I hear any more of your lip!' The spectators on the sideline jeered Micilin as he walked off.

'Get off the ground will ya and stop your messing!' Brendan said to the young player when Micilin was out of earshot. With that Sean jumped to his feet and did a short jig to mock his opponent for being sent off. There were more cheers and jeering and Brendan blew his whistle again to get the game back under play. It had been a busy few days with long hours and little sleep, but with everyone working together along with the efficiency of the new machinery, the harvest and their futures had been secured.

'Here ya bowsey!' said Kate good naturedly as she handed Micilin a bottle of Guinness and a great big meat sandwich on a plate when he sat down on the sideline beside the priest.

'You are much nicer than that new husband of yours!' Micilin said as a way of thanks when she sat down beside him. 'There's no justice, Father. None at all!' he said to the priest.

'What are you on about?' he replied. 'You do the crime you do the time! Sure, it's only fair,' said Father Michael in defence of Brendan's decision to send him off.

'I know, Father,' he replied. 'But how come he sends me

off for such a little thing like that, yet he won't send his brother to jail for trying to kill him?' Micilin looked at him, perplexed at the way in which Brendan and the priest had organised to have his brother released without charge and put on the boat to America with a one-way ticket. 'I'd have had him hanged!'

'For what?' asked Father Michael, amused at the big man's belligerence.

'For trying to kill him!' Micilin said in exasperation. 'Sure, a blind man could have seen it.'

Father Michael laughed. 'He knew the gun was going to explode!'

'Go on!' Micilin stared in amazement. 'How did he know for God's sake?'

'Because he booby-trapped it,' explained the priest. 'He told me that it's something a lot of the pilots do over there to make sure that their own gun is not used against them if they are captured by the enemy. As far as he was concerned it was an unfair advantage. You can't charge a man for blowing his own hand off!' Father Michael added.

'Jayzis, that's some story all the same,' said Micilin and took a swig of his Guinness. 'Sure it has a happy ending no less!' he said to Kate and nodded in the direction of Brendan's parents sitting together with Grace asleep on his mother's lap.

'Thanks to this fellah!' Kate said looking at Father Michael.

'Thanks be to God!' he replied.

Thanks

To Kate and Paddy who showed up in my life at the most unexpected of times and have inspired me ever since in the telling of this wonderful story. To Victor for dropping in the way he did, teaching Paddy to fly and organising the Shelbourne Hotel. Heroes all ... for all heroes are true romantics at heart.

To Barbara Keating - my Fairy Godmother, who wove her wand through the early manuscripts. For more of Barbara's magic see – To my daughter in France. Blood sisters. A Durable Fire.

To Jim Schmitt - for Molly and Malone and all of the great flights that we shared and Warren Denholm and the team at Avspecs for technical support. See www.warbirdrestoration.co.nz

To Rosie my researcher ... thanks Mam.

To Pat Ingoldsby, writer, poet and lover of life. Thanks for the liquorice all sorts.

To Paul Manson, Christine Smith and Paul Engles for helping me to keep the Faith.

To my editors Cynthia Mc Kenzie and Lorraine Bretnall - sincere thanks for dotting the I's and crossing the T's

To the amazing Debbie (Brown Dog Design) for the front and back cover ... bow wow!

To all of my trusted 'test pilot' readers who helped to console and encourage me every time I got shot down. Your opinions are worth far more than all of those agents and publishers who will forever regret the BIG ONE that they let get away!

Special Thanks

To Conor Makem for allowing me to quote the lyrics for his father Tommy's song 'Ever the Winds'

To Buffy Sainte-Marie for kind permission to quote the lyrics from her wonderful song 'Johnny be fine'

Share the BIG IDEA

Check out our website. If you like the BIG IDEA behind 'The Christening' and would like to share the dream and help me to make it into a BIG MOVIE then please ....

Send me an e-mail telling me how much you love the story. I will update you with regular news flashes as we progress towards making the movie. When it comes time for auditions I will let you know well in advance so that you can come and 'try out' for a part.

E-mail everybody on your contact list. Get them to share the BIG IDEA by buying the book from www.trysoftaproductions.com Encourage them to spread the word to their contact list. It won't take long before we get the whole world involved.

That's the BIG IDEA!

Again thanks a million!

e-mail: gary@trysoftaproductions.com

Wing Commander Brendan ('Paddy') Finucane, (DSO, DFC and bar) from Ireland became one of the most decorated Spitfire Ace's during the Battle of Britain. With the highest number of 'kills' (32), Finucane was the youngest Wing Commander in the RAF all before his 22nd birthday. Paddy was both the leader of his Squadron, and an inspiration to his pilots and ground crew. With his Shamrock crested Spitfire emblazoned with his initials, he achieved one of the highest scores in RAF history.

Doug Stokes - writer and historian helped me to maintain authenticity during the telling of this story.
For more of the facts see Doug's books

Paddy Finucane: Fighter Ace
and
Victor Beamish: Wings Aflame